ABBOTS FOR

The Abbots Ford Trilogy covers the
Twentieth Century, tracing four
generations of a family in a Somerset
village, focussing mainly on the women.
Through two World Wars, and
unprecedented social change, these
women strive to keep their families on
course, and their working lives viable.

THE AUTHOR

Elizabeth Davison was born and lived in
London, but spent much time in Somerset
staying with her mother's best friend.
Her visits continued for many years and she
always enjoyed the time she spent there.
This book is a reflection of her impressions
and feelings of her love of life in the
West Country.

Elizabeth Davison

This book is published by
Grosvenor House Publishing Ltd
Link House
140 The Broadway, Tolworth, Surrey, KT6 7HT.
www.grosvenorhousepublishing.co.uk

A CIP record for this book
is available from the British Library

ISBN 978-1-83975-819-5

Return to the Hill

ELIZABETH DAVISON

Book Two of
The Abbots Ford Trilogy

Grosvenor House
Publishing Limited

RETURN TO THE HILL

Return to the Hill follows four primary characters who have
grown up in a Somerset village at the start of the
Twentieth Century, and been changed by the experiences of loss
and diminution during the First World War, find their way
in life elsewhere. It joins them in 1935 when Alice has become
a lady's maid in London and Dorothy a nanny in Scotland,
while Eddy and Seth remain in the village to farm.
Their lives are changed again with the outbreak of World War II.
Dorothy returns home to nurse her sick mother and take
care of her father and brothers. Having given her life to the
service of others, in her forties, she falls in love with an unlikely
man and begins a new and exciting chapter in her life.

Chapter One

JANUARY 1935 – JUNE 1935

The bus trundled along the lanes towards Abbots Ford leaving bustling Bristol behind. It had been a long journey; the train had been delayed, and even her trip to Paddington Station had proved traumatic. Enough of that though. Enough about the trouble she had been having with the Duchess of Taversham, her employer, enough about her love affair with Steven. Time to think about her mother and grandmother now that Grandad Will had passed away.

Alice looked out at the familiar Somerset countryside and it all came back. The slow, almost plodding way of life; the steady reprise of the seasons, the measured response of the village folk. How different from the life she had experienced in London these past four years. London! She decided she must really put it to the back of her mind, even though the contrast with where she now found herself kept recalling it like an echo. Down the hill past Salisbury House, along to the crossroads, beyond Redford's the general store and abattoir, the bus came to a halt near the small square just outside the Partridge Inn. Alice struggled down the steps with her suitcases.

"Hello, girl." Malcolm Smythe, publican of the Partridge, came out of his front door as she alighted, greeting her as though she had only been away a week.

"Hello Mr Smythe."

"Sorry about your Grandad. Come home for the funeral?"

"Yes."

"Do you want help with your cases? Jacob's lad's here."

"Thanks – that would be nice."

He turned back towards the pub and shouted. Almost at once, a handsome lad of about seventeen came running out.

"Hello. You the lady who needs help?"

"Yes, thanks. Can you manage one and I'll bring the other."

They walked towards Church Lane. The lad seemed shy, but Alice could not be bothered to make small talk. Perhaps he would think she was stuck-up. Too bad. Her heart was too heavy to worry. The smell of the piggery opposite Orchard Cottage assaulted her nostrils before they reached the small house.

"Thanks. I didn't catch your name?"

"Don. Short for Donald. My Dad is Jacob Smythe. 'Bye."

She stood looking at Orchard Cottage. It had not changed; uneven grey blocks jutted out here and there, covered with ivy as far as the roof. It sat sideways-on to the lane, facing the hill, its windows staring out benignly. The plum-tree orchard ran alongside the cottage and the length of the garden. Beyond the sturdy grey stone wall which was the boundary, lay the churchyard. Alice smiled to herself as she remembered how she and her younger sister, Dorothy, used to scare their little brothers with ghostly stories and then dare them to walk near the churchyard wall in the dark, when they visited their grandparents. She had arranged to stay with her grandmother, Louise, on this occasion. Her parents, Flora and Seth, still had her two brothers living at Plumtree Cottage, so it made sense to stay with gran. She went slowly down the two steep steps; it looked bleak, different. Was it because Grandpa Will had gone, or was it just because it was January? She was putting off opening the door. It looked smaller. She tapped on it. A young man opened it; he was the image of her Uncle Bill.

"Hello," she said. "Remember me?"

"Hello, Alice." said young Will, Bill's son.

She went in, trying to adjust her eyes to the darkness of the room.

"Hello, Alice." Another young man came through from the kitchen.

"Hello, Charles. I hardly recognised you," she told her Aunt Louise' son.

"I'll tell Gran you're here," he said.

Alice took a deep breath and looked around. The coals glowed through the bars of the range and the black lead shone darkly. There was a new sofa but everything else appeared exactly the same. The massive dresser containing all her grandmother's pottery, crocks and china stood against the wall opposite the range. A maroon velour cloth still covered the large table which stood in the middle of the room like an altar to family life. A wireless now stood on a table at the far end of the room near the tiny window which gave glimpses of the orchard towards the main road. The throaty 'churtling' of the chickens made her smile as she peered out; she had forgotten how ridiculous they sounded. The two young men moved around the cottage quietly, making tea and sandwiches. The door to the staircase opened slowly, and Louise came down the stairs one at a time. Grief had etched pain on the elderly woman's face, Alice could see that. She was shocked how much her grandmother had aged in her absence. Louise Henty was stick-thin, her hair pure white. She moved stiffly towards Alice.

"Hello, my dear. Good of you to come," she said, kissing her granddaughter. Alice thought she must be in her late sixties, which meant that her grandfather would have been turned seventy; a good age.

She wished she had not stayed away so long; wished she had not been so taken up with the glamour of London and its people.

"I'm so sorry, Gran, so sorry".

Her grandmother seemed to be trying hard to keep her emotions under control, and the way she could do it was to stand and sit ramrod straight, not accept any sympathy and not to weep.

"He went the way he wanted to go – he worked till that last day".

"He said he felt alright, Gran, didn't he?" offered young Will.

"Yes, dear, he did."

"When does Dorothy arrive?"

"Tomorrow, and your Mother said she'd be along to see us all in the morning."

As the evening wore on, her cousins disappeared for a time and her grandmother made the two of them a meal. It was starkly sad and muted, alien to how she remembered Orchard Cottage; but then she supposed, it would never be the same again. She looked forward to seeing her mother, father and brothers – but especially Dorothy. Sensible, ordinary, placid Dorothy.

+ + +

"Mother, you're looking well. I'm very sorry about Grandpa." Alice greeted Flora after four long years away.

"Shame it had to be a funeral to get you home," commented her mother.

Alice had the grace to blush. She experienced another twinge of conscience over her protracted absence. It was strange to be home, seeing them once again. It was as though they had ceased to exist while she pursued another life.

"Now then, Flora, dear," said Louise.

"Mother, will you be coming along with Alice for tea?"

"Dorothy arrives this afternoon. I'll stay here for her," said Louise.

"Good. So you'll come with me to Briersham to see your Father and brothers, Alice?"

"Go back with your Mother, dear. I'll be fine," assured Louise.

Her brown eyes seemed faded and tired.

"Will you be alright, Ma, are you sure?" asked Flora.

"Yes. I have things to do in preparation for Dorothy's arrival. I'll keep busy."

Alice was relieved to leave behind the prevailing gloom, and though Flora was desperately upset about her father's passing, it was tinged with joy at seeing her daughters again after so long. They walked briskly towards Briersham.

"Your Dad's expecting you. He'll be in for his dinner soon," said Flora.

"How is he? How are you, Mum?" Alice searched her mother's face.

"We're fine. Working hard. Your Dad runs the Smithy still and the boys work at Drakes Farm. 'Course your Grandad James can't do so much now."

They talked about the family and Flora told Alice how everyone fared. Alice could hardly wait to see Plumtree Cottage again. Nothing had altered. The cottage nestled up a cart track off the main road which ran through the hamlet of Briersham, two miles from Abbots Ford. Alice looked up at the grey stone house which had been her childhood home. They approached through the gate in the low wall and walked up the path to the back of the cottage, going into the scullery. Alice spun round, taking it all in. The well-worn pine table and chairs, made as a wedding present for her parents by her great-grandfather, still stood at one side of the room. There were the two small battered chairs on either side of the small fireplace and the pots, pans and utensils which her mother had used for as long as she could remember, hung on the walls.

"Oh, Mum! Nothing has changed!" she cried delightedly.

"No reason why it should, Alice, is there?" responded her mother acerbically. "Just because you have posh London friends and forget where you come from, doesn't mean we have to change as well."

"Mum, you're telling me off again!"

Flora worked in the scullery preparing the meal, while Alice walked around all the rooms, touching the ornaments and fingering the highly polished furniture. It was cosy and welcoming, cared for and reassuring. A grandmother clock ticked calmly in the corner of the neat living room, measuring their lives. The small front window allowed little of the grey wintery light through and shadows fell, allowing her only profiles of the solid furniture. Pretty embroidered antimacassars protected the chairs and sofa and two cats snuggled on the worn rug in front of the range. Delicious aromas tempted her senses, transporting her, in a moment, back to her childhood.

"It even smells the same, so wonderful!"

"Make yourself useful and lay the table, if you're not too above yourself to do that," said Flora crisply.

There was a rumble of male voices and before she could reach the door, her father and brothers were in the scullery rolling up their sleeves to wash, having all arrived at once.

"Hello, my girl." Seth grinned like a Cheshire cat.

"Hello, Sis," Eddy greeted her casually.

"Hello, Sis," echoed young Seth shyly.

She kissed them all, to their embarrassment. It was their way to pretend that nothing was unusual, nothing special was occurring. They had not met for four years, yet any sign of undue emotion was not welcome. They sat around the table and tucked into the meal.

"You had a good journey, our Sis?" enquired Eddy.

"Don't ask," laughed Alice.

"How's Gran today?" asked young Seth.

"She's quiet; she'll be enjoying the company," said Flora.

"Dorothy arrive today?" asked their father.

"Yes. Gran said she's coming this afternoon."

Alice looked at her family. How she had missed them, missed this house. They would never know how she had felt when she first left for London at twenty-one; there had seemed no future for her at home. She had not met anyone she wished to marry, she was not remotely interested in farming, nor her Aunt Louise' shop, nor dressmaking. She had had to find a way to earn a living and had gone into service in Bath at seventeen. She had done well and swiftly been offered a job as lady's maid to the Countess Daventry. The Countess had taught her well, and during the London Season when Alice was twenty-one, the Duchess of Taversham had poached her. She had travelled all over the country and all over the world, but there was nowhere sweeter than the cottage here at Briersham.

Seth, her father, was still a handsome man of forty-nine. His dark hair was flecked with grey, but his eyes were bright, and he had grown a moustache. Her mother looked much the same; her dark hair was 'pepper and salt', her face more lined, but her eyes radiated the same warm intelligence as ever. The biggest change was evident in her brothers: Eddy who had been a thin seventeen-year old had filled out to handsome young manhood of twenty-one. Seth was nineteen and the image of their father at the same age.

The atmosphere eased as they conversed through the meal, and Alice became more her 'home' self again. She had not realised how much she had changed through her experiences and her life away from Abbots Ford. Suddenly, the men all got up and went off to work again. Alice had forgotten the long hours they had to put in, in the country, and not waste valuable daylight, especially when the days were short, as now.

Flora was clearing up. She always was busy, but now there must not be a minute left to think. Alice put the drying-cloth down and put her arms around her mother, to Flora's consternation.

"I've missed you. I'm sorry it took so long. I'm sorry it took this, Mum."

Briefly, her mother responded and then she dashed off upstairs as if it was a sin to show emotion, to weep. Even when your father or grandfather had died, even when children returned home after years away, even when you loved too much.

+ + +

Thoughts jostled inside Alice' brain as she returned to Abbots Ford. She was glad to see them all looking so well. The village was sweetly familiar; the square grey stone tower of St Mary's Church peering through the bare branches of the surrounding trees. The school next to it appeared smaller than she remembered. She peeped in as she passed the chapel and it too, looked smaller. She thought about the harvest suppers and weddings which had taken place in the old iron village hall at the far end of the village, next to the Smithy where her father worked. The very scale of the village in comparison with the metropolis which was London, made her feel secure. She could feel the memories of her childhood folding around her like a cloak. She was still full of sentimental reminiscence when she reached Orchard Cottage and went down the steps, mentally preparing herself for her grandmother's mourning. She was surprised, therefore, to hear laughter. Dorothy turned as she opened the door.

"Alice!" Her sister rose and came to greet her with a warm embrace and kiss on the cheek. She held her at arms' length and cried, "Let me look at you!"

Alice was taken unawares. She had been so involved in her own thoughts and memories that she had forgotten that Dorothy had arrived that afternoon.

"You're looking well! And so sophisticated!"

Alice was confused by the effusive welcome from her younger, quieter sister. Now twenty-three, Dorothy had been away from home since she was eighteen. She had gone to London to begin training as a nurse. After two years, she had decided to change course and train as a nanny. Her reasons were the same as Alice. There was nothing she had wanted to do at home. Circumstances had not allowed the two girls to meet up and Dorothy's 'family' had recently moved to Suffolk, from where she had travelled now. She had managed to make the trip home annually, for her employers were not selfish.

"You've changed," said Alice warmly, looking her sister up and down. Dorothy was tall and slender, almost thin. Her dark hair was cut in a bob and swung, shining as she moved. Her brown eyes were framed by straight, dark brows, and her high cheek bones lent a kind of beauty to a face which verged on the plain. She wore a plaid skirt with a serviceable, neat white blouse and bottle-green cardigan. Her eyes lit up as she smiled at Alice and their grandmother in turn.

"What was the laughter about?" asked Alice.

"We were recalling last New Year's Eve when your Grandad thought he was the Prince of Wales after coming home from The Partridge," explained Louise.

"Grandad Will?" exclaimed Alice disbelievingly.

"Yes, Grandad Will! He could be a bit of a lad at times," her grandmother told her.

They shared a meal and stayed talking for a long while about old times, before the girls returned to their room, where they carried on chatting late into the night. They were in the room which had once been their mother and aunt's bedroom. It had changed little, if at all; indeed there were even some of their old books stacked on the shelves under the sloping roof.

"Girls Annual 1900, Hetty at Priory Park," read out Alice.

"Good Lord, these books are older than we are!" chuckled Dorothy.

"Poor Gran," said Alice thoughtfully. "She'll miss him."

"So will Mum, we all will," observed Dorothy.

"Oh, come on," said Alice.

"What do you mean?" asked Dorothy, hurt.

"We've been away, living our lives. We missed him by not being here!"

"You know that isn't true," Dorothy protested. "I came home as often as I could."

"Let's not argue, not now," Alice was regretting what she had said.

"But we had to leave, didn't we?" Dorothy insisted.

"Yes I suppose so."

"Lets' get some sleep. Big day tomorrow."

They nestled down, but neither girl slept. There were too many memories, too many regrets.

The crowing of a cockerel betrayed what rest they had achieved, and they had to rise, wash, eat, and bury Grandpa William.

+ + +

Friday dawned, covered in thick snow which had blanketed the world overnight. Dorothy had arrived just in time, for the village was cut off, by road at least. It was a 'big' funeral, as the local term would have it. William Henty was well-liked and respected in the village. *Not many like him left* they had said of him. His family was large, his friends were many, and most of the village turned out in the raw weather to see him off.

Michael Orrins was still the vicar at St Mary's and Tom Bates the retired blacksmith who continued to help Seth, was the man to supply a handsome black gelding to pull the funeral carriage. Bill had arranged everything, and the wake was at Orchard Cottage, scene of so many happy events and celebrations.

The carriage was brought down the lane silently in the snow, complete with coffin, to leave from the cottage, his home, for the last time. Snow drifted gently on to the pall, and on to the horse's jet-black plume.

Tom led Ebony down Church Lane, and around to the church. William's widow Louise had decided to follow him on foot, so she and her family, including Beatrice, her dead son's widow and their son Charles, followed Will to St Mary's. No sooner had their feet made prints in the snow, than they were filled. It was as if the Heavens mourned the passing of a good man; a man who had worked hard all his life, loved his family and harmed no one. The monochrome scene lent an added solemnity to the occasion.

They had arrived at the church. All the ladies waited while their menfolk bore the coffin inside. Only relatives carried William: his remaining son, two sons-in-law and five grandsons. Every woman in the church wore deep mourning.

Louise did not cover her face; she remained dignified throughout. She had always been a good wife to Will and she would not let him down now. She was surrounded by their family; their love and her courage would see her through.

Through Death's dark vale I fear no ill
With Thee Dear Lord beside me
Thy rod and staff my comfort still
Thy Cross before to guide me.

Louise faltered at the first line. Death. Where is Thy Sting? Thy Victory? *There shall be no victory, Will,* she thought. *It shall not part us.* The moment passed and she regained her composure. Her daughters would not give way while she held on; she would be strong for all of them. That was her way.

They buried him near his parents in the graveyard. Everyone had been civil and said wonderful things about him. Now it was all over. Louise felt as though her own life was over.

"Gran, can we speak with you?"

"Yes, my dears. How elegant you both look in black," she said vaguely, distracted.

"We have both arranged some time off..."

"Yes?"

"May we stay with you, here, for a while?"

"Good gracious! Is that it? Of course. That would be truly welcome."

They went to their parents and told them of their plans. For the first time, their mother allowed herself a tear.

"Gran will love that. What nice timing." She smiled. "Maybe you can come for the day on Sunday; we'll all be together. Dad will like that too."

The visitors melted away, like the snow, till there was only family left.

"Ma, anything at all – let us know what you need," instructed Flora. "And I'll be along tomorrow."

"Remember, Ma, we've all got room for you if you want to get away," reiterated Louise.

"Don't worry about anything," reassured Bill.

"You're all wonderful children," she told them. "You always were. I have all of you, and your Dad is with your brother, Charles. Nothing to fret about. Not any more. Not now."

FEBRUARY 1935

Flora was visiting Ellie before going to see her mother. Ellie Bates had been the village midwife who had initiated post-natal visits for six weeks to help the new mothers. This innovation had proved to be both popular and successful, for infant deaths had dropped dramatically in the area. In 1908, Ellie had detected an innate ability in Flora when she had coped with delivering her sister-in-law's baby unaided, and had persuaded her to join her in the work in order to train her. Ellie had recently retired when her own daughter, Jenny, had qualified under Flora's tuition. Ellie's husband, Tom, had been the village blacksmith, but had handed over the bulk of the work to Seth when he lost heart after losing both his sons in the Great War. The older couple still lived at Smithy Cottage, next door to the forge, where Flora now paused briefly to speak to Seth. The Smithy was housed in a massive old barn with a brick forge and chimney at one end. The earth floor was strewn with hay and tools and pieces of timber and metal were neatly stored around the walls. The noise, heat and odour of molten metal invaded Flora's senses as she tried to attract Seth's attention. A chestnut mare stood waiting passively, munching hay to pass the time.

"You alright, love?" He had stopped hammering to talk to her.

"Yes. Busy morning. Got a lot to do?"

"Sir Matthew wants me to see about some iron gates."

"Will you manage all the work?"

"Should do. Going to see Ellie?"

"Yes. How is she today?"

"Haven't seen her, but Tom's not been out."

"I'll see you later."

"Bye, love."

Flora knocked on the door of Ellie and Tom's house and waited.

"Come in, dear." Ellie was looking frail. She was only sixty-three but suffering from arthritis nowadays.

"How are you?" asked Flora.

"Not too bad".

"Has Bonnie been round yet?"

"No, dear. David's mother isn't well. She's gone round there today."

"What about Jenny?"

"Says she'll see you at the Heyes Farm at eleven."

Flora made them all tea, for Tom had joined them.

"Hello, love. You alright?" he asked.

"Yes thanks."

"How's your Mum bearing up?"

"She's alright. Has off days. It's early yet."

They sat in a friendly silence for a while, mulling over life and its ups and downs.

"I'd best go round and see her now."

Flora washed up the cups and saucers and bade them farewell.

"May come back later."

"Alright, dear. Always nice to see you."

As Flora walked with her bike through the village she stopped to talk here and there. When you deliver most of the babies in a place, you know almost everyone. Flora was finding that she was now delivering babies to mothers whom she had delivered; it gave a sense of continuity, but made her feel old.

When she reached Orchard Cottage, sunshine bathed the trees in its weak and watery light. She still was not used to having only her mother there, even though for much of the time, Will had been up on Peartree Farm when she visited.

"Hello, Ma," she called.

Louise came out from the kitchen.

"Hello, dear. I have the kettle on. Come and sit down."

They gossiped for a time. Alice and Dorothy were still staying with their grandmother, but both had gone off to Steeple Burstead to help their Aunt Louise with stocktaking, prior to the new season.

"Flora, I have an idea."

"Yes, Ma?"

"Only an idea...."

"Yes."

"It's hard to say. You've lived out at Briersham for, what? twenty-eight years, ever since you and Seth got married."

"Yes, Ma?"

"Dear, this house is too big for me now."

Flora looked at her mother.

"Would you and Seth consider moving here?"

"What about you?"

"Well, I'd move down to the front room and you and Seth would have my..."

"Ma! Oh no, not yours and Dad's room..." Flora was horrified. "Ma, I couldn't..." She remembered when her father had so proudly built it, how he and her mother had loved the views from the three windows.

"You come here every day to see me. Most of your work is in and around the village and Seth works here as well."

"No, Ma. You're not giving up your home. It's been easier since we got the bikes."

"Think about it, Flo. Louise and Gordon have built that lovely big house at Upper Abbots and Bill and Jessica will never move now from Peartree Farm House. How many years since they moved in? Must be fifteen," she mused.

"Nothing more to say, Ma."

"Talk to Seth; he's always had sense."

They discussed it no further and it was time for Flora to collect her bicycle from the front garden and meet Jenny.

"Don't forget to tell the girls about that invitation, Ma," she called as she left.

"Right, dear, 'bye for now."

MARCH 1935

Bill, Flora's younger brother was taking time adjusting to the loss of his father. He had always got along with Will, more so than his idolised older brother, Charles, who had been tragically killed in the Great War. Bill had helped on the farm since he was a small boy, but Charles had been the obvious heir. That was not to be, for he had moved away to Salisbury with his wife, Beatrice, even before going off to war; she had made remaining in the village an unacceptable option, because she had created a family feud. So Bill had helped to keep the farm going, and Will had come to rely on his son absolutely. Bill had married the pleasant, friendly Jessica at the end of the war and had two sons and two daughters of his own. Young Will was fifteen and they were pleased that Grandpa Will had lived on to see him join the team. His youngest, John, was five and the girls, Anne and Louise, were sixteen and nine years old.

Bill came in from milking that spring morning looking forward to his breakfast. The smell of bacon drifted into his nostrils as he opened the kitchen door. He kicked his boots off and left them in the porch, padding across in his stockinged feet to give Jessica a peck on the cheek.

"What's that for?" she grinned.

"Cos you're cooking my favourite breakfast," he told her.

"But you always have eggs and bacon for breakfast," she laughed.

"That's what I mean!"

He sat down at the table and Jessica turned to pour their tea.

"Where's Will?" she asked.

"He'll be down by and by," he informed her.

"Louise went with your Louise and Gordon," said Jessica.

"She loves working in that shop. Strange that even their own children aren't as keen as our Louise," commented Bill.

"And her just a little thing, with a few more years at school! Pity Anne doesn't really know what she wants out of life!" said her mother.

"She'll be alright, give her time," advised Bill tolerantly.

"There's a few letters," Jessica pointed out.

"Bill tucked into his breakfast first and then opened an official-looking envelope. Jessica did not notice at first that the blood had drained from her husband's face. He read and re-read the letter and Jessica realised that he was perturbed.

"What's wrong, love? You look as though you've seen a ghost."

"I can't believe it." Bill told her. "Says here I have to go and see the solicitor bloke about the 'lease' for the farm. Our Dad owned it, the farm."

"Are you sure it says 'lease'?"

"Look for yourself." He handed her the letter.

"He always spoke of leaving the farm to me and our lads…"

"Definitely says 'lease', doesn't it?" said Jessica, shocked. "How were Louise and Gordon able to build their house on this land if it's all leasehold? What does this mean for them?"

"Hadn't thought of it that way. What about this house, come to that?"

"Does it say how long the lease is? Let me read it again," said Jessica taking the letter from him.

"If we don't own it, who the hell does?" asked Bill.

"When do you see the solicitor?"

"Have to phone to arrange it," replied her husband.

"Well, sort it out as soon as you can. We have to know where we stand," pleaded Jessica.

"And I'll have to tell our Louise as soon as she and Gordon get home," he added.

They poured another cup of tea, and sipped it, silent and stunned. Bill's thoughts ran wildly on. How could Will, his father, not have told him what the situation was? He must have realised that it would all come to light after his death. Perhaps Louise knew already? He drained his cup.

"I'm off again, love," he told Jessica. "Try not to worry about all this." He sounded more confident than he felt. It was as if the earth had caved in beneath him. The security of his home, his job and his family was under threat. Worst of all, if it was true about the leasehold, he felt betrayed by his own father. He could not broach the subject with Louise, his mother, for she was still grief-stricken, and if she did not already know, he did not want to add to her problems. He would have to await the outcome of the meeting with the solicitor and pray that it was not as bad as it appeared.

+ + +

The house built by Flora's sister, Louise and her husband Gordon, was on Henty land at Upper Abbots. Although their shop at Steeple Burstead continued to thrive, they still preferred to live at Abbots Ford, and they had bought a car to travel back and forth together. Their eldest son, Charles who was eighteen, worked for his parents. Their elder daughter, Emma, had joined them when she left school two years earlier. Only Victoria, who was twelve, was left in the village each day at school.

They arrived home early because they worked a half-day on Saturdays. They dropped young Louise off at Plumtree Farm House, and Jessica ran out to the car.

"Urgent business! Bill had a solicitor's letter this morning... Can you come round this evening?"

"What's the matter?" asked Louise.

"Very involved. Bill will explain later. Alright?"

Louise nodded, and shrugged her shoulders to Gordon as they drove towards their own home.

"Not like Jess to make a mountain out of a molehill!" she observed.

Later, that evening, they all sat round drinking tea.

"What's all this about then, Bill?" asked Gordon. "We're intrigued."

16

"You'll be more than intrigued when you know what it is," said Jessica ruefully.

"It seems that the farm and all the land are leasehold, not freehold, as we'd thought," explained Bill.

Both Louise and Gordon blanched visibly.

How...? What...? Louise was opening and closing her mouth like a fish, as all the unasked, unanswerable questions disappeared on the air of her shocked silence.

"So our house is on leasehold land?" said Gordon.

"That's what we want to find out. What happened when you thought you bought the land?" queried Bill.

"Just that. I thought the land was given by your father. He even gave us money to help with the building of the house, and we borrowed the bulk of the cost as a mortgage."

Jessica and Louise sat quietly, not taking anything in.

"The bank must have been satisfied about the ownership of the land..." said Bill.

"Do you want one of us to go with you when you see this Mr... or is Jessica going?" asked Gordon.

"Yes, you should come, Gordon," agreed Bill.

They continued to discuss the situation with all the combinations of solutions and explanations there might be, but were none the wiser.

"I must say I am surprised that Will did not make the facts clearer, not like him at all," said Gordon as they left. Louise had not voiced the thought. It seemed disloyal to her father. The sense of disillusion hung in the air about them, almost tangible.

"Does Flora know?" asked Louise, as an afterthought.

"I haven't spoken to her," said Bill. "I suppose she'll get Orchard Cottage... anyway, we can ask her if Pa said anything."

Louise and Gordon left to return home.

"I hope it is still our home," she said as they closed the door behind them. "I don't know how Pa could do this to us," she said, her voice breaking as she burst into tears.

"Now then. Wait until we know for sure. Will wouldn't have put us in this position," Gordon reassured her. He had faith in his late father-in-law, and sent up silent prayers that he would be proved correct and that faith rewarded.

+ + +

Beatrice Henty, Charles' widow, and her son, Charles had a cottage on her father's land. After her husband's death at the beginning of the First World War, she had returned to Abbots Ford to live with her parents while she awaited the birth of her baby. Her son was now twenty-one and unable to settle to anything. Both his grandfathers had provided for him and he had been spoilt by both families; sadly, he had grown into a selfish and devious man. More recently he had demonstrated an interest in the Smithy, and in the absence of enthusiasm from his own sons, Seth was trying to encourage him. Although only a nephew by marriage, Seth seemed to bring out the best in the boy, even recognising something of himself as a young man.

Charles had been working intermittently at the forge for a few weeks, when, to Seth's amazement, he had a visit from Beatrice. He was working on a piece of ornamental iron-work and so engrossed in what he was doing that he did not know how long she had been standing watching him. He pulled an arm across a perspiring forehead and caught sight of her. Flora had never felt that the time was right to tell her husband the full extent to which his brother-in-law, Robert, had been unfaithful to Rebecca, but Seth did know Beatrice had been involved and was a dangerous woman. What was more, Beatrice had always been unpleasant to Flora and the family. In a small village, they maintained a veneer of amiability between them all, being related by marriage, but it remained an uneasy truce.

"Hello, Seth," said Beatrice, looking at him from beneath lowered lashes.

"What can I do for you, Beatrice?" he asked, business like.

"It's the wheels on the trap..."

"You want me to sort it out for you? I'll come round to have a look later," he told her.

Dismissed, she turned on her heels and left without another word. Beatrice was forty-six and was still an attractive woman.

There had always been whispers about her, but she had not married again, to the surprise of all who knew her.

Seth arrived at the cottage at tea-time and knocked on the front door. She was wearing a fitted tweed skirt and pink twinset, with pearls at her throat and ears.

"Come in, Seth," she purred. He stood awkwardly in the small hall, waiting to be shown the work to be done.

"Cup of tea?"

"No, thanks. Flora's expecting me home."

"Ah, yes." She led the way through the house and out to a shed at the back. The wheels were leaning against piled up boxes and Seth examined them.

"No problem there. I'll collect them in the morning." He was aware she was standing close to him, much too close for politeness or comfort. She ran her hand up his arm to his shoulder. He did not know, afterwards, why he did not immediately move away and leave her in no doubt that the attention was unwanted.

"Seth?" He turned towards her and she put her arms around his neck. Almost involuntarily, his arms went around her waist and he bent his head down to her upturned face. It seemed churlish not to kiss her. Seth was embarrassed. "I've got to go…"

She nodded, smiling secretly to herself. She knew that he had enjoyed the experience. He, in turn, felt guilty and manipulated. As he walked down the path, he could have kicked himself for his foolishness. *Just a kiss,* he thought. He did not even like Beatrice, but she had a certain magnetism and he had felt drawn, unable to check his reactions. He walked home, trying to think of a way to get himself out of mending the wheels. Charles could collect them! He lived there, after all. He could show Charles what to do, and allow him to deal with his mother. Seth arrived home at Orchard Cottage happier for having solved the problem. He greeted Flora cheerfully, only becoming irritable with her later in the evening as the thought of that kiss teased his memory, and the guilt jarred his conscience.

+ + +

Esmée (Thorndyke) Mortimer had lost none of her spirit. She was seventy-three but still flaunted luxuriant titian hair which many swore was a wig. She and Barnabus, who had just turned eighty, had been married eighteen years, a second marriage for both of them. The beautiful house where they lived dominated the far end of the village towards East Hartness, because many trees and shrubs had been removed, revealing the mansion to public gaze. After her first husband's death, Esmée had spent some years in a depressive wilderness and had allowed the house known as Fourwinds to deteriorate. Fortunately, as a talented artist, her gift had saved her and she had recovered to welcome her son and daughter back into her life. Over the years she had made Abbots Ford a pilgrimage for artists and sculptors in the West Country, for she had introduced exhibitions at her home even before the First World War. The mood during the war had precluded such perceived frivolities, but with peacetime came a return to the popular annual event. Some local people complained of the influx of motor cars during the week-long opening of the house, but others were grateful for the additional revenue it generated. Esmée's daughter, Madeline, and ex-Naval officer husband, Algernon, had eventually settled in Bath. They and their two children, Oliver and Ophelia, were attending the first day of the exhibition. Esmée's son Giles, now in his fifties, was about to make one of his rare forays to see his mother. Years ago, on his return from a lengthy posting to India, Giles had fallen in love with one of his mother's oldest friend's, Anna. Esmée disapproved because of the twenty year gap in their ages. Consequently, the relationship between them all had foundered; nor had Giles ever had a family of his own.

"I think that's everything," said Esmée with some satisfaction. "It all looks presentable. The idea of having new artists in the library is a good one. Oscar Stevens shows much promise," she added. Barnabus was sitting in a comfortable chair near the range in the huge kitchen, with a small dog on his knee. He nodded in agreement.

"Would you like some lunch now?" she continued.

"What do the others think?" he queried.

"They've dashed off home to prepare for this afternoon. It's only we two." Esmée looked at Barnabus as she pottered about, making sandwiches. He looked tired. He was still a handsome man; tall, thin, white haired, with a bushy white moustache and a goatee beard. He adored Esmée and always enjoyed the exhibitions, especially when he was showing a piece of his own work. He was a sculptor, who used different media and materials, and often persuaded Seth to do some soldering for him when using metals.

"There's time for you to have a rest after this, Barny, if you wish," she told him, as they ate.

"I don't need a rest," he muttered crossly.

"You've been working so hard, too hard."

"Hard work never hurt anybody," he told her irritably.

They heard the doorbell jangle, and shortly, the maid came through, telling them that Madeline and her family had arrived.

"She's early," groaned Esmée. Barnabus said nothing.

"Show them into the salon and I'll be along directly," she instructed. They finished their snack and Barny opened a bottle of white wine which they took, with four glasses, through to the salon.

The room glowed warmly from a fire roaring in the enormous grate. Cream silk sofas sat close by, luxuriously fringed, and cream silk curtains graced the massive windows at each end. Family photographs were grouped on occasional tables and on a baby grand piano. A Chinese carpet provided a splash of colour in the neutral room, which made an elegant and suitable backdrop to the paintings on exhibition.

"Hello, my dears." Esmée greeted her family warmly.

"Hello, Mother. Everything is ready, I see," commented Madeline. They walked slowly around the exhibits, sipping wine and remarking upon the qualities of each painting or piece of sculpture. Oliver and Ophelia, Esmée's grandchildren, were now of an age, at fourteen and twelve, to appreciate their grandparent's works.

"How long did the bronze take, Barny?" asked Algernon.

"I've been working on it, on and off, for eighteen months," Barny told him.

"May we go and look round the garden?" asked Ophelia sweetly.

"Of course, dear," said Esmée.

"Watch out for the dogs! You're wearing a new frock," warned their mother as they disappeared.

"They're looking well. They've grown since Christmas!" Esmée told her daughter and son-in-law.

"We miss them now that they're away at school," said Madeline.

"They soon grow up…" said Esmée.

People began to trickle into the house and by the middle of the afternoon there was hardly room to move.

"You know, Mama, flowers would add something…" suggested Madeline.

"This is an art exhibition, not a flower-show," rebuked Esmée.

The older woman mingled with her guests, talking and gossiping, guiding people around, explaining interpretation. Madeline was engrossed in conversation with one of her mother's oldest friends, also an artist, when she noticed someone who was tantalisingly familiar. For a moment, she could not place him but then realised with a frisson of shock, that it was Giles, her brother. She had not seen him for many years. She made her way through the groups of people talking, and those studying the pictures, and went quietly to him.

"Hello, Giles." He turned, and she was stunned anew at his appearance. "How are you?" she asked.

"Maddy! How wonderful to see you. Is Algy here?"

"Yes, somewhere about. Mother didn't say you were coming."

He looked the same somehow, still tall and slim, but much, much older. She supposed that he must be similarly surprised upon seeing herself. A woman appeared at his side, stylish and elegant, but undeniably elderly. Madeline did not recognise her.

"Hello, Madeline." It was the voice which identified her.

"Hello, Anna. How are you?" she said politely. It crossed her mind to wonder if her mother knew that they were here.

"Have you seen Mother?" she asked him.

"No. Hoping to. How is she?"

"She's keeping very well. We came at Christmas, to stay for the festivities. Barnabus is frail," she told him. She noticed that her husband was being bored to death by Major Frankland, and made her excuses to rescue him.

"Algy, Giles is here and Mother doesn't know yet," she whispered urgently. "I don't want them to meet for the first time in years quite so publicly. Can you make an excuse to take Mother out to the water garden and I'll bring Giles out?" She knew that Algernon would be discreet, and when she noticed that Anna was inspecting the sculptures in the library, she went straight over to Giles.

"Come and see the garden and tell me what's been happening to you all this time," she invited with a smile.

He explained that he and Anna had never married, but everyone assumed that they were.

"It just didn't occur to us," he told her.

"Anna must be a similar age to Mama," said Madeline.

"A year younger."

"Are you happy?"

"Depends upon what you mean by 'happy'," he replied. "We get along."

"Have you seen the children?" she asked, deliberately changing the subject.

"No, but I expect I shall," he smiled.

They walked along the crazed and bricked path, chilly in the weak spring sunshine and came upon Algernon with Esmée in a recessed bower.

"Mother," said Madeline gently. "Look who's here."

Esmée looked round, smiling, and her face crumpled in recognition. He was so like his father, and the shock of seeing him unexpectedly had caught her unawares. Yet if they had said he was here, she might have refused to meet him.

"Mother?" Madeline and Algernon strolled away arm in arm towards the sound of their children's shouts and laughter, while Esmée embraced her son.

"How are you, my dear?" she asked, watery-eyed.

"I'm well. You look well, how have you been?"

23

"Mostly good. But tell me about you. What have you been doing with yourself?"

"Still in the Diplomatic Service. Still with Anna."

He had said it. She had not wanted to ask, but she wanted to know. "I see." Her generous mouth was set in a firm line. "Is she here?"

"Yes, Mother, she is. She wanted to come and I could not have left her behind."

Esmée admired him for that. He was loyal, if ill advised. Though she had to admit that their partnership, and love, had lasted longer than many a marriage.

"Will you come and see her?"

Esmée was hesitating, when suddenly Anna appeared and joined them.

"Hello, Esmée. How lovely to see you again."

"Hello, Anna. Good of you to come," said Esmée graciously.

"The exhibition is impressive, and what a lot of people!" said Anna.

"Yes. It has become a date in people's diaries," agreed Esmée.

"I'd like to see Barnabus before we go," said Giles.

"He's resting, but you can see him. The crowds sometimes overpower him. He's only in the kitchen!"

She took the couple to see her husband.

"Look who I've brought to see you!" she said.

He turned his rheumy eyes upon them.

"Hello, my boy," he said, genuinely pleased to see his stepson.

"Hello, Anna." He had stood to greet her. She leaned forward to kiss his cheek, for they had been old friends.

"We're leaving shortly, but wanted to say 'hello' before we go," she explained. Esmée stood by, looking at them while they spoke to Barnabus. They spoke of the success of the exhibition, of how Fourwinds was looking, of the niece and nephew Giles still had not seen, everything, except their feelings.

"We'd better be off now. It's been wonderful to see you both," said Giles.

"You must come again, soon," offered Esmée.

"That would be nice," said Anna. Giles kissed his mother and assured her that they would be in touch. When they had gone, Esmée was not sure how she felt about them. It still seemed such a waste, because Anna had been too old to have children when she met Giles; thus he had been robbed of the chance to have a family. She did not have time to ruminate further, for Madeline sought her out to request the use of towels: Oliver had pushed Ophelia into the pond and was dripping weedily on to the Chinese carpet in the dining room.

+ + +

Alice and Dorothy had created quite a stir in the village on their extended holiday, with all their fashionable clothes, modern ways and shorn hair. Alice was as vague and capricious as ever, which did not preclude her being quick-witted and sharp-tongued when she liked. She wore many of the Duchess of Taversham's cast-offs and maintained her short bobbed hair in fashionable honey brown waves. Her pale blue eyes would skim over everything and everyone, seeming not to take anything in, but she was shrewd enough. She had had many love affairs but was not ready to settle down. Yet she experienced real heartache when an affair ended, as the one with Steven had, just after Christmas.

Dorothy with her brown button eyes and kind smile loved the children in her charge. She had loved a man once, and only once. She did not see why she should become involved with many men, when she wanted only one. When it had not worked out, she had thrown herself into her work, which was easy, because of its very nature.

Eddy, their brother, had fallen head over heels in love with a pleasant girl called Elizabeth. When the couple realised that the girls were to return to their employers imminently, they decided to bring their betrothal celebrations forward in order to cheer the family after the sadness of Grandpa Will's loss. The party was arranged for the Saturday before the girls' departure.

The cottage was overflowing with family and friends. It had been a pleasant early spring day, but a chill nipped the air as the evening wore on. The grandparents called in at teatime, staying long enough to complain about the latest songs crackling loudly from the gramophone speaker.

"What about a sing-song around the piano?" asked James Hawkes.

The young people took no notice of him, and Flora raised her eyes to the heavens.

"These young folk don't know what they're missing, do they?" she asked Charlotte.

"I quite like it myself!" replied her mother-in-law, jigging about to the rhythm. Seth's sister, Rebecca, called in with her husband, Robert. Rebecca knew Elizabeth well and had come to congratulate her friend.

Alice and Dorothy were sad that their lengthy sojourn was coming to an end. They had both enjoyed the time at home. Alice needed a quiet moment, and walked outside to the orchard, through the old scullery door. She picked a piece of bark from a tree and leaned against it, thinking of her return to the frenetic pace of London life. The cold pure air cleared her head, as she inhaled the smells of the countryside. She did not hear the footsteps across the scrubby grass.

"Hello, what are you doing out here?" The voice was soft. "You've grown up, Alice. Attractive girl now," he continued.

She was in a strange mood. She knew he was flirting with her but she did not care.

"You're not bad yourself for an old 'un," she laughed.

He had always had an attraction for women; it was not immediately obvious, but he managed to make them feel special.

"Got any boyfriends?" he asked.

"A few."

"Anyone special?"

"No one I'm saving myself for," she commented, provocatively.

He stood close to her, beneath the tree.

She looked at him with her ice-blue eyes, heavy-lidded the way she had practiced in her mirror, when the thought crossed her mind that she looked a little like Bette Davis.

He stood even closer, close enough to kiss her. She was playing him like a fish and he did not know. They kissed, while languidly she rested against the tree.

"A woman like you could drive a man mad," he laughed nervously. "Meet me."

"Where?"

"Anywhere we can be alone."

"I'll meet you in Bristol on my way back to London."

"Bristol?" he hesitated. "Alright. When do you go?"

"Tuesday."

"It's awkward, but I'll be there."

"There's an hotel near Temple Meads Station called 'Traveller's Rest'. Meet me there at three o'clock."

He kissed her again, impatiently.

"Alice!"

Dorothy's voice registered the shock she felt. She had not meant to call out, but her amazement at finding her Uncle Robert kissing her sister, a girl young enough to be his daughter, had not prepared her.

"Just a farewell gesture, Dotty," laughed Robert, embarrassed.

"Yes. I took him by surprise," said Alice convincingly.

"Grandma and Grandad Hawkes are leaving. I was sent out to find you."

"I'll have a smoke out here," said Robert.

The girls went back to the party together.

"I hope you know what you're doing." Dorothy could not fathom her sister or her attitude to men and relationships.

They drank a final toast to Eddy and Elizabeth, who made a lovely couple, for Elizabeth was a pretty dark-haired girl with honest grey eyes. Eddy was like his father, Seth, but with grandfather Will's mid-brown colouring.

"When's the wedding?" asked Auntie Ruth.

"Not till this time next year. We're saving for one of those new houses being built on the edge of the village," explained Eddy.

"Good for you. Sensible pair!" said Grandad Hawkes.

Elizabeth's parents and family were leaving at the same time as the Hawkes family.

"See you at the wedding! Thank you for a lovely time," they said to Flora and Seth.

"Not like you two," smiled Louise. "You couldn't wait to get married. Your Dad and I worried at first..." she continued to smile at the memory.

"You were right, of course."

+ + +

Louise was sad to see the girls go. She had enjoyed their company and the house would be quiet without them. The spring was well underway now; daffodils and primroses welcomed the better days once again. She sat thinking of her memories: she and Will as young lovers, as friends, as parents and grandparents. Will's strength of character and love; he had taken everything in his stride. He always maintained that he was like that because he loved his work, being close to the earth and God's creatures. Whatever it was, he had been strong enough for all of them and more. She knew she would not get over his passing – come to terms with it, yes, but not recover. They had been together too long for that – she was part of something which had lost its soul.

The girls had brought their luggage down earlier and were going round to catch the bus to Bristol.

"Goodbye, my dears. It has been lovely having you here," she told them.

"Bye, Gran. We won't leave it so long next time," said Alice.

"Look after yourself, Gran. I'll write," Dorothy promised.

Their mother had come along to see them off; they had said their farewells to their father and brothers the previous day.

"Try to come sooner next time, Alice," said Flora pithily as they struggled with the suitcases and bags. "Write and let us know how you are."

The bus rattled towards them and a passenger got down to help them, tipping his hat as they sat down.

"Bye Ma," said Dorothy, while Alice waved mutely, swallowing the tears. They sat in silence as the bus trundled through the village and puffed up the hill past Salisbury House. They gave a small wave here and there as villagers saw them and realised that they were leaving. At Steeple Burstead they watched out for Aunt Louise in her shop as the bus drove past, waving furiously when they managed to catch her eye. Then they sat back again holding in their sadness at leaving. Their eyes devoured the familiar countryside as they travelled through it, trying to save up the sights for when they were feeling low and far from home.

They began talking, as the outskirts of Bristol were presaged by a build-up of houses, new and old, with new parades of shops at their core. It was as if, mentally, they were putting Abbots Ford behind them; as if there was no room for their Abbots Ford personae within their London or Suffolk selves.

Alice had arranged that Dorothy's train left first. She saw her into the station, leaving her own cases too, and waved her off on the train which would link with one in London taking her on towards Ipswich. She had a lump in her throat as the train drew out, its energetic snorting and belching of smoke making it appear like a living thing. She watched until Dorothy's dark head with its little red hat was a tiny spot on the side of the train, then until the train itself was a tiny spot, and finally disappeared.

Dorothy had a carriage to herself. She took off her hat and put it with her bags. Then she took out her handkerchief and cried all the way beyond Bath. She missed her family so, and had not really wanted to move away. Once she had completed her training and secured a position with another kind family, she had begun to make a life for herself. The Marshalls were friendly and genuine people; he was a banker, and they had a place in London and a property between Ipswich and Norwich, called Pelham Hall near the small village of Saxmundham. Dorothy was looking forward to seeing her charges once more; she hoped that the under-nanny and governess had maintained standards of behaviour in her absence. Tobias was seven, Rupert five, Julianna four and Daisy two. As the train thundered towards London, she could feel her pleasure mounting at the thought of taking care of them all and organising their routine. Abbots Ford is lovely to go back to, but the children are my life, she thought, and began making plans for surprises and treats to delight their childhood.

+ + +

Alice had gone back outside the station and walked purposefully towards the hotel called 'Traveller's Rest'. It had seen better days, having been built at the height of Victorian baroque. The furnishings looked blowsy and overdone, not to mention being extremely dirty; the site near the station during the age of steam did not help.

"I have a reservation. I am Mrs Black," she announced to the little man behind the desk.

"Ah, yes, Madam. Your husband is already here. Have you any bags?"

She answered in the negative and was shown up to a room which looked almost as filthy as the vestibule.

"Hello, darling," she approached Robert with confidence and planted a kiss on his cheek for the benefit of the little man from downstairs.

"Am I late – so annoying!"

She turned and saw that he was still standing there.

"Thank you so much," she said, giving him a tip, and expertly manoeuvring him out through the doors. Robert stood dumbfounded at this evidence of expertise.

"Have you done this before?" he asked, only half-joking.

"No, of course not."

"Did you have a good journey?"

"Yes, and you?"

"Yes, but I have to catch the four-thirty bus home."

"Shall we order some tea, or not?"

"No, I'm going to have a smoke first."

Alice undressed and got under the bedclothes, while Robert had a cigarette. They made small talk, studiously avoiding mentioning the family. Eventually, Robert joined her in bed and they made love. It was almost passionless; it was certainly mechanical. He wanted her young body and she wanted a man. It did not seem to occur to either of them that it was wrong, for all kinds of reasons. He explained that her being away so long made him think she was a different person to the little girl he used to know.

"Thank goodness for that, you naughty boy!" she teased.

If either of them had thought through the processes which had brought them to this tryst, they might not have been so complacent. It was as though they were completely unaware of the social morés which governed behaviour; they deserved each other. Such is the complexity of the human psyche that Robert was able to return home and behave like a loving husband and father. Similarly, next time Alice went home and met her Aunt Rebecca, her father's sister, it would not dawn on her how she had betrayed her. Yet Alice was not an intrinsically evil person; she had many good points and was often excellent company. Both she and Robert were emotionally derelict in that area of their lives. Alice dressed and gathered her things. She stood at the door in her elegant suit.

"I'll see you the next time I'm home," she smiled.

She turned and left the tawdry room, went down the stairs and out into the March afternoon. An hour later, she was on her way, in the train, towards London, and her other life.

MAY 1935

Esmée's husband Barnabus had died peacefully in his sleep after a short illness. It was not a large funeral, their artist friends who lived locally attended, but Esmée did not contact the numerous acquaintances they had made over the years they had been married. The children from his first marriage attended with their families, and of course Madeline, Algernon and their children. Giles turned up alone, to Esmée's relief. She knew she would not have been able to cope with her feelings about Anna while she was emotionally fragile.

The sun shone brightly on the cortège as it moved slowly along the main road towards the church. Esmée remained dignified and in control throughout the service, and moved among her guests at Fourwinds afterwards, ever the attentive hostess.

"Mama, why don't you come back home to Bath with us?" asked Madeline.

"You know you're welcome," smiled Algernon gently.

"I know, my dears and I thank you most affectionately. But I shall remain here. Perhaps I could come for a long weekend later in the summer, if I can find someone to take care of the dogs!"

"I could come and dog sit for you, Mama," offered Giles, arriving behind them and catching the tail-end of the conversation.

"Oh, there you are, dear," said Esmée. "What are your plans?"

"I thought I would stay tonight. At least, if there's room," he added unnecessarily. Esmée was taken aback. Giles had not stayed overnight for years.

"Off course, dear. I'll tell Johns to make up your bed."

"Have you any other overnight guests, Mama?" enquired Madeline.

"My old and very dear friend, Sonia, is staying the week," Esmée told her. Madeline nodded, satisfied that her mother would be kept occupied during the next few vulnerable days. She gathered her children and after sad farewells to Esmée, the family left for Bath. By teatime, everyone had gone, except for the house guests. Sonia went up to her room before dinner, sensing that Esmée and her son wanted to talk privately.

"I am so sorry about Barnabus, Mama. He was the very best of men," said Giles.

Esmée sniffed and blew her nose. It had been a trying day. They sat in the morning room looking out on to the water garden.

"I know you'll miss him terribly," said Giles.

Esmée nodded. After a while, she spoke.

"We had eighteen wonderful years. I married two unusually excellent men."

Giles acquiesced, and they sat in silence as the evening light turned to gold across the garden.

"Mama, Anna is very ill." He spoke quietly, confiding in her.

She turned her blue eyes on him, their expression mirroring her concern.

"She's dying."

"Giles, how awful. I am so sorry, dear boy. What do they think it is?"

"Cancer. They've given her three weeks rather than months."

She continued to look at him as he spoke. Suddenly it was too much for him, and he wept. His mother rose and went over to sit next to him on the sofa.

"You know I understand," she stated. She put her arm around him and stroked his cheek. She knew he truly loved Anna, and her sympathy for them welled up in her. Her regret for the wasted years and her own grief for Barnabus left her feeling sick and empty; too empty for tears, she merely felt numb.

"Giles, bring her home, to Fourwinds if she will come."

He turned and held his mother in a tight embrace, then pulled away, shaking his head.

"I'm sorry, Mama. I didn't mean to..."

"Think no more of it, son. Bring your Anna home and we'll look after her together."

"Thank you. Oh, thank you."

"No, thank you. I'm not saintly. I need a chance to make amends, if it's not too late."

They sat until it was time for a dinner they could not eat, watching the sun set on a phase in both their lives.

JUNE 1935

The legal repercussions in Bill and Louise' discovery that Peartree Farm was, in reality, a leasehold had taken weeks to unravel. Bill and Gordon had travelled to Bristol on three or four occasions to clarify and protect their position. They drove home to Abbots Ford filled with relief after the last meeting. Jessica and Louise were waiting at Peartree Farm House for their return.

"How did you get on?" asked Jessica. Both women were at the end of their tether with anxiety because the security of their homes was threatened. They waited patiently while the two men came in and settled themselves after their journey. Tea was brewed and they all sat in the comfortable living room.

"Well?" repeated Louise.

"The news is good," said Gordon to put them out of their misery. "Indeed, the news is excellent."

"Tell us, tell us!" cried Jessica.

Bill smiled as he looked at his wife and began to explain the outcome.

"The houses are safe!" he said exultantly.

Jessica and Louise hugged one another, and listened open-mouthed.

"It seems that Father bought the land this house stands upon, and the house, years ago, in case he and Ma wanted to live here," said Bill.

"Then, when we wanted to build a house," carried on Gordon, "he secretly bought the land so that we could."

Louise began to weep silently.

"I knew Pa wouldn't have let us down," she whispered.

"The other news is that the farm is definitely leasehold: ninety-nine years," continued Bill.

"How do you feel about that?" asked Louise.

"Relieved about the house, sad about the farm."

"So, how is it financed?" asked Jessica.

"Pa bought the lease at the outset and the amount which I'd understood was some kind of pension payment in trust, is really a ground rent."

"So there's nothing to leave the children?" said Jessica sadly.

"Well, yes, there'll eventually be the house, and the lease runs on for another fifty-seven years," said Bill.

"We can breathe easily now anyway," said Gordon. "Nothing much will change."

"Who really owns the farm?" asked Louise.

"Apparently, there's a management company, who aren't saying who the outright owner is," elucidated Bill.

"I suppose they had to contact you because the lease is in your name now that Pa's gone?" put in Jessica.

"Yes. But it still gave us all a fright!" replied Gordon.

"Did you mention it to Flora or Ma?" enquired Louise.

"Haven't said anything to Ma, but I did say something briefly to Flora. She knew nothing about the farm and assumed the same as we did. She said it was because Pa had mentioned to her that Charles' son was 'taken care of' and that she and Seth would have Orchard Cottage one day. So she thought Pa must have 'taken care' of us as well.

"Let's get out the sherry then!" suggested Jessica.

They laughed loudly and made silly jokes, letting go of all the worry. Bill shook as he poured the drinks into wedding-present glasses, retrieved from the back of the china cabinet. They all stood up to toast themselves.

"Here's to us, and our homes," said Jessica, with moist eyes.

Bill looked at his wife, at his brother-in-law, and finally at his sister.

"Here's to our Pa. Thanks Pa!" he said emotionally. "Sorry for doubting you."

They took a sip of the smooth sherry and felt it warm their throats as it slipped down. While the knowledge that their homes were safe warmed their hearts.

+ + +

Flora and Seth were still in love. Their relationship had neither gone sour, nor weakened. They strived to spend time with each other, but too often circumstances intervened: work, family or friends, which made it difficult to arrange. They had decided to take the chance, spend the money and give themselves a week away in Minehead. Tom was able to cope for that length of time in the Smithy, and Jenny could manage alone for a short time; unusually, no babies were due then anyway.

They had organised everything so that Eddy and Seth would not starve in their absence; someone would go in and see Louise every day. They were packed and prepared for the journey.

"All happy?" asked Seth.

"More or less, I'm sure I've forgotten something," said Flora.

"We're just not used to things like holidays," said Seth, grabbing her around the waist and swinging her backwards in imitation of a Latin lover.

"Mind your back, you daft fool," she scolded.

Eddy, who had a broken-down old van, arrived to transport them and their luggage to where they were picking up the bus.

"All ready you old folk?" he called.

"Enough of 'old folk' you cheeky monkey," said his father good-naturedly.

"Let me help you, Mum." He took her heavy bag and put it in the van.

"Oh I do like to be beside the seaside," sang Eddy, and Seth joined in, full of high spirits as they drove along. They were approaching the junction with the main road, when Jenny's husband, Alan came racing along on his bicycle.

"Thank God," he panted.

"What's wrong, Alan?" asked Flora.

"It's Ellie – been took bad." He struggled for breath.

They left him there as Eddy turned right to go along the main road towards the Smithy. Flora and Seth ran up the path to the cottage and went straight inside.

Dr Tanner was examining Ellie and Tom, Bonnie and Jenny stood around helplessly.

The doctor turned to look up at Tom.

"There's nothing to be done, lad. She's gone."

"But surely…" Flora stepped forward, involuntarily, and Seth put out his hand to stop her.

"Mum?" Insidious panic made Jenny's voice shake.

Bonnie was crying quietly, but Jenny would not accept it. Tom stood inanimate. Alan rushed back in.

"Sit down, Tom," said Seth quietly. "Sit down, man."

He did as he was told. Bonnie had turned away from the dreadful scene and Jenny's Alan put his arm around her. Flora had sat down because her legs would not hold her.

"Mum?" repeated Jenny.

"She's gone, Jen," said Seth.

"We've got to do something..." She began crying hysterically and this brought Flora to her senses.

"Stop it, Jenny."

Jenny went over to Ellie's body and was obviously about to attempt resuscitation.

"Take her upstairs, Alan," instructed Flora.

"Brandy for Tom, Seth. Have you got any?" asked the doctor.

Seth thought afterwards that the doctor himself had been in need of a brandy. He had worked with Ellie for many happy years. They had co-operated and worked side by side in what, traditionally, was a fraught relationship. Ellie's personality had been ideal for the job. She had never given offence in her dealings with her mothers, always being aware that they and their babies were individuals, and as such, were experts about themselves. They needed her expertise and experience at delivery and in the first few days, but thereafter, Ellie had never been dogmatic. She had been the same with her family and friends and they had loved her well. Now, suddenly, she was gone. Admittedly, she had seemed weaker in recent months, but there had been no sign, no warning, that her heart was so damaged.

Word went round the village like wildfire, and her shocked husband and daughters were buoyed up momentarily by the waves of support and affection towards them. Everyone was grief-stricken and Bonnie and Jenny found themselves comforting others who found their mother's passing too much to bear. They would mourn later and longer.

Her funeral was on a sunny day at the end of June. Relatives and friends who had travelled were put up in the village. Flora was the mainstay in organising the wake, which was taking place at Smithy Cottage. Tom prepared Ebony and the carriage himself; he would not allow Seth near them.

People came from far and wide to be there. There was not sufficient room in the church and churchyard and people stood the length of the main road, from church to forge, lining the path of her final journey.

Ebony gleamed, his mane silky and swinging. The harness sparkled in the sunlight and the carriage shone. Tom led the horse himself and her family followed behind. No child squirmed or cried and it was silent except for the clopping of Ebony's hooves, the jangling of the harness, and the weeping of the women. It was right that the sun should shine, for she would not have wanted all those children to get wet or cold. They sang *There's a friend for little children* at the service. They spoke of her love of people, and especially of children.

"She would not wish for sadness on this day," said Michael Orrins. "Let us celebrate instead, her life, and her contribution to our community."

It seemed as though everyone attended the wake, after they had laid her to rest. The company spilled out past the field, beyond the Smithy and out on to the road. Tom was only aware of a blur, a sea, of faces. They came at intervals and shook his hand, murmuring words of comfort and condolence. And then they were gone; it was over, all over. They had to learn to live their lives without her, while remaining grateful that she had been there at all.

+ + +

Chapter Two

SEPTEMBER 1935 – JUNE 1937

The long, elegant façade of Pelham Hall always gave Dorothy a thrill of pleasure when they returned to it. The pink-red bricks glowed with a Mediterranean blush in the soft Suffolk countryside. The family was returning from a month in Scotland and the children were excited to be coming home. Horses munched grass in the home field and looked up as the motor cars drove noisily past, crunching over the gravel drive.

"Nanny, do look, we're almost there!" cried Rupert.

"I liked Scotland" averred Toby.

"They killed all the birds," stated Julianna, sadly.

Daisy sat on Dorothy's knee, looking around, interested in everything.

"We're home," Dorothy told her.

As the cars drew up, a number of servants came down the steps to help everyone inside. The second car contained all their luggage; Sir Philip and Lady Stephanie were following on later.

"Welcome home, Miss Hawkes," said the butler.

The three elder children ran up the steps as fast as they could, closely followed by Iris Clark, the under-nanny, whom they called 'Nursey'.

Once inside, they had to climb four long staircases and two smaller ones to reach the nursery floor. Before they went up, Dorothy consulted with the housekeeper as to what was available for the children's tea and staff supper.

The children were overjoyed to see their rooms, beds and toys once more. Even little Daisy seemed to recognise everything. Dorothy organised refreshing baths for them all and they sat in the day nursery before the fire which had been lit, having tea in their dressing-gowns.

"Tell us about Abbots Ford," suggested Rupert.

"It isn't so very different from the countryside near here," said Dorothy. They loved hearing about where she had lived when she was a little girl, a concept they had difficulty in assimilating.

"Were you big when you were little?" asked Julianna.

"Of course she was silly," said Toby.

"I think some people are becoming very tired after their journey," commented Dorothy. Iris was cradling Daisy and Dorothy suggested that she should settle the toddler, while she, Dorothy, read the others a story.

"Cavemen!" shouted Toby.

"Brer Rabbit!" shouted Rupert.

Dorothy calmed them down and read to them. They listened avidly, for this was a routine they followed wherever they found themselves. After they had said their prayers and were tucked into crisp, cold, sheets, Dorothy left Iris in charge and went to the day nursery. It was a pleasant room, furnished as a sitting-room, but with all the paraphernalia related to children. The maid had set the table for two, where later, Dorothy and Iris would share a meal.

The children were so tired after their long journey that they had settled down at once. Dorothy went on the long trek downstairs to see Mrs Watson, the housekeeper.

"How are they, dear? All settled?" she enquired.

Dorothy asked about news and gossip in their absence, and related the same about the family in return. It was a pleasant household; their employers were interested in everyone as a family and the staff were interested in their turn.

After a cup of tea, Dorothy went back to her domain to unpack everything and to set about organising the children's laundry, which she and Iris did between them. A laundry maid would assist them tomorrow as they had just returned and had more than usual. The governess did not join the family again until next week and in the meantime, Dorothy enjoyed the freedom they had to roam the estate and surrounding countryside on what the children called 'ventures'. She expended all her energy during her busy days, so it was no wonder she had little chance of a social life, except with house staff and other nannies. She just had time to write to her parents before supper. She had been so busy preparing for the visit to Scotland that she had been unable to reply to her mother's sad letter at the beginning of July, telling of the unexpected death of Ellie Bates. She had also received a gossipy letter from Alice, saying the most outrageous things about the Prince of Wales and a so-called friend; apparently rumour was rife in London. *That girl,* thought Dorothy fondly, *exaggeration should be her middle name!*

NOVEMBER 1935

Alice could hardly contain her excitement. Mrs Simpson had been seen with the Prince of Wales yet again. Indeed the Duchess had spoken to them, no less!

"You're tugging my hair, Alice. Do take care," said her employer coldly. "It really is too much," continued the Duchess. "She is such an awful person – hardly one of us at all."

Alice made no comment.

"Which gown did we decide upon?"

"The slinky pale grey crepe, Ma'am," said Alice.

The Duchess was extremely glamorous. She had blonde, curly hair and brilliantly blue eyes, but wore no 'paint' as she called it. "Too vulgar for words" was the verdict.

"Slinky? Whatever do you mean?"

There was a knock on the door and at her command, it opened. It was the Duke.

"Good evening, darling" he said, completely ignoring Alice. "Are you almost ready?"

"Just a few more moments. Alice isn't concentrating."

"I'll order the car round then, shall I?"

"Of course."

"See you downstairs." He departed, leaving an impression of elegance and worldliness.

The Duke was forty-one, his Duchess eleven years younger. They were thoroughly involved in the social scene and attended all the prestigious events. The household was kept equally busy with functions at Elton House, one of the most elegant addresses and homes in London.

When her mistress had departed, Alice returned to her own quarters. She had a sitting room, bedroom and tiny bathroom to herself, and she was able to have visitors as long as she was discreet. Tonight, it was just a girl friend, a fellow lady's maid who was coming for a meal. They would sit and gossip, try on clothes and dance to music on the wireless. Later, Janet, her friend, would have to dash home to be available when her 'Lady' came home from an evening out.

Alice looked at a photograph of her parents which was placed on a bureau. *If only you knew the life I lead here, you would be horrified.* Her visit home earlier in the year had unsettled her, because although she remained busy, she could not get rid of a nagging doubt in her mind. Perhaps it was because of Grandpa Will's death... was she suddenly aware, for the first time, of her own mortality? Surely she would hate running a house? She knew she was too selfish to look after a husband or care for children – Heaven forbid! She could hardly look after herself. Still, the doubt remained. Was what she was doing worth anything? Mother had written so eloquently in the summer about her friend and colleague Ellie Bates; the sadness of her loss and the worthiness of her life. *What would people say about me?* she thought. The butler came to save her from further introspection by announcing her friend's arrival.

"Thanks, Webster," she called. "Bring her on through!"

JANUARY 1936

There was sadness once more in the country. King George V had died. He had been a private man, and it had taken some years for the British public to take him and his withdrawn wife, Mary, to their hearts. He had at last been convinced of the nation's love on the occasion of their Silver Jubilee the previous year. Now they mourned him and the popular Prince of Wales became King Edward VIII. Rumours had abounded in the capital for many months but the public were, as yet, unaware of the threat to the throne.

Most people had never seen the Royal Family in the flesh, but the news was worth a mention in Abbots Ford. Prayers were said at St Mary's for the new King and the rest of his family. The passing of a monarch always seemed to represent the passing of an era and to herald a new beginning.

There was a new beginning for Eddy, Flora and Seth's eldest son, and his betrothed, Elizabeth. They were in the middle of preparations for their wedding in March. The burden of organisation was on Elizabeth's mother, but the house the couple were buying was now complete. It was on the outskirts of the village towards Steeple Burstead. Part of a row of houses, it was semi-detached and had three bedrooms. Members of both families were invited to view the new home and they marvelled at the modern conveniences: electric light and running water which could be heated by a boiler in the kitchen, a bathroom and toilet upstairs plus a toilet attached to the outside of the house downstairs. The garden was fenced round, but there was not enough land for them to keep animals, or even chickens. Everyone had rallied round giving them pieces of furniture, but they had bought an electric cooker.

"I'd never manage with one of those," stated Flora categorically when she saw it. "Wretched new-fangled thing."

Elizabeth's mother bemoaned the folly of omitting to build a range in the house and condemned electricity as being dangerous, saying "It'll never catch on!"

Eddy and Elizabeth were a popular couple in the village. Everybody knew the Hawkes family and Elizabeth had worked in Wilton's the drapers since leaving school. She was an excellent needlewoman and supplemented her income by making children's clothes. Now, she applied her skill to creating soft furnishings for her new home and they both worked hard on the house. Eddy returned home and immediately continued his work digging over the garden, making Flora smile to herself, recalling Seth's endeavours when making their home habitable almost thirty years previously.

Flora and Seth were facing a dilemma, for Louise, her mother, had been trying to persuade them to move to Orchard Cottage ever since Will had died. Then, Flora had been jolted by Ellie's death, because although she thought she had experienced tragedy during the war through losses to the village and the death of her elder brother, Charles, her friend's passing made her realise that her mother would not be there for ever. While they were making the decision, young Seth took up with a girl, and looking to the future they chose to move and leave Plumtree Cottage for him, thus settling the issue.

MARCH 1936

The spring became a frantic time because while Eddy was in the process of transporting his belongings to his new home, Flora was going through the accumulation of thirty years' family living in order to decide what to keep, what to leave for young Seth and what to dispose of. In the meantime, Seth was busy painting and decorating at Orchard Cottage, prior to their moving in. Louise Henty found it all exciting and was delighted with her newly-decorated downstairs bedroom. The room already had an attractive Victorian fireplace, decorated with tiles at the sides, and new wallpaper and curtains made it look bright and cosy. She spent ages carefully placing her favourite treasures and photographs around the room on shelves, mantelpiece and cupboards, standing back with a sigh of satisfaction at the effect she had created.

One evening at Plumtree Cottage, as they sat beside the range in the living room, Flora admitted to Seth that she would be sad to leave.

"Of course, my duck. So shall I. But this is a good idea, Flo," he replied.

"Remember when you built the wash-house?"

He laughed.

"Will I ever forget! Our Arthur rushed off and left me for dead when the stone fell on me!"

They sat for a while, thinking about the life they had lived there. All at once, they both said, "Do you remember when..." and stopped, laughing, "when I had Alice?" she continued.

"Oh, I remember a lot, girl," he said fondly. "It's a while since I chased you around that table there!"

She flushed, remembering some of the storms of their marriage.

"I've improved, haven't I?" she said.

"Well," he hesitated, deliberately teasing her.

"Remember when we had Eddy?"

"Mmm, good times," murmured Seth.

"Good and bad. It was during the War and Ellie and Tom had just lost their Paul," said Flora.

They did not speak for a time, while they thought back to those days.

"And now he's going off tomorrow to start a new life of his own."

"Yes, we'd better get to bed to look our best for his big day. Come on my duck." Seth pulled her up out of her chair and put his arms round her.

"You'll always look your best," he said as they went up the pine stairs together, arm in arm.

+ + +

Flora had made a new dress and jacket for Eddy's wedding. She could have chosen whatever she liked from Louise' shop, but opted to go her own way.

"You can't wear green to a wedding," Louise had said, horrified.

"It isn't green, it's nearer yellow," protested Flora.

"Greeny-yellow!" laughed her sister.

Dorothy had said the same thing when she arrived.

"I wish you'd all leave me alone and think about your own clothes," Flora told her waspishly.

Dorothy had caught her father's glance and said no more.

Young Seth looked distinctly ill-at-ease in his best suit and tight collar waiting with Eddy in the front pew. The two young men whispered together and something Seth said made Eddy smile broadly. Watching them, Flora was relieved. She had not thought it would be one of the boys getting married first; she had been sure they would have had a wedding before this, Dorothy perhaps.

The organ music echoed stirringly around them as Elizabeth approached on her father's arm. Flora looked at Eddy and, catching his eye, smiled reassuringly. He returned the look and then his eyes were drawn to his bride as she advanced towards him. She looked stunningly beautiful in a lace and crêpe dress; she wore a diadem of pearl flowers from which a plain full-length veil fanned out. There was an ethereal quality about her which shone from her eyes as she looked at Eddy. A gentle smile played about her mouth as her father symbolically handed her over to Eddy, and she nodded imperceptibly to him in gratitude and filial love.

The marriage service evoked many emotions within each member of the congregation, depending upon their own marital state and phase in life. Once outside, a photographer took a picture of the bride and groom.

"That's it! Smile! Good. Now the parents and bridesmaids. Lovely!" He jollied them all into a neat group and encouraged smiles from them.

"Don't they look lovely," said Charlotte Hawkes fondly.

"Nice young people," agreed the other grandmother.

"Good to see you out and about, Tom," said James Hawkes as Tom went by. Tom nodded in acknowledgement. He had not recovered from his loss, but at least he was there.

The wedding breakfast was at Elizabeth's parents' home just outside the village. Groups of people stood about the packed living room or closeted themselves for a gossip. When the time came to cut the wedding cake, Eddy's friends heckled him good-naturedly while he responded 'Your turn next!' to one or two of them. He made a hesitant, amusing speech while Elizabeth stood proudly beside him, quiet and calm. The time flew by and before long, the bride emerged in a brown-trimmed cream coat and dress, ready to leave on honeymoon.

Dorothy hovered close to Flora, knowing instinctively that the couples' departure would leave her mother sad.

"Thanks for everything you two." Eddy kissed his mother and shook his father's hand. Young Seth lined up to kiss the bride and to shake his brother's hand. To her surprise, Dorothy found tears springing to her eyes. They looked so perfect together, and here was her younger brother starting life as a married man.

"Be good to her," she whispered as he gave her an unaccustomed kiss on the cheek. They all stood watching and waving as the car taking the couple to Steeple Burstead to catch the bus, disappeared over the hill and out of the village. Flora and Seth stood for a while watching the empty scene, until Dorothy put her arm round Flora's shoulder.

"Come on Mum, Dad. Time to go home."

They turned to say their goodbyes and the four walked home to Orchard Cottage in thoughtful silence.

APRIL 1936

Giles and Esmée were still reeling from the experience. Anna had agreed to move to Fourwinds to be nursed, but she had been more resilient than the doctors had given her credit for, because she had lingered on for another eight months. She had been a good patient but her suffering had wrung from her carers the last dredges of emotion. Her funeral had been exceedingly quiet, for she had no family. A few of Esmée's friends gathered at the church with her and Giles, but Madeline opted not to attend. After the many months of attentive ministration, both of them found it difficult to settle down to anything. Esmée felt unable to paint, and Giles wandered through the house and round the garden like a wraith. Anna had meant so much to both of them, yet the relationship between her and Giles had blighted the long friendship between the two women. Grief had a strange effect upon people. At least, her final months had bound the three together.

Giles had been invited to the hunt on Lord Strickland's Estate. He did not want to go anywhere, let alone any kind of social gathering. His mother had begun to be perturbed at the extent of his grief.

"It's been three months, and you've hardly left the house, Giles," she entreated. He did not demur, but he still refused to go. Esmée spoke with Lady Strickland on the telephone, which resulted in a visit from Euphemia Strickland, one of the daughters of the house. She was a contemporary of Giles' and a good enough friend to be able to pick up the relationship where it left off at their previous meeting, years before. Her interest lifted his spirits, and she eventually persuaded him that a change of scene was in order. He agreed to attend, on the understanding that he was free to withdraw to his room if it all became too much.

"What a nice girl!" enthused Esmée when Euphemia had gone.

"Hardly a girl, Mama, she's only two years younger than me!"

"Well, she seems like a girl to me," laughed his mother.

"Her daughters are in their late twenties, indeed, the eldest is thirty-one" he informed her, as if to prove a point.

"Be that as it may, company, of whatever age, will do you good."

He had only agreed to achieve some peace and quiet. He would go for this one weekend, and then perhaps his mother would leave him alone to grieve.

MAY 1936

Flora had not realised how much she would enjoy living at Orchard Cottage again. It was much bigger than Plumtree Cottage and she had brought many of her treasured belongings with her. Some furniture had been given to Eddy and Elizabeth, but much of it remained where it was for young Seth's use.

Louise, her mother, allowed her to take over as chatelaine, helping unobtrusively when needed; it was an ideal arrangement. There were still a few hens pecking around in the orchard, and Seth bought a dozen more. Even though Flora now took care of her mother, she could not get used to having no children at home at all. She had long ago adjusted to the girls' absence, but almost overnight, both Eddy and Seth were no longer there. Seth either managed for himself at Plumtree Cottage, or went to his grandparents for meals, because it was nearer.

Flora had managed to make the garden pretty at the front of the cottage, something she had not had time to do before. She was still working with Jenny but they split the duties and each had a pupil midwife with them; the two girls were state registered nurses. Rachel Hughes and Gillian Brown were pleasant young women from outside the village. Rachel had trained in Bristol, and Gillian was a Londoner; both were in their early twenties.

Every ten days or thereabouts, Flora found herself reversing her journey of thirty years, and going out to Briersham to clean her old home for her son. She arrived one Tuesday morning to find Seth and a girl sitting at the pine table in the scullery.

"Hello, there. Not interrupting am I?" she asked breezily.

It was odd that they were there together alone, and they seemed miserable. Flora started working around the living room dusting and polishing; it had remained tidy as Seth hardly used it.

She heard them whispering and vowed that she would advise him against having young women home on their own in future, for fear of the girls' reputation.

"Not at work this morning?" she asked pointedly.

"Mum, can you come and sit down? We want to talk to you."

Flora made them all a cup of tea and joined them.

"Mum," he began again, reluctantly, "we have a problem." He looked at Helen, who looked rueful.

"Helen thinks she's..." He could not say the word.

"We love each other," Helen said defiantly.

"Are you telling me that Helen is expecting a baby?" asked Flora.

"Yes."

"When?"

"Well, I've missed two."

"So what are you going to do about it?" said Flora.

"We want to get married."

Flora sat and thought about it. There was nothing she could say. Seth had met Helen at Christmas and they had been seeing a great deal of each other, but he had not mentioned that his intentions were serious.

"It's something only you two can decide on," said Flora. "Does your Mother know?"

"No."

"I think she should."

"We were going to decide by ourselves and then tell her."

"Your Dad will have to be told, Seth," said Flora.

"I know. What do you think he'll say?"

"Nothing he can say, son. It's one of those things. Just make the right decision."

"The only decisions are giving the baby away or keeping it and getting married," said Helen.

"Whatever you decide, your Dad and I will back you up," Flora told her son. "And you, Helen."

"Thanks Mrs Hawkes. You've been good about it."

Flora did not carry on with her chores that day, but got on her bike and went back to Orchard Cottage. Louise was sitting outside and Flora fetched a chair to join her.

"I think about your Dad a lot, Flora," she said apropos of nothing.

"I know, Ma."

"Are you glad you moved back here?"

"Of course, you know we are."

"You. I mean you. Are you happy, girl?"

"Yes, Ma." She wanted to tell her mother that Seth could be in real need of Plum Tree Cottage, but she ought to tell her husband first. She got up and went to start the meal, kissing her mother on the head as she went.

Louise was not sure what, but she knew something was worrying her daughter; she would be told all in good time. She put her head back and enjoyed the warmth of the early summer sun.

JUNE 1936

Bill and Jessica's home was comfortable. Peartree Farm House stood back from the road, in the middle of a large plot, surrounded by garden. The porch was at the side which looked strange at first sight because the house did not stand sideways-on to the road. No doors were seen from the front, and the windows surveyed the road running through Upper Abbots with a dark, vacant stare. Inside was cosy and countrified; stairs ran straight up from a tiny square hall just inside the front door, leading to three bedrooms. The kitchen, which had a bathroom tacked on to the side, was large and untidy and led straight into the living room. Bill sometimes enjoyed sitting in the tidy silence of the dining room because its windows faced the hill and farm. He remained the easy-going, pleasant man he had always been, while Jessica calmly managed everything in the home. Theirs was a happy, tranquil life, punctuated by the events of the farming year.

One warm summer evening, when Bill had finally settled for the day, there was a knock at the front door. Most people approached by the back door, so much so, that the gate at the front path was permanently stuck. Someone must have wrestled with it to arrive that way. It was Jessica who answered it, returning to say "Someone for you, dear," and leading in a tall, sandy-haired young man.

"Hello. Sorry to intrude." He smiled. The accent was not local, but London, posh London.

"What can I do for you?" asked Bill politely.

"I'm staying with people locally. I'm down with my Mother, actually. She suggested I came along to say hello."

"Oh yes?" Bill still had no idea who the young man could be.

"My uncle thought I should pop in too. Says you and he had tremendous fun when he returned wounded from the Great War!"

It began to dawn on Bill that his visitor must be a relation of Captain Julian Johnstone, to whom he had been general factotum because of the Captain's disabilities.

"Oh Lord, yes," he said, relieved, laughing. "And you say you're here with your Mother... you are Oberon's lad?"

"No. Mother is Fidelia, Fiddy. She talks about you often and the fun you three, no four, had. Said I ought to come and see you."

Bill scrutinised him. Yes, he could see it now. The slanting green eyes and that hair! Not such a dark russet, but hers all the same.

51

"Is your Father down as well?"

"No, Father died in the war and Mother never remarried."

"I'm sorry, er...?"

"My name is Joshua." He leaned forward, and belatedly, they shook hands.

Sensing a release of tension, Jessica offered him tea.

"No. I hadn't meant to stay, thanks. I really wanted to have a chat some time, go for a pint perhaps?" he raised his eyebrows enquiringly at Bill.

"Yes – yes, that would be fine."

"What about tomorrow night?"

"Yes," Bill nodded.

"At the Partridge, about nine?"

"Yes, yes. Good."

They shook hands again and Jessica guided him towards the back door. He walked across the concrete to the path and disappeared around the corner of the house. Just as he reached the corner, coming the other way at the same speed, was Anne, Bill and Jessica's eldest child. She was a pretty seventeen-year-old with her mother's blonde hair and blue eyes. They collided, sending Anne crashing to the ground.

"Oh, I am so sorry," apologised Joshua.

"Catching a train?" asked Anne, sarcastically. Then she looked up, as he helped her to her feet, into the handsome face and green eyes.

"Are you alright?" He was concerned.

"No thanks to you!" She laughed, teasing him.

She brushed herself down, and Joshua waived once more to Bill and Jessica, still standing at the back door.

"Who on earth was that?!" she enquired. "He's nice."

Bill explained who the visitor was, and told of the plan the following evening.

"Can I come?"

"A pub is no place for a nice young girl," said her mother.

"Only joking, Mum."

"I should think so too."

Bill stood at the dining room window, looking out over his land and up at the hill. They had been good days for him, apart from the war which was not good for anybody. He had often thought about Fiddy, but had not seen her again since that magical summer; he had never mentioned it to anyone, certainly not Jessica. He was glad that she had found happiness with someone, he had known she would. He looked forward to hearing about the family again.

+ + +

Seth and Helen were getting married. It was to be a quiet wedding, but it did not turn out that way. They had decided upon marriage as soon as they knew for certain about the baby. Helen's mother then began to organise everything. They agreed to a white wedding, *Or what will people say?* her mother had said. They only wanted close relatives and friends, but her mother had other ideas, and a big family.

Their home was not a problem, as Seth was already ensconced at Plumtree Cottage. Helen gradually introduced changes in the weeks leading up to the wedding, which caused some arguments between the couple.

"Why, isn't it good enough for you? It was good enough for my Mother", Seth had asserted harshly, after Helen wanted to throw out some old chairs.

"If it's going to be my home, I want to choose at least some of the things in it," she had shouted back.

"Why spend money when we don't have to," responded Seth.

"Because I want something I've chosen, something of my own."

"The baby will be your own," he had muttered.

Helen had become hysterical at that.

"Not yours as well, then? I did it all on my own, of course!"

"I didn't mean..." he began.

"You meant it alright, you selfish, you brutish..."

She crumpled in a heap on the floor, unable to think of a bad enough word to describe her fiancé.

53

"Don't, don't cry." She shrugged him off.

"I won't marry you. I'll manage on my own."

"Don't be silly, I love you," he said quietly, cradling her in his arms. Seth was tall, dark haired and blue-eyed like his father; but his character, while similar, was more complicated. There was an arrogance, a selfishness which was not part of the older man. Helen loved Seth, but, often, she felt that he did not feel the same. Except on the few occasions when they had made love.

Now their wedding day was upon them. Helen had given in over the furniture, and the ancient chairs still graced the living room, but with new covers.

"Good morning, Flora – Seth," said Michael Orrins. "We gather yet again."

"Yes. Hello Reverend Orrins." They went into the church, which was decorated with summer flowers, their perfume pervading the atmosphere.

Helen was a lovely bride. Unlike the fashion of the time, she wore a full-skirted gown of white brocade. Her two sisters were bridesmaids in pale blue, and two tiny nieces wore white trimmed with blue. Her mother had done her proud. They had the wedding breakfast at the village hall, and such was the size of the family, and it's character – there was Irish blood somewhere – that the festivities went on right through the afternoon and evening.

Eddy's Elizabeth was taken ill, and they had to admit that they had just discovered that she was pregnant, but had not wanted to take any attention from Seth and Helen's big day. Both Alice and Dorothy had managed to come home for the weekend, and had travelled from London together. During the evening, Robert had cornered Alice and propositioned her.

"What, with all these people here?" she laughed, "You're mad!"

"Mad for you. You look good enough to eat," he said, hungrily. "I often think of our afternoon in Bristol."

Always ready to exploit such an opportunity, Alice agreed. They strolled casually away from the village hall, and round the back of the Smithy where Seth stored his hay and straw in a half-barn. Robert moved bales around to make a sheltered nook and

Alice prepared herself immediately, taking off her outer clothes. They were in the middle of the act, when childish laughter and shrieks disturbed their concentration.

"No, no, Uncle Seth – don't be monsters any more!"

"Grrrr..." There was more laughter, as with a suddenness the distance of the laughter had belied, Bill's two youngest came upon their cousin Alice with her uncle-by-marriage, in flagrante delicto, closely pursued by their Uncle Seth.

+ + +

The bride and groom were having a week away in Devon, with one of her aunties. They were all travelling together the following day, so Seth and Helen were to spend their first night of marriage at Plumtree Cottage. Half-way through the evening, while dancing with his bride, Seth noticed his little cousins, Louise and John, running into the hall, obviously upset and crying. Seth excused himself and went to his Uncle Bill and Aunt Jessica's to investigate. Before he could reach the group, Bill was making his way towards the rear exit with some speed, which alerted Flora, among others, who also followed.

Thus it was that Bill, Flora, young Seth and others, went out to find that Seth had punched his brother-in-law Robert soundly and that he had blood coming from his nose and mouth. With great presence of mind, and not a little embarrassment, Seth had pushed his eldest daughter behind the piled up bales and, through clenched teeth, ordered her to make herself decent. So that when the audience arrived, what they saw was Seth, having dealt with Robert, now manhandling him down towards Smithy Cottage.

"What in God's name is the matter, Seth?" pleaded Flora.

"Not now," barked her husband.

"Anything I can do, Dad?" asked Seth.

"No, son. Go back to your wedding."

"Let me help," said Bill. But Robert was offering no resistance and Seth told them all to return and forget about what they had seen. Bill and Flora walked back together, talking earnestly, and their sister Louise met them.

"What on earth is going on – someone said Seth hit somebody?"

"It's not clear what happened. Best forgotten for now," suggested Bill.

Flora did her best to put a brave face on the situation but she knew her husband, and that it must have been something serious to make him take those steps on such an important and socially sensitive occasion.

+ + +

Alice knew of a path which ran all the way along behind the cottages, the bakery, newsagent and Dr Tanner's house, and came out at the crossroads. She ran and stumbled, fell and crawled all the way along; scratched by brambles, tripped by trailing undergrowth, her delicate summer clothes were ripped to shreds, and so was she. She waited until no one was in sight and made a dash for Church Lane, then ran without stopping to Orchard Cottage, down the steps, inside and up to her room where she threw herself on the bed, sobbing and in shock.

She would never forget the moment as long as she lived. Her father had caught her making love with his sister's husband. It was as if she suddenly saw it through her father's eyes. Not from her own point of view, that of a London sophisticate moving on the perimeter of a society whose lax morals were the talk of ordinary people, but from the point of view of her blacksmith father, living and working in a country village, where strict moral codes prevailed, with good reason, in such a small community. She cringed. Her Father... Uncle Robert... The awfulness of it all dawned on her consciousness and her conscience. Mercifully, the black enveloped her as emotion overcame her, and she passed out in a dead feint.

+ + +

Flora and Seth had been sad that young Seth's marriage had been precipitate, but delighted about the idea of a grandchild. Now they knew that Eddy's wife was expecting a baby as well; two in a short space of time!

They had managed to keep the details of the fracas at Seth's wedding private and Seth and Helen had gone off happily.

Dorothy had travelled back to Ipswich via London alone, as Alice was in no state to return.

After the events of that day, she seemed to undergo some kind of breakdown. She slept continuously, did not eat, and when she was awake, cried all the time.

"It's her conscience worrying her," Seth opined. Although Flora had been shocked when told the details, she felt some sympathy for the plight in which Alice found herself. She knew Robert of old, and while she gave him credit for reforming and bringing up a nice family, she felt sad for Rebecca, his wife. What she did not perceive, was that her daughter was culpable: all she saw was her suffering, and attributed it to other causes. Instinctively, her father knew better, knew that her nature was akin to that of Robert. He could not confront that concept and so reacted with anger.

As she emerged from the crisis, Alice was aware that the whole experience had been cathartic. She had been uneasy about her life for many months, had questioned her existence. She could not afford to give up her job, she had a good position, but she pledged to herself that she would change. She would be less vacuous, more giving. She did not know how she would do it, but she would find a way. She did not know then, that what is evil in the world had a perfect opportunity in store.

JULY 1936

Bill said no more to Flora about the scene at the wedding. His children had told him what they had seen, and of course, they had witnessed everything. They had not fully understood but they knew that their cousin Alice had been doing something which had made their Uncle Seth more angry than they had ever seen him. They were not really aware of who Robert was; the families saw each other, but not that often. Rebecca had not found out, thanks to the discretion of all concerned. Seth was sorely tried over it all, but could not put his sister through any more pain. In any case, he could never have told her who had been involved. Flora had never revealed all she knew of Robert; her motive had always been the continuation of Robert and Rebecca's marriage and family life. She saw no reason to tell Seth now.

Bill had met Joshua for a drink one evening, and enjoyed hearing about how well Julian Johnstone had adapted to life in London. He had married but there were no children. Naturally, the villagers knew all that anyway, but Joshua was able to tell Bill how Julian really was. Subsequently, there was no need for them to meet, but Joshua was interested in Anne, and found excuses to appear at the house more and more frequently. Then Joshua began taking Anne out; he had a sports car and would arrive outside, honk the horn, and gesture to Anne to come out. She always told her mother where they were going, and they saw no reason to stop her.

"He'll soon tire of our Anne, she's not really his type," said Jessica. But he did not tire of her, and she blossomed with his attention. Then, Anne came in one evening and announced that she had fallen in love; not only that, but Joshua loved her in return.

+ + +

Giles had thoroughly enjoyed the weekend at Darnley Hall, the vast manor house which was Lord Strickland's family home. The whole family was delightful and welcomed him at once, like one of their own. Even Euphemia's sisters remembered him from his days in the army, when he was a dashing young officer. 'Before you dashed off to India' as one of them had jokingly recalled. He had been equally popular with them and had been included in several more gatherings. He was invited to Lord Strickland's birthday ball and found himself looking forward to it. He had not worn tails for as long as he could remember and tried his suit on with trepidation in case it did not fit. 'Not bad' he told the mirror.

At fifty-four, he looked ten years younger. His hair had retained its Viking colour and his weight remained constant. The only change was in his eyes; the unfulfilled promise of his expectations lent them a pensive expression. Any lines around his features merely accentuated his craggy good looks.

The ballroom twinkled and sparkled. The candlelit room vied with the final rays of the setting sun to illuminate the beauty of the ladies as they danced. Giles' partner was Euphemia's eldest daughter, Penelope. She was a tall girl, a woman really, being almost thirty-two. Her dark hair was trimmed into a short, sleek bob, like a cap. Her hazel eyes sparkled as she responded warmly to Giles. Politely, he danced with Lady Strickland, Euphemia and her sisters during the evening. The air of tragedy which created his aura made him appear vulnerable even though he was mature, and the women were drawn to him. He was attentive to each of them, enjoying the company after the months of isolation. He was equally at ease in masculine company, having had experience of command. He was speaking to Lord Strickland in a group of men when Penelope approached and dragged him, laughing, on to the dance floor. Suddenly, there was an interruption as the master of ceremonies called the company to order, and a trolley was wheeled in, carrying an enormous cake, upon which burned innumerable candles. Applause broke out as the patriarch advanced towards the stage. They sang 'For he's a jolly good fellow' and the candles were extinguished, with assistance from his family. Lord Strickland thanked them all for their attendance and good wishes and the band struck up again to continue the dancing. Penelope suggested that she and Giles should go out on to the balcony. Chinese lanterns were dotted around the parapet and couples sat at tables on the wide gallery. Giles and Penelope walked slowly to the far end and she sat on the balustrade, looking out over the landscaped twilight beauty of her father's garden.

"Mother told me about your wife."

He said nothing, sipping wine from his glass.

"I am so sorry."

He shook his head, looking down.

"I shouldn't have said anything..." she offered.

"We never married, you know," he told her quietly.

Sensing that he wanted to talk, she did not speak.

"She was very ill. In the end I think she was glad to go." He ran his finger up and down the stem of his glass.

"You must have been very much in love," she said.

He looked at her shadowed face, sensing her sympathy and understanding from the softness of her voice.

"Yes, we were," he admitted.

They remained silent, each deep in their own thoughts, for what could have been an age. Then Penelope stood, and reaching up, kissed him gently on the mouth. Her elegant hand stroked his face and she left without another word, returning swiftly to the house.

AUGUST 1936

Sir Philip and Lady Stephanie Marshall were spending the holidays at Ruthven Farm. Dorothy always enjoyed their time in Scotland; she adored the scenery and found the people friendly and down to earth. Dorothy and the under-nurse had taken the children north two weeks before their parents joined them, so they had all settled in. The weather had been glorious, the children thriving in the clear, fresh air. Lady Stephanie was recovering from a miscarriage and stayed quietly in her room most of the time. It was not discussed with Dorothy or Iris, the under-nurse, but the two girls demonstrated their sympathy in subtle ways.

Dorothy had cultivated a friendship with the nanny and children of a local family, who always looked forward to their visits to Scotland. They were planning on having them to tea, and the children were tidying their toys in readiness for the visitors. The old farmhouse did not allow for a nursery suite. Instead, the children had bedrooms upstairs and a day-nursery downstairs. Cook had been alerted to extra people for tea and had produced a gooey chocolate cake especially. The children greeted each other delightedly and the group, seven children, two nannies and the under-nurse, set off for a walk. They stood quietly watching rabbits playing, then went to the stables to see the horses. Dorothy and Caroline, the other nanny talked companionably as they strolled, sometimes addressing the children who skipped and frolicked around them. Caroline confided that she was leaving the family to marry her sweetheart. "Do you think you'll ever marry, Dorothy?" she asked.

"I never seem to have the time to meet anyone!" replied Dorothy cheerfully. "When's the big day?"

"October."

"Where are you going to live?"

"In the village. Robert is a policeman so we're given a house."

They made their way back to Ruthven Farm for tea, and amidst the changing of shoes and washing of hands, Dorothy noticed that Rupert was looking extremely pale. She felt his forehead and face and found that he was clammy. She had been aware that he had been quiet on their outing, but put it down to getting used to having other children with them.

"Aren't you feeling very well?" asked Dorothy calmly.

He shook his head, looking sorry for himself.

Dorothy organised tea and with apologies to their guests, left Iris to deputise while she took Rupert up to his room. She gave him a tepid bath first, and when she was towelling him dry, he vomited without warning. Although Dorothy had not completed her state registered nursing training, she knew that his symptoms warranted intervention by the doctor.

The ambulance took half-an-hour to get out to the farm, by which time Rupert was a seriously sick little boy. Lady Stephanie had been told, and waited silently with her son. The small tea-party finished early, and Iris maintained the other children's routine as closely as she could. It was decided that only Dorothy should accompany Rupert to hospital because his mother was still feeling weak. Rupert was taken at once for an operation on his appendix. Dorothy waited, deeply distressed. She could not sit still, but paced up and down, pushing her fears from her mind. The minutes dragged like hours as she strived to occupy her thoughts and remain optimistic. Other people came to sit in the dingy waiting room: an elderly man smelling strongly of tobacco sat coughing in a corner. A young woman with four children, and in a state of advanced pregnancy, screamed relentlessly at her energetic brood. Dorothy usually enjoyed observing people, but unusually, she felt impatient with these fellow citizens. She got up and walked along the corridor, stopping to look out of a window. The sun was still high and bright in the sky, even though it was well past tea-time. People were hurrying about their business, going home from work, returning for duty. The calmness of standing, just watching, relieved her anxiety and she allowed herself to think of her small charge, who was at this very moment, under anaesthetic, undergoing a life-saving operation. She brushed her hand across her eyes as she pictured his small body, vulnerable and undermined, when she had bathed him earlier. Other images of him presented themselves: Rupert standing dangerously near the top bar of the main gate; Rupert running across a meadow, curly hair flying; Rupert fast asleep, angelic and irresistibly beautiful. Tears sprang unbidden in her eyes, and she fumbled for her handkerchief in her uniform pocket.

"Can't be that bad, surely?" said a pleasant male voice.

Dorothy turned, embarrassed, and found herself looking into the laughing brown eyes of a passing doctor.

"The little boy I look after is having an emergency appendectomy," she explained.

"Oh, I'm sorry. How long has he been in?"

"An hour and a half."

"Would you like a cup of tea? I'm just going off duty."

She hesitated.

"I'd bring it to you here... you'll be ready to hear how he is..."

"Alright, thank you." She gave him a watery smile.

He disappeared around the corner giving her a friendly wave. They were drinking the weak tea when a nurse approached.

"Miss Hawkes?"

"Yes."

"You can see Rupert now. He's in Recovery." The nurse smiled encouragingly. "He's still a bit woozy, but he's asking for you." Dorothy turned to go, thanking the young man for the tea.

"Can I see you again?" he asked her.

"My 'family' are at Ruthven Farm, Brechon Village," she told him. "Get in touch if you like." She followed the nurse to where Rupert lay on a trolley, gradually regaining consciousness.

"Hello, Rupert." Relief surged through her as he turned his head, opened his eyes, and said, "Nanny?"

She stayed with him until he was transferred to the ward. She found a telephone to give the good news to Lady Stephanie and the anxious people waiting back at the farm. Rupert was staying in hospital for a few days, and there were no facilities or rules which allowed anyone to remain with him, other than at strict visiting times. Dorothy was allowed to see him again before she left, when a car picked her up to take her back home. It was the farm manager who collected her.

"Are you feeling alright, Miss Hawkes?" he asked as they drove through the darkened countryside. Dorothy nodded. She felt exhausted, drained. It was as though Rupert was her own flesh and blood; that was why she was good at her job. But she must remember in future that that is what it was, a job.

SEPTEMBER 1936

Louise and Gordon continued travelling back and forth daily to their shop, in Steeple Burstead. They were doing well enough to consider expansion, especially now that Charles and Emma were proving useful. They decided to open a shop in Abbots Ford, close to the one at Steeple Burstead and open a larger one at East Hartness.

"Dad and Emma will run the further one, while you and I will take care of the local one," Louise told her son delightedly. There was much excitement in the family over the plan. They sat around the large dining table discussing it.

"We'll need to take on more girls at the Bath workshop," commented Gordon.

"Especially now that Gran can't sow any more," agreed Louise. "And Ma's time is mostly accounted for with her work. It's not like when we first began," she smiled.

They gathered up the dishes and trooped out to the kitchen to wash up. Their house reflected their success in business; built of local stone, it was double-fronted and graced by an oak front door which was reached by a shallow arc of drive. The hall was timber-panelled and double doors led to the spacious drawing room which ran the full length of the house. On the opposite side were the dining-room, kitchen and study. The children had a bedroom each, but there were endless disputes over the only bathroom when they were all preparing to leave in the mornings.

"Anne is seeing a bit of that young man, isn't she?" probed Louise while her daughter wiped a plate dry.

"He's nice," sighed Emma non-committally.

"Not our sort of people, I'd have thought," pressed her mother. "Is she getting serious about him?"

"I don't know, Mum," retorted Emma firmly, implying it was none of their business. The two cousins were close in age and close as friends. Anne had confided in Emma about her romance with Joshua from the beginning. As the weeks passed, Emma had been gradually sucked into the group of friends.

On a glorious Saturday evening in early autumn Joshua and his cohorts arrived in three cars; Anne ran up the drive.

"Come on, Em! You don't need to change!" The excursion was unplanned and Emma had spent her afternoon off unpacking the new seasons' fashions. There was a brief scrabbling while Emma threw on a different frock and in a fog of carbon-monoxide and raucous discussion, the vehicles disappeared down the narrow lane towards the main road.

"I hope those young men are careful drivers," said Louise. "Do you think they'll really get to Weston and back by ten o'clock?" she continued.

"Don't worry, my love," comforted Gordon. "She'll be back safe by ten."

They settled down for the evening beside the fire which had been lit to take the sudden chill from the evening air.

"I always love the autumn best because of the lovely days and cosy evenings," said Louise, hugging her cardigan around herself.

They talked about the opening of the new shop and their move to Abbots Ford.

"We won't lose any customers. They'll only have to come two miles, after all," said Charles before he left to go out for the evening. While she chatted to Gordon, Louise played cards with her younger daughter, Victoria, before it was time for her to go to bed. When she had settled her in, she returned to her own room and sat at her dressing table brushing her hair. She enjoyed their bedroom, it was cheerful and pretty, featuring floral wallpaper which she and Gordon had chosen together. By now, Emma was late but Louise did not worry, she would be home soon, she was a good girl.

"Do you want some cocoa?" Gordon called from downstairs.

"Yes, dear. I'll be down in a minute."

They drank the hot, soothing liquid and talked. They pretended not to notice time passing and the hands of the clock approaching midnight. Charles came home and went up to bed without comment. Finally, Gordon said he would take the car and drive along the main road towards Weston.

"What's the point of that?" asked Louise irritably.

"I might see them," said Gordon reasonably.

"Alright then. I'll stay here."

He drove along the narrow, pitch-black lanes to the main road and turned left towards Weston. He drove as far as East Hartness, almost half-way to Weston-Super-Mare, and decided to return home in case he had missed them.

She was not home. Louise was in tears and making yet another hot drink when he returned.

"Should we tell the police?" suggested Louise.

"Not yet. They would contact us if..." he did not need to complete the sentence.

"She's not alone. Anne is there as well."

It had not occurred to them to check with Bill and Jessica, but it seemed unlikely that she would be there, knowing they would worry.

"Try to get some sleep, hon," suggested Gordon.

"Alright. I'll try," she said miserably. She went upstairs and crawled into bed, but could not sleep. She tossed and turned, read, tried to sleep again and finally got up and went back downstairs. It was four o'clock.

Gordon was dozing, alert immediately she went into the room.

"They must have crashed – contact the police," she begged, rising hysteria catching in her throat.

"No – we'll leave it 'till daylight. I'll go over to Bill's early and see what they think".

She lay on the sofa. The fire had gone out and the autumnal chill made her shiver.

"I'll get you an eiderdown," he offered. Gordon had not undressed. He collected the quilt and tucked his wife in. He put the kettle on for another drink, and then gathered the bucket, shovel, newspaper and ashcan required to clear the grate, in preparation for laying a fresh fire.

As soon as it started to become light, he walked up the lane to Bill and Jessica's. He rapped on the back door and Jessica answered it almost at once.

"Come in."

"No sign of them, then?" asked Bill.

"You did expect Anne home last night?"

"Of course."

"When shall we bring in the police?"

"I thought about nine o'clock," suggested Bill.

They offered him breakfast or a drink but he said he ought to get back to Louise. When he arrived home, both Charles and Victoria were up and worried about their sister. Louise was making eggs and bacon for them, and it smelled so inviting that she and Gordon managed to eat some as well. Just as they were enjoying the meal, they heard a car draw up and reached the door as Emma was coming in.

"Where have you been?" Louise' worry and panic was suddenly transmitted into fierce anger.

"Where is that young man?" asked Gordon, peering out into the drive, but they had gone.

66

"We went to Bath instead," said Emma quietly. "There was a nightclub..."

"A nightclub!"

"I said I didn't want to go..." She began to cry. "I knew you would be worried," she clung to her mother.

Louise' anger suddenly transferred itself from her daughter, to the young man who had not delivered her home in good time.

"Gordon, you'll have to speak to him," she ordered.

"Yes – or even Joshua," agreed Gordon.

"It wasn't Josh's fault," said Emma.

"Whose fault was it, dear?" asked her mother.

"Nobody's really."

"Wasn't Anne worried?"

"No. Anyway, she and Joshua are going to get married."

"I don't see what that's got to do with this," said Louise.

They all sat down and Louise made breakfast for her wandering daughter.

"Thank goodness you're safe, anyway."

Silently, Louise promised herself that she would have a word with Bill, so that nothing like this happened again.

OCTOBER 1936

Esmée powdered her nose and scrutinised her face in the glass. She was still an attractive woman and always took care over her wardrobe, even if some of her more Bohemian styles were avant-garde. She still missed Barnabus and grieved over him, but Giles' return to live in Fourwinds was a boon. He had invited Penelope Fitzwilliam for drinks, prior to their attendance at the Hunt Ball. Esmée was intrigued by the couples' relationship, for he had been seeing a great deal of the girl, who was twenty-two years his junior.

Poor Giles! First, Anna, twenty years his senior and now Penelope! As she descended the stairs, she heard their voices talking, laughing and teasing. Interesting.

"Ah, Mama!" He turned towards her and led her over to the sofa. Penelope rose to greet the older woman, putting her sherry glass on a side table.

"You look wonderful," Esmée told Penelope.

Giles stood near the fireplace smiling proudly.

"What will you have, Mama?" he enquired.

"Gin and tonic, dear." Esmée asked after Penelope's grandfather, whom she knew well. She watched attentively as the attractive young woman told her of his latest escapade. She seemed a pleasant, sincere person. *No reason why she shouldn't be,* thought Esmée. *They're a good family.*

When it was time for the couple to leave, Esmée sent regards to the girl's parents and grandparents.

"Lovely to see you again," said Penelope as she departed.

Giles settled her and her gown into the car, and waving to his mother, walked round to get into the driver's seat. They were passing the church when she spoke.

"You're like her."

"D'you think so?"

"Yes. She's nice. She's wondering about us, though."

"Lot's of people are 'wondering about us', including me."

He looked straight ahead, concentrating on the road.

"What do you mean?"

"I like you. Like you a lot," he told her.

"Mmm?"

"I like being with you."

"I like being with you too," she said.

"How much?"

"A lot."

He laughed. He could see that the conversation was getting him nowhere.

They were nearing the gates to Darnley Hall, and soon they would be joining crowds of people. They were always with crowds of people. He realised with a shock that he wanted to be alone with her. It was twilight, and he turned the car down a lane and parked on the edge of a copse.

"What are you doing?" asked Penelope.

He turned to her, seeing only the outline of her face and features in the fading light. He could smell her perfume, and the fur collar of her cape framed her face.

"I more than like you," he said softly. She was motionless. He leaned towards her, and putting a hand on each shoulder, pulled her nearer to him and kissed her. She did not resist, and he put his arms around her, pulling her close to his chest. They kissed passionately, their pent-up desire finding release at last. They pulled apart, breathless and ecstatic.

"Giles!" Penelope chuckled low and huskily. "You surprise me!"

"Don't see why!" He pulled her towards him again, placing his hands beneath her cape. They both knew that this would have to stop. Quite apart from moral considerations, they were expected at the Hunt Ball.

"Penny, I love you."

"Give us both time to think, Giles," she laughed. She could feel her pulse racing and a churning sensation in her stomach. She was happy and excited. She already knew that she loved him, and had confronted the perceived problem of the difference in their ages. She did not care. He was the man she wanted. He was courtly, gentle, kind; he had a colourful past, and if they fulfilled one another physically as well as liking each other, nothing would stop them. She patted her hair, reapplied her lipstick and straightened her gown and cape.

They arrived at Darnley Hall where they were welcomed by her grandparents.

"Why you look radiant this evening, my dear," commented her grandmother, Lady Strickland.

"I'll wager you're the cause," Lord Strickland told Giles.

Such was their involvement with one another, that their obvious feelings caused comment that evening. They thought that they were behaving normally, but their every move and glance, even from opposite ends of the ballroom, betrayed their love.

"Young lady," said Euphemia Fitzwilliam, hissing angrily at her daughter. "Come into the study, I want a word with you." They stood glaring at each other, a library table between them.

"I'm not a little girl, Mother. I'm a grown woman. Whatever it is you're about to say, I'll do what I feel is right." She looked defiantly at her mother.

"He's old enough to be your father! He's almost the same age as me, indeed, he's older than I am!"

Penelope folded her arms and turned away.

"There's been gossip about him. He has a chequered history with women," her mother pleaded.

"He was faithful to Anna for years and years," defended Penelope.

"You'll disappoint a great many people if you continue this liaison with Giles Thorndyke," stated Euphemia.

"Liaison!" shrieked Penelope. She moved closer to her mother. In a low, determined voice she spoke to her.

"This is no mere liaison Mama. Since I laid eyes on him, I have known I wanted him for my own. Mother, I am going to marry Giles, regardless of what you, or anyone else, say." She swept out of the room, banging the door behind her, leaving Euphemia standing open-mouthed and aghast.

+ + +

Flora was delighted that Eddy and Elizabeth were so happy. Elizabeth had suffered morning sickness until the third month of her pregnancy, but once that had worn off, was fit and well. Eddy had always been the most amenable of her children, he took after Grandad Will. Where Alice had been other-worldly, Dorothy straightforward and Seth temperamental, Eddy had always been conciliatory and poured oil on any troubled waters. He was an ideal husband, Elizabeth a quiet and doting wife. When Eddy went to work at Drakes Farm, Elizabeth often went to her mother's. She was there when it began. The first Flora knew of it was when one of Elizabeth's sisters pedalled down to Orchard Cottage like a maniac, around midday.

"Flora, Mrs Hawkes – Mum says you must come, and quick."

"What's the matter," asked Flora, wiping her hands.

"It's Elizabeth."

"Oh my God," she isn't due until December."

"I know. Mum's frantic, please let's go."

"You go on," said Flora. "I'll just get my bag."

There was no time for Flora to change into her smart dark blue uniform, so she collected a fresh apron and cuff-bands, and her bag, and pedalled through the rain.

When she arrived at the house, Elizabeth's mother was extremely anxious. It was obvious that Elizabeth was in premature labour and all Flora could do was to help her as much as possible.

In the middle of the afternoon, Elizabeth became severely distressed. Flora realised from her demeanour and breathing that she would have to involve Dr Tanner, and she knew by teatime that the child would not survive. The doctor who arrived was not Dr Tanner but a young man.

"I'm standing in because he is not well," he explained. "I am Martin Blake."

He examined Elizabeth and turned at once to Flora.

"You're aware what we are going to have to do?" he asked.

Flora organised what was required and told the family to stay in the living room. Eddy had arrived home and had pleaded to be allowed to see his wife. She was in such a distressed state that Flora acted both in her professional capacity and with a mother's compassion, and refused.

When it was all over, Eddy went in. He already knew that there would be no baby. He accepted that, as long as Elizabeth was going to recover.

Neither Flora nor Dr Blake left, and a sense of oppressive sadness hung over the house and everyone in it.

Eddy's father, brother and Helen and some of Elizabeth's married siblings gathered. Neighbours and friends called in, said a few words and left again. The other midwives called and offered to take over, but Flora would not leave Elizabeth. Eddy's grandma, his Aunt Louise and Uncle Bill – all called in. It was as if everyone knew.

Eddy was with her all the time.

"I'm here my love, my darling. Everything is going to be alright."

"My baby..." she murmured weakly.

"Everything's fine, just rest, dearest girl," he said.

"I love you, Eddy."

"And I you – forever and always."

She slept, at last, and her dark lashes feathered her alabaster cheeks.

At one o'clock that morning she slipped quietly away. The young doctor felt her pulse and shook his head at Flora. Flora knelt down beside her son, and placed an arm round his young shoulders. She leant her head towards his. In a few moments, the doctor crept out, and Seth, his father, came in.

With her husband to support her, Flora told him.

"She's gone, son, she's gone." Seth bent and put an arm around his son and the other around his wife. Eddy was stroking Elizabeth's hair. He did not weep, nor speak, nor move, for more than an hour.

Elizabeth's mother and father quietly came in and joined the vigil.

"Son, it's time to go – for now. Come with us and try to sleep."

He allowed himself to be led away, and they took him home to Orchard Cottage. They did not attempt to go to bed, but sat in chairs or on the sofa, to be with him. Flora was exhausted, but her instinct to watch over her son in his need precluded sleep.

Louise, his grandmother, came from her room and sat beside him.

"I've been thinking and praying. None of that will help you for a while yet," she said quietly, slowly, pausing between phrases. She continued, "Last year I lost your Grandad. He was old, but my love for him was not. He was withered and wrinkled, but my love for him was not." Louise put her arms around her grandson as he began to weep silently. Flora and Seth, and his brother Seth sat and listened.

"Forty-four years ago this day, I gave birth. It was Jacob. Forty-one years ago this day, Jacob passed away. A cruel twist of fate. A cross to bear. You will wonder if the bitterness of the cross was worse than this. I'll not speak to you now, of faith, son. I've lived a long time, this pain will pass."

He sobbed into his grandmother's thin and withered chest, but her love and compassion for him were young, and the others sat and listened.

NOVEMBER 1936

He said he only wanted family. Any more would be too much and he was determined to be there. The village mourned; everywhere closed, even though it was market day. Curtains throughout the village were drawn: they wanted him to know they understood.

Tom prepared Ebony again, and when he led him through the village to collect Elizabeth and her baby Edgar, not a soul was about.

Elizabeth's family was devastated; three cars followed the horse and carriage at snail's pace, carrying her parents and relatives, and Eddy and his family.

The service was short but, unusually, John Williams, the headmaster, said a few words. He spoke of Elizabeth as a small girl, as a star pupil, as a valuable member of the community. He spoke of God's 'lending' people to us here on Earth, some staying a while and others staying longer. He said equally laudable things about Eddy, whom he knew also, and asked for prayers for him especially.

They were laid to rest in the churchyard, near Elizabeth's grandparents. There was no wake and the families shook hands warmly and kissed and went back to their own homes for tea and sandwiches. It was too painful; they only needed their closest people around them. Eddy would always be special to them, but on this day, the families mourned alone.

DECEMBER 1936

It was while the Hawkes family was still recovering from tragedy that disaster appeared to overtake the whole country. King Edward VIII decided to give up the throne in favour of his younger brother because he wanted to marry a woman with two ex-husbands still living. On 12th December, he abdicated and George VI became King, his wife Elizabeth, Queen and his daughter Elizabeth, Heir Apparent.

People were divided on the subject; some were sad while others felt that he had not wanted to be king, ever. At a time when people looked to the Royal Family for moral leadership, the effect on society looked ready to reach seismic proportions. The only advantage seemed to be the popularity of the family taking over.

Christmas for Flora and Seth would be quiet. Neither of their daughters could manage to visit home; their employers needed them. Eddy went to work at the farm and kept himself busy, even though it was a relatively quiet period.

Young Seth and Helen were happy, and awaiting the birth of their baby, who arrived with the minimum of bother on Boxing Day. Jenny and Rachel Hughes were at the delivery, for Flora and Seth, along with her mother Louise and Eddy, had gone for lunch to Louise and Gordon. There was a knock on the door at four that afternoon. Gordon answered it.

"Hello, Gordon. Is Flora here?" asked Jenny.

"Come in, I'll get her." He showed Jenny into the study.

"Flora, your Seth is a dad. Helen had a boy at two o'clock. Weighs seven pounds five ounces," she told her quietly when Flora joined her.

"Thank you, Jenny. Thanks for coming. Is Helen alright?"

"She's fine – he just popped out, like shelling peas!"

She said goodbye and left. Flora went into the drawing room and Seth looked over at her.

"Who was that, Flo?" he asked.

"It was Jenny. Helen has had her baby." She hesitated, while ascertaining Eddy's response.

"Well?" asked Louise.

"It's a boy!"

"That's grand," said Eddy at once. "I'll go and see them."

Flora was relieved as there would be no need to skirt around Eddy's feelings; he had defused the situation by offering to go. Typical Eddy.

As good as his word, he went to Plumtree Cottage immediately. Flora did not offer to go then; she and Seth would visit tomorrow and see their first grandchild.

He knocked at the door and his brother called "Come in".

"Congratulations, 'Daddy'," said Eddy, smiling and shaking his hand.

Seth was surprised to see him.

"Can I see the little fellow?"

"Yes. Of course. They're up here."

Seth led the way upstairs and through the first bedroom, to where Helen lay, exhausted but happy, with the child at the side of the bed.

"Hello, Eddy. Nice of you to come. Here he is," she said.

Eddy leaned over the crib.

"Oh yes. A Hawkes if ever I saw one – all that black hair!" He looked at Helen. "You alright then, girl?"

"I'm fine, Eddy. Fine."

"Shall we have a beer?" asked Seth.

Eddy had thought to leave, but was easily persuaded to stay.

The boys had their beer up there in the bedroom and gave Helen her stout. It seemed incongruous that in the room where only hours ago, Helen had given birth, the three of them now sat drinking beer, with the tiny child asleep in his crib.

"We're starting him in good habits, anyway," said Seth.

"He'll be down the Partridge with me in no time," agreed Eddy. He asked about the birth and they told him how Seth had fallen down the last few stairs in his efforts to help, and had to be tended by Rachel when they thought he had broken his ankle. Eddy laughed at that.

"Ed, about his name..." hesitated Seth.

"Yes?"

"We'd like to call him Edward...?"

"Or Edgar," put in Helen.

He was silent for a while. "Edgar. Call him Edgar," he said confidently.

The brothers stood and Seth clasped his arms around Eddy and clapped him on the back. Seth could see Helen's face over Eddy's shoulder, and she could not keep the tears from falling. He looked at her, while he held his brother, and his love for her shone from his eyes and made them moist too.

"You'll be his godfather, then?" asked Seth.

"That I'll be," said Eddy.

MARCH 1937

The romance between Anne and Joshua continued unabated and they were talking about a formal engagement. One evening, the newly installed telephone rang and Bill answered it.

"Hello, Bill," said a female voice.

He knew her at once.

"Hello, Fiddy."

"Can we meet?"

"Meet?" he repeated vacantly.

"Yes, have a talk somewhere."

He knew she did not mean a visit to either house.

"Where?"

"Can you get away?"

"Not easily."

"What about now?"

He thought about his excuses to Jessica and then agreed.

"Walk down to the main road. I'll pick you up in fifteen minutes."

He stood, collar up, waiting in the freezing night. He pulled his hat down hard over his eyes and stamped his feet. Where was she? A moment later a car drew up and he opened the door and got in.

They roared off towards Weston.

"Where are we going?" he asked.

"Nowhere, just the edge of Gryphon Wood."

"How are you?" asked Bill.

"So, so."

"Seems a bit cloak and dagger."

She said nothing and they drove further on. Eventually, she signalled and pulled over to a clearing at the edge of the wood.

She opened her bag and took out a cigarette case and lighter. As she lit up, he watched her face. She had not changed in the intervening twenty years. Her hair was the same colour, and her face was, if anything, even more beautiful, because it exhibited more depth of character than before. She looked at him from under her lashes and then flicked the lighter out. She drew on the cigarette, and slowly exhaled.

"You've no idea, have you?" she asked eventually.

"About what?"

"This is no secret lover's meeting, Bill!"

"Then what…"

She laughed, "You were willing to come when you thought…" she laughed again, mirthlessly. "Oh, Bill."

"Why are we here?"

"Anne and Joshua are too serious. It cannot be."

"Now, Fiddy, our Anne is a lovely girl. If your Joshua thinks he's too good…"

"Our Joshua."

He knew what she meant at once, but could not believe it.

"Our Joshua," he repeated tonelessly.

"Yours and mine."

"My son?"

"Yes."

"When was he born?"

"January 1917 – believe me, he is yours."

"I didn't know."

"I tried to tell you. I went away to have him. At first I thought about – you know – but couldn't go through with it. And I've never regretted it."

"He told me his father died in the Great War."

"I had to tell him something, Bill. Certainly not the truth."

"I can't believe it."

Bill was assimilating the secret she had shared, so he had not yet recognised why she had told him. He was thinking of it purely in terms of how it affected himself, Fiddy and Joshua. He knew he did not want Jessica to find out, or his other children. His other children! Anne. He groaned.

"Oh my God."

"You can see now why I have had to tell you?"

"They're half-brother and sister".

"What are we going to do? They think they love one another," said Fiddy.

"Well, we'll have to stop them."

"How?"

"I'll tell Joshua he can't see Anne anymore."

"And what reason will you give?"

"I'm her father, she's under twenty-one."

"And you think that will do it?"

"I'll try."

"And what will you say to Anne, have you thought about that?"

"Oh God," he repeated. "This is too much to take in."

They drove back to Abbots Ford and Fiddy dropped him where she had picked him up. They made no other arrangements to meet.

"Bye, Fiddy – and, thanks for telling me."

"I had to. Cheerio, Bill." And she was gone.

+ + +

It was the anniversary of Eddy and Elizabeth's wedding. Everyone was in church because between them, Eddy, Seth and Helen had chosen that day for Edgar's christening. Eddy had spent much time with Elizabeth's parents and explained to them how much his little nephew meant to him. They encouraged him, and Elizabeth's mother had visited Helen and baby Edgar.

The christening was after matins and many of the congregation stayed. It was a moving service and little Edgar behaved impeccably. Dorothy was home to stand as godmother and Louise' Charles was godfather, and of course, Eddy. Flora looked at her sons, feeling exceedingly proud. Seth had been pitched into fatherhood sooner than he had planned, and Eddy had seen fatherhood snatched cruelly away, but their love for one another had made the best of the situation and they were helping each other. Helen was a lovely girl whose sympathy and understanding towards Eddy had rapidly endeared her to the family. Nothing could ever take away Eddy's pain and grief, but, Flora ruminated as she stood at the font, the March sunshine slanting in on the group, the timing of this little boy's birth had been aptly correct after all.

APRIL 1937

"You will do as I say, young lady." Bill shouted at his daughter, and Jessica could not understand why he was making such a terrible fuss.

"You don't understand, Father," she responded. "We love one another and we are becoming engaged whether you like it or not."

"You are under-age and I will not give my consent."

"Bill, dear, it would be an excellent marriage for her," interjected Jessica.

"Be quiet woman, you don't know what you're talking about."

Bill had never spoken to his wife so harshly before, and both she and Anne were taken aback.

"Why don't you like him, Father? I thought you two got on well." Anne spoke more rationally; she was genuinely perplexed by her father's reaction.

"You must trust me, I am looking to your best interests," he told her.

Privately, Jessica thought that Bill was merely jealous, and unwilling to part with his eldest child, or reluctant to accept she was grown-up. So, secretly, foolishly, she encouraged Anne and plotted with her to carry on seeing Joshua. An engagement party was planned with conspiratorial glee. Fiddy was being kept in the dark as well, on the premise that when she and Bill were confronted with a fait accompli, they would relent.

Lady Moira Johnstone was no fool, and knew her daughter. When she had seen Fidelia's violent opposition to her son's romance with Anne Henty, which was the antithesis of her usual laissez-faire attitude, she realised intuitively that she must drop some hint of the coming celebration. Nothing specific was ever said between them, but it was tacitly understood that the joining together of these two young people must be avoided at all cost – even the cost of their desperate unhappiness. Fidelia had contacts, as did her parents and between them, they arranged for Joshua to be taken up by the Diplomatic Service and whisked away to some distant part of the Empire, before he could plight his troth with Anne, and with the minimum of time to say goodbye.

JUNE 1937

Alice was home for a fortnight. She had been home for Elizabeth's funeral, but had had to dash off again afterwards. She marvelled that her parents could welcome her so wholeheartedly, for guilt had riddled her soul since last year's debacle at Seth's wedding.

"Don't be silly, Alice," said her mother. "You're our daughter."

"Oh Mum, I'm so pleased to be home."

"We're pleased to see you."

They talked about Seth and Helen, and how Eddy was, and his love for little Edgar.

"He's working harder than ever," Flora told Alice.

They gossiped about the family, about her cousins, and trouble with both Aunt Louise' Emma and Uncle Bill's Anne. Flora told of how the new shop her aunt and uncle had opened in the village had almost burnt down, only to be saved by Uncle Robert, of all people.

While they talked, there was a bang on the door.

"Good gracious, who can that be, making that noise?"

Flora went through to the living room to find a tall, fair, bearded gentleman standing there.

"What can I do for you?" she asked frostily.

"I'm told the Smith lives here," he grinned showing beautiful strong, white teeth.

"You're told right, but he's not here, he's at the forge."

At that moment, Alice walked through the short passage from the kitchen and stood, staring at the apparition.

"Hello," he said jauntily.

"Hello," Alice repeated, as if in a trance.

"This is my daughter, Alice," explained Flora.

"Hello Alice! What a lovely name."

Flora explained where the Smithy was, and Alice offered to walk along and show him. He introduced himself.

"I'm Theodore Weston," he told them. "It means Gift of God."

He was so cheeky that they both laughed, and Alice relaxed. They went outside and she saw that he had his horse with him.

"Hup, Chessie," he said, as he untied the reins.

Alice walked alongside Theo as they went through the village towards the Smithy. People greeted her as they went; she had only arrived home the previous day and villagers were pleased to see her again.

"You've been away?" he asked.

"Yes."

"Where?"

"London."

"Oh London, eh? I've been to London."

"What were you doing there?" she asked, intrigued.

"You tell me first."

"I'm a lady's maid."

"Aah," he said, as if comprehending something.

"Why 'aah'?" she smiled questioningly.

"You're different."

"Different to what?"

"Just different."

"So are you."

"Then that's two of us."

"You haven't told me what you were doing in London."

"I'm in the Army."

"Which regiment?"

"Coldstream Guards."

"So why have you a beard?"

"I've been on leave."

"Why here?"

"You must be the most inquisitive filly I've met in a long time," he told her, but he did not answer her question.

They had arrived at the forge.

"Dad, this is Theodore Weston. He came to Orchard Cottage looking for you."

Seth came forward to deal with the young man's query.

Alice said goodbye and left straight away. She knew she had been snubbed.

"Bye," she called.

"Oh, cheerio," he said absently, and continued speaking to Seth. "And thanks."

"Any time." Alice was happy as she walked back through Abbots Ford. She had worked hard for the duchess and needed a rest. Two whole weeks to look forward to! Time with her family. A little nephew. She felt at peace with herself.

+ + +

"Mum, I knew it was his doing. I'm sorry to go, but I'm not staying here, living with him, knowing what he did. He's ruined my life."

"I don't see how it could have been your Dad, dear," said Jessica. "If Joshua had to go, he had to."

"He didn't want to, I know that for sure."

"You're too young to leave home, live in a big city."

"I'm eighteen, Mother, and I'm going." Anne was implacable.

"Explain to your Dad then, dear. Don't go like this."

"You know I've been planning it, but you wouldn't believe me."

"You'll break his heart."

"He broke mine."

"What time is your bus?"

"Half-past-two."

"I'll help you with your cases." Jessica knew there was nothing she could do. Bill was far up the hill, busy baling. Anne had a place as a student nurse at St Mary's Hospital, in Paddington, London. She would be living in the nurse's home, where they were strict with the girls. She had organised everything herself.

The familiar bus chugged along and came to a halt at the stop which was supposed to be opposite the Partridge Inn, but took up the whole road. Anne put her bags on the bus and turned to kiss her mother.

"No crying now, Mum," she ordered.

"Take care of yourself, dear. You're very precious to us."
Jessica took out a large handkerchief and blew her nose.

"Bye, Mum," called Anne. Jessica stood and watched as the
bus went along the road, up the hill to the bend and out of sight.
She felt empty, bereft. She knew that Anne had to leave home
sometime soon, but not like this, not so far away. She turned and
began to walk slowly home.

+ + +

Chapter Three

AUGUST 1937 – JUNE 1941

Penelope Fitzwilliam was a determined young woman. She had had to be, for she and Giles had faced strong opposition from her family. Giles had not foreseen, nor intended, the marriage. He had been as surprised as anybody about his love for Penelope, and even more, hers for him. He had spent settled and satisfying years with Anna, and had not fully recovered from her death when Penelope had appeared on the scene. He was being swept along on the vehicle of Penny's youthful enthusiasm, always aware that it probably was an unsuitable match. Her energy and verve were infectious and he found himself doing things he had thought were beyond him. They had spent a fortnight skiing in Austria with friends that winter. He was riding more and rode with the local hunt. They went dancing in Bath and Bristol and travelled all over the country visiting friends and enjoying weekend house-parties.

Esmée was quietly thrilled at the turn of events, while understanding the family's disapproval. Had she not been in a similar position for years? The difference was that if the couple achieved their ambition to marry, despite the antagonism, they would still be capable of producing a family, God willing. Esmée tried not to influence her son, but encouraged him with sagacity.

Penelope finally persuaded her parents to allow the betrothal by dint of threatening to elope. Euphemia and Richard knew their daughter well enough to believe that she could lure Giles into agreeing to the outrageous plan, and so a celebration was arranged at Darnley Hall.

"You look good enough to eat," said Giles appreciatively as she descended the stairs towards him. He held out his hands to her. "Excited?" he asked.

She nodded, the beads on her headband sparkling and shimmering, reflecting the light. She was wearing deep emerald green, heavily beaded, and her eyes kindled as she looked at him, for he was looking more handsome than ever tonight. His blue eyes crinkled at the corners as he returned her look. He tucked her hand into his arm as he escorted her into the library for drinks.

"Here they are!" cried her grandmother cheerfully.

Euphemia and Richard were welcoming and polite, but both still regretted the engagement. While they talked among themselves, Giles took Penelope to a quiet corner and presented her with a small velvet box. She took it delightedly, aware of what it contained. She stared at the substantial emerald, which was surrounded by diamonds, for a long moment.

"Put it on for me!" she entreated. He took out the ring and placed it on the third finger of her left hand.

"There! We are betrothed." He kissed her tenderly and a ripple of applause broke out behind them. They turned and went towards her family, who could not help but be mollified that a daughter of the house should look so radiantly happy. Richard shook hands with Giles, and Euphemia kissed him on both cheeks.

"Time we were going downstairs to greet our guests," suggested Richard.

One of the first people they saw was Esmée, accompanied by an old friend of herself and Barnabus. They were greeted warmly and served champagne. Euphemia took Esmée to see the generous gifts the couple had received already.

"Don't be too downhearted Euphemia. I do sympathise, my dear." said Esmée. "But Giles is a good man, he'll be kind and loving to Penny, and he has a great deal to offer."

The younger woman nodded, not wanting to commit herself, yet knowing that what Esmée had said was true.

The dance went off well, for they had friends in common. "When's the wedding?" was the oft-asked question, to which they replied vaguely, "Sometime next spring."

Later, Giles crept into Penelope's room to kiss her goodnight; she was a modern-minded young woman and willingly invited him into her bed. However his feelings of gallantry would not allow him to make love to her before they were married. Penelope could not understand the illogicality of this stance because he had lived for almost two decades with Anna without being married.

"On this of all nights," she complained. "Don't you find me attractive?" she asked seductively as she slid her negligee from her shoulders, revealing a thin silk nightdress skimming her lithe body.

"Of course I do," averred Giles, sorely tempted. "But you're my bride. It isn't long to wait." He kissed her again and returned to his room, thinking about the future, realising how lucky he was to have been presented with a chance to have a family. Did he love Penny as much as she loved him? He chased the thoughts to the shadows of his mind; he knew he loved her. It was not wrong to look forward to children at the same time, he told himself. He removed his dressing-gown, folded it neatly, and climbed into his own bed, drifting immediately into a deep, untroubled sleep.

SEPTEMBER 1937

The Harvest Festival service was held on the first Sunday in October. The whole village turned out for the occasion, because in a farming community it was not only traditional to celebrate the fruits of Gods' gifts, but genuine gratitude: it was their living. Flora and Jessica had arranged the produce around the altar, and Gordon Bartrup had made a loaf the shape of a sheaf of corn, as a centrepiece. Children from the school walked up the aisle at the start of the service, carrying small boxes of fruit and vegetables to add to the display. Later, these would be distributed to the elderly and poor of the parish. Heartily, they sang the well loved hymn: *We plough the fields and scatter the good seed on the land.* Reverend Orrins gave his customary humorous sermon, at the end of which he announced his retirement at the close of the year. There was a gasp of disbelief from the congregation; he had been in the village for so long, and appeared ageless and so full of energy that they had not realised that he was almost seventy. Usually, rumour and gossip heralded these events in the village, but he had kept his secret well; it was a complete surprise. While they were still murmuring, he continued: "Reverend Douglas Glover, his wife Esther and their four young children will be coming here to live. I know that you will extend to them a warm welcome when the time comes." This news prompted more whispers, and he added, "However, I cannot bear to leave my flock, and have decided to remain in the village upon my retirement." He concluded the prayers and dismissal and followed the choir to the back of the church as they returned to the vestry. The villagers filed out quietly, they were so shocked at the news. Michael Orrins had guided and supported them through the great events in their lives: marriages, christenings and funerals for nearly forty years. He had encouraged and given them heart in time of loss during the Great War and they could not imagine anyone who could take his place.

"We'll have to mark his retirement," muttered Flora to her husband as they walked towards the lych-gate.

"He can't go just like that", agreed Seth.

They walked home silently, mulling over the change which Michael Orrins' retirement would mean to Abbots Ford.

Catherine Redford caught up with them just before they reached Orchard Cottage. "Flora!"

Flora turned and greeted her friend. Sometimes, Flora had thought that Catherine was inclined to be inquisitive and that running the General Stores was a way of fulfilling her need. In time, she had realised that Catherine meant well and that far from being malicious in any way, the interest in people and the circulation of news served a valuable purpose; elderly or vulnerable customers who were not seen for a few days were checked upon. Catherine had often discreetly told Flora or the other nurses snippets of news or relevant details which helped in their dealings with their young mothers. The communication of information only ever travelled one way, for Flora and her colleagues were too professional to indulge in gossip.

"What are we going to do to mark his retirement?" she asked breathlessly.

"I was just saying to Seth that we'd have to do something... we can't just let him go," agreed Flora.

Seth nodded and carried on into the house, for he did not trust Catherine.

"Let's call an emergency meeting of the committee to decide," suggested Catherine. "Put word around to meet at my house on Wednesday."

"Alright, Wednesday it is. See you then," said Flora. She followed Seth, her head full of ideas.

"Has Seth told you the news, Ma?" she asked.

"Yes, so sad isn't it? But he is getting on, you know," replied Louise.

"Catherine Redford caught up with us to suggest an event to mark the retirement. Got any ideas?"

"Do you know, he has always enjoyed the gathering on Christmas Eve, but that's usually at the vicarage, so we can't expect to have it there now," said her mother.

"I'll mention it to Catherine. He leaves at the end of December. In some ways, Christmas is a good time to go, so joyful. In some ways it isn't good, all the memories. Either way, we'll give him a Christmas Eve he won't forget!" promised Flora.

+ + +

The meeting the following Wednesday was run with customary efficiency by Catherine. They were sitting in the fine dining room of the splendid house she and Angus had had built many years ago. It sat back from the road, further up the lane from their premises, towards Upper Abbots. It was constructed with red bricks and had a dark grey tiled roof. A small, plain front door was set in the middle with windows on each side, like a doll's house. The iron railings which decorated the perimeter of the garden were painted grey. The high ceiling of the dining room boasted an elegant three-lamp gas light fitting, which now illuminated proceedings. They sat around the walnut dining table discussing how they could honour the man who had been their vicar for so long.

"We'll need somewhere large, because the whole village will want to come," said Flora.

"What about asking Esmée Mortimer to hold it at Tradewinds?" suggested Maisie Wilton, who had recently retired from the drapery business, but still lived in the village.

"Good idea. There'll be no going in the garden at that time of year! Tradewinds would be the right size as we'll all be inside," commented Emily Blake, the wife of the locum.

"Who will approach Mrs Mortimer?" asked Flora.

"I'll ask her next time she comes into the shop," said Catherine.

"What about funds?" asked Molly Saunders tentatively.

"I say that the money raised at the Harvest Supper this time should pay for it," said Catherine.

"And we could run a raffle," added Winifred Smythe.

They agreed on the details and discussed last minute arrangements for the Harvest Supper Dance before closing the meeting.

"Any news of Anne?" Catherine asked Jessica chattily.

"Yes, she's settling in well. They've done their induction course and they'll be going on the wards soon." Jessica Henty seemed to have accepted her eldest daughter's absence with equanimity. Flora overheard the exchange and made a mental note to go and see Jessica to find out how she really felt.

NOVEMBER 1937

Everyone had been heartened and amazed by the effect on Eddy of the birth of his little nephew, Edgar. He doted on him and as the child quickly developed a personality and began to recognise him, so Eddy spent longer at Plumtree Cottage seeing him. The contrast between the cosy home Helen had created there, and his own empty shell of a house, with all its bitter-sweet memories, could not have been greater. He was always made welcome and included in meals without question, so that it became routine for him to spend all his time with Helen, Seth and little Eddy, only having to return home to sleep, or when he was visiting his parents at Orchard Cottage. Helen felt sorry for him and Seth hardly noticed, he was so used to having his brother around. As the winter began to bite, Eddy became more loath to leave the warmth and security of his brother's home and return to his cold and empty house. One evening towards the end of November, he fell asleep in the chair and it seemed churlish to turn him out into the cold night to walk the two-and-a-half miles home. Helen made up a bed in the downstairs bedroom and Eddy spent the night there. Next morning, he stretched and yawned expansively as he strolled into the scullery.

"Haven't slept like that for months!" he said. "What's for breakfast?" Then he ate a plateful of eggs, bacon and toast, drank his tea and went off to work at Drakes Farm without a word. After that, it seemed taken for granted that he was living with them.

Helen broached the subject just before Christmas.

"When is Eddy going to go and live in his own house?" she asked quietly in their bedroom one night.

"Why?" said Seth absently.

"Well, we never have a moment on our own together now," she replied.

"He's still getting over Elizabeth and the baby."

"It's over a year," she said gently.

"He likes it here," stated Seth. "He loves little Eddy."

"I don't mind him coming sometimes, but living with us is too much," she said firmly.

"You're always selfish!" he shouted, turning on her. "Think of somebody else for a change."

"That's unfair," she cried. "He's your brother but I'm the one who does all the work."

"I'm the one who brings in the wage, you'll do as you're told," he countered.

She turned away, utterly dejected. Seth pulled on his trousers again, and snapping his braces on to his shoulders, stomped off back downstairs. Helen heard the low mumble of voices until she fell asleep, crying softly into her pillow.

DECEMBER 1937

It was warm for the time of year. A constant stream of ladies had been beating a path to Esmée Mortimer's drive all afternoon, carrying containers, tins and dishes of all shapes and sizes. A car laden with china crunched over the gravel and drove gingerly round to the rear of the house.

"Esmée!" Emily Blake, the doctor's wife, tried to locate the chatelaine. "Wait here a moment please, Mr Baker," she said.

"Esmée! Are you there?"

"Mrs Mortimer is laying out tables in the salon," the maid told her.

"We've brought tons of plates and so on. Can you help Mr Baker and me to unload?"

All three were trudging to and fro with boxes when Esmée and her daughter, Madeline appeared.

"My dear! Are you coping? You should've called."

"I did, but you were busy, so we just carried on. Hope you don't mind?"

It transpired that there were teams of helpers in various rooms, laying out food and organising the last minute details of the farewell to Michael Orrins, and his wife Virginia. There was an underlying excitement because it was Christmas Eve, and everyone was looking forward to the festivities.

"What have you arranged with Michael?" asked Mrs Tanner, the senior doctor's wife, who was the vicar's contemporary.

"I just said he was invited to a hot toddy after the early evening service," said Esmée.

"So he has no idea?"

"Not as far as I know."

"Good. Virginia is in the dark as well. It should be a pleasant surprise. If they seem as if they'll get here too soon, I'll waylay them," she grinned.

Flora and Seth walked arm-in-arm around the corner to St Mary's. They were in a happy mood, for their family was all present. Both girls had been able to arrange to spend Christmas at home. Eddy and Seth arrived with Helen and Edgar, and only Louise was left at Orchard Cottage, keeping an eye on the hams simmering on top of the range.

Murmuring greeted the family as they entered the church. Reverend Orrins only had tonight, tomorrow and one more

Sunday before he would end his working life as a minister. Most of the villagers could hardly recall the previous incumbent, if at all. The congregation settled into silence and a pure, perfect soprano voice sang *Once in Royal David's City*. Flora's heart warmed to the familiar carol; she had heard it introduce the service of nine lessons and carols every Christmas Eve for as long as she could remember. First, as a small child, full of excitement at the idea of the surprises and treats to come, and overpowered by the Nativity scene, tree, candles, holly and gold and white altar cloth decorating the church. Later, as a young married woman, attending with her handsome Seth and her parents and family; being accepted as an adult member of the community, and remembering secretly the naughty fun she and Seth would have in private later and feeling blasphemous for thinking of it in church. Later still, attending with her excited children, and thinking of all the tasks and chores still to be done at home after a frantically busy day, but knowing that this was an oasis of contemplation, calm and thankfulness. She was jolted back to the present as Reverend Orrins cleared his throat to read the first lesson. His kindly grey eyes peered at them all over his spectacles while he read the words as though hearing of the miracle for the first time. His grown up children were all in the front pew with their families. There was no sermon, and the minutes flew past, until they were singing *O Come All Ye Faithful*. He gave the blessing and after a few moments' prayer, followed the choir to the rear of the church, and stood, ready to bid his parishioners well for the season. He may have been surprised at the brevity of their greetings, for they were all in a hurry to make their way to Tradewinds.

He and Virginia and their family eventually found their way to the big house. Lights shone from all the windows, and a huge Christmas tree could be seen clearly through a window, exciting his grandchildren.

"They must have a large party for Christmas, dear," said Virginia. They knocked at the door. There was a delay before someone opened it wide and exposed all the children from the school, standing on the wide staircase and in the hall, who began singing, *Away in a Manger* unaccompanied. He was taken aback, and listened, pausing on the doorstep. When they had finished, he thanked them effusively, still unaware that most of the villagers were in the house.

"What a wonderful surprise! Thank you all very much. How kind of you to stay out on such a special night."

The warmth and light enfolded the family as they were welcomed inside. They were greeted by applause and cheering as they approached the salon, and people spilled out to shake his hand and clap him on the back.

"We couldn't allow you to go without a proper farewell!" Catherine Redford told him.

Michael and his wife circulated, stopping longer here and there with older parishioners. Sandwiches and punch, or cups of tea were passed round and the atmosphere sparkled with the warmth of true friendship. Reverend Orrins seemed bemused, but was obviously enjoying himself; similarly his family, grateful that he was being thanked for all the years of work and service. Giles Mortimer stood on the steps in the salon and cleared his throat to attract attention.

"Ladies, gentlemen... Reverend and Mrs Orrins..."

The sound of conversation and laughter died away as they turned towards him.

"We are gathered here..." A ripple of laughter erupted at his ecclesing of the words used on many occasions when Michael Orrins had married them. "...to honour and to thank the man who has been our help and support in good times and in bad."

"Hear! hear!"

"Thank you Michael, Virginia and family for your cheerful, happy presence among us for nigh on forty years."

One of the youngest children stepped forward with an album almost as big as herself, and presented it to him.

"What is this, Ruth?" he asked, smiling at the small girl. She was too shy to explain, and Esmée spoke up.

"We have collected mementoes and photographs of your time here, and mounted them in here."

"How lovely. Wonderful!" he exclaimed, obviously moved.

There was silence, and he gazed around the room at the expectant, sad faces.

"It has been my pleasure to be vicar of Abbots Ford for many years," he said quietly. "I feel I know you almost like my own family, for I share in not only the most important occasions, but also in your everyday lives. I am getting on now, and it's time to hand on the torch to a younger man." There was a murmur from the assembled company. He continued: "I know that you will welcome Douglas Glover and his charming family, and quickly make them feel part of the village. Virginia and I will not be far away, we are settling in Abbots Ford for our retirement. Thank you for all your love and support, for the fine gift which we shall enjoy perusing, and for this party." There were tears in many eyes as they applauded his speech. They shook his hand as they left in groups to go home and prepare for Christmas Day.

"Thank you, Esmée, Giles and whoever else helped to arrange this for us. We've enjoyed it tremendously, haven't we, Ginny?" His wife nodded in agreement.

"See you tomorrow," said Esmée warmly. "Happy Christmas."

The Orrins family went out into the clement night with the gratitude of the community to enhance their Christmas and their memories to brighten their retirement.

JANUARY 1938

The older Seth struggled along the snowy track. The cold spell had come unexpectedly and no one had been this way since the last fall of snow and it was hard going. His breath came in short bursts crystallising on the cold air. He glanced around at the scenery but had to look quickly down to place his footsteps cautiously. He stopped for a moment to catch his breath and take a longer look around, placing his hand on his knee while his foot rested on a mound. It was on days like this that the heat of the forge was most welcome, that and the warmth of the horse he was shoeing made the Smithy almost cosy. He took in the picturesque view, the snow covered cottages in the distance and the familiar countryside dressed in winter garb. The hill presented itself in all its beauty today – the patchwork of the fields up its side, for once a single colour. The winter sun shone weakly, catching a sparkle in the trees or on a hedge. There was no sound bar the crunching of his own feet. He set off again and came to his destination, a small cottage standing alone at the end of the track. When he knocked, he was surprised that an attractive young woman answered it. He had been going to carry straight on in as he usually did when he called to check up on old Mrs Matthews.

"I'm sorry! I'm Seth Hawkes and I…"

"Come in lad, come in," called Violet Matthews.

"How are you today?" he enquired.

"I'm alright," she told him.

"Auntie Vi is a bit under the weather. I came yesterday, but thought I'd stay until she improved."

Violet coughed a deep fruity cough which suggested infection on the chest. As she struggled to recover she tried to speak.

"My great-niece from…"

"Don't worry, Auntie Vi. I'm Eileen," she explained, laughing nervously. "I'll make a cup of tea."

She disappeared out to the scullery. Seth screwed up his hat in his hands and turned it over and over.

"Flora said is there anything you need?" he asked.

"You're so kind to me, you and Flora," she began.

"Let me have your list and Flora will get it today," he told her.

"Well, Eileen could go…"

"No, she's better off staying with you in the warm."

Eileen emerged from the scullery carrying a tray with three dainty bone-china cups and saucers upon it, as well as the matching teapot, cream and sugar.

"How do you like it, Mr Hawkes?" she asked.

"As it comes, thanks, love – long as it's hot."

Seth felt self-conscious while he watched the young woman pour the teas. Mrs Matthews seemed oblivious and was fiddling with linctus and a spoon while her shawl got in her way.

Eileen shook as she handed the cup and saucer to him. Their eyes met and he could see that she was equally interested in him.

She was not as young as he had thought when he first saw her. He reckoned she must be well into her thirties.

"It's kind of you to get Auntie Vi's errands," she said. "I could do it, truly..."

"No. You stay here. Flora will get the shopping and I'll bring it round later."

Seth drank the tea and reminisced about winters past with Mrs Matthews.

"I'll be off now," he announced, muffling himself up once more against the weather. "See you later," he grinned.

Eileen smiled with her eyes and thanked him, making him feel like a young man again.

"See you later," she echoed.

Seth had always had an eye for a pretty face and in the early years of his marriage had occasionally misbehaved. Flora had had such grave doubts about his behaviour with her sister's two bridesmaids that she had berated him in front of his workmates, and it had culminated in Seth forcing himself upon his wife, such was their anger and passion over the affair.

He had easily rejected Beatrice' advances because he disliked the woman so intensely, but on his travels he still liked to flirt and had come close to being unfaithful again even in recent years. He thought of Eileen as he made his way back through the village; her firm bosom and shapely waist, even in a thick winter skirt and jumper, her friendly, welcoming brown eyes and brown curly hair. She was neat and yet accessible and Seth could not stop thinking about her. He wondered if she was married – he had not noticed any rings on her hands. Suddenly, he felt ashamed of himself for his lewd thoughts. Flora could not be bothered with 'all that' as she called lovemaking now. He thought that perhaps something was amiss with her for she had muttered about 'women's problems' when he had tried to cajole her. They got on well together and there was deep love between them, but he was disturbed by the feelings Mrs Matthew's niece had revived.

He quickened his step as the road became easier where others had walked and greeted the brave souls he met along the way. Throughout the day his thoughts kept returning to Eileen and the fact that he would see her when he delivered her aunt's groceries. He knew that she would be as pleased to see him again as he would be to see her. A shiver ran through him at the thought of her and he tried to concentrate on his work, throwing himself into the strong physicality of it, attempting to dissipate the unbidden feelings.

SPRING 1938

Sadly, Reverend Glover was not to have the pleasure of officiating at what was the wedding of the year, as far as Abbots Ford was concerned. They thought of marrying in the cathedral in Bristol, but after much deliberation, they decided that the marriage should take place in the tiny chapel beside Darnley Hall. There were over three hundred guests being invited and although they could not all attend the ceremony, the problems of transporting them would be eliminated: they would find their own way there, and then find their own way home. As the day approached, chaos broke out simultaneously at the home of the bride's parents, Caversham Park, at Darnley Hall and at Tradewinds.

At Caversham Park, Euphemia thought she would never organise Penelope's trousseau in time. Part of the problem was the girl herself: never available for fittings, always changing her mind, and flitting here, there and everywhere. Penelope had never been so happy. She had not reached the age of thirty-two without having had the odd affair now and then, but they had always been with men whom she now regarded, with hindsight, as callow youths. She giggled and whispered with her girlfriends, and had engrossing conversations with her married friends. She spent hours on beauty therapies leading up to the big day, determined to be as much like a goddess as possible for Giles on their honeymoon.

Euphemia travelled endlessly between her home and her parent's, at Darnley Hall, organising and planning the wedding breakfast and reception, and the ball which would take place in the evening. She consulted with her mother over everything, to the extent that Penelope complained that 'Grannie is arranging my wedding!' Gradually, however, the different strands were converging and completed, until the tasks which were left could only be done on the day.

In the meantime, Penelope had initiated some changes at the newly named Tradewinds, which was going to be their new home. Esmée had encouraged her and so she had had to agree to whatever Penelope wanted. It was some time since the décor had been renewed, and both women threw themselves into the task in hand, consulting Giles only when they had already made up their minds. The house had been overrun with builders and decorators, people overseeing soft-furnishings and carpet-layers, for what seemed like months.

"She certainly brings new life to this place!" observed Esmée warmly after one of Penelope's visits. "Just what it needs!"

Two weeks prior to the wedding, a pantechnicon drew up at the front door. It contained furniture belonging to the bride, personal belongings, and vast quantities of clothes and books. There were plants and pictures, lamps and photographs, cushions and ornaments – and her bottom drawer linen.

"Good grief, darling! I hope Tradewinds is large enough to contain all of this – and you!" exclaimed Giles as the removal men began bringing everything inside.

The day broke promisingly. It was bright but chilly, and Penelope's teeth chattered as she leapt out of bed to look at the weather. At least it isn't raining, she told herself. It suddenly occurred to her that this was her last day in her parent's home as a single woman. She had been so busy and so sure, that there had not been time for reflection. She shivered and put on a warm dressing gown.

"Darling, what are you doing wandering about? Breakfast will be brought up to you this morning," chided her mother. "All brides have breakfast in bed."

"I'll need Mary to come and light the fire then," she called over her shoulder. Later, she was eating a boiled egg when her mother came in.

"How are you feeling?" she asked solemnly.

"I'm being married, Mother, not executed!" laughed Penelope.

"It isn't too late to put a stop to it, even now," said Euphemia hopefully.

"Oh, Mother! Not today of all days!"

"I know, Penny. But I thought I ought to say it."

"I love him, Mummy. I really do. Don't worry about us." She reached over and put her arms around her mother's neck.

"We only want you to be happy." Her mother sniffed and searched for a handkerchief.

"Oh, Mummy, you're not going to cry, are you?"

The two women laughed, each relieved that they had reached an understanding. The mother aware of the pitfalls any marriage can hold, and the daughter believing she was aware of them.

The organ announced the arrival of the bride and her father and the congregation rose. Giles did not turn to watch her but kept his eyes fixed on the stained glass window above the altar of the chapel. He could feel his mother's eyes boring into his back, and knew that she was not looking at Penelope either. The music welled up and echoed through the small building and soon she was at his side. Her gown was simple: brocade cut beautifully, plainly, to display her still-girlish figure and elegantly long limbs. A sweetheart neckline framed the pearls Giles had given her for a wedding gift. On her head, she wore a small tiara, from which a lace veil billowed; she carried a bouquet of spring flowers. Giles turned to look at his bride and was overcome with love and pride. They made their vows while their families and friends looked on, marvelling at the quixotry of the situation.

After signing the register, which was done on a table behind the altar, the organist played a toccata to accompany the first steps of their journey together. They emerged from the little church to the cheers of villagers and staff who were waiting to see them. The families followed and threw confetti while a photographer attempted to record the event.

When he had what he thought were good enough pictures, the wedding party made their way up to Darnley Hall, followed, with good-natured frivolity, by their guests. The ballroom had been transformed into a tented bower. Pink and white muslin billowed from the ceiling and walls, gathered at intervals with sprays of spring flowers. The long tables echoed the colour scheme and Penelope laughed delightedly when she saw it.

"Oh, Giles! Grannie has gone too far as usual!"

"It's beautiful, my dear," he commented, bemused.

Servants moved among them bearing trays of glasses filled with champagne.

Penelope's elegant friends came at intervals to whisper in her ear, followed by gales of girlish laughter. They made a handsome couple, standing between her parents and Esmée, greeting guests.

When they had enjoyed the wedding breakfast and it was time for speeches, her father brought tears to Penelope's eyes with his tribute to her and tears of laughter at his witty quips at her expense. Giles' contribution was sophisticated and urbane as he complimented his new young wife. Her friends could begin to see what the attraction was for her, for he looked handsome in his morning dress. Even Euphemia wondered if she had been wrong about the match.

The tea-dance was well underway when Penelope went upstairs to change into her going-away clothes. There were cries of appreciation when she appeared wearing cream silk trimmed with peach, topped with an elegantly flattering peach hat. Everyone seemed to kiss everyone else in the mêlée as they left, and Penelope sat back in the car breathlessly after turning to wave to her parents once more.

"Did you love it?" she asked Giles, elated.

"It was wonderful, darling. So are you."

The hotel for the first night of the honeymoon was in Bath, then they would travel down to Portsmouth to catch the ferry for the continent. After a relaxing meal in the restaurant, they retired to their room. Giles disappeared to the bathroom, returning after a long interval wearing his pyjamas and dressing gown. Penelope remained where she was, sitting near the long window smoking a cigarette.

"Are you getting ready for bed?" he enquired.

"Silly! Does it look as if I am?" she laughed.

"Come along…"

"Can I pour you a drink?" she asked.

"No, thank you. I've just cleaned my teeth."

"Well I'm having another."

"Don't you think you've had enough this evening?"

"This is my honeymoon. If I can't have a little more than usual tonight, then when can I?"

She clanked and clattered the glass and decanters as she poured herself a gin and tonic, and returned to her chair. When she had lit another cigarette she inhaled deeply and looked out at the elegant crescent.

"It's been an exciting day, hasn't it?" he ventured.

"Mmm," she agreed.

"Come on, Penny. What's the matter?"

"Nothing. Really."

Giles had been spoiled by the women in his life so far: first, his mother, and then by Anna. These older women had always accommodated him and his whims. Now, instead of spending time finding out what was obviously worrying Penelope, he left her to her own devices and, removing a book from his luggage, settled down to read it on a sofa at the other side of the room. Tears threatened Penelope's eyes, but she took a deep breath and another sip of her drink.

"You're so unromantic," she blurted out eventually. "I think that you don't really love me!"

"What is all this about?" he asked, genuinely perplexed.

"You're so... correct," she said.

"Mmm?" He placed his book carefully on the table and moved towards Penelope's chair. "What is all this about?" he repeated, lamely.

"We're on our honeymoon, Giles," she said, as though it explained everything.

"It's been a busy day. Why don't you get into your night things and come to bed?"

It was true. She was tired. Obediently, she stubbed out her cigarette, drained her glass and went to the bathroom to change into her most beautiful, diaphanous trousseau nightgown. When they lay side by side in the luxurious four-poster bed, she felt better.

"Happy?" he asked.

"Yes. I love you," she replied, turning towards him.

It had been a long time to wait. He had refused to consummate their love because she was his bride, and his gallantry meant saving her for this occasion. He did not know of her affairs, for she had always been discreet. In any case, they had been genuine love affairs and the men involved were gentlemen who would not discuss her. They kissed and he held her tightly to him, while she stroked his hair, and neck, and chest. She nibbled his ears and kissed his body, pressing herself firmly against him and murmuring softly of her love for him. When she asked him if he loved her and there was no reply, and at the same moment realised that there was no movement from him, she looked into his face and saw, to her utter disappointment, Giles had fallen into a deep sleep.

+ + +

Seth and Tom Bates had been asked by the Reverend Douglas Glover to replace the wrought-iron sconces in the church. They stood in the nave of St Mary's looking up at the distempered walls.

"Could do with cleaning, couldn't it?" observed the vicar.

"And a coat of distemper," added Seth.

"That's an idea! How long since it was decorated?" continued Reverend Glover.

"Do you know, I can't recall," admitted Tom.

"Must be a long time then?"

"Good heavens, yes. I'll ask Flora's ma when I go home," offered Seth.

"Either way it would be nice if it was done," maintained the vicar. "I'll look into it."

"In the meantime, we'll get on with these candle fittings. I'll go up the ladder, Tom," said Seth.

They carried on with their work, and Douglas Glover disappeared into the vestry. He was a pleasant man of thirty-two. Tall, with thinning hair and spectacles, which made him appear studious and scholarly, as indeed he was. His wife, Esther, who was the same age, looked Scandinavian but was Scottish. She was friendly and approachable and kept busy with her young family of four. James was eleven, Iris, nine, Jeremy, seven and Hazel, five. The villagers were slow to accept them completely, for their loyalty to Michael Orrins and his family ran deep.

Seth and Tom worked until they had removed all the fittings, and were gathering their tools together when Reverend Glover returned.

"I've been making some enquiries, and it's possible that we can redecorate the church if I can summon up some voluntary help," he told them.

"I'm willing to give some time," offered Tom.

"You can count me in," agreed Seth.

"That's a good start, thank you. I'll mention it on Sunday, and we'll see what sort of response we get."

Esther Glover joined them just as the two blacksmiths were leaving.

"Don't let me chase you away," she smiled.

"Time we were off anyway," said Seth.

Douglas told her about the mornings' work, and Esther laughed.

"Shame we can't do something with the vicarage as well!"

"One thing at a time. They'll probably enjoy refurbishing their, our, church." He put his arm around her waist. "I'm hungry. Is it nearly lunchtime?"

"Yes. All ready. The children will be home in fifteen minutes, so don't be side tracked and forget!" She went out through the vestry to return to the vicarage.

Her husband stood looking up at the vaulted ceiling of his new church. He was aware that it would take time to settle in and be accepted by the congregation, and could picture the gatherings in health, joy or sadness which must have taken place beneath this roof, under the ministration of his predecessor. He accepted his position and enjoyed his job. He turned to make his way home, to join his family for the midday meal, humming his favourite hymn as he went.

MAY 1938

Eddy was still living at Plumtree Cottage with Seth and Helen, returning at intervals to check on his own home. Seth still failed to see Helen's point of view, but little Edgar sometimes appeared confused.

"He thinks he has two daddies," she said wryly when both men were playing with him one teatime in the early summer.

"He doesn't! He calls me 'Uncle Ed'," laughed Eddy.

Helen ran her hand wearily through her hair. She found it exhausting to look after two men and a baby, for she was doing all Eddy's laundry. There had been no further discussion other than the argument in their bedroom that night, and Eddy had taken it for granted that he could stay. He sat with them in the late evening, listening to the wireless, so that they were never alone together, except in bed. They were snuggling down one night, and Seth cuddled up behind her, running his hands over her body.

"Leave me be, I'm tired," said Helen.

"Come on," he coaxed, beginning to climb on top of her. There had been no preamble. He felt the urge to make love, regardless of the fact that he had hardly addressed a word to her, let alone said anything romantic or loving.

"Get off, Seth. I don't feel like it. I'm tired," she complained.

"You're always tired these days," he grumbled.

"So would you be if you had to look after two grown men and a baby."

"Oh that's it! My Mother managed to look after six people, and had a cheerful smile for us when we came in."

"Not everyone is as perfect as Flora," said Helen wearily.

"You used to be keen enough," Seth commented quietly, bitterly.

"So were you! You were gentle, caring. Now it's just jump on, wham, jump off. You hardly seem to even care that it's me." Her voice was rising as she told him how she felt.

"Be quiet. Eddy will hear."

"The devil with Eddy," she shouted, becoming angry as she thought of the unfairness of it all, of Seth's selfish attitude. Seth put his hand over her mouth and leaned down close towards her face. In the guttering candlelight, he appeared dark and cruel.

"Don't talk about my brother like that, he's worth a dozen of you. You'll do as you're told." He turned away from her on the far side of their bed and appeared to go straight to sleep. Helen lay as shocked as if he had struck her. She loved him and always would, but he had a streak of cruelty and selfishness which was tarnishing their relationship. Now, his intransigence over the issue of Eddy's living with them was beginning to tarnish their marriage. She was sorry for Eddy's tragedy, and had done all she could to help, but it was time for him to stand on his own feet, to lead his own life again; after all, he was only twenty-three. She would speak to Flora, appeal to her sense of what was right. Eddy had been with them for over six months; surely their mother would see that it was wrong, if she, Helen, had had enough of it? She went to sleep, only to dream of dark caves full of indescribable monsters with two heads. She awoke to little Ed's cries and got up to take him down the pine stairs which led directly into the scullery. She felt tired and drained, but calmer than she had been for some time. Quietly, efficiently she prepared breakfast and fed her baby. When the men left for Drakes Farm, she cleared away, stoked the boiler in the wash house, and washed, dressed and prepared herself to face her husband's mother, to see if Flora could succeed where she had failed, in appealing to Seth. If not, the end of her marriage was in sight.

AUGUST 1938

The faces in Abbots Ford were gradually changing, though the essence of the village remained the same. It was time for Dr Tanner to retire as his health had not been good for two or three years. He had been a popular and friendly doctor and had practiced in the village for most of his working life. He did not want any presentations and left quietly with his wife, retiring to the Highlands of Scotland. Young Martin Blake, who had been assisting him for two years, took over the practice.

Yet more homes were being built on the outskirts of the village, thus bringing new families and blood to the area, in greater numbers than ever before. More motor traffic was on the roads and fewer people kept horses. Electricity was available in the new houses and some of the older properties were being converted. Some places, like Orchard Cottage, had electricity for their lighting but steadfastly refused to cook with it. Flora maintained her range, which was extended to provide hot water in a tank.

The harvest was underway when Reverend Glover announced that the plans for refurbishing the church were to begin the following month.

"Anyone who can spare time to clean the church first, washing walls and so on, helping out by covering pews and fittings, and packing away anything that moves, will be exceedingly welcome."

After the service, Catherine Redford and Flora went to see him and suggested putting up a list to which willing participants could add their names and the jobs they felt able to do.

"Excellent idea, ladies. I'll do it in time for the evening service."

"It's a shame it's just now. It's so busy, what with the harvest and all," said Catherine.

"There'll be plenty of time. The professionals don't start until mid-September," he assured them.

"What about services while they're doing it?" asked Flora.

"It'll be topsy-turvy while the work is underway, but, have no fear, we shall be open for worship," he grinned.

Flora had caught up with Seth and he asked what Reverend Glover had been saying. She explained, and he cursed for the timing of the work, because it precluded his helping.

"When I've finished at the Smithy, they'll need all the help they can get at Drakes Farm."

"Don't worry, there'll be more than enough people to help," she said.

While Flora was dishing up the Sunday dinner, Seth asked her mother about the church.

"Can you remember when it was last cleaned and distempered, Ma?"

"I believe it was the year of Queen Victoria's Jubilee, Seth," she told him.

"About time it was done again then!"

"Is it all arranged? Is it being done?" asked Louise.

"Middle of next month, Ma," said Flora.

"I wish there was something I could do to help," said her mother.

"You help by helping me on your good days, and being cheerful for us, Ma. More than enough. Don't fret. You've done your share in your time."

They sat down to a roast beef dinner and drank cider with it, a merry trio, full of good humour. Later, when they had finished, Flora and Louise cleared away and washed up, while Seth had a short nap before joining the workers at Drakes Farm. Louise went to the small front room downstairs which was her bedroom, to have a quiet hour, and Flora settled herself with her sewing.

"May I come in?" The voice woke Flora with a start. It was her daughter-in-law, Helen, with baby Edgar.

"My dear, come in. I must have fallen asleep!" She looked around for Seth but there was no sign of him, and mentally she noted that he had probably gone back to the harvesting.

"I need to talk to you, Mrs Hawkes, and I've been plucking up courage for weeks to do it, nearly came a few times."

Helen could not bring herself to call Flora 'Ma', nor could she call her 'Flora', that would be too disrespectful, so 'Mrs Hawkes' it was.

"What's troubling you?" asked Flora dangling her grandson on her knee.

"It's Seth. Well, Seth and Eddy, really," she began.

Flora listened attentively.

"Last November, when it was cold, we put Eddy up for the night – and he's stayed ever since."

Flora nodded.

"We know how much Eddy has been through..." Helen paused, waiting for Flora to say something, but she merely nodded encouragingly again.

"Seth doesn't see why it shouldn't just carry on, but I..."

"You want him to return to his home?"

Helen nodded, her face crumpling under the strain of it all.

"Don't worry. You've done well sheltering him all that while. Do you want me to have a word with Seth?"

Helen agreed, wiping her eyes.

"Thank you, oh, thank you," she mumbled into her handkerchief.

"We won't say any more about it, or to the menfolk," Flora told her, and she understood.

Louise Henty joined them and dandled Edgar on her knee. The little boy gurgled and spoke his own language to them, encouraged and adored by all three women. Helen felt so close to them, and watched as they played with her baby. Perhaps Flora really understood. *Did wisdom come with age?* she thought, or had Flora always been sensible.

"All the hearts you're going to break, little man," crooned his great-grandmother, "just like your rascal of a father!"

SEPTEMBER 1938

Flora's husband, Seth, and Eileen could not meet often enough. Their affair had begun shortly after their first meeting at her aunt's cottage. Eileen had stayed with Violet until the weather cleared in February, and Seth had made excuses to return. Sometimes Mrs Matthews was in bed upstairs and the couple had the fire to themselves, which was when Seth had stolen his first kiss from her. She had been shy at the beginning but as the weeks wore on she became increasingly eager. On the occasions when her aunt was downstairs, Seth would follow her to the scullery which led straight off the living room and they would snatch a kiss or an embrace.

"You'll be glad when the good weather comes, Seth," commented Mrs Matthews one morning. "I can never repay yours and Flora's kindness to us."

"Don't you be fretting now, Mrs Matthews," he said. He winked at Eileen, who had the grace to blush. And so they met throughout the spring and summer. Their feelings did not go completely unnoticed. Eileen was unable to act normally whenever Flora was about.

"I think you've an admirer there, Seth," she remarked, smiling. "That should make you feel younger."

"You've no sense, woman," Seth commented, laughing, reassuring.

But the lovers had consummated their love in, if not exactly, the same place where Seth had found Alice with Robert, not far off, the warm hay he stored for use in the Smithy.

Eileen watched as Seth hammered a horse-shoe into shape on the anvil, admiring his sinewy, brown sweating torso.

"What shall we say I've come about, if anyone comes in?" she asked, once he stopped striking the metal.

"Don't worry, I'll think of something," he told her offhandedly.

She wandered about looking at everything, touching and examining.

"Bit messy in here, isn't it?" she teased.

"Just you mind yourself," he told her confidently. "I don't allow cheeky wenches in here you know."

She went to the horse he was shoeing.

"Good boy, good boy," she whispered.

Seth began to fashion the shoe again and she patted the horse, trying to shut out the metallic, rhythmic sound. When he stopped again, she moved nearer to him.

"When will I see you?" she asked in a small voice.

"God, you look a picture today" Seth told her, wiping his brow. "You know you're making me hot under the collar don't you?"

"Seth, I want you," she said, looking unwaveringly at him. Later, she was not sure how it all happened so fast. He had come towards her and, taking her arm in a firm grip, steered her out of a side door and into a half-barn where there were bales of hay. He took her in his arms and pushed her roughly against the wall behind them. They could still be seen from the outside, so he pulled her down onto the floor, kissing her hard and strongly. They explored each other's bodies with eager hands and there was nothing going to stop their rising passion. Afterwards as they lay together, kissing each other softly, Tom Bates came blundering in, completely unaware of their presence. He almost tripped over them.

"God – I'm sorry," he mumbled and made a hasty retreat.

"Oh Christ," cussed Seth.

"Who was that?" panicked Eileen, hastily pulling her clothes on and tidying herself up.

"He's my friend, Tom. Don't worry love, it'll be alright," he comforted. "He won't say anything." He helped her up and brushed her down.

"Will I see you later?" she asked again.

"Better leave it for today, love. I'll come out your way the day after tomorrow," he suggested.

"Do you still love me?"

"Course I do – more than ever. Now shoot off out of here," he said briskly, patting her on the bottom.

The horse had stayed, tethered, waiting patiently for his new shoes.

"Sorry about that delay, old lad," murmured Seth, patting him on his velvety nose. "You know how it is…" He threw himself into the work he loved. Fleetingly, it crossed his mind what he would say by way of explanation to Tom. The two men had shared many thoughts and feelings over the years, but nothing along these lines. *Nothing he can say – not really his business,* thought Seth as he tried the shoe for size.

OCTOBER 1938

They all gathered on the Saturday after the Harvest Supper dance. Even some of the men from the farms were there, as the harvest was safely gathered in. The professional decorators had been delayed, and the villagers were to begin cleaning the church. They had gone about it methodically, and had ladders and pulleys, scaffolding and buckets. The younger women were to assist in washing down pillars and walls, while the older ladies were covering the pews and stripping the church of all the hymnals, hassocks, chairs, cloths and anything they could remove. These were being stored in the vicarage and school, wherever there was room. Flora and her sister, Louise, were draping dustsheets over the font when Maisie Wilton and Miriam Redford approached carrying baskets.

"We've brought sandwiches and pasties to save people going home if they don't want to," they explained.

"That's a good idea. Perhaps Reverend Glover could tell everyone," said Flora.

When this was done, and they had stopped for an impromptu picnic, Esther Glover asked some of the ladies to help to carry teas across to the church.

"Talk about the feeding of the five thousand! I'm amazed at how much food came out of those baskets," quipped Seth.

Tom gave Seth a sidelong glance full of meaning.

"What's that look for?" Seth asked quietly.

"You – quoting the Scriptures," Tom told him, half under his breath.

"What do you mean?"

"You know what I mean – you've been avoiding me because you know what I mean," said Tom.

"What are you men muttering about?" asked Flora.

Neither answered, but Tom got up, carrying his pasty and strode out through the church.

"Have I offended him?" She glanced at Seth for a response.

"No – you know how odd Tom can be. I'll just go and see what's bothering him."

Seth followed and made his way across the hummocky grass between the graves. He found Tom right at the bottom of the churchyard where the water tap stood, next to the foul-smelling pile of dead flowers and plant refuse.

"Grmph." Tom greeted him grudgingly.

"You said I've been avoiding you, and you're right," agreed Seth.

"Right I'm right," Tom told him. "You're too ashamed to meet my eye, lad."

"I'm here now. Say what you have to."

"I need to say nothing. You're a man over fifty – you should know how to behave by now. You're taking that young woman – out of wedlock – while you have a treasure of a wife at home. How many commandments are you breaking to do it?" demanded Tom.

"I couldn't help myself... I needed her," Seth told him lamely.

"Rubbish. What if Flora were to find out? What about the hurt you'd cause her and your family? That girl can't be many years older than your own daughters. I hope you're ashamed, Seth Hawkes."

"She's thirty-four."

"Like I said, not much older than your Alice."

"It's different, Tom. It's not like you think."

"Don't try to pull the wool over my old eyes, lad. There's nothing different – I saw for myself in that barn. What are you going to offer her – marriage? Course not!" he added triumphantly. He munched the last of the pastie, and said quietly, "What if she were to get pregnant, Seth, where would you be then?"

They continued to argue until the others called them, accusing them of not working hard enough.

"Lazy buggers," shouted Jack Watling, a crone of Tom's.

"Blasphemy in the Lord's garden," said Catherine Redford piously.

"We're coming," called Seth.

"Heed what I've said, boy," reiterated Tom. "It's not worth upsetting the whole applecart for."

Those who could, continued to work until the light began to fade. Douglas Glover and his wife joined in, scrubbing at the walls vigorously, removing the dust and grubbiness of decades.

"We'll come along early in the morning to remove the dust sheets for early communion," Angus Redford assured the vicar.

"I cannot thank you all enough," Douglas told them gratefully.

When everyone had gone, he and Esther stood in the middle of the chaotic church and marvelled at what had already been achieved.

"Well, it is their church," said Esther. "It's one of the cornerstones of village life."

"Are you happy?" he asked her.

"Yes. I like the village, and I think the people are beginning to like us."

He hugged her and they made their way back to the vicarage where one of the Sunday school teachers, Margaret Watkins, was kindly keeping an eye on their family.

"Is the church clean now? Can we look?" pleaded Hazel.

Douglas laughed. "Tomorrow you shall see it. Yes, we're all working hard to make it clean, but it is very messy just now," he told his daughter.

"May we help tomorrow, Papa?" asked his two elder children.

"Yes, that would be welcome, just as long as you're not in the way."

The family settled down for an evening of relaxation in preparation for the busiest day of their father's week. Douglas Glover rewrote his sermon, incorporating his gratitude to the people of the village. For the first time he felt as if he belonged.

DECEMBER 1938

Excitement pervaded the atmosphere, for the first service after the church was decorated and reassembled would be the nine lessons and carols on Christmas Eve. Snow had been falling gently for two days, transforming Abbots Ford into a winter scene from one of the Christmas cards they were sending to family and friends. Tom Bates and Seth were among the people who were heaving the pews back into place the day before Christmas Eve. People worked in groups all through the building, setting up the altar, returning cupboards, arranging evergreen foliage and the Nativity scene. They were delighted with the result. The stained glass window had been cleaned and shone darkly as the weak afternoon light faded. The new iron sconces contrasted elegantly against the white walls, and the pews had been polished to a high gloss. The ladies of the village had combined to make new tapestry covers for the hassocks which were proudly put in place. The celebration at the vicarage on Christmas Eve was going to double as the party to mark the refurbishment of the church. Seth took the strain of pushing the last pew into place while Tom manoeuvred it. Suddenly, Tom collapsed without a sound and lay motionless in the nave. Seth called out, alerting the people around them. Flora ran across and felt for his pulse. A shocked group stood around, not saying anything. There was no panic; it was as if they knew. They waited while Flora tried to do what she could, but he was gone. Someone ran across to Dr Blake's house, and he came from his regular surgery, only to confirm what they already knew.

"Where are his daughters, does anyone know?" he asked.

"I'll look for them," offered Louise, Flora's sister.

Flora and Seth stayed with Tom until transportation arrived to convey him home, and then they accompanied him. Jenny and Bonny and their families were waiting for them at Smithy Cottage, and Flora and Louise did their best to comfort them.

Tom's passing made for a subdued Christmas; everyone in the village knew and liked him.

"He hadn't recovered from Ellie's death," said Flora sadly.

Seth had never confided in Flora that, many years ago, Tom had broken down shortly after the news had come through of the loss of Tom and Ellie's second son in the Great War. Tom had lost heart and spirit and had begun to hand over the Smithy to Seth's care from then onwards. Seth did not reveal the secret now. He respected the man and his feelings, an extremely private man, who had rarely allowed his emotions to show. Seth knew that it had been hard for Tom to speak to him of his affair with Eileen. Tom had rarely interfered in anyone's business and it had demonstrated the strength of his feelings about it that he had broached the subject to Seth at all. Seth felt guilty and ashamed that he had caused a decent man to worry. Tears sprang to his eyes and he fought down the lump rising in his throat.

"We'll do our best to give him a good send-off, the way he did for everyone else," he said.

"The girls are taking it hard," went on Flora.

"We've all got to go when our time comes, and leave behind our loved ones," said Seth, amazed at his own duplicity.

"I worry about when Ma's time comes," admitted Flora. "She's aged a lot since Pa died."

Tom was laid to rest next to Ellie, in the snow, the day after Boxing Day. Many of the villagers turned out, despite the weather, and even Flora's mother, Louise, was taken round to St Mary's for the funeral. Douglas Glover and his family were as sad as any, and Reverend Glover had privately voiced his distress that Tom had died while helping out in the church. Tom's daughter, Jennifer, heard about it and went to the vicar to say that there were three places where her father would have wanted to end his days: in his bed, in the smithy or in his church.

Seth went for a long walk up to the top of the hill after the funeral, and Flora knew that he wanted to be alone. Tom had been like a second father to him, and Seth was almost a surrogate for the sons Tom had lost. They had been similar in many ways: men of few words. Seth had no words now, and gazed out across the Somerset countryside as if he could glean answers or strength from the familiar landscape. He stood for a long while, and then made his way back home.

MARCH 1939

There was still great unrest in Europe. The Spanish Civil War was coming to an end, but the British Navy had been mobilised the previous autumn. All of this passed by the people of Abbots Ford, who were struggling to maintain their own lives. The Hawkes family suffered a sad loss when Charlotte, Seth's mother, died suddenly just before Easter. The Hawkes children and grandchildren gathered around James to comfort and support him, and there were enough of them to do so.

Eddy had finally returned to his own home, ostensibly his own decision. Flora had hinted as much to him, saying that it was not fair to Seth and Helen as a couple, always having a third party there. She had told him gently that it was time for him to lead his own life, and he had heeded her words. He went to work at Drakes Farm, and returned home, and that was his life. He hardly cooked for himself and the house was neglected and run down, which was why it suited him so well to live with Seth and Helen:

even his responsibility to himself had been taken from him. Eddy had altered since Elizabeth and Edgar's deaths, and the abject grief had faded. What people did not realise was that he suffered a deep-seated depression. They knew that only time would heal his spirit and did their best to keep him cheerful day by day. So Flora was shocked when, unusually, she called at the house in which he and Elizabeth had started their married life so full of hope in the future. She had been careful not to step on her daughter-in-law's toes and had only visited their home when invited. There was really no need, for the young couple had called in at Orchard Cottage regularly; there had not been a precedent for Flora's visiting. She was only calling in after visiting her sister-in-law, Rebecca, who lived at that side of the village.

Flora approached the house and it struck her that there was an air of neglect about it. The small front garden was overgrown, and pieces of rusty machinery were scattered about, and an old bicycle lay near the hedge which now grew around it. The door was unlocked, and Flora knocked, called out and went in. The kitchen was not untidy for it was obvious that it was never used. Instead, a general grubbiness pervaded the place where it had not been cleaned for a long time. The other rooms were the same and in the bedroom, a pile of dirty clothes lay, witness to the fact that Eddy had never learned how to wash them. It made Flora sad rather than annoyed. She rolled up her sleeves and did what she could to clean in the time she had available. Then she left the tin of cakes she had baked for him in an obvious place, and taking the pile of dirty laundry with her, left for home. *Maybe he was better off living with Helen and Seth,* she thought. *He could always return to Orchard Cottage...* she was deep in thought as she walked through the village. She would talk to Seth about it, and of course, her mother Louise. *I wonder if we ever stop worrying about them?* she thought. *Probably not.*

SEPTEMBER 1939

Even more serious worries pushed family concerns aside. At the end of August, the rest of the British Fleet was mobilised and on the third of September, war was declared, after Poland was invaded by German forces. Great Britain and France mobilised and the world found itself at war for the second time in less than a quarter of a century. All the men between the ages of eighteen and forty-one were called up for active service, unless they were a reserved occupation. For those who remembered Word War One, with all the loss of life, sadness and worry, it was a desperate period.

Alice immediately gave in her notice to the Duchess of Taversham who was dismayed, and applied to St Mary Abbots Hospital School of Nursing in Kensington, an area she knew well.

Dorothy was up in Scotland, where Sir Philip and Lady Stephanie had already decamped with their family for the duration of the war.

Young Seth continued to work on Drakes Farm, because James was retired, and only Arthur and David remained of all the uncles, and of course Eddy. Seth and Helen were settled and happier. Edgar would soon celebrate his third birthday, and his parents announced that they hoped to provide him with a baby brother or sister the following summer.

Louise and Gordon still had their shop at East Hartness, but they were beginning to struggle. Their family was splitting up, for Charles had been called up and joined the Royal Air Force as a gunner. Emma and Victoria became Land Girls, 'Digging for Victory' as the saying went.

Towards the end of September, Louise Henty became poorly, and Flora thought that the idea of yet another war was too much for her. In the first week of October, she died peacefully in her sleep.

OCTOBER 1939

Many more older faces were missing around the village. Now it was the turn of the lady who had been a tower of strength to her family. Flora, Louise and Bill were heart-broken, but it was Eddy who seemed to take it the worst. She had been such a comfort to him in his time of need, and he had always adored his Grandma Henty.

Flora and Louise were sitting in her little downstairs bedroom at Orchard Cottage, trying to feel, once more, her presence. It was the day before the funeral, and Flora had lit the fire. Louise sat in her mother's chair, crying quietly. She had already been depressed by her son Paul's leaving to join up. Now, she looked round at her mother's things through the tears. Flora brought them both cups of tea and put the tray down on the small table near the bed. The fire played and danced inappropriately, casting light on the pale flowers of the wallpaper. The bed was still made up with its attractive quilt, which their mother and father shared.

"I don't think I can bear it," wept Louise. "Pa, and now Ma. Gone." She burst into a fresh spasm of weeping. Flora sat quietly, sipping her tea.

"Her poor hands," Louise muttered, almost to herself.

Flora gazed impassively around the room. Her eye caught sight of a bag she had not noticed before, tucked into the head of the bed. She rose and idly plucked it from its sanctuary. Gently, she opened it, inquisitiveness turning to surprise. Gradually, beautifully embroidered material emerged through her hands, revealing itself to be an altar cloth. On examination, they realised it was not quite finished. Even so, it was exquisite. It was triumphal, for use at Christmas and Eastertide. The design was intricate, incorporating a gold cross with all the plants and flowers, foliage and wildlife of the two seasons. Tiny red berries shone from green leaves, and the red was echoed in a tiny robin's breast. The delicate tracery of pale spring flowers and leaves was intertwined with the purple touch of crocuses. Both women were speechless. They stared at the work with tears running down their faces.

"She must have been doing it for the church," said Louise brokenly.

"Look, she's written down when she started it. She'd been working on it for over a year," said Flora.

They were stunned. Neither had had any idea that their mother had been producing such a treasure.

"What shall we do with it?" asked Louise.

"Present it to the church. It'll be like a memorial."

"It isn't finished."

"We'll finish it."

"Should we?" said Louise tentatively.

"Don't see why not."

They folded it carefully and replaced it in the tissue paper. They both felt a warmth, a comfort, as if they regarded it as specific proof of their mother's existence; as if such a thing were needed. Now they could anticipate her funeral the next day with equanimity.

The rain did not cease all day. It poured from the ivy leaves on Orchard Cottage and dripped from the edges of the porch roof; it ran down the lane, and it soaked the good earth. Louise Henty was conveyed to church in a hearse, with wreaths made up from the deep red and orange chrysanthemums which she had loved, laid upon the casket. Her children and grandchildren mourned her, but knew that they had given her much joy in a long life. Those of her friends who were left, joined the family and Reverend Orrins emerged from his retirement to share the officiation at the funeral service of one of his oldest friends and parishioners.

The wake was held at Orchard Cottage. Flora and Louise chose the occasion to show the assembled company the work their mother had almost completed on the altar cloth. The two ministers were deeply moved, and Douglas Glover vowed to use it that Christmas if they were able to complete it in time. Somehow, the specimen of Louise Henty's work exemplified her life; the purity and care, the commitment to her faith and love for her family. It made the occasion less sad, more hopeful, and took away the sting of her death. Bill, who had been pathetically grief-stricken, ran his hands over the fabric and embroidery, marvelling that his mother had been capable of producing such intricate work when she had suffered so badly with arthritis in her hands.

"Trust Ma to leave us something to remember her by!" he said wryly.

"Oh, I think she's left more than that," said Flora, putting her arm through her brother's. "You're like her, I'm like her, so is Louise. And look at all the grandchildren!"

Bill patted his sister's hand.

"Good old Flora. Yes, you're very like her, thank goodness."

"Come and see me any time you're feeling low, Bill. That's what families are for." Then she enquired casually "Do you hear from Anne these days?"

He shook his head sadly.

"Well, anyway, don't grieve alone. Ma wouldn't have wanted that. We've got to stick together, we Henty's." She smiled.

"You're a Hawkes!" he told her.

"By marriage, maybe. In my heart I'm still a Henty. By blood, I'm a Henty. But don't let on to Seth!"

Bill was comforted. The family. A warm cloak to wrap around you when the cold wind of despair blew through your bones. This was the legacy their mother and father had bestowed upon them all. He made up his mind then that, come what may, he would mend the schism between himself and his eldest daughter. Nothing and no one was worth the splitting of families.

+ + +

Seth had been unable to drag himself away from Eileen. The physical attraction between them was so strong that even though he knew that what Tom had said was right, he continued to risk everything he loved to satisfy his passion for the girl. If they had been seen around the village, no one had stumbled on the truth, and there was no gossip and no rumours. Perhaps people could not believe it of Seth, or a respectable young woman like Eileen. However, they had reached an impasse. Eileen had realised that Seth was never going to leave Flora for her, something she had increasingly tried to coerce him into doing. They discussed it endlessly, because when Seth was in thrall to her, he deluded himself that what she demanded was feasible. He prevaricated in the end, trying to have it both ways. Flora had noticed that something was on his mind, but she put it down to various things, including his sadness at Tom Bates' passing which had affected him deeply. He missed Louise, her mother, and naturally, everyone was worried about the war. Ultimately, it was the war which came to their rescue. Once Eileen realised that there was no future with Seth, that his loyalty to his wife and family would even over-ride his feelings for her, she decided to go to London and take part in the war effort. She was not sure what exactly she would do; she might even join up, she told him.

In a way, Seth was relieved. In truth, he never envisaged having to leave Flora, it just was not an option. He had not bargained for someone of Eileen's age falling in love with him to the extent that she wanted to marry him. He missed their meetings, their lovemaking, and was depressed for a few months, but he knew it had to be that way. Eileen went off to her new life, bolstered with thoughts of 'beating the Hun' and 'doing her bit' for England. A number of the younger generation were leaving the village for the same reason, and there were tears, smiles, waves and brave faces to see them off at the bus-stop opposite the Partridge Inn. Malcolm Smythe became used to pouring medicinal brandy for parents who had just seen off their sons or daughters. The fact that it was the period of the phoney war fooled nobody: was it not the second time this century that they were having to teach the Germans a few manners? No, the war was going to part those free to love and those who were not. In either case, it made no difference when you lost them.

DECEMBER 1939

Esmée stood in the hall looking at the Christmas tree.

"Lovely, isn't it, Mother?" said Giles emerging from the salon.

"Yes, dear. And this time next year there'll be someone very special to share it with."

Giles put an arm round his mother's shoulders. She had been looking her age of late, but the news of Penelope's pregnancy had put a renewed spring in her step.

"It'll be wonderful, won't it?" he agreed.

Penelope came slowly downstairs. Pregnancy did not come easily to her and she spent most of the time feeling poorly. A miscarriage earlier in the year had left everyone depressed and

Penelope weak. She had made an effort this evening because her parents, grandparents and a few friends were coming for pre-Christmas drinks.

"Hello, darling!" Giles turned towards his wife.

"Come and sit down, dear," said Esmée solicitously.

Penelope hated the cloying concern surrounding her, but as she felt so ill, she accepted it without demur. They were sitting discussing the war when their guests began to arrive. Euphemia knew that Penelope did not look well but said nothing. Her daughter had not confided in her, but she felt that there was something more underlying the young woman's lack of vitality, than the problems she had experienced with pregnancy. They had an enjoyable and sociable evening, but Penelope retired to her room as soon as they had gone. Giles had suggested separate bedrooms when they had been married three months, giving as a reason his restlessness in bed, caused by an old wound to his back. Penelope prepared for bed, and the maid appeared with hot milk.

"'Night, ma'am," she said quietly as she closed the door.

It was almost two hours later when Giles knocked gently on his wife's bedroom door to kiss her 'goodnight'. Receiving no reply, he popped his head around the door because he could see through the slit in the frame that her light was still on. To his horror, he saw her slumped on the floor near the bed. He rushed over calling her name again and again. He raised the alarm, and, leaving someone with her, went to telephone the doctor to attend her urgently.

Penelope had lost the baby. Christmas held no joy in the household at Tradewinds then. Giles and Esmée were as upset as Penelope herself. Her room was filled with out-of-season flowers and baskets of fruit, but she took no interest in anything or anybody. She was completely transformed from the happy, energetic person who had promised to love, honour and obey Giles only twenty short months before. Giles' own disappointment meant that he withdrew into himself and thus was unable to give his wife the support and unconditional love she needed. Esmée, in turn, could not summon the strength to encourage her son to look to the future. The war, the waiting, and the machinations of the countries of Europe jostling for power, all dragged her spirit down. With no contemporary in whom she could confide her fears and sadness, she came down with a severe bout of influenza and they feared for her life.

JANUARY 1940

Bill continued to 'Dig for Victory', with his large farm working at full strength. His lad, Will, now seventeen, pulled his weight and Bill hoped that he would be allowed to remain there because he was needed. They would have to wait to see if the country needed him more as the war progressed. Anne hardly ever visited them. She had travelled to Bristol to meet her mother once, but still refused to see her father.

Beatrice remained a thorn in the family's flesh and her son, Charles, now twenty-six, had spent the duration of the war thus far trying to avoid taking part in it.

Flora was celebrating her fifty-first birthday. Seth was fifty-four and with the death of James, his father, just as the New Year began, they were coming to terms with being senior members of the family. Flora had begun to hand over the general work of midwifery to Jenny, Rachel and Gillian, whose catchment area had increased because they were now employed by the local council health committees. She covered emergencies and holidays and occasionally, follow-up visits, seeing new mothers for six weeks after their baby's birth, a service which had always been peculiar to their area and had been initiated by Ellie Bates. Flora had long since ceased taking home the new mother's bed-linen to wash, though.

Alice paid a flying visit home. She was enjoying her first year at St Mary Abbots Hospital, but her parents fretted about her being in London.

"Don't worry," she told them. "Nothing's happening."

For this was still the period of the 'phoney war'.

She was full of enthusiasm about her work, and her parents could see a definite change in her. They breathed a sigh of relief for they had discussed and worried about her endlessly. She described to them the rambling, florid Victorian buildings which constituted St Mary's; it's enormous, cavernous wards filled with rows of people. She aped the martinets who ran the wards and described the flamboyant caps the sisters and nurses wore. She made them laugh by recounting the antics of the student nurses, medical students and the patients themselves. They knew that it was not all jokes and fun, but took it that sadness and loss were part of her job.

She was in Redford's General Store on the day she was returning to London, when he came in.

"Hello, there," he said pleasantly. "Are you home for a while?"

For a split second she did not recognise him because he had shaved off his beard. It suited him.

"Going back this afternoon."

"So am I," he smiled. "Which train are you catching?"

"The three twenty-five," she told him.

"How nice. So am I."

She was unsure how to proceed, so she gathered her shopping and told him that perhaps she would see him on the train.

"I'm motoring to Bristol and leaving my car at Temple Meads to be picked up. May I give you a lift?"

"That would be nice," she agreed.

"I'm leaving at two-fifteen. I'll pick you up then."

She went home and told Flora that Theodore Weston had turned up again, and what she had arranged with him.

Flora made no comment. They did not know the Weston family, so they must be new to the area; but he had seemed a nice man at that brief summer meeting nearly three years ago. Alice was thirty, and sensible enough to run her own life without advice unless she asked for it. They were sad that her visit had been so short, but had enjoyed seeing her. Flora stood by the wall of the cottage as the car disappeared down Church Lane. Her heart fluttered for a moment, and her mouth went dry; she felt a chill of apprehension. Understandable, she thought to herself, when Alice was returning to the capital. How long does a 'phoney war' go on?

SEPTEMBER 1940

The school was preparing to begin another year. Miss Taylor had long since retired, and her place had been ably filled by Thelma Wright, a dynamic young woman in her twenties. John Williams had retired that summer, and the whole village had turned up to witness the children singing songs, reading poems and thanking him. His replacement had arrived to take up residence at School House in the summer holidays. Matthew Ashton was an energetic man of forty-two, balding, with a fringe of still dark hair around his head. His wife, Lydia, was an attractive blonde woman of forty, with a vivacious personality. They had three children: Diana who was eighteen, Simon fifteen and Vera, twelve.

School House was similar to the Vicarage; pebble-dashed and trimmed on the corners with red brick. The windows exhibited an ecclesiastical influence, which was logical, since St Mary's was the church school, and both it and School House had been built in the middle of the last century to educate the village children. Iron railings had once graced the boundary on to the road, but they had recently been removed for the war effort. Seth, who had taken them down, replaced them with wooden palings, held together with wire.

"Won't keep the blighters in," he had joked, "but it'll slow 'em down!"

It was a long time since School House had rung with children's voices; it had always been off limits to pupils. It was a pleasant house, with small, cosy rooms and heavy wooden furniture. The curtains and carpets were worn to nothing because John Williams had not noticed their gradual deterioration. Now, with the country at war, Lydia could not enjoy refurbishing their new home. She gave it a thorough clean, assisted by her daughters. Her son dug over the lawn at the front, in readiness for planting potatoes and sowing vegetables. Matthew spent most of his time in the study, preparing the coming years' curriculum, or in the school itself painting the classrooms. Cunningly, he placed a notice at the front of the school asking for any senior pupils, male or female, who had a few hours to spare, to come along and help him to brighten the school.

On the first day, Flora was amused to see how grown up little Edgar looked. He was going to be four in December, and was eligible to be in the nursery class in the mornings. His mother, Helen, had brought him and his three-month-old sister Louise, along. Flora looked around at all the bright little faces, recognising many of them and their older siblings because she had delivered them. Among them were Rebecca and Robert's grandchildren. *How the years fly,* she thought. Even Flora, little Flora, named after herself because she had delivered her, was now thirty-two. Each generation of children came, grew up, reproduced; each generation came, grew up and were sacrificed at the altar of politician's schemes and dreams. When would it end? Flora shuddered in the September sunshine as she watched the children troop into school.

As the month wore on, dreadful news of the attacks on London continued. On the 7th September the Luftwaffe mounted it's heaviest aerial attack so far and the damage to life and property was catastrophic. Londoners continued to fight back by not giving in. They cleared up as soon as they could, and the routine of living, as far as circumstances would allow, carried on defiantly.

Hearts swelled after the Battle of Britain and 'the few' won. German aeroplanes lost: 1,733; RAF losses: 915. This still represented a price too great, but it did mark the turning point.

DECEMBER 1940

The war was no longer seen as the prerogative of the capital and other 'chosen' city ports. The Germans had bombed Bristol beyond recognition, and there had been numerous fatalities. Fifteen miles away, it brought the reality of war much closer to the people of Abbots Ford, even though most of them were already touched by it. Another generation of husbands, sons and fathers had been called up to serve their country; willingly, they had gone, except for Charles Paul Noel Henty, whose birth had cheered a family and the village, in the dark days at the beginning of World

War One, and who now had to be coerced by the military police to join the Second.

JUNE 1941

Louise and Gordon had to close their shop at East Hartness owing to the start of clothes rationing. They had been hard put to keep going, through reduced business and difficulty finding staff. Both of them ran the Abbots Ford shop. Emma had married but her husband had gone away to war only a few days later, with the Royal Navy. They did not bother to set up home, and she continued to live with Louise and Gordon, who said they had plenty of room for Stephen whenever he returned.

A few days after her fiftieth birthday, Louise called in on Flora at Orchard Cottage. She had no particular reason, but she knew that Seth was keeping busy, even though there were fewer horses about, because he mended farm machinery and tools, and even made a few pieces of equipment out of old metal. So he would be at the Smithy until teatime. She felt sad; life was changing and everything was different to when she and Flora were young. They sat drinking tea with the front door and windows wide open. The sky was clear blue, birds twittered and fluttered between the plum trees in the orchard, butterflies flitted from flower to branch, elegant in flight.

"I'm lonely, Flo," she confided.

"Lonely? Don't be daft, girl," snorted Flora.

"I am. Charles is away God knows where, Emma is here but she's really somewhere else, and as for Victoria, you just can't speak to her."

"You've got Gordon."

"Oh, Gordon. Yes, I have Gordon, love his cotton socks, but he's just – Gordon."

"You're lucky to have him. Count your blessings."

"You sound just like our Mum. Oh Flo, I do so miss our Mum." She collapsed on to Flora's shoulder and cried her heart out.

"There, there, Lou. I know how you feel. There's times I miss her sorely as well."

"She was so strong, so good. She always knew what to do." She broke into fresh sobbing.

"There, don't upset yourself," murmured Flora.

"Do you know, sometimes I hardly noticed she was there!" she said, looking at Flora with red, flooded eyes.

Flora laughed, ironically.

"I know what you mean," she said.

"I'm so fed up with this war," she complained.

"We have it quite easy, really, Lou," said Flora.

They sat side by side, thinking about all the problems of living and bringing up families, and the war.

"I'll make another cup of tea," suggested Flora.

She had just poured it, when Gordon appeared at the door. His face was ashen.

"I've been looking for you everywhere," he said tonelessly.

Louise knew as soon as she saw him.

"Charles?"

He handed her the telegram.

'Missing, believed killed in action', it said.

Irrelevantly, stupidly, it passed through Flora's mind that she had thought 'they' telephoned people with bad news. Maybe there were just too many now.

They sat drinking tea they could not taste, while silently, screamingly, ragingly, they took in the news.

+ + +

Chapter Four

NOVEMBER 1941 – EASTER 1946

News was through that H.M.S. Ark Royal had been sunk. The sinking of a ship always seemed to catch the imagination of the people in a way that reports of hand to hand combat, or planes crashing out of the sky, never did. Perhaps it was historical; echoes of the Spanish Armada, England against the might of the oppressors, and so on. It always affected morale.

Alice reported as much when she came home for a few days. People were feeling low, the war seemed not to be abating. Rumours abounded about the rationing of food, and it seemed that it could not be long before it was.

In the midst of all the trauma and heartbreak of war, Alice was happy. She and Theo were very much in love. They met as often as they could in London, which was difficult because Theo was often away. They conducted their romance in the pubs and restaurants in and around Kensington and on the occasions when she could sneak him into the nurse's home. He was everything she had ever looked for in a man. War invested a devil-may-care attitude into such encounters, and although theirs was more serious than the odd encounter, the affair was kept on the boil because everyone's link with life was tenuous at that time.

So it was strange to be in the relative calm of the village. She spent the time seeing family and friends, especially her Aunt Louise, who had not recovered from the loss of her son Charles.

She spent time with her brother Eddy, at his house. He permitted her to do some perfunctory tidying and cleaning, which he would not usually allow, not even to Flora. While he saw his family regularly, especially Seth, Helen, Edgar and little Louise, he was gradually withdrawing into himself.

While she was home, she saw her Aunt Jessica and Uncle Bill and gave them news of Anne, whom she met often; their hospitals were not far apart – a short bus journey, and she liked her cousin. Too soon, it was time to go and with everyone's good wishes ringing in her ears, she returned to London.

DECEMBER 1941

No one could believe it. On the 7th December, the Japanese attacked Pearl Harbour. The general consensus was that this would alter the complexion of the war, and it did. The United States of America, who had so far been reluctant to become involved, could not help but sanction retaliatory measures. Britain was no longer on her own.

FEBRUARY 1942

Dorothy loved Scotland. She took in the news of the war, but it seemed far away. Her charges had grown; Tobias was fourteen and away at Eton; Rupert, now twelve was in his final year at a local preparatory school, but the girls, Julianna, eleven and Daisy, nine, were still in her care. The governess, Miss Vanessa Simms, completed the ménage. Four other girls who lived nearby joined them for classes each day and Dorothy gave them all lemonade and biscuits, or lunch when required.

It was a good life. They had not travelled abroad since the outbreak of war, but it was an enjoyable existence. The family owned the property in the Highlands where they now lived, and except for Sir Philip's absences, their routine resembled that of an eternal holiday.

The snow was deep, and Miss Simms and Dorothy had taken the children out on a nature walk, to play in the snow and watch out for wildlife. One of the servants came running out, legs leaping, to wade through the snow, saying that there was an urgent message for Dorothy; someone had telephoned, could she telephone the post office at Abbots Ford?

Flora was poorly, very poorly. Seth had contacted their younger daughter, because he knew that no one else would be suitable. Her sister Louise was in no state to look after her as she was suffering a form of breakdown after the loss of her son. Many people were willing, but Seth knew that she needed Dorothy.

It was a sad little group who waved Dorothy off.

"Shall you come back?" asked Daisy, bravely attempting to hold back her tears.

"I hope so, when my Mother is better," said Dorothy, smiling a tight, taut smile. She, too, was emotional about leaving them, with no date of return.

"We really love you, Nanny," the older girl told her.

Lady Stephanie came into the nursery.

"All ready, Dorothy?"

"Yes, Lady Stephanie. My bags are downstairs."

"Say 'goodbye' then, girls," she told them.

It was all Dorothy could do not to break down in front of them; it was only her thought not to upset them further which enabled her to maintain her composure.

"I'll come and see you soon," she promised.

She bade them all farewell, kissing the girls on the cheek.

"Goodbye, Dorothy. Safe journey," said Lady Stephanie.

"Goodbye, Dorothy, keep in touch," Vanessa Simms told her.

Dorothy could say no more, the lump in her throat threatened to choke her. She went down to the car which would take her to the station, away from the family she had grown to love, away from the children she secretly regarded as her own, and back to Abbots Ford; home to Flora.

MARCH 1942

Dorothy found Flora much changed; she had not managed to travel home since before the war, and she saw that her mother had aged. Her hair was completely grey and her brown eyes seemed weary and sad. She was in so much pain that she could do only the minimum of work in the cottage, and on some days, could do nothing at all. Seth could hardly bear to see his spirited Flora fading away, and he not only carried on working, but stayed out as much as he could. Young Seth's family had expanded again, with the birth of William in January, and Helen brought them for short visits to see their grandma. Eddy called in every day, and was his quiet and gentle self with his mother, bringing the ghost of a smile to her face.

Dorothy took over the running of the cottage, and Eddy often joined them for the evening meal. Seth would deliberately pass on the gossip at table, trying to interest Flora in the people she knew, and to divert her attention from the pain. Michael Orrins called in now and then and they sat discussing old times and people they had known. The young doctor was endlessly supportive, doing his best to alleviate her suffering with the remedies available to him. The nurses, Flora's old colleagues and friends, Jenny, Rachel and Gillian made a point of one of them calling by each day, even for a few minutes. Flora was glad when the first signs of Spring came; she had always loved Spring, and it reminded her of when she and Seth had married thirty-five years previously. As she sat looking out of the window up at the hill, she believed she even felt a little better.

APRIL 1942

Alice was coming home. It was only a flying visit, but she wanted to see them all, especially her mother. Flora had never seen her looking so lovely, she was blooming. Her hair had a healthy sheen and her blue eyes sparkled. It was a shock for Alice to see her mother looking so poorly, but she was nearing the completion of her nursing training, and the letters she had received from the family had alerted her to the possible gravity of her mother's illness.

They had chairs on the path in front of the cottage, so that the three of them could enjoy the sun. They sat talking companionably about the visit they had received from Helen and the children the previous day. Even Flora laughed, painfully, when they recalled the funny things the children had said. Flora reminisced about some of the numerous things they had said themselves, when young; so Seth arrived home for his dinner to gales of laughter.

"What's all this, then?" he asked, smiling, pleased to see Flora happy.

They told him, and he added his contribution of memories about their antics as children.

"Remember when the boys brought the frogs home, and within two days, there seemed to be frogs all over the scullery?"

"It wasn't that funny," Flora spluttered. "The dogs thought they were playthings hopping about, and I fell over Lassie as she chased one. Nearly broke my arm!"

"Mum, remember when Dotty and I decided to run away, and spent the night up in a tree, and Dotty fell out of it?"

They all roared with laughter again, including Dorothy, who commented that it had not been funny at the time because she had broken her collar-bone.

They helped Flora inside, as it was time to serve the meal. Just as they were about to start, Eddy and Seth arrived together.

"What's this? A party?" asked young Seth.

Dorothy went to collect two more plates and dished up the meal for them. The girls spoke again of the escapades they had recalled, and their brothers remembered even more. By the end of the meal, Flora was weaker than ever, with laughter.

When they had finished, and were sitting chatting generally, Alice spoke up.

"As you're all here, I've something to tell you."

They looked at her expectantly.

"I'm going to have a baby."

This was not, on the face of it, good news. Alice was an unmarried woman of thirty-two and there was a war on. They all knew of Theo, and the itinerant nature of his job, especially now. But these were the very reasons why it was good news.

"Oh love, are you pleased?" asked Flora.

"Couldn't be happier! We'll get married quietly as soon as we can," she told them.

The gathering immediately turned into a celebration and the men toasted Alice, Theo and the baby in ale, while the ladies toasted her with tea.

"When is it due?" asked Dorothy.

"December," said Alice.

They talked excitedly about the quiet wedding and the baby. It was something to look forward to, when there was so much to grieve over. Something for Flora to look forward to.

Seth kissed Alice on the cheek.

"Atta girl, Alice! Show 'em what you're made of," he said.

"Don't worry, Dad. I can cope! Finals, wedding, baby; I'll manage it all!"

OCTOBER 1942

Flora had enjoyed the summer. At times, they thought she would recover as she appeared to be in remission. There was celebration when they heard that Alice had passed her finals.

At the end of the season, as the days began to draw in, and the leaves perished, Flora deteriorated. As the trees became bare, and the cold began to bite, she worsened. Alice was alerted, and she and Theo, who had married quietly up in London, prepared to go home. Even though married they had had to continue to live separately: Alice in the nurses' home and Theo at the barracks. In any case, she was due to return home to Abbots Ford for the birth of her child.

Then came an unexpected bombshell of another kind. Theo was given urgent embarkation orders. He could not tell her where he was going; he did not know himself. They met for a last night, in an hotel. Alice was nervous and upset.

"Have a gin or something, it won't hurt you now, will it?" he asked.

"I'll have a brandy," she said.

They both had more than one brandy, and the fears lessened.

"You're very beautiful when pregnant," he told her, tracing a line around her breasts and down to her swollen abdomen, as they lay on the luxurious bed.

"I love you," she told him. "I've never loved anyone the way I love you."

"I know that." He was not being over-sure of her, he knew it to be true. He felt the same about her. She was an unusual woman, and he had known many women. He never knew how she would be when they met; she was always different, never boring. Her vagueness, her whims, her changeability; characteristics which would drive many men away, he found lovable and he understood. He also knew that there had been other men for her; but they both knew that they were soul-mates, that their marriage would never become dull, that there would always be the spark of something to ignite them.

They made love, passionately, hungrily, lovingly.

He joked about their unborn child, about the fact that all three of them were there, just before he was going off to war.

Just before dawn, when he would leave, they made love again, tenderly, touchingly and cryingly.

"Don't say 'goodbye' when you go," she begged.

"Take care, my love. Take care of our boy."

She clung to him.

"My love, my dearest, my husband."

Gently, he extricated himself from her arms. He put on his great-coat, but held his cap; his kit-bag stood at the ready by the door.

He kissed her one more time, and her tears drowned them.

"I have to go," he said, his voice husky with love and regret. "So long."

"So long," she repeated, and he left, striding down the plush corridor. He turned to wave, one last time. She turned back to the room, and went to the window, trying to catch a last, final glimpse of him in the dark morning street. He was gone.

She stayed there, tears falling down her face, for a long time; for an age, until she had no more tears to shed. She put her arms around her unborn child and stood, watching the sky, until the sun began to waken the October dawn.

NOVEMBER 1942

Alice tried to gather her thoughts. It was time to go home and stay; it had been arranged, but was postponed until Theo had gone. Flora was dying, she knew that. The sooner she went home, the better. She was at a friend's flat, having left the nurse's home.

In the morning she hurriedly made her way to Paddington. But while descending the stairs, she tripped, badly fell and was knocked unconscious.

When she awoke, she was in St Mary's Hospital, Paddington, where her cousin, Anne, was nursing, though Anne was not aware of her presence yet.

A doctor came and gently told her that she had lost her baby, but that she would recover from her injuries. It was fortunate that she was still in shock, for she took in none of what he had said, and lay resting, numb and oblivious to everything around her.

She and Theo had already lived through the London Blitz and all the bombs the Luftwaffe had dropped on the city and its people. They had survived, albeit with a few near misses. What happened to Alice seemed so unfair and so, so sad.

MID NOVEMBER 1942

They did not tell Flora what had happened to Alice. She probably would not have taken it in if they had, for she was suffering delirium associated with the final phase of her illness. Dorothy nursed her mother with unfailing patience and love, and even young Seth and Eddy helped her. Her father could not. He was incapable of accepting what was happening, and did his best to deny it, to himself most of all.

Dorothy had remained strong when they received the news about Alice, though Seth went away on a long walk and was out most of the night, returning home exhausted and drained early the next morning.

Young Seth had ranted and raved, cursing the war and everyone. Eddy had been permanently anaesthetised by his own tragedy and did his best to support their father and Dorothy.

Flora died in her sleep towards the end of the month. She had suffered so much that, initially, they felt only relief, for her sake.

Her husband could not carry on and closed the Smithy for the first time for as long as anyone could remember.

The Reverend Douglas Glover suggested that Michael Orrins emerge once again from retirement for this occasion and share the officiation of the funeral service. Seth moved himself to organise the carriage, though Ebony had died. He was lent a beautiful black shire horse to transport Flora. She had been only fifty-three, a long way short of the allotted three score years and ten. People were shocked and saddened by her passing, and her family inconsolable.

Alice was still too ill to travel and missed the funeral, on a cold, drab, wet November day. They packed the church to thank God for Flora's life and work, and then trickled away, leaving the family alone to lay her to rest. Seth, her husband, stood bare-headed in the rain at the graveside. He did not picture the sick, wasted woman of the last weeks. He remembered only her shining, straight dark hair, the laughing brown eyes and the unbridled spirit of her youth. He did not recall the suffering and irritability of delirium, but remembered instead their love and loving, their laughter and the energy and greenness of their knowing years. It did not occur to him to regret his infidelities because they were no relation to his love for her, to the family they had raised and what they had been to each other. Now it was all over. As he stood mourning, their life together and all it had meant to them, his spirit, his very soul, felt dissolved by the rain, and dissipated into the earth around her grave.

"Farewell, Flora, my love, my wife," he thought, he whispered.

Dorothy put her hand into his, and his sons took each arm.

"Come on, our Dad," said Seth.

"Time to go home, Dad," said Seth.

"Time to go home, Dad," comforted Dorothy.

But Seth shook his head, slowly, as they led him back. He knew it could not really be home any more, ever again. Not without his Flora there. He would go, though, and not upset his children any more; they walked back to Orchard Cottage through the rain.

+ + +

At the end of November, a message reached Theo's family in Abbots Ford. It said that Major Theodore Weston had been killed on active service, during the allied invasion of North Africa.

MARCH 1943

Alice had been home a few weeks, and her dear friend of training days had stayed with her, for a while.

Seth was hard to live with, having become bitter at Flora's early death. He went about his work grumpy and silent. Dorothy was glad to have female company. It had been hard work nursing her mother for all those months, and now that her father was being difficult, it was a diversion having Alice and her friend Sue to stay. Not that Alice was an easy companion; her injuries had taken time to heal, and the loss of both husband and baby had rendered her emotionally unstable.

Dorothy still kept in contact with the Marshall family in Scotland by writing often. Lady Stephanie, spurred by the wish to see Dorothy again and sympathetic to all she had suffered since her return home, invited her back for a holiday, sending funds for her fares and expenses. Dorothy decided to go. Her Aunt Louise offered to make the main meals for Seth, and Alice was well enough to do day-to-day tasks. Her father became grumpier than ever when she told him of her plans, and on the morning she was leaving, he ignored her altogether.

Dorothy resolved to put it all behind her as she sat on the train at the station. She was excited at the prospect of seeing the girls again. She liked wearing her good green suit and dark green felt hat; she had had no cause to wear her beautiful tan shoes and bag while she had been at home. Her lisle stockings felt strange on her legs, and it was odd to sit and do nothing, even on a train. She would read when it got underway; it was enjoyable to sit and look at all the diverse people. Later, as the train sped north towards Scotland, she began to feel guilty about leaving her family. A strong cup of tea in the restaurant car soon dispelled her qualms. On her return to her carriage, she removed her hat and slept a while. She awoke when a young man accidentally kicked her overnight bag, and the noise startled her.

"Gosh, I am so sorry," he apologised.

"Don't mention it," she replied politely.

"I didn't mean…"

"Not at all, don't give it another thought."

"Where do you get off?" he enquired.

"Kingussie," she told him.

"Are you visiting family?"

"No. I'm going to stay with my old employer."

"What do you do?" he asked pleasantly.

"I'm their Nanny. Or I was," she said, somewhat flustered.

"I'm sorry, I'm embarrassing you – too many questions."

"I'm Angus McBain. We have a farm in the Highlands," he volunteered.

They spent a pleasant hour sharing histories and talking about their families. It was good to speak to someone who was unaware of all the tragedy the Hawkes family had weathered; somehow refreshing. She declined when he invited her to a meal in the restaurant car; she was too well brought up to accept that from a strange man.

"Thank you anyway, it was good of you to ask," she told him. So he went off by himself.

At the end of the journey, he gave her his telephone number but she again declined to give the Marshall's, for fear of upsetting them.

"Do ring me. I'd like to see you again," he told her as they parted at the station.

The girls were exultant at seeing her again. They had a new nanny, a charming girl of about twenty-eight, named Marion Thomas. Lady Stephanie greeted Dorothy warmly, and showed her to a guest room herself.

"You are here to rest. Make yourself at home, and do anything you like," she said.

Dorothy felt cossetted; it made a welcome change. For too long she had been at the beck and call of others, though she gave of herself willingly.

On her first day, Marion asked if she would like to accompany herself and the girls on a walk. She agreed with alacrity and they set off for the village. Julianna and Daisy walked on each side of her and told her all their news. They in turn asked Dorothy about her 'Mummy' and were sad to hear that she had died.

They played games of 'I-Spy', and wove elaborate dreams into stories, beginning with 'If I had a wish I would....' They bought 'sweeties' at a local shop, for which Dorothy had saved her coupons specially.

When they returned, Dorothy opted to have lunch with Marion and the girls, and afterwards, they read to each other.

"Come and hear my piano exercises," implored Julianna, who was a gifted musician for her age. Tears threatened Dorothy's eyes as she listened, for Julianna had chosen to play one of her mother's favourite pieces of music.

That evening, with the girls in bed, Dorothy and Marion talked of their work and told of previous employers, experiences and children. For both of them, the Marshall's were only the second family and they had grown to love all 'their' children as their own.

"Do you think you'll ever have a family of your own?" Marion asked.

"Yes, one day. When I meet the right man," Dorothy laughed.

The peace and tranquillity of the well-run house and its location in the Scottish Highlands did much to revive Dorothy's spirit. Her enjoyment of the children and the time with them completed the transformation.

"You look so much better, my dear," Lady Stephanie told her at the end of the week.

"Thank you so much for having me. It was so kind, and I have enjoyed it," replied Dorothy.

"It's no trouble. Come whenever you like; we're always pleased to see you."

Dorothy was sad to leave but felt that she had made a new friend in Marion Thomas. The girls knew that Dorothy would return to see them again, and the farewells were not as tearful as before.

"Don't forget to write," they called as the car taking her to the station pulled away.

"Nor you. Be good," she replied.

On the train, she attempted to adjust her mind to going back to the tribulations at Abbots Ford, and found it difficult. Her thoughts kept returning to the two bright little girls with their parents and nanny.

Perhaps I should reconsider, she thought. *Perhaps I should go back to work.* It was something to think about as the train thundered south, and home.

MAY 1943

Almost as soon as Dorothy had returned home, she had been pitched into work for the Red Cross. This involved helping local families who had been evacuated to the country, and also organising the care of the new-born and toddlers generally.

Jenny had volunteered her for the job in her absence, knowing that as well as her training as a nanny, she had completed two years of an S.R.N. course. Rachel had gone off to join the army and they were severely short-handed locally.

"I knew you wouldn't mind, Dorothy. It runs in the blood, dear. Flora would want you to do it," said Jenny candidly.

She also knew that Dorothy probably needed something like this voluntary work to fill the void in her life. Anyway, she could do it until she made a decision about what to do in the future.

There was a problem at home. Alice had returned to nursing in London, and Eddy had given up his house to move to Orchard Cottage, so there were two men to look after. Eddy would arrive in, covered with all sorts of farmyard muck and Dorothy would have to spend the day scrubbing and cleaning.

"At least get your boots off before you come in!" she shouted at him. He was so used to treating his house badly, that he would not compromise, and it led to many arguments between them.

"Give over, you two," Seth would growl.

"Well he would try the patience of a saint," Dorothy protested.

"Leave him be," insisted Seth, unable to see Dorothy's point. She was glad to get out and do her voluntary work.

Part of her work involved meeting with Matthew Ashton, and his wife Lydia. Matthew had made quite an impact on the village during his three years as headmaster. He had modern ideas about education which some of the parents were not happy about.

"Art? Who needs art?" they would say. "Teach them reading, writing and arithmetic, that's all they want."

Lydia's involvement came about because she acted as her husband's secretary, and all the details of new arrivals, or explanations about disappearing evacuees, had to be imparted to her. On the other hand, details of social deprivation or unusual circumstances had to involve the headmaster himself. Dorothy liked Lydia; she was an effervescent person, full of enthusiasm about everything, always willing to organise events, and with unbounded energy. 'Hello, my dear!' she would greet Dorothy, 'and how are you today?' and she would listen to the answer, if there was one. Her children were equally sociable, though Simon was shy with strangers. Diana had almost finished teacher-training and Simon was hoping to go to university to read law. For the time being, Vera helped at school, working with the other teacher, Thelma Wright. They were a pleasant family and Dorothy was delighted to accept when Lydia asked her to join them for a meal.

"My dear, I know how hard you work looking after your father and brother, come and have someone else cook for you, for a change," she offered.

Dorothy had a lovely time, with much laughter and witty conversation. Sentimentally, it reminded her of how her own family had been, when they were all growing up, but still at home; reminding her painfully of when her mother was alive.

SEPTEMBER 1943

For many years now, Beatrice had been a respectable member of society, her affair with Robert, and the trouble she caused, forgotten. She had had a great many problems with her son, Charles, who had gone through life trying to live up to his father whom people in the village regarded as a hero. Seth had tried to interest him in the Smithy; Bill had tried to encourage him into farming, like his father and grandfather before him, but nothing could tie him down. The problem was that his grandfathers had made sure he would be financially secure, so he did not bother to work. What he failed to realise was that these resources were not infinite.

Beatrice was causing a scandal in the village, by becoming romantically involved with a man twenty years her junior, who had made his money in unspecified business to do with the war. Her family were horrified, her son ashamed; the man was only a few years older than himself. When Charles confronted him, and cast doubt about how he had earned his money, Derek Tyler stood up to Beatrice' son and told him his fortune had been honestly earned, and that he had served his country before being wounded, which was more than he, Charles had done. Punches had been thrown, and Beatrice was torn between her lover and her son, a situation not entirely unknown to them.

One evening, shortly before the wedding, Beatrice and Derek were having a drink in the lounge bar at the Partridge Inn, and Beatrice had consumed rather more than was good for her. She spotted Robert in the saloon bar, and began to describe her conquest of him, all those years ago, to her fiancé. The family had managed to keep the whole affair secret, in order to protect Rebecca, and the whole pub quietened, listening agog to what she had to say. The younger folk knew the parties involved, even if they could not believe what she was saying.

Robert could listen to no more. He crashed through the door dividing the bars and stood before her.

"Silence, woman!"

"Who do you think you're talking to?" demanded Derek, standing up.

"Sit down," Robert ordered.

"You still have feelings, don't you, Robert," Beatrice sneered.

He raised his hand to hit her, but Derek was the younger, stronger man. He fended off the blow.

"I wouldn't if I were you."

"Come on now, gentlemen," said Joshua. "Let's not spoil the evening."

Robert backed off, muttering "Bitch", and the embarrassed clientele began talking again in low voices.

Beatrice got up and flounced out, saying loudly, "I'm not staying here," and Derek followed.

Robert sat down, determined not to lose face even further by skulking off out, so that everyone could talk about the altercation behind his back. After a suitable interval, he finished his drink and left, vowing to deal with Beatrice one day, even if he swung for it.

JANUARY 1944

Seth and Helen had just had an addition to their family. Flora Mary had arrived at Plumtree Cottage with the same ease as Edgar, now seven, Louise, nearly four, and William two and a bit.

"The perfect family," said Seth, "two girls and two boys."

"Well, it's all you're getting," laughed Helen.

"We'll see," teased Seth.

Another little granddaughter cheered her Grandad Seth miraculously. He took more of an interest in the Smithy than he had since Flora died. He decided to re-build it at the edge of the orchard, which fronted the main road. If he put a gate in the hedge, people could ride their horses straight in, or even drive, if they arrived by car, to see him about tools to be mended, or ornamental iron work. Yes, he would convert the old barn and build a new forge, and when he went to work, he would only have to walk up the path and out to his own orchard. He liked the idea greatly; he would put his plans into action immediately.

You'd have liked this idea, Flo girl, he thought to himself. *You would have been out there chivvying me all the time!* He smiled inwardly, remembering how she would tell him off at times. Then he realised, with gratitude, that it was the first time he had thought of her, without wanting to end it all. The thought of her and how she had been, was a comfort and not a torment, a torture. There was a renewed spring in Seth's step as he went about his business.

APRIL 1944

The war ground on. Monte Cassino was finally destroyed by Allied bombers. People did not know it yet, but the D-Day landings were in the planning stages. The war still conspired to keep people who loved each other apart. Louise and Gordon's daughter Emma had only seen her husband, Stephen, once since they married in 1941, and she had a lovely little girl as a result, whom she had called Margaret. The attractive little grandchild had helped both Louise and Gordon to come to terms with the loss of Charles, and she was even more entertaining now that she was almost two. Their other daughter, Victoria, was twenty-one and preparing to marry a local farmer in the summer. The shop kept them busy and gave them a living, but Louise had lost her verve and eagerness to create anything different, because of the dearth of fabrics, trimmings and coupons.

Bill and Jessica had become used to not seeing Anne; the war would probably have parted them in any case. Will was twenty-one and planning to marry in the autumn. He worked hard on Peartree Farm. Louise was eighteen and helped her aunt and uncle in the shop; she was keen to design clothes but this was very difficult at the time. John was nearly fourteen and keen to work full-time on the farm, but he had to carry on at school for a further term. He complained loudly and long, but Matthew Ashton persuaded him and others like him, to use the time effectively by introducing woodwork classes, and also by persuading Seth to give metalwork classes to groups of boys. For the girls, he arranged for Jenny to give talks on nutrition and child care, and Mrs Salmon to teach cookery and needlework to final year girls. It gave the young people a new interest during their last year in school, and made parents who had been looking forward to an extra wage, feel that their offspring were not wasting their time.

AUGUST 1944

On 25th August the Allies liberated Paris. The end was in sight. People were elated.

Dorothy continued with her work, though there were fewer evacuees now. She ran a weekly clinic for mothers and babies, where the babies were weighed and the mothers given advice.

"Sometimes it's just like working with Flora, your Mum," Jenny said one afternoon.

Dorothy laughed at the compliment. She had been sorely tried in recent weeks, while her father had been organising the new Smithy in the orchard. He had required help fetching and carrying, needed advice which he did not take, and all in all, had almost driven her to despair. She had been secretly pleased to see him more his old self again; and she was happy to be compared to her efficient mother. She turned to see who was next in line, and shouted with surprise and delight. Alice stood there, pretending to be part of the queue.

"Alice, how wonderful! I didn't know..."

"No, it was a whim. My friend Sue isn't well, so I said I'd take off and bring her little girl with me. Hope you don't mind?"

"Of course not." Dorothy turned to the small child standing close to Alice.

"Hello. What is your name?" she asked.

"Marina," the child told her.

"How old is she, she's sweet, isn't she?" commented Dorothy.

"She's almost three, very well behaved," Alice told her reassuringly.

Marina was a chubby little thing, with sleek dark hair, not unlike Dorothy's own. Her slanting hazel eyes looked enquiringly about her.

"I want to go toilet," said the child.

"We'll go on home, shall we?" said Alice, laughing.

"Yes, see you soon, I'm nearly finished here. Oh and remember, Dad is working out in the orchard now. You won't get a minutes' peace."

Alice walked with Marina the short distance from the chapel where the clinic was held to Orchard Cottage. She deposited their bags, took the little girl to the lavatory and went to find her father.

"Hello! Dad? Are you there?" she called.

She and Marina stood at the door of the Smithy.

146

"This is nice, Dad!" she enthused.

"Hello, my love! Didn't know you were coming."

He kissed her on the cheek.

"You're looking well," he told her. Then he noticed Marina.

"Who might this be?" he asked kindly.

"This is Marina. She's Sue's little girl. Remember Sue, who came home with me after my fall?"

"Ah yes."

"Marina stayed with her Grandma then, because she was only a baby. But she's a big girl now, and is able to come on holiday with Auntie Alice, aren't you?"

Marina nodded.

"Would you like some chocolate?" asked Seth.

Marina's eyes lit up, she had not been used to chocolate but she knew what it was. They went and got it from Seth's secret cache. When she had eaten it, the small, pretty child spoke.

"Please, can I have some more?"

"Oh yes," said Seth, "I can see that Marina and I are going to get along famously."

Alice laughed. She had known her friend's little daughter would be spoiled and petted here, which was just what was required for a baby whose life thus far had resounded to the roar of enemy planes and doodlebug bombs.

AUGUST TO SEPTEMBER 1945

The atomic bomb had been used to destroy the city of Hiroshima, which resulted in victory over Japan. On 2nd September the Second World War was over. Britain had been battered and bombarded, had stood alone for much of the time, but her spirit had never faltered. Ordinary people had endured open warfare in a way never experienced before, when civilians were killed and maimed. They had suffered deprivation in every area of their lives, some worse than others, and they fought on and triumphed.

The new King and Queen had proved their worth. The shy younger brother of Edward VIII had turned out to be a man for his time, supported and encouraged by his Queen. They had visited people all over the country after bombing raids, and walked among them, talking to them; commiserating, comforting, in a way Kings and Queens had never done before. They were more popular than ever.

The cost of the experience was to be counted for years to come. The country was deeply in debt, there were shortages of everything; food rationing continued into the next decade. Personal cost had to be counted also. There were children who had grown up not knowing their fathers because they had been away at war. Couples apart for years had to rebuild their marriages, if they could. The fabric and infrastructure of the country itself had to be rebuilt in the same way.

Yet none of that mattered. Peace was worth celebration; no more partings, no more bombs. London was en fête. The Royal Family appeared on the balcony of Buckingham Palace with the hero of the age, Winston Churchill. The crowds went wild; young, middle-aged or old, it made no difference. They were of one accord, peace had been achieved, the dictators slain.

It took a while for it to sink in. In Abbots Ford there had been other celebrations, when that summer Victoria Chapman, Louise and Gordon's daughter, became Mrs Alan Stokes. Alan was a local farmer and the couple had been courting for four years. They were taking over a cottage at Hilltop Farm, and were using great ingenuity to make it into a home, what with lack of resources and the utility furniture.

Now it was Will Henty's turn, Bill and Jessica's son. He was marrying Polly Robinson, who was a lively girl, popular and busy. She worked behind the counter in Redford's Grocers' and intended to carry on after her marriage.

Jessica was pleased with the frock and coat she had bought for the wedding from Louise. Jessica's own Louise had helped with the choice.

"It's nice to think we'll soon be able to have new things whenever we like – as long as we have the money!" chuckled Jessica.

"I still can't believe the war is over, I thought I'd be more excited," said the older Louise.

"It'll take a while, dear. Life's changed so much for everyone," said Jessica sagely.

Young Louise tried to lighten her aunt's words by focussing both her and her mother's attention on her wedding finery.

"I think that this aquamarine coat is perfect for you, Mum," she said.

"Isn't it marine blue?" asked Jessica.

"Whatever it is, it looks nice. The print frock will go well with it and you can wear it later on when its' time to take off your coat and dance," said her daughter.

"It's at the village hall, isn't it?" asked the older Louise.

"Yes, Polly's mum is arranging everything, but we're all helping with the wedding breakfast."

She pirouetted in front of them and added a lovely hat.

"Mother of the bridegroom!" said her daughter.

It crossed the elder Louise' mind that was something she would never be; but she had adjusted to her grief.

"I'll have these. I feel comfortable," said Jessica.

"Have you someone to open the shop for you on the day of the wedding?" she continued as her daughter and sister-in-law wrapped the garments in tissue paper.

"Yes. Don't worry, Gordon and I will be there," she said.

That evening, Jessica modelled the coat and frock for Bill.

"Very elegant," he said appreciatively.

"You look nice for an old 'un," said her younger son, John.

"Cheeky!" she laughed.

It was a perfect September day, with the added ingredient of euphoria, a result of the end of the war.

The familiar old church was filled with autumn flowers, the rust, gold and peach colours along with the dark green foliage, looking effective against the grey stone. It was to be a big wedding with many guests, some arriving from the North East of England.

Dorothy had managed to have Seth's old best suit cleaned for him. He was looking forward to his nephew's wedding. Eddy, who hardly ever wore a suit nowadays, had asked Dorothy to press his for the occasion. All the cousins were attending, and Louise Hawkes, Seth's five year old daughter, was to be one of the bridesmaids.

The wedding was perfectly lovely; the bride was radiant and the bridesmaids beautiful in their ivory parachute-silk frocks. The newlyweds were returning to their cottage for the honeymoon.

Young Seth Hawkes was proud of little Louise, and even tiny Flora was toddling about and amusing guests. His boys, Edgar and William, were nine and three and a half. Helen looked attractive and he was proud to show off his family on an occasion like his cousin's wedding.

He went outside the hall for a cigarette and stood, hand in pocket, head up and eyes narrowed, exhaling the smoke through his nostrils. He looked out over the countryside that surrounded Abbots Ford, which was steeped in a September evening haze. It had been a glorious day and the last glints of gold and pale blue tinged the sky on the horizon. The woods and trees appeared like woolly ghosts scattered around which were being dispersed by the mist. He felt good. They had taken a long time to recover from Flora's death, she had been the linchpin of the family. He would always miss her and at times, like today, would think to himself, *she would have enjoyed this.* Everyone had hated the war, but in many ways, Abbots Ford had escaped the harsh, dreadful reality in their day to day existence: no bombs had fallen there. He had almost finished his cigarette when he was aware that someone had joined him.

"Sorry! I made you jump."

"No... I was just going in."

"Lovely, isn't it?"

"What?"

"Out here."

He had been so engrossed in his thoughts that he had not been seeing any more.

"Oh yes."

"Seth Hawkes, aren't you?"

"Yes."

"I'm Iris Murchison."

He showed no sign of recognition.

"I was two years below you at school."

He looked at her properly then. The light was not good, but he was aware of softly shining blonde hair and her eyes glinted in the twilight. She was small, only reaching his shoulder.

"You still don't remember me, do you?" She laughed, which erupted as a delicious gurgle.

He was embarrassed; he knew she fancied him.

Helen came out at that moment.

"Hello, Iris."

"Helen."

"I was just getting some air," explained Iris. "It's stifling in there."

"Time we were making a move, the children are getting fractious," Helen told Seth.

"Bye then," Iris called after them as they went to round up their brood. Before they left, they were able to wave Polly and Will off on their new life together.

As they chugged back to Briersham in their ancient car, Helen asked him about Iris.

"What was she doing out there?"

Seth was vague. "Don't really know, she just appeared."

Helen's attention was diverted by an argument between Louise and Edgar.

"Come along now, you two. Soon be home."

They had been good and it had been a long and exciting day.

Helen began singing "There'll be bluebirds over the white cliffs of Dover" and they joined in happily as they trundled on towards home.

NOVEMBER 1945

Esmée had not come to terms with the absence of grandchildren. After years of acceptance of the situation when Giles was with Anna, her hopes had been raised again when he married Penelope. She gleaned great comfort from her beautiful garden, and although

Mr Birch, a retired farmer, did most of the heavy work nowadays, Esmée enjoyed pottering about. Much of it had been turned over to growing vegetables and fruit during the years of war, but the water garden remained. It had been unseasonably mild that autumn and the pruning had not been completed. Mr Birch was planning a bonfire and so she took her secateurs and went to work on the rose bushes and lavender. She hummed 'Lili Marlene' under her breath as she worked, placing the dead pieces of stem in her trug.

Giles and Penelope were having early dinner because they were travelling to Bath to the theatre, and there was no sign of Esmée.

"I'm sure I told Mother our plans," said Giles, mildly irritated at being kept waiting. "Did she ask to be served in her room?"

Penelope rose to ask one of the servants if they knew where Mrs Mortimer was planning on dining and returned flustered when they knew nothing.

"I'll pop up to her room. She's become forgetful recently, she's probably pottering about or napping," said Penelope reassuringly.

She returned, increasingly perturbed, as no one knew where her mother-in-law was. Giles went to question the staff and ascertained that his mother was last seen in the garden that afternoon. He took a torch, and with some of the staff, went outside to search. Penelope and one of the maids scoured the house.

It was Giles who found her. She was slumped across a rose-bed and it was too late. He stood frozen, knowing that she was dead, but unable to say a word. In the darkness, the others did not see her and bumbled over to him.

"Can't see her over here, sir. Shall we get more help to search?"

Giles was like a statue, neither moving nor speaking.

"Sir?"

Then they realised. She was carried carefully inside and the doctor was sent for. Penelope went out to bring Giles in, and he did as he was bid, sitting obediently beside the fire in the morning room. Doctor Blake suggested a brandy for him.

"He's in shock, taking it hard. Give him time, he'll come round," he told Penelope confidently.

"I'll ring Madeline and Algy. They'll need to know, and Maddy may help him," she replied.

"And I'll organise the necessary services."

Doctor Blake left them and Penelope telephoned for her mother to come at once. She felt unable to cope with her husband's catatonic state. On her return to the morning room, she found him gone. His mother had been put in her bed, and lay with the sheet tucked under her chin. She looked peaceful, her blue eyes closed, to look no more upon a troubled world. Penelope found him standing beside the bed, staring down at her.

"She knew a great deal of grief," he said in a monotone.

"She knew happiness, also," his wife comforted.

"I did not fulfil her expectations," he lamented.

"Come, my dear. Don't torture yourself. Maddy will be here soon."

He allowed himself to be propelled downstairs again, to await the arrival of his sister and her family.

Esmée lay alone in death, her life having been, not tragic, but a balance of happiness and fulfilment, and worry and sadness, like that of most people. She had been blessed with many gifts, and a long life; she would have been content with that much.

DECEMBER 1945

Dorothy was used to the routine at home now. She had to accept Eddy's eccentric ways, and her father Seth was not much better. He would bring pieces of half completed equipment, and sit beside the fire working with it and leaving bits and pieces all over the rug.

Her work with evacuees was finished but she continued to organise the weekly mother and baby clinic, which she enjoyed. Her friendship with Lydia Ashton was even stronger and the two women spent much time together organising events for both school and church. Along with Esther Glover, the vicar's wife, they were a powerful triumvirate. They had arranged a visit to see the pantomime 'Little Red Riding Hood' at Weymouth that first Christmas after the war.

Alice had come home for Christmas and brought her friend Sue's little daughter, Marina with her. They had so enjoyed her visit that summer, that it was clear she would be welcome again.

They sat around the table at supper time. Seth and Eddy had both arrived home earlier than usual.

"So how are you doing, Alice?" asked Eddy.

"Busy," she grinned.

"And who have you brought to see us?"

Marina smiled; she liked these two people. They did not talk down to her but treated her as if she were grown up, and small though she was, she could see the humour in the approach.

"Marina said she would like to come and see you again."

"Do you still like chocolate?" enquired Seth.

Marina nodded.

"I might have some upstairs, for after tea," he confided.

The adults exchanged news and discussed the changes the ending of the war had brought.

"So what about the pantomime? When do we go?" asked Alice.

"The Saturday before Christmas," Dorothy told her.

"How many are going?"

"Two coaches, church and school, you see."

"Marina, will you like that? We'll be here for a week, then we'll have the church treat to the pantomime and then I'll take you home to Mummy on the Monday in time for Christmas."

Marina had no idea what a pantomime was, but she liked 'treats' and going in coaches. She nodded.

The meal over, the women cleared up while both Seth and Eddy disappeared again.

"What do they find to do at this time of the year?" asked Alice.

"And at this time of night!" laughed Dorothy. She had put water on to give the child her nightly wash. They carried the jug upstairs and put it on the marble top of the wash-stand.

"Do you know, Alice," said Dorothy suddenly, "I can remember Mum doing this in our house, with a jug just like this."

"I know. Weird isn't it? And our Mum and Aunt Louise shared this room, remember?"

It was Dorothy who soaped the flannel and washed Marina's little pink-cheeked face. The child stood patiently, waiting to be rinsed, and then the huge fluffy towel descended, blotting out the light while Dorothy dried her. When she was clean, she was put into a nightgown and lifted into the soft, cloud-like featheriness of the mattress. Both women tucked her in and kissed her.

"Isn't she sweet?" said Alice.

"Night, night. Auntie Alice will be up soon," Dorothy told her.

They left the light on low and returned downstairs. They made a hot drink together and took it to sit beside the fire.

"How are you these days, Alice?" asked her sister.

"Alright," Alice replied.

"A lot's happened."

"That it has. Three years gone since Mum went."

"Three years since Theo, and the accident...."

"You don't forget, do you?" said Alice.

"No. There'll always be those people with us wherever we go, whatever we do. They're part of us."

"Do you ever regret having to come home?" Alice asked Dorothy.

"No time for regrets. I write to the Marshalls and the children write back, but they're growing up. No, family comes first."

"I don't know what Dad and Eddy would do without you. I couldn't look after them."

Dorothy laughed at that.

"Sometimes I find it impossible as well."

They gossiped about people in the village. Dorothy told Alice all about the Ashton's and Esther and Douglas Glover and their family.

"So many of the people we knew have gone, and it's not even as if we're old ourselves," said Alice plaintively.

"You poor old thing," mocked Dorothy. "Come on. Time for bed. We'll take Marina round to say hello to people tomorrow."

"It's nice to be home," yawned Alice. "Maybe I'll stay too."

+ + +

Seth had been surprised when Iris turned up at Drakes Farm asking to buy eggs.

"Not enough around the village for you?" he asked.

"I was out this way anyhow," Iris told him.

Drakes Farm House was now occupied by David and Peggy, Seth's brother and his wife, and their son Albert and his wife, Betty, and family.

"Go and see if Peggy's got some," he told her.

"Aren't you in the darts team at the Partridge?" she asked.

"No, I'm not. I've got to go now. Sorry. 'Bye."

Iris went and bought her eggs from Peggy.

"There you are my love," she said as she packed them up and handed them over.

She was about to leave when Betty came in.

"Hello, Iris! How are you?"

Peggy looked surprised, so Betty explained that they had been in the same class at school.

"Can you stop for a cup of tea?" she asked.

They swapped gossip and Iris told Betty that she worked in the post office at Abbots Ford.

"I haven't seen you in there," said Betty.

"Only odd times," explained Iris. "I still help Mum at home."

Betty introduced her four children and then Iris said she should be making her way home. As she was leaving the farmyard, Seth was driving out of the gate. He wound the window down.

"Need a lift?"

"That would be nice, I'm late," she said.

"We always seem to meet in the semi-dark," Seth laughed. "I still can't remember you from school."

"You always used to pull my hair."

"I pulled all the girls' hair," he laughed.

She liked being close to him. He smelled of farm, but it was a pleasant, earthy, rankly smell. The old car bumped over the uneven road towards the village.

"Where do you live?" he asked.

"Top end of Mill Lane," she told him.

"When they arrived, she asked him if he would like a cup of tea.

156

"No. I've got to be getting off now thanks," he replied, and crashing the gears of the car, reversed up and drove away.

+ + +

It was the day of the Christmas treat. The coaches had lined up outside the school and church, and Dorothy was seeing people on board. There was tremendous excitement and the adults seemed as caught up in it as the children.

"Have you got the boiled sweets?" Dorothy asked Alice.

"Yes, and the flannels and newspaper."

"Sounds as if she's ready for a disaster," said Lydia.

Gradually people arrived, and with much fussing about and taking off coats, sat on the coaches in noisy anticipation.

The outing passed in a medley of impressions for Marina. She had never experienced anything like it before and found it truly wonderful. Afterwards, all she could recall was the red cape Little Red Riding Hood wore, the frightening wolf and the feeling of many kind grown-ups taking care of her, but most of all, Dorothy. Alice was kind and caring but Dorothy engendered a feeling of confidence and love and the child was drawn naturally to her. On the way home on the coach, she fell asleep snuggled closely next to Dorothy. Most of the children fell asleep on the journey back while the adults discussed the show. Matthew and Lydia Ashton sat just in front of Dorothy and Marina and were part of a happy group as the coach sped back to Abbots Ford through the darkness. Dorothy thought she had not been this happy since her time with the Marshall family. She cuddled Marina to her; *perhaps Alice' friend Sue would allow her to have the child to stay at Easter. Yes, that would be something to look forward to,* she thought to herself.

SPRING 1946

Charles Henty, Beatrice' son had arrived back in Abbots Ford. No one knew where he had been since the military had conscripted him in 1940. It was three years since Beatrice and Derek had married. Gossip had died down, but the couple still excited comment; she was now fifty-six and Derek thirty-six. Derek had moved into the turn-of-the-century house Beatrice had lived in for years when they married, and now Charles joined them there.

There was to be a dance at the hall because they were trying to raise money for the church roof. It was one of the first occasions since the war when the young people could attend such a function, and they were looking forward to it. A local band was playing all the up to the minute popular tunes and the girls were doing their best to have new frocks.

Coloured lights had been draped around the edge of the stage where the band would perform and there was an atmosphere of expectancy, not to say apprehension. A whole generation had never been to a dance. They arrived in small groups and couples, and the hall filled and came alive with the music and the enjoyment of Abbots Ford's young people.

Charles Henty had gone to the dance with some of his old cronies. He retained the ability to draw people to him. He noticed her about half-way through the evening. She was slender and had dark wavy hair which reached down her back. Her red frock skimmed over her bust and hips, flaring out at the hem. She was in a group of fellows and girls but did not seem to be with anyone in particular.

He went over and asked her to dance. She turned and smiled at him, and it reached her hazel eyes.

"What's your name?"

"Amy," she said.

"Do you live in Abbots Ford or have you come from somewhere else abouts?"

"You don't remember me, do you?"

"Should I?"

"Well, we're sort of related – by marriage." She laughed at the expression of surprise upon his face.

"Really?"

She concentrated while she thought about it.

"Your Dad was the brother of one of my aunts-by-marriage."

"That's too complicated for me to think about!" he laughed.

They danced together for the rest of the evening, including the last waltz, when he held her close and she did not pull away.

"Can I see you home?"

"Yes, don't see why not," she replied.

They talked as they walked together through the village in the crisp night.

"Can I see you again?" he asked.

"Maybe."

"When."

"When I'm free!"

"When are you free?"

"When do you want to go out?" She laughed again, and he caught her and kissed her full on the mouth. She melted in his arms and responded in spite of herself.

"Meet me tomorrow."

"Alright."

"I'll come for you at seven."

He kissed her again, slowly and then, touching her nose with his finger, left her, waving when he reached the gate.

She went into the cottage humming some of the songs they had played during the evening.

"Have a good time?" asked her mother.

"Wonderful – just like old times, before the war."

Her mother was pleased she had enjoyed herself. The war had robbed some young people of good times. Amy was thirty-two and had had chances before the war, but she was the spoilt youngest daughter. Her brother Robbie was twelve years her senior and even her nearest sibling, Flora, was six years older. She had been born after her parents had weathered more than usually serious problems, when a false accusation had put her father in prison for a while, and her mother into a mental hospital for many months.

"Meet anyone nice?" asked her mother nonchalantly.

"Mmmm."

"Was that him at the gate?"

"Yes, Mother – and I'm seeing him tomorrow!"

"Anyone I know"

"Charles Henty."

Rebecca knew of Charles' reputation and the trouble he had caused over the years. She knew, too, of the gossip about his mother in the village. But most of all she knew that her husband, Robert, had an all-consuming hatred of Beatrice and would not allow her name or any mention of her in the house.

"Is that wise?" she asked.

"Wise?" asked Amy.

"You know what he's like," said her mother.

"I know he's wonderful. I've liked him ever since we were at school, but he never noticed me – till now."

"Don't let Dad know you're going out with him, dear," pleaded Rebecca, "he hates that woman."

"Doesn't worry me. Dad's an old stick in the mud. Feuds are so silly," stated Robert's daughter.

"Well, be careful anyway. You know what they say ...."

"Don't worry, Mum. He isn't like that at all."

Rebecca said no more, and Amy went up to bed to dream of her dream come true – a date with Charles Henty.

+ + +

Lydia and Dorothy had been to Bath together to look at the shops. They had lunched in a pleasant, expensive restaurant, and later, eaten cream cakes in a tea-room. Dorothy felt very much the woman of the world in her mauve suit, which she had made herself. It was a light wool tweed dress and jacket, finished off with a purple velour hat with a large brim and purple velvet ribbon trim.

"You look nice, dear," Lydia had said when they met to catch the bus.

"Thank you," Dorothy had blushed.

They had bought fabric and paper patterns, knitting wool and chocolate.

"My feet are so sore," complained Lydia as they walked around the town. "It's these dratted hard pavements."

"Here's a seat, we could rest here," suggested Dorothy.

"Good idea," said Lydia, sinking gratefully on to it.

"Isn't it nice just being able to go about our business," observed Dorothy.

"Yes, I still can't get used to it."

"It was so awful, perhaps there won't be any more wars."

"I certainly agree – not after this one."

They looked again at their purchases and discussed what good bargains they had found.

"Do you ever wish you'd married?" asked Lydia suddenly.

Dorothy was surprised.

"Well, no, yes. Yes and no," she stumbled. "Why do you ask?"

"It's so surprising. A nice woman like you, not married."

"Nobody's asked me," laughed Dorothy.

"I'm sure that's not true," parried Lydia.

"There's been no one serious. I've been too busy," explained Dorothy.

Lydia shook her head in disbelief.

"Too busy giving your life up for everybody else."

Dorothy did not reply. She did not see it like that. Not her jobs as a nanny, nor her looking after her parents and brother at home.

"I have a brother. He too is unmarried. Come and have dinner next week and see what you think," said Lydia.

Dorothy laughed aloud.

"You are incorrigible," she told her friend.

"Will you come?"

"Yes. I'll come."

"Good, that's settled then," said Lydia, satisfied.

They gathered their bags and made their way to where they would catch the bus home.

Dorothy was having Marina down for Easter and now she would have a date as well; she was looking forward to the next two weeks.

+ + +

Seth had got used to Iris popping up wherever he happened to be. She was an extremely attractive girl and pleasant into the bargain. She often arrived at Drakes Farm to see Betty, and Seth would dally over a cup of tea with them. Invariably, she persuaded him to give her a lift back to the village and they would be alone in his car.

One afternoon that spring they were travelling along when suddenly the engine spluttered and gave out.

"Oh damn," moaned Seth. Iris was happy, it meant a few more minutes alone with him.

He got out and told her to sit in the driver's seat and showed her how to pull the hand brake off when he shouted, so that he could push the car off the road and out of the way, while he mended it. He worked on it for a while, to no avail. He decided he would walk back to the farm for a spare part, but before he went he sat down dejectedly on the blanket Iris had spread on the ground while she waited.

"You could have walked home by now," he told her.

"I'd rather be here with you," she said looking at him straight in the eyes.

As if hypnotised, he leaned forward and kissed her slightly parted lips. Iris reached her arms around his neck and pulled him down onto the blanket.

Seth had been married to Helen for ten years and had always been a faithful husband; there were those to tell Helen had it not been the case. She had been his first and only real girlfriend, and they had had a happy marriage. What assailed him now was an attractive woman who was making no bones about wanting him and he could not resist. They made love passionately with little preamble or love-talk; even so, it was an experience the like of which Seth had never had in all his years with his wife.

"Oh my God," he groaned when it was over.

"I love you," said Iris baldly.

"No, don't say that," said Seth.

"I do. I have for ages."

He turned to face her, amusement growing on his face.

"Is that why you've been pursuing me, you minx?" he asked.

"You didn't run very fast!" she retorted.

"We've got to go," he said suddenly, realising how it would look if anyone went by.

"I'll walk home, Seth," she offered.

"O.K." He grabbed her as she turned to leave and asked her when they could meet again.

"Come round tomorrow. Eight o'clock. Mum 'll have gone to bed."

He kissed her roughly and let her go, and her heart sang as she walked towards Abbots Ford.

EASTER 1946

Dorothy prepared for the evening carefully. She had washed her dark hair in rainwater and put cream on her face. She dabbed lightly at her skin with a pale powder and slapped her cheeks to make them pink. Dabbing lavender water behind her ears, she picked up her bag and went downstairs. She had on a dark brown skirt and a cream blouse with an Edwardian collar, which she had adorned with her mother's cameo.

Seth looked up as she opened the door at the bottom of the stairs.

"You look nice, girl. Where you off to?"

"I told you Dad, Lydia and Matthew invited me to dinner."

"Dinner, eh? This time of night? I had my dinner at dinner-time," he teased.

"I'm off now. Got everything you want?" she asked.

"Yes. I'm fine. Have a nice time."

She was overcome with love for him, her dad; so she kissed him on the forehead as she passed his chair. He looked up.

"What's that for then, eh?" he smiled.

"Nothing. Just behave yourself while I'm gone."

The room looked inviting. Lydia had painted it a dark colour; terracotta, she had said it was. A white linen cloth sparkled on the table, and glasses shone, reflecting the light of the candles.

"Sit down, Marcus; sit here Dorothy," she instructed.

Matthew poured the wine.

"So you had a good journey, Marcus?" he asked.

"More or less," replied his brother-in-law.

Lydia brought the first course in. It was soup. They talked pleasantly together; there were only the four of them, Diana, Lydia's eldest daughter had completed her teacher training, married and gone to live in Wells. Simon was reading law at university and Vera had begun teacher-training, so none of them was at home. The conversation was scintillating; Matthew put forward his views on politics, education, philosophy and theology, while Marcus bounced his ideas in return. Lydia and Dorothy could hardly put in an opinion edgeways, but Dorothy enjoyed it all the same.

When the ladies were in the kitchen while the men sat and continued their conversation, Lydia whispered,

"Well, do you like Marcus?"

"He's a lovely man," Dorothy replied with conviction, "but I don't think he's noticed me particularly!"

"Oh yes he has. I can tell," said his sister.

Dorothy was sorry when it was time to return home. She had enjoyed the company and the meal. Lydia and Marcus were in the middle of a family discussion when Dorothy made a move to leave, so it was Matthew who walked her home along the main road and down Church Lane.

"Goodnight, young lady," he said as she went in.

"Goodnight, Matthew and thanks again for a lovely evening."

"We must do it again some time," he called as he left.

In her bedroom, Dorothy mulled it over. *No, I don't think he's the one for me – nice though he is,* she thought. She had an early start next day because Alice was bringing Marina down from London to leave her for the week. She climbed into the comforting feather mattress and lay for a while, planning what she would do to entertain the little girl whom she was looking forward to having to stay.

+ + +

"Well, you've got bigger since Christmas, haven't you." Dorothy was genuinely surprised at how much Marina had grown.

"Yes. I'm big now and I'm nearly four."

"No you're not," laughed Alice. "You aren't four until September."

"Shall we go to the post office and buy a post card to send to Mummy telling her you've arrived safely?" asked Dorothy.

"Yes please," replied Marina. She allowed Dorothy to help her with her cardigan and then held her hand as they walked to the post office. Iris Murchison was behind the counter.

"Who's this then, Dorothy?" she asked. Dorothy explained.

"Do you like Abbots Ford?" She addressed the question to the child.

"Yes, thank you," responded Marina.

"What a sweet little girl," enthused Iris.

They posted the card after writing a message on it for Sue, and walked back to Orchard Cottage. Dorothy had an uneasy feeling about Iris. She had been unusually pleasant, and Dorothy could not think of a reason why.

+ + +

Charles and Amy had gone to the cinema in Bristol on their first date. Charles drove them in his MG, speeding along the winding lanes and hairpin bends carelessly and expertly. Afterwards, they had gone to a restaurant for dinner.

"You know how to win a woman over," said Amy, looking at him from under her lashes.

"Nothing to it, they just fall at my feet," he boasted, not untruthfully.

They ate their meal, Amy enjoying food she would not usually have eaten. Charles had chosen red wine to accompany the meal and he kept filling her glass before the waiters could reach them. It was late when they left Bristol, and he put the hood up on the car. He did not drive as fast on the way back, and Amy rested her head against the seat and relaxed on the journey. Just before they reached

Abbots Ford, he turned into a copse on the edge of a wood and switched off the engine. He turned and looked at her in the darkness.

"You're a funny girl," he told her.

"Why funny?"

"You are just yourself, you don't put on a front."

"What's funny about that?"

"Lots of girls feel they have to......"

"I'm too old for all that. I'm thirty-two, you know."

"Same age as me – when's your birthday?"

"June."

"I'm younger than you. Mine's not until Christmas Day."

He leaned forward and kissed her without touching her with his hands. He was gentle and tentative. She sat passively allowing him to explore her lips.

"What are you doing on Easter Saturday?" he asked.

"Family thing. Spending the day at Uncle Seth's."

"Flora was my auntie, Dorothy's my cousin. I'll come," he offered.

"Should you?" she asked.

"No reason not to," he said breezily.

"Isn't there something between our families?"

"Not that I know of, other than that they're a lot of gossipy, jealous old biddies."

"Charles!"

She was aghast that he should say such things, even if secretly amused. The village did have its share of older chattering ladies, but not in the family as far as she knew.

He kissed her again, this time taking her in his arms and kissing her eyes, nose and face as well as her mouth. Then he turned back to the wheel of the car and turning on the ignition, reversed up and carried on towards her home.

"I'll come and fetch you and we'll walk along together," he told her.

"No. No, I'll meet you there," she insisted.

"Alright, then, if that's what you want."

So it was arranged; for the first time in many years, Charles was returning to Orchard Cottage.

He kissed her gently on the lips and said goodnight. She got out of the car, wishing that she could have fought him off, had he given her the opportunity. It was going to be an education getting to know Charles Henty.

+ + +

Dorothy had enjoyed the two days so far with Marina. She loved the routine of looking after the child: bathing and washing her, laundering her clothes. Alice had stayed two nights and then returned to London, and Marina had accepted the arrangement without comment. She was as happy with Doris as with Alice, who, in fact, she knew much better. Dorothy took the little girl along to Peartree Farm to have tea with Jessica, and to show her the farm animals. Jessica was pleased to see them, and the two women gossiped while Marina played among the chickens.

"How's Will settling down?" asked Dorothy.

"He's fine. Polly is such a nice girl, and we often see them here."

"When did Anne last come home?" probed Dorothy.

"You know what she's like with her Dad," said Jessica dejectedly. "She pops up now and then, but hardly says a word to Bill."

"What was it all about? What does Uncle Bill have against Joshua?"

"Dotty, you know as much as I do. Bill got a bee in his bonnet about the boy, and nothing could change his mind."

"They say that Joshua's family was against it as well – but some of them are stuck-up anyway. With Uncle Bill, I never understood what got into him."

"Well I never thought it was worth a rift with Anne. I don't care who she marries as long as she's happy," said Jessica.

"I agree, but it gave some of the gossips in Abbots Ford something to get their teeth into!" laughed Dorothy.

Jessica was thoughtful. "It hasn't made your Uncle Bill any happier, you know. He broods a lot about it. I can tell by the look on his face when he's in a certain mood. Sometimes, even a stroll up the hill doesn't bring him the peace he seeks."

"Maybe he won't find that until he makes his peace with Anne," commented Dorothy.

"You sounded just like Flora then, dear," smiled Jessica.

Marina skipped back and slipped her hand into Dorothy's.

"We'd better be on our way. It'll soon be time to get supper," said Dorothy.

"Thank you for having me," said Marina without prompting.

"You're a polite little girl – you can come again," said Jessica approvingly.

"Tell Will and Polly to call in on their way one day," said Dorothy. "I'd love to see them."

"Alright" said Jessica, and waved them off as they walked hand in hand down the lane.

EASTER SATURDAY 1946

Dorothy had been baking. She was an excellent cook because she had been taught by Flora and Louise. Naturally, Easter biscuits were a choice for this occasion, chocolate cake, which Seth adored; trifles and delicious sandwiches, ham, tongue, and a fruity lardy cake completed the spread.

Marina had been well behaved as usual, fascinated by all the preparations.

"Who is coming?" she asked.

"Lots of people. Family and friends," said Dorothy.

"Why?"

"It's Easter and Easter is a happy time, like Christmas, you remember, when we went to the pantomime?"

Dorothy felt unequal to the task of explaining the symbolism associated with Good Friday, so ignored it.

"Why is it happy?"

"Because Jesus came back," said Dorothy.

The conversation went on, while the child asked questions and Dorothy answered.

"So we share a happy time with family and friends," concluded Dorothy.

Seth came in from the Smithy to wash.

"What time are they coming, girl?"

"Three o'clock, Dad."

"Who's coming?"

"Louise and Gordon, Jessica and Bill if he can make it. Your Rebecca and Robert, Amy, Ruth, John and Isabelle, some of the cousins...... and Lydia may pop in."

"Is there room for all these people?" he asked tetchily.

"Of course there is, Dad."

Seth spotted Marina in a pink and white striped frock, decorated with a frill from shoulder to shoulder.

"Will you introduce me to your fine friend," he requested in an exaggerated display of courtliness.

Marina laughed delightedly.

"You know it's me, Grandpa Seth," she giggled.

"Bless my soul, it's little Marina," he gasped.

There were voices at the door.

"May we come in?"

"Hello, Bill, Jessica, of course. Come in," called Dorothy.

She made an enormous pot of tea and soon the extra chairs were filled, as people sat drinking and talking. All the ladies had worn their brightest frocks, and as it was not often that they gathered together in this way anymore, especially at Orchard Cottage, there was a sense of occasion even though they were not celebrating anything in particular.

"It's as if Flora's going to come out from the scullery or kitchen," said Aunt Louise.

"Is Eddy coming?" someone asked.

"I told him about it but he disappeared this morning and hasn't been seen since," Dorothy laughed.

Seth and Helen and their family joined the group at teatime and their Grandpa fussed over them. Little Louise was an ideal companion for Marina and they ran around the cottage between the adults, playing 'Hide and Seek'. Amy tried to amuse them half-heartedly, but they were content with their own games.

At five o'clock Charles Henty arrived. He was Seth's nephew by marriage and Seth welcomed him warmly. Charles sought out Amy and stood talking to her and some of the cousins. He leaned forward, laughing, to kiss her, just as her father, Robert, looked over at them.

"What the hell do you think you're doing?" shouted Robert, completely forgetting himself in the heat of the moment.

"Dad," pleaded Amy.

"Rob," said Rebecca, surprised at his reaction.

Everyone had stopped talking, stunned into silence by the tension in the air when Robert spoke.

"Leave my daughter alone, you scum of the earth."

"Uncle Robert," began Dorothy, but her father had stepped forward.

"You'll not create a scene in my house lad, will you?" said Seth authoritatively.

Robert was the only person there who recalled the dreadful scene in the old scullery, when Charles' mother Beatrice had admitted that it was she who had sent the letter to the police with the dastardly accusation against him. Flora and her brother, Charles, were gone, and Beatrice uninvited today. Thirty six years' bitterness erupted as Robert called out in torment:

"It was his bitch of a Mother wrote the letter that put me away."

Some of the ladies had removed the children to the garden by now, and embarrassed younger people murmured and made moves to leave discreetly, whispering thanks to Dorothy.

Unspoken questions hung in the air, but they all believed him. His wife Rebecca sat, shocked, while her widowed sister Ruth put her arm about her shoulders.

"What do you mean, Robert?" asked Seth, only seconds later, but it seemed like hours.

"You only have to ask the Jezebel, she'll tell you."

Charles had stood immobile while all this was being said. He knew what he had witnessed while he was growing up, and did not instinctively jump to defend his mother. He did not know the facts of the accusation, but his own credibility and survival were at stake. He could not win. If he defended her, it would be wrong, but his silence grew, and magnified the crime, of which he had not even been aware. A son not defending his mother's honour! He turned, and without even a glance at Amy, marched out of Orchard Cottage.

Robert seemed suddenly to become aware of the disturbance he had created, and was confused.

"I'm sorry," he said to nobody in particular, and stumbled out of the cottage and up the two steps to the lane.

"Seth, go after him," said the elder Seth.

Dorothy was horrified that the assembly had ended in this way. It crossed her mind, briefly, that it was fortunate that only family had witnessed the quarrel. That was bad enough! How could anyone believe that there would be peace in the world when families maintained feuds for decades!

Amy was crying quietly in the corner near the grandfather clock, but no one took any notice of her. The older members of the family were worrying about Rebecca. Had the fabric of nearly fifty years marriage crumbled away in moments? Why had Beatrice done such a poisonous thing all that time ago? The happy Easter gathering dispersed into the spring sunshine, as they went home wondering.

+ + +

Chapter Five

AUTUMN 1946 – MAY 1950

Eddy had become more and more secretive as the years wore on. He and Dorothy hardly exchanged a word nowadays; he merely came in for his meals, ate them, and left. At least, she had persuaded him to leave his filthy rubber boots at the door of Orchard Cottage. Every so often a transformation took place in her brother. When he had finished his work on the farm, he would have a bath in the kitchen on a Saturday afternoon, sleek down his hair, which was beginning to thin, put on his best suit and disappear until Sunday afternoon. Dorothy assumed he had a lady-friend somewhere, though obviously not in Abbots Ford, or she would have been notified of the fact before now. It would never have done for her to ask him where he went; in any case he would have told her to mind her own business. He was withdrawn and reticent in the extreme. He went about his business, even downing a pint or two at the Partridge Inn, with no one any the wiser about him or his interests and opinions. During the week while he worked on Drakes Farm, his clothes could only be compared to those worn by tramps. His things were laundered by Dorothy, yet he never seemed to wear anything clean. His shirts, mended by her, were always torn and bedraggled. His trousers were kept up with braces, yet he wore a raffish tie around his waist instead of a belt. If he combed his hair, it never appeared to benefit from it. In winter, he topped the whole thing with the sort of coat and cap which anyone else might have put on their scarecrow. Dorothy had long since washed her hands of him; her patience had worn thin. During one of their last rows, she had rebuked him, telling him frostily that he was becoming a laughing stock in the village and that his way of life was no memorial to his wife and son, gone these last ten years. He had looked her in the eye long and hard, too angry to reply, since which time he had retreated into himself completely.

The harvest had just been gathered and completed when the first clue as to what Eddy was up to came to light. Someone had seen a photograph in a newspaper in Wales and brought it home to Abbots Ford. Nobody would confront Eddy with it directly, but there was much gossiping and muffled laughter at the Partridge Inn. It was not until Seth became aware of it that the family was enlightened.

"Ballroom dancing champion?" said Dorothy, astonished. "Eddy?" she added disbelievingly.

Seth laughed.

"That's what it says. It's him, alright."

They examined the blurred photograph again.

"He's with a girl!"

"I know," replied Seth with a ribald laugh.

"No wonder he's not been saying anything," giggled Dorothy. "Who's going to broach it?" she added.

"Better be me. I'll tell him tomorrow at the farm. He's got to know that everyone knows," said Seth reasonably.

"How long has it been going on?"

"It says here the heats began last year."

"Good heavens! I still can't believe it. What a dark horse our Eddy has turned out to be!"

"I'll go and tell our Dad now," said Seth mischievously, looking forward to their father's reaction.

"How I'm going to keep a straight face when I see him, I don't know," said Dorothy. "It certainly puts a different complexion on him, that it does!"

NOVEMBER 1946

Louise and Gordon had a houseful. Their daughter Emma, her husband Stephen and four-year-old daughter were still living with them. A cousin whose husband had died had come to stay while she recovered, and they were entertaining a young man who had flown with their son Charles, before he was killed.

Louise had taken a painfully long time to assimilate the losses in her family. No sooner had she recovered from her mother's passing, than her son had died. She had only just come to terms with that when Flora died. She and Flora, always extremely close, had drawn even nearer after the loss of their mother and Louise' son. Gordon had feared for her reason, but their little granddaughter had come along at a fortuitous time: there was a new reason to live, an investment in the future. Now Victoria's baby was due any day and Louise was looking forward to the new addition. She went up to Hilltop Farm to see her daughter, taking with her yet more completed baby clothes. Victoria was pleased to see her, for she had been confined to the house for the last month due to swelling in her ankles. She looked at her mother, relieved to see that she appeared to be much better than of late. Personal grief, aggravated by worries about the shop, had taken their toll on her and she had not been looking well.

"How are you, dear?" asked Louise.

"Fine, Mum. Feeling fine. It's stopped moving. Midwife says he's 'engaged'! I just think he's too big to move any more."

Louise chuckled.

"Just as long as you don't do what I did to your father when I had your brother."

It was the first time she had mentioned Charles light-heartedly. The story of how Gordon had delivered his own son was well rehearsed in the family.

Victoria laughed ironically.

"If Alan was involved, I'd end up delivering it by myself. Calves and lambs? Easy! A baby of his own? Never!"

They brewed a cup of tea and sat talking and looking at the layette.

"Only two weeks until Polly's baby is due," reminded Victoria. "It'll be nice for mine to have a 'cousin-once-removed' so close in age!"

"I must pop in and see Jessica and Bill," said Louise, almost to herself.

"How are things going at the shop, then?" asked Victoria.

"The same, dear. Rationing keeps business depressed. There's little or no material for making new things, and the trims are non-existent. Young Louise has been going to jumble sales buying garments for the buttons and trimmings."

"Good idea," said Victoria. "It won't go on for ever, Mum. It's got to end soon."

"I certainly hope so. I'll never know how the country discarded Churchill last year. I've lost my faith in everyone."

"This new lot have some good ideas. Health care for all, and they promise to take care of us from the cradle to the grave."

"As long as there are no more wars, that's all I really worry about. I worry about this new generation."

"Try not to, Mum. The future should be bright for them."

"I was in Bristol last week. The future holds lots of building for them, it's a mess."

Louise cleaned some windows for her daughter before she prepared to leave.

"Look after yourself, dear. Not long now," she comforted.

Victoria stood at the door waving to her mother and pondering on the events in her life in recent years. Bad though it had been for Louise, it was no better and no worse than life had been for the majority of the population of the British Isles. The war had taken its toll on everyone; it had worn everybody out. *Maybe I can look forward because new life is stirring within me,* she thought. *What have Mum and Dad got to look forward to now?*

APRIL 1947

New housing being constructed after the war had led to a further influx of people into the area. People were escaping, too, from the destruction of their cities during the war. Men returning home from fighting wanted more for their families and settled in the clean air of the Somerset countryside. Doctor Blake decided he would need a partner to help when the new National Health Service was formed the following year. He had spent some weeks interviewing young men for the job, and had not yet found anyone whom he felt fitted the bill.

"They're all so young, so green," he told Emily, his wife. "Half the people in the village probably wouldn't accept them, and the other half would take advantage of them."

Then along came Jack Ingrams, who was the last person to be interviewed.

"That isn't why I've chosen him," Martin explained to his wife. "He's just perfect."

Jack Ingrams had qualified at the end of the war, and had spent two years with the army, at the tail-end of operations. He was unmarried, but that was no particular drawback as far as Martin Blake was concerned.

"We can put him up while he looks for a place to live, can't we?" he suggested.

Emily raised her eyes to the heavens and agreed, laughingly.

"One more won't make much difference, I suppose," she sighed.

Their two children Olivia and Justin were twelve and ten respectively. Justin attended the village school, but Olivia spent weekdays at a secondary school in nearby Glastonbury.

"It shouldn't take him long to find something, suitable," comforted Martin. "In any case, he's a very nice chap."

Thus it was that Abbots Ford found that it had a new doctor. He was, as Martin had promised, a 'very nice' chap.

He did his best to fit in with the family while learning about the village and his new patients. When he had been with them for six weeks, he came across a cottage up the lane from the Redford's property, which was central enough to be convenient, and just the right size for the few pieces of furniture he had managed to collect. His benefactors were invited to a house warming drink or two when he moved in. He showed them around the tiny, picturesque cottage and they admired his efforts at homemaking.

"To you, and your new home," said Martin jovially, holding his glass aloft.

"To your new home, may you enjoy many happy years here!" repeated Emily.

The sound of the telephone rent the air and Jack deposited his glass to answer it. He returned to the room stony-faced.

"Penelope Thorndyke at Tradewinds. Says it's serious. Her husband has collapsed," he reported.

"Come with me," said Martin. "You haven't had any contact at Tradewinds as yet, have you? Now's as good a time as any."

The two men gathered their coats and bags, and with apologies to Emily and the children, left in Martin's car.

Someone was at the front entrance awaiting their arrival as the car crunched over the drive.

"This way, Doctor," said the man, trying to be calm and efficient when he was obviously badly shaken. They were shown into the morning room, where a fire was lit despite the warmth of the early spring day. Penelope Thorndyke was leaning over her husband, who was lying prone upon a sofa. The two doctors approached swiftly and Doctor Blake examined Giles. In a very short time he turned and, putting a hand on her shoulder, told Penelope that there was no more to be done. It was upsetting for them to see her response. Both had, on numerous occasions, imparted sad news to relatives, but the effect of seeing this sophisticated, worldly and elegant woman weeping hysterically over her dead husband was unnerving.

"Now, now Penelope. Is there someone we can call to be with you?" asked Martin Blake.

"No, no, no. Please no. I want to be alone with him," she wept.

"I want you to take one of these," said Doctor Blake, giving her a tiny number of pills. He left the room to give instructions to the senior servant about calling her family, and Doctor Ingrams stood awkwardly, not knowing what to say.

"You say he's had a massive heart-attack?" Penelope turned her tear-stained face towards him.

He nodded. "There was nothing anybody could have done," he reiterated.

She was stroking her husband's head and murmuring to him. "Nothing to be done, nothing to be done."

"Do you want a glass of water to take one of the pills Doctor Blake has given to you?" he ventured.

She seemed not to hear him. He noticed a tray set up in the corner of the room and investigated to see if there was water available. He poured her a tumbler full and taking it to her, motioned to the pills, untouched on a coffee table. Doctor Blake had by now returned, and informed her that all the necessary arrangements were being put in hand and that a member of her family was on their way. They saw to it that she took the pills, and voicing their commiserations, they left. Neither man spoke until they were driving down the main road.

"Another piece of village history gone," said Martin flatly.

"No children, then?"

"None. He had a sister living in Bath. Don't know if she's still there," Martin told him.

They drove on towards Jack's new home in silence, each deep within thoughts of his own.

"Thanks for the lift. See you tomorrow," said Jack.

As Martin opened his front door he could hear the sound of his son's laughter, bright and full of energy, looking forward to the Easter holiday.

"I'm home!" he called, and went to join the family fun.

DECEMBER 1947

It had cheered the country enormously when the King's eldest daughter married Lieutenant Philip Mountbatten, a handsome Nordic looking Greek prince, who was also descended from Queen Victoria. After wartime privations, some of which they still suffered, it was a joy to see Royal ceremonial again. It was said that Princess Elizabeth had had to save clothing coupons for her gown and trousseau. The newspapers were full of the young couple, and it was obvious to all that it was a love-match and not an arranged marriage in the usually accepted sense.

Seth and Iris had continued with their illicit affair. He lived in constant fear of being discovered, for they snatched moments at her mother's house when they crept back late at night. They drove out into the country and made love in Seth's disreputable old heap of a van, but rarely could they go out together as a couple for fear of being spotted. Inevitably, Seth's relationship with Iris had a detrimental effect on his life with Helen. He became ever more dissatisfied, picking quarrels with Helen, and snapping at the children. At times, he realised that one day he would have to choose between them, and he could not envisage leaving the children.

Towards Christmas, Iris had some news for him: she was pregnant. He was out of his mind with worry, torn between loving Iris, and the pull of his life with Helen and the children. He became so short-tempered that Helen challenged him one evening.

"Have you got a fancy woman? Seth, I asked you a question. Have you got a fancy woman?"

He sat sullenly behind his newspaper.

Running out of patience when he refused to answer, she snatched the paper away from him. If she had been attempting to elicit a response, she succeeded, because he jumped up from his chair and grabbed her by the shoulders.

"Don't ever – ever do that to me again, woman," he growled between tightly gritted teeth.

The effect was menacing and Helen was shocked. He released her and she took a step backwards, realising that his arm was raised ready to strike her.

"It's – it's true, isn't it?" she stammered.

They looked at each other for long, tense moments, both wondering how they had come to this.

"There's been talk. Is it Iris Murchison?" asked Helen, endeavouring to remain calm.

Seth nodded, like a man in a trance.

The tears welled up in her throat but would not come. He had been acting strangely for many months, but when she thought about it, she could not pinpoint when the deterioration had begun. They still made love intermittently, but without passion. She had thought that their busy family life was taking its toll on them, and had made excuses for him in her mind. She shivered and her knees felt weak. A wave of nausea swept over her as she knew with certainty that her marriage was all but over. Seth had always had a cruel side to his nature, always giving her the impression that he had never fully given himself to her, always keeping the total essence of himself apart. Seth collected his coat and cap and left to go to the Partridge Inn, while Helen rocked herself to and fro, screaming silently deep within herself.

SPRING 1948

There was a 'big' funeral in Abbots Ford that spring, and much sadness. Angus Redford, the pater familias of the Redford clan, died in his sleep. He had always been there working in the butchers department of the shop, or so it seemed, for as long as most people could remember. Even Catherine, his wife, still helped out for a few hours a day in the grocers, though she was well past seventy. Their eldest and only son, Graham, had long since carried responsibility for the complex, but now his son, Nigel, had been sharing in the running of the business for some years. Graham's sisters, Phoebe and Rosamund ran the grocers, with the help of Maud and Millicent, Phoebe's daughters and Judith, Rosamund's daughter.

The church was packed on the day of the funeral, mostly with his vast family, but also a goodly contingent of friends and villagers. Seth organised a horse and carriage for his old friend, and the village came to a halt for one of their most influential number to be laid to rest.

Young Doctor Jack Ingrams drove slowly behind the cortège on his way to Will and Polly Henty's house at Hilltop Farm. He had been summoned by the midwife when the birth was taking longer than expected. When he finally arrived it was decided that the forceps were necessary to help the baby into the world. Polly was a sensible young woman but had become distressed during the protracted labour. The midwife was Jenny, Ellie's eldest daughter, now an experienced nurse of fifty. She and the doctor worked hard to assist Polly and late that afternoon, a baby girl was born. Fittingly, they called her 'May'. Just before the birth, the other nurse on duty, Jenny's partner, Sarah, arrived.

RETURN TO THE HILL

"Hello all. Hello Penny," she greeted them all cheerfully. "Where's little Janet? At your Mum's?" she asked.

Janet was now a lively eighteen-month-old and her grandmother, Jessica, had whisked her away to Peartree Farm when Polly's labour had begun. Bill was attending the Redford funeral. Sarah took over and bathed the newborn child, while the doctor and Jenny attended to Polly. Jack Ingrams had fitted in remarkably quickly and well, and the nurses found him easy to get along with. In passing, he whispered to Sarah.

"Fancy a drink after this?"

"Not in uniform, Doctor," she replied mockingly.

"I don't mind if you remove it," he responded.

She rolled her eyes at him.

"Not in front of the child, if you please."

"I'll drive you home to get changed," he offered.

"I'm on duty till nine and then I'm off home," she informed him.

"When are you off duty? For a whole day I mean?"

"Friday."

"Damnation. Can't make Friday," he cursed.

"I'm free Sunday afternoon," she announced.

"Sunday afternoon it is. I'll call for you at about two. Does that suit you?"

She nodded, and finished dressing the baby.

"Here she is! All clean and lovely to see Mummy." Sarah handed the sweetly-smelling infant to her mother, and Will was invited in to the room to meet his new daughter.

Doctor Ingrams left and the two nurses put the room in order.

"You be alright?" asked Jenny. She turned to Will. "You'll be staying all the time?"

He nodded and assured her that his wife would not be left alone.

"Mum is keeping Janet for tonight."

"I'll be back in the morning to see how you both are. Seven and a half pounds was a good weight," said Jenny. The two women went out to their bicycles.

"After a date was he?" asked Jenny, grinning.

"Mmm, he was," chuckled Sarah.

"He's very handsome. I could quite go for him myself if I was a few years younger," she admitted.

"When you've got handsome Alan at home?"

"Are you going out with him?"

"Maybe," said Sarah, non-committally. They rode off through the evening, each hoping for respite to drink a cup of tea before the next emergency presented itself.

+ + +

It was a warm late spring morning, and she stretched luxuriously, having woken naturally for a change and not to the shattering sound of her alarm clock.

"I've brought you a cup of tea, dear. I thought I heard you stirring," said her mother. "Aren't you meeting that nice young doctor today?"

Sarah turned over and informed her that he was calling for her after lunch.

"Coming here?"

"Don't fuss, Mum. He won't be coming in, he's only picking me up."

"Well, it's a beautiful day. Where is he taking you?"

"I don't know." Sarah laughed, exasperated. "It's only a date, Mum, not an engagement."

"Drink your tea before it gets cold," said Mavis her mother, hurt at the implicit dismissal.

Sarah was twenty-seven years old and so involved in her job that her mother had begun to fear that she would be left on the shelf as there seemed no time for a serious boyfriend in her life. Relatives had begun to comment, as though there was something wrong with her daughter.

"You take your time," comforted her father. "You wait till you find the right one, my love."

She studied herself in the mirror, piling her curly blonde hair high up on her head. *No, I'll leave it loose, maybe just tie it back,* she thought. Her hazel eyes scrutinised the summery floral frock she had on. She was pleased with the result. When they had eaten lunch, she sat reading the Sunday papers.

"How you can sit there all calm, I don't know," commented her mother.

"Leave her be," said her father tolerantly.

When his wife had left the room, he fiddled with his pipe. "Your Mother only wants you to be happy. That's why she's fussed."

They sat quietly together with no need for further explanation.

"That sounds like him," he said, when they heard a car draw up outside.

Sarah gathered her things.

"Bye, Mum," she called, knowing that both her parents would be peering through the window as they drove away.

"Hello! How are you today?" Jack jumped out and ran round to open the door for her.

"Thanks. Beautiful day, isn't it!" she enthused.

He glanced to check that she was settled and comfortable and drove off down the lane towards Briersham.

"There's a little pub out towards Steeple Burstead I thought we'd call at first," he suggested.

"Sounds fine to me," she smiled.

He was telling her a convoluted joke when they arrived and she burst out laughing as she got out of the car.

"I knew we'd get on well. Any woman who laughs at my jokes is a winner!" he told her, taking her elbow, guiding her to a seat outside. They gossiped about colleagues and about the hospitals where they had trained. His keen grey eyes always met hers directly and she judged him to be a transparently honest man. His light brown hair was combed tidily back from a high forehead and his cheeks and nose were finely chiselled. He was perhaps too thin but Sarah liked his gangly elegance.

"I thought we'd go for a run – see where we end up?" he ventured, when they had finished their drinks.

She nodded in agreement. *I know where I'd like to end up,* she thought. He was every bit as nice as he had at first appeared. They shared the gallows sense of humour often found in the medical profession and she spent much of the afternoon laughing.

When they reached Bath, Jack parked the car and they walked around the centre of the quiet town hand-in-hand. Everywhere was closed, it being Sunday, but they met other couples and families out enjoying the clement weather. They window-shopped and found that their tastes coincided. He joked with her again: "We're meant for each other!" He leant towards her and placed an explosive kiss on her cheek. Sarah laughed and felt close to him, wondering if it was possible to fall in love with anyone so swiftly. On the journey back to the village, he was quieter.

"Shame nowhere is open on Sunday evenings for a meal," he said. "I'd invite you back to my place and rustle something up to eat, if I didn't think you'd think me fast!"

"Is that an invitation, doctor?" she queried.

"Most certainly is, nurse," he replied.

"Are you a good cook?" she asked, tentatively.

"Best bacon and beans at Barts," he chortled, stressing the *b* sounds in mock-American accent.

"God, for a minute I thought you could add Cordon Bleu cooking to your many talents, Dr Ingrams," she said with mock-relief.

"Don't underestimate some of my talents, Nurse!" He grinned lasciviously at her before turning his eyes back to the road.

"Seriously, shall we go to my place?"

"Jack, I'd love to ... but ...," she was thinking of the gossip it would generate if she was ever seen at his cottage.

"I understand. Don't worry - another time, perhaps."

As they neared Abbots Ford, she began to gather her cardigan, bag and gloves together.

"When can I see you again?" he asked.

"My day off is Friday," she told him.

"Blast – I'm on duty."

"No time for a drink one evening?"

"Not unless I change my on-call time with Martin," he said thoughtfully. "Tell you what, I'll see what I can do and give you a ring." They had arrived at her house.

"Thank you for a lovely afternoon. I have enjoyed it," she told him sincerely.

"So have I. Hope to do it again very soon." He smiled deeply into her eyes and gave a little nod.

"I'll ring you," he reiterated.

She stood and waved as he drove away, then turned to walk up the path and round to the back door, where she knew her mother would be waiting with suffocating concern, to hear about the afternoon.

SPRING 1949

Young Louise Henty was over the moon with excitement. There was a rumour that rationing in the form of coupons was coming off clothes at long last.

"It won't make much difference straight away remember, dear," her Aunt Louise warned her.

"They'll still need money, which remains in short supply," put in her Uncle Gordon.

She turned with shining eyes towards them.

"Does it mean that I can go to college at last?"

They had planned this for years, looking forward to the day when business picked up.

"Yes," said Gordon, with quiet pleasure. "We'll make enquiries and perhaps you can start in September."

They made a cup of tea to celebrate and were enjoying it when the lights inside the shop suddenly failed.

"Oh no," groaned Gordon. "Not again! I thought I had put it right."

As it was daylight, they were not plunged into darkness, but it was gloomy and dull. The shop had not been refurbished since before the war and needed a new coat of paint. It was stylishly fitted out in a similar fashion to the shop at Steeple Burstead, where Louise and Gordon had started their business over thirty years ago. The floor was polished wood, and the mahogany cupboards lining the shop contained garments which were taken out individually to serve a customer, or 'client' as they called them.

"I'll telephone for an electrician this time," said Gordon resignedly.

It was not long before the young man arrived. He wore a boiler suit and carried a tool box. Breezing in, he turned a cheeky grin on young Louise.

"Having trouble with your electrics?"

"Yes. I'll get my uncle," Louise told him primly.

The repairs did not take long, while the two women tidied the cabinets and drawers between attending to only one or two customers. Young Louise had almost forgotten that he was there, when he appeared silently at her side as she folded shawls and scarves.

"Are you doing anything tonight?" he asked.

"No. Yes, I am why?" she countered, becoming flustered.

"Do you want to come to the pictures?"

"No. I can't. I don't know you anyway."

"You do now. My name's Barry. Barry Harris."

"No. I can't, I'm sorry."

"Don't worry. Perhaps another time." He spoke to Gordon and went off, banging the door and whistling.

"Cheeky thing!" said the older Louise. "He wanted to take you out, didn't he?" She smiled at her niece, who shrugged it off. "Nice looking though, wasn't he?" added her aunt.

Later they closed the shop and made their way home through the village. Young Louise bade them goodbye as she turned in at the gate of Peartree Farm.

"See you tomorrow."

As she walked up the farm track towards the house she heard a low whistle. Turning, she saw the young electrician who had been at the shop earlier was waiting for her near a tractor.

"What are you doing here? How did you know where I live?"

"Easy. I asked at the newsagents. I said 'Who's that lovely bit of stuff in the posh dress shop?' and they told me."

Louise was horrified.

"You didn't really say that did you?"

His grey eyes danced merrily, teasing her. The quiff of his hair fell over one side of his forehead as his lopsided grin taunted her.

"Come out with me and I'll tell you," he promised.

"I can't tonight."

"Friday? We'll go to the pictures. There's a good film on."

"Oh alright," she agreed at last.

"I'll collect you in the van at seven o'clock. Alright?"

She nodded and he set off down the track to the road.

"The van's around the corner," he smiled. "Didn't want to let on I was here, in case you took fright."

Louise shook her head as she went slowly, towards the back door. *Pushy and cheeky* she thought. *Maybe I shouldn't have said I'd go.* She opened the door and the delicious smell of her mother's cooking tempted her nostrils.

"Hello, Mum, I'm home," she called as she closed the door behind her.

+ + +

Alice was nearly forty. She had not yet met another man with whom she felt she could share her life. She was happy enough, for she had bought a flat in the poor part of Portobello Road in West London, a complicated journey from St Mary's Hospital Paddington, where she was a nursing sister. She was a respected member of staff, but often laughed up her sleeve at some of the antics the student nurses became involved with, especially as they thought that they were the first ones to discover whatever it was they were doing.

Alice arrived home exhausted from duty one evening. An envelope was on the shelf in the hall, addressed to herself. She plodded up the four flights of stairs, dragging her shopping bag with her. All she wanted to do was make a snack, have a warm bath – and sleep. She put the kettle on and, kicking off her shoes, flopped into her comfortable armchair. Opening the envelope, she saw that the letter was from her good friend Sue, mother of Marina, the small girl whom Seth and Dorothy had taken to their hearts and who had begun to stay regularly at Orchard Cottage. Sue had dropped it through the door herself, for she lived only a ten minute walk away. Sue had only written a few lines but the crux of the matter was that Sue's husband was leaving her and that she wanted to see her as soon as she could. Alice made her snack and instead of the bath and bed, she went to Sue's house.

Sue and her husband lived in a row of houses edging one of the elegant garden squares, in Kensington. They rented it cheaply because the house still suffered dampness in the basement due to the damage inflicted during the war. Marina was still up when she arrived, and greeted her delightedly.

"Hello! Have you come to see me?" she asked, jumping about excitedly.

"Yes. You and Mummy," Alice assured her.

"Look, I've lost a tooth," exclaimed the child.

"My goodness, and did the tooth fairy leave you something?"

"Yes. Sixpence," said Marina.

"Time for bed now. Go on up and I'll tuck you in," Sue told her. "Don't wake the others!"

She kissed Alice goodnight and went off upstairs.

"So what's been happening to you and Ben?"

Sue told her the whole sorry tale of Ben's affair with a woman at work, and how he had been spending less time at home with her and the children. They had had a stand-up row culminating in her accusations and his admission of the situation. He had packed a bag and left the previous day, and now Sue was left to pick up the pieces and explain what had happened to their children.

"I'm so sorry," said Alice. "I thought you two were perfect for each other."

The two women sat up talking until the early hours, when Alice had to return home and sleep because she was on duty again early the next morning. She had succeeded in making Sue look on the bright side and to give Ben a second chance if he returned.

Alice changed wearily into her nightdress. She would have a bath in the morning. As she brushed her hair she told herself that though she sometimes felt lonely, she had avoided all the trials and worry which marriage and a family involved. She knew that she was becoming introverted and selfish, and that it was a strategy for survival in the world on her own.

SUMMER 1949

Jack and Sarah had known from their first date that they would marry. At first, they both pretended otherwise, not wanting to be hurt, but they were so obviously soul-mates that the more they learned of each other, the more they wanted to be together. Gradually, they became almost inseparable and then at Christmas Jack had produced an engagement ring and asked her to marry him. Her mother was ecstatic and threw herself into preparations for the wedding almost at once. Sarah was to move into Jack's cottage for their start to married life, and she would continue working part-time until they started a family of their own.

Their wedding day was glorious but windy. As she arrived at St Mary's with her father, her veil blew around her shoulders making her bridesmaids work hard to keep it under control, laughing and beautiful as they did so. Jack's family were all there from Surrey, waiting within the austere greyness of the little church which always took on the mood of the ceremonies it witnessed. Deep pink roses decorated the vases, the same as the bouquet Sarah carried. Jack turned to watch as she and her father came up the aisle towards him, the pride glowing from her father's eyes like beacons. The organ music swelled around them, enclosing everyone in its grandeur, lifting their hearts and bringing a lump to the throat. Reverend Glover waited while the echoes subsided and Sarah gave her flowers to the chief bridesmaid.

"Every wedding is special to a couple and family. But this wedding is special to our village too because two of its best-loved people are joining in holy matrimony. It seems more than two years since Dr Jack Ingrams joined us...." He waited while the congregation suppressed their laughter. "... and by that, I mean how quickly we have taken him to our hearts." The service continued in the time-honoured way and Sarah's mother wept all the way through, managing a watery smile for her daughter when they signed the register.

They had a marquee in the large garden of her parent's house with the motif of deep pink roses everywhere. Outside caterers ensured that everything ran smoothly and it was a most perfect day for them all.

They were honeymooning in France and stayed at an hotel in the country on their way to Portsmouth, where they were catching a ferry. Sarah was quiet at the start of the journey.

"Been a big day, hasn't it?" said Jack.

"Mmm," she agreed.

"I think everyone enjoyed it, didn't they?"

"Mmm," she repeated.

"I hope you're not having second thoughts – it's too late now, Mrs Ingrams!" he joked.

"No, oh no, darling. I'm just thinking about Mum. She always meant well, you know."

"I know that. Just so long as you do too."

"You get on with her, don't you?"

"Doesn't everyone?"

"Mmm." Sarah sounded doubtful.

"I think you were just the target for her full attention, and you're quite similar in some ways," he opined.

"Heaven forbid," she laughed.

"Forget all that now. We're on our honeymoon," he advised.

There was champagne awaiting them at the hotel and more flowers. When they had seen their luggage to their room they walked around the exquisite gardens before dinner.

"You're so beautiful," he told her, kissing her cheek. "I have died and gone to heaven. Beautiful surroundings and a beautiful girl – who is my wife."

The idyll was shattered by the sound of pounding feet on the grass and shouts of "Doctor Ingrams!" A waiter ran up to them, out of breath.

"Sorry to trouble you, Doctor Ingrams! A gentleman has collapsed in the foyer – can you come quickly?"

Jack hurried away with the man, leaving Sarah to follow on. When she caught up with them, Jack told her that the man had suffered a heart-attack.

"Here are my keys. Get my bag from the car," he ordered, turning swiftly back to his patient.

It was fortunate that a doctor had been on the spot, for the man's life was saved. An ambulance had been called and Jack went with him to the hospital, until the doctors there took over. Sarah followed in the car to bring him back to the hotel. The staff had saved what they could of the dinner the couple had been looking forward to, and they drank to each other with the remainder of the champagne. Afterwards, they fell into the luxurious bed, and in a haze of exhaustion, happiness and alcohol, drifted off to sleep at once.

In the early hours, Sarah thought she must still be dreaming as she slowly surfaced from sleep to find that Jack was kissing and caressing her. Tentatively at first, she responded and, for the first time, they consummated their love and their marriage.

"Oh God, Jack, how I love you," she breathed, as they reached the climax of their lovemaking.

"Sarah, Sarah, my love," groaned Jack.

They lay entwined, panting, replete.

"Is it always going to be like this?" asked Sarah, finally.

"Christ, I hope so – for the first sixty years, anyway."

"No, not this, you idiot! You – being on call everywhere?"

"Oh, that," he sighed dismissively.

"Yes, that. It could have ruined our wedding night," said Sarah, sounding hurt.

"It's a fact of life, my darling. People can't choose when or where they have heart-attacks or accidents. I can't just switch off either. You know that - nurses are the same. You do what you can." He said it all kindly, tracing her mouth, nose and eyes with his fingers. His hands moved down to caress her breasts and then they were making love again. Sarah giggled.

"What's the matter?" he asked.

"Did they tell you at Med. School that this was possible?" she asked.

"What?" he asked obtusely.

"Twice in fifteen minutes."

"Oh, that," he said. "No, all they said was that it would drop off if we did it more than fifteen times in half-an-hour!" They muffled their laughter with pillows and snuggled up together, a lifetime ahead of them. Whatever it held, Sarah had no doubts about the man she had chosen – there would never be a dull moment.

JANUARY 1950

Seth was sixty-four and still working as hard as ever in the Smithy. There were enough horses about in that part of the country for him to keep his hand in, and he continued to make and mend tools and took on the occasional ornamental ironwork commission. He still had work as a wheelwright, fashioning the iron rim of the wheel around the wheel stone. He enjoyed having the older boys from the school, to teach them the rudiments of metalwork, and was proud of the fact that a few had chosen to follow the craft as a job.

Dorothy had just turned thirty-eight and was fully occupied looking after her father and brother, doing her voluntary work at the baby clinic and church, and regularly having Marina and other friends or relatives to stay at Orchard Cottage.

Young Seth had caused a scandal in the village when he and Helen parted. She moved away to Bristol, taking their children with her. He saw no reason why he should not remain at Plumtree Cottage, for he still worked at Drakes Farm, which was how Dorothy found herself, like her mother before her, traipsing back and forth each day to tidy the cottage and leave snacks for her brother when he was out late or very early.

Iris had miscarried the child she was expecting, but she and Seth still carried on with their affair while she continued living at home with her mother. The parting between Seth and Helen caused a terrible row between him and his brother. Eddy, who thought the world of Edgar, Seth's eldest son, perceived that Seth was taking his family for granted. He felt that Seth was ignoring his children and using his wife, and accused him of neglecting his duty towards all of them.

Louise and Gordon, having struggled through the war, had been assisted by the removal of clothing coupons in the spring of last year. They revelled in the four grandchildren their daughters had provided.

Jessica and Bill still did not see Anne, who had stayed in London permanently since the war; they received word of her through Alice now and then, but the wounds inflicted over her love affair with Joshua had been too deep for reconciliation.

Young Louise continued to work with her aunt and uncle in the shop whilst attending college in Bristol and had taken over most of the driving to Bath, thus allowing her to become more involved in design decisions.

Charles Henty and Amy had spent many months apart after her father had challenged him at Orchard Cottage, but the attraction between them could not be ignored and they had met in secret. That was not Charles' style, nor was he an ardent or selfless lover. Amy had to make most of the running while conspiring to allow Charles to think that he was.

Eventually, they had moved to Bath to live together as man and wife. Rebecca was sad that Amy had opted for that alternative, but as she was thirty-four when she left home, it was seen as preferable to becoming an embittered old maid. Robert would never view it philosophically; his opinion was that, after almost ruining his family, Beatrice and her son had now stolen his beloved youngest child, for he rarely saw her nowadays.

+ + +

Lydia had to go to hospital for a routine check and had asked Dorothy to travel with her for the day out. It was cold and miserable as they waited for the bus and Lydia stomped her feet to keep warm.

"I hope this doesn't take too long today, Dorothy. We want to be able to look at the shops and still get back before it's dark, don't we?"

"Yes, and I really need to get some shirts for Dad and Eddy, too," replied Dorothy.

The bus came and everyone climbed on, talking about the cold weather and the misery that was January. As they left Abbots

Ford, Lydia looked out at the passing countryside, silently taking it in. Ever sensitive to peoples' mood, Dorothy did not intrude on her thoughts.

At the out-patient department, the mêlée was off-putting. People were everywhere, sitting on row upon row of wooden bench seats. The department had not been painted for years; bottle green cracked and chipped walls lent gloom to an already worrying experience. Short tempered nurses barked at patients who had the temerity to enquire when they might be seen, after they had already waited two hours. Dorothy stayed with Lydia and they chatted in muted tones, looking at the examples of humanity they saw around them. People were looking tatty and tired.

"I'll be glad to get out of here!" Lydia confided.

"What do you suppose can be wrong with so many people?"

It was a rhetorical question; Dorothy had done her bit in out-patients during her two year stint in training.

Eventually Lydia's name was called, loudly, and she went in to see the doctor. Considering the length of time she had waited, the consultation was brief. She did not comment when she emerged from the little room; she had not said much about the problem to Dorothy, but gave her to understand it was to do with 'women's problems'.

"What would you like to do now?" asked Dorothy.

"Have a cup of tea and an enormous cake," grinned Lydia.

They set off in the direction of Fuller's tea-room, and Lydia put her arm through Dorothy's as they walked.

"Thank you for coming with me," she said.

"It's no trouble. I needed a day out, away from Dad and Eddy."

"How is Eddy?" enquired Lydia.

"Well, he took it badly when Helen took the children when she and Seth split up. Especially Edgar. You know he worships that boy."

"I know. It's very difficult. Helen did what she thought best, but Matthew was upset when she uprooted all the children from a school they knew."

"He goes to see them about once a month. It's all the time he can spare from Drakes Farm," said Dorothy.

"Do you think they will really divorce?" asked Lydia.

"It seems serious. Helen will never trust him again, and anyway, he's still infatuated with Iris," explained Dorothy.

"They don't go about openly though, do they? Or anyhow, I haven't seen them."

"No, Seth knows Dad doesn't approve. I can't say I do really."

They had arrived at the tea-room and found a table. The waitress took their order, which included the enormous cakes they had promised themselves.

"I've got some good news," said Lydia happily.

"Do tell."

"Diana is expecting a baby in May."

"Oh how wonderful, Lydia. You'll be a Grandma."

Dorothy was pleased for her, because she knew Lydia had missed having her family about her. She had let her children go freely, and although none lived too far away, they were all busy with their own lives and careers. She and Matthew were exceedingly happy together; while they were good company to have in a crowd, they were equally happy to be on their own. Both were optimistic, contented people who were, at the same time; sensitive.

"I suppose we should go and catch our bus," said Lydia.

They paid the bill and gathered their belongings and made their way towards the bus station.

"Marcus is staying next weekend. Can you come and have a meal with us on Saturday?"

"Yes, I'd like that. What time?"

"About 7 – dinner at 7.30." Lydia told her.

They met one or two villagers getting on the bus and gossiped and laughed with them while they waited for the journey to begin.

As they juddered and rattled home Dorothy felt comfortable and secure. Lydia was like that, friendly and open, so that it was easy to be oneself in her company.

They arrived home and went their separate ways. Dorothy decided that she would repay Lydia's generosity, and return their hospitality with a meal at Orchard Cottage in the spring.

When she opened the door to the cottage, Seth looked up. He did not look well and Dorothy was alarmed.

"Why, Dad, what's the matter?" she cried.

"I don't know, girl," he replied painfully.

"Where does it hurt? How long has it been like this?"

"It's my chest, Dotty." He seemed to struggle for breath; it hurt him to breathe.

"Let me get the doctor."

"That young chap's no good," moaned Seth.

"He's not that young, Dad! Let me get him."

"No. I'll be alright. A good nights' sleep. Let me breathe in one of your concoctions, I'll be alright."

Dorothy infused some herbs and poured the liquid into a bowl. Seth put a towel over his head and breathed deeply. He sat till the water had cooled, breathing slowly, deeply and painfully.

"Any better, Dad?" Dorothy was anxious.

"Yes. It's eased now, love."

"Best get you to bed, eh?" she asked.

He agreed to go to bed; it was almost time anyway. When her father was settled, Dorothy made a hot drink. While she sat beside the fire enjoying it, Eddy came in.

"No supper tonight then Sis?" he said, surprised.

This had never occurred before.

"I've just put our Dad up to bed, he was taken poorly."

"Aye?"

"When I came home from Bristol, he was in here having trouble with his breathing," she told him.

"Probably got a cough on his chest. He spends hours out there in that barn," said Eddy.

"I've got pasties for supper, I'll do them now." Dorothy got up as she spoke. She was still worried and promised herself that she would get the doctor in the next day if her father was no better. She and Eddy sat alone eating their meal.

"I'm going up to Bristol myself next Sunday." He said suddenly.

"Oh yes?"

"Seeing Helen and the children. That boy Edgar's nearly fourteen. He needs his Dad around now."

Divorce was not commonplace in the West Country, or anywhere, at the time, and Eddy disapproved.

"Give them my love. I've knitted jumpers for all of them," said Dorothy. "Meant to give them for Christmas but William and Flora's weren't ready."

"Aye"

"What time are you going on Sunday?"

"I'll drive, and leave after breakfast."

"Right. Are you having dinner there?"

"Yes, I expect to. You said Dad was having trouble breathing?"

"Yes. He had pains in his chest. If he's the same tomorrow, I'll call in Dr Blake."

"He'll not like fuss," Ed told her.

"He'll just have to put up with it then," replied Dorothy sharply.

They continued eating in silence, each lost in their own thoughts. Eddy got up and sat in his leather chair reading the paper, not waiting until Dorothy had finished her meal. She did not comment; she was used to Eddy's quirky ways. They argued as much as ever, Dorothy for justice, and Eddy because life had treated him badly. Dorothy cleared up when she had finished her meal, washing up in the dull loneliness of the big, old kitchen. She was suddenly overwhelmed with the futility of it all, of her life nowadays, of the day. She knew instinctively that her dear friend Lydia was really ill, and now her father was showing signs of age and infirmity. Dad. Big, tall, strong, handsome dad. The love of her mother's life. *Good job you're not here to see him poorly, Mum,* she thought. *You wouldn't have liked that!* She said goodnight to Eddy as she went through the living room and opened the door by the latch to go upstairs. She listened at her father's door and tapped on it.

"Alright Dad?" she said quietly. There was no reply.

She went to her room in the sloping roof and peered out at the stars through the dormer window, before closing the curtains. She sat on the stool in front of the dressing table and looked in the mirror. She had the same straight hair her mother had had, and since the twenties had cut it in a bob, swinging straight and shining round her head. The brown eyes looked back at her and she observed that lines were appearing round her mouth as well as her eyes. "You're getting on," she said quietly to herself. "What have you got to show for it?"

She thought again about her father and sad, ungrateful brother. Tears began to trickle down her face. *Stop it,* she thought sternly. *Self-pity never got anybody anywhere!*

She was a gentle, kind, matter-of-fact person who gave constantly to everyone and everything else and had rarely expected anything for herself. She got ready for bed, and climbed into the clean, stiff sheets and soft feathers. Turning off her light, she buried her face in the downy pillows and cried herself to sleep.

+ + +

Eddy was up early to see to his herd and have his breakfast before driving to Bristol to see Helen, Seth's estranged wife and their four children. He took with him the four cardigans and jumpers which Dorothy had knitted and some bookshelves Grandad Seth had made for their bedrooms. He also took a large box containing milk, butter, eggs and cream, and some of Dorothy's bottled plums. He packed the car up and said goodbye to Dorothy and his father.

Dorothy was having a cup of coffee with Lydia before church and she left the cottage soon afterwards. Seth was going to work in the Smithy.

"Morning!" Lydia's cheery face welcomed Dorothy and she showed her into the drawing room where Matthew was talking to Simon and his wife Theresa, Vera their youngest daughter, and Diana and her husband Donald. A chorus of voices hailed Dorothy as she went in.

"Nice to see you," said Matthew. "How are you this fine day?"

Dorothy had a special word for Diana who was now six months pregnant. Vera went out to help her mother with the drinks. They were a pleasant family of whom Matthew and Lydia were justly proud. Diana had been teaching until giving up work to have her baby; Simon was a lawyer, and Vera also a teacher. When they were together like this, they were witty and entertaining and there was much laughter and jocularity. Matthew had to be dissuaded from talking 'shop' with his daughters, because teaching was an all consuming passion for him. Lydia joined them and sat down and Dorothy noticed that there was a momentary shadow of pain across her face before the customary cheerfulness returned. They talked of the coming child and how Matthew and Lydia would be grannie and grandad. Dorothy wondered if the family were aware that all was not well with her. They were going to morning service together and all scattered, collecting coats, hats and scarves.

"Are you alright, Lydia?" asked Dorothy quietly.

"Yes, dear," replied Lydia gratefully. "I'm fine."

Reverend Glover greeted them at the door. Douglas Glover and his wife Esther were friends of the Ashton's. Dorothy enjoyed being part of their gatherings, and mixing with families similar to her own. After the service, she returned to Orchard Cottage to make lunch for herself and Seth; it seemed quiet after the sociability of School House.

Eddy arrived at the Bristol house where Helen lived, just in time for lunch. All the children were pleased to see him, especially Edgar; the mutual affection between them was obvious. He distributed the gifts and gave Helen some money in an envelope, from himself. They all told him how they were getting on at school, for even little Flora had been at school a year now. 'Uncle Eddy' played almost as much a part in their lives as their father nowadays. Helen served pudding and then she and Eddy settled down with cups of tea while they shared gossip. Sunday school was held at the local church, and shortly, Helen got them all ready to walk along to St Peter's for the three o'clock class. Eddy went with them for the fresh air. Edgar was too old for Sunday school now, so he and Eddy kicked a ball around the local park for a little while, before a group of Edgar's friends joined them. Laughing, Eddy decided to give in gracefully against half a dozen youngsters, so he and Helen carried on back to the house. She put the kettle on for a cup of tea and was standing in the kitchen daydreaming when Eddy suddenly put his arm around her waist and kissed the back of her neck.

"Eddy!" she was shocked. She knew that Eddy had become eccentric, and had shut away any feelings he may have had about women, since the death of Elizabeth, but she had always felt safe with him and was able, until now, to be completely natural and friendly in his company.

"What do you think you're doing?" She turned to face him. He was confused.

"I ... I'm sorry, I didn't think you'd...." He had turned and gone to the living room.

"You were going to say you didn't think I'd mind, weren't you? Weren't you?" She demanded.

"I'd best go," he said, gathering his coat and hat.

She began to feel sorrow instead of anger.

"It's just, I didn't expect that from you. I thought you were my friend."

He said nothing, but prepared to leave.

"We can still be friends. Not that sort though."

"I'm sorry, Helen. I don't know what came over me. It was just that......."

She saw him to the door.

"Thanks for bringing everything. Thank Dorothy and Seth. Thanks for the money. Find yourself a nice woman, and settle down Ed."

"Bye. Tell the children 'sorry' not saying goodbye to them."

He drove away in his battered old car. Helen waved, then went back inside. Life could be dreadful. She knew how lonely he must be, and that he felt relaxed with her and loved the children. But he was still her estranged husbands' brother. Even if she liked him, it was not acceptable, either to her or to society. She felt irritable and let down. It was not an easy life, bringing up four youngsters on her own, but she had had to leave Abbots Ford. She could not turn a blind eye to the affair between Seth and Iris and anyhow, Seth had assured her that it was no mere affair, that Iris was the love of his life. Helen had had no alternative; now she felt more lonely than ever. Her link with her children's father and his family had been damaged by Eddy's neglect of convention.

There was a loud knock on the door and she went to let in her noisy family.

"Hello, Mum," they shrieked as they tumbled in through the door.

"Can John come to tea?"

"I want Melanie to come to tea!"

"I didn't know we could have friends to tea."

"Quiet, all of you. No one to tea today." And she went about organising her children and getting their Sunday tea.

EASTER 1950

Marina was coming to stay and Dorothy was elated. Even Seth was looking forward to the visit, for of all the young people and children who visited Orchard Cottage, he liked little Marina best. The child was now seven and a half, and they enjoyed seeing the changes in her as she grew.

"I'm going to Bristol to collect her off the coach, Dad." explained Dorothy. "I'll do some shopping first, so I'll be leaving early. Your lunch will be on a plate in the larder. Alright?"

"Yes, girl. I can manage," he said irritably, although the last thing he could do was manage to get a meal for himself.

"We'll be home about four."

"Right oh."

Dorothy put her hat on in front of the mirror, and struggled into her coat.

"I'm off then, bye." Dorothy departed to catch the ten o'clock bus.

On arrival in Bristol, Dorothy took herself to Fuller's tearooms for a cup of coffee and a cream slice. A wander around Dingles' resulted in the purchase of a fetching bottle green velvet hat with a bow at the side. She even bought a white short-sleeved blouse, and mused that her mother and Aunt Louise would be shocked at the waste, when such an item could so easily be 'run up'. Dorothy could sew, but she enjoyed knitting more. Soon it was time to go to the bus office in Cathedral Street to wait for Marina's arrival. Dorothy went to the counter window at the far side of the grubby brown and cream waiting room, to enquire about the coach from London, Victoria and its estimated time of arrival. It was due in at two-thirty, and, according to the snooty woman behind the counter, was running on time. Dorothy sat on one of the long, leather-covered bench seats in the waiting room and stuck a stamp on the post card she had bought, in readiness for Marina to write to her parents telling them of her safe arrival.

Dorothy stood stretching on tip-toes, looking in at the windows of the coach which had just arrived outside the bus office. She caught sight of Marina just as Marina saw her, and they smiled and waved at one another delightedly. The passengers slowly alighted and eventually Dorothy held the little girl in her arms in a welcoming embrace.

"Hello, Marina. How are you? Did you have a good journey?"

"Yes, thank you, Aunt Dorothy. That lady looked after me on the coach."

Dorothy nodded gratefully to the woman who had stepped off the bus just after Marina.

"What a lovely little girl," said the woman.

"Thank you."

Dorothy collected Marina's small suitcase, and they went to sit down and write the postcard. Once it was safely dispatched, they went to catch the bus for Abbots Ford. Marina was tired, but obviously excited to be visiting them again. She sat watching avidly as the bus travelled through the suburbs of Bristol and out into the countryside. She drank in the houses and walls built of local stone, the hilly countryside and the steep streets.

She watched fascinated while the bus negotiated the hairpin bend in a village along the way. It was only the skill of the driver which prevented scraping the bus along the walls of nearby cottages. Local people going about their business stopped momentarily to watch as the man manoeuvred the vehicle round the sharp bend. Once they were safely on their way again, relief made passengers laugh and joke. Dorothy could feel the excitement rising in Marina as they approached Abbots Ford.

"Will Grandad Seth be at home?" she asked.

"He certainly will, dear," assured Dorothy.

The amazing thing about Marina's visits was that Seth and Eddy and young Seth always greeted her as though she had never been away, as though there was nothing unusual about a little girl suddenly appearing at Orchard Cottage. They always called her 'Lucy' for no reason anyone could think of, and she in turn, had always accepted it and answered to the name.

"Well if it isn't young Lucy!" Seth came in and sat down at the table for supper. He asked Dorothy how her shopping trip had gone but made no other comment about Lucy's arrival.

Eddy walked through the living room to wash in the kitchen, greeting no one, and on his return sat down and began to eat.

"You got the salt and pepper, Lucy?" he asked.

"No, Uncle Ed," she replied.

Dorothy cleared away the first course and brought in a fruit pie.

"Custard's good for you, Lucy," said Seth when Marina said she did not like it.

After they had eaten, both men left the table to carry on working. When she had cleared away the debris and dishes of the meal, Dorothy suggested that she and Marina should play a game of draughts before the child's bed time. While they were playing, Lydia called round to see them and suggested an outing together during Marina's stay. The two women laughed as the little girl told them some jokes she had read in a comic. The child was so attractive and intelligent, it was easy to love her and enjoy her company. While they were talking and laughing, Seth returned.

"Hello, Mrs Ashton. You've met our young friend before, haven't you?"

"Yes, Mr Hawkes, I certainly have."

"I have chocolate here. Does anyone want it?" asked Seth.

He was reaching into his pocket when he suddenly collapsed against the table, looking very ill indeed.

"Dad, what is it?" Dorothy was at his side in seconds. With Lydia's help they gently lowered him to the floor.

"I'll get Dr Blake," said Lydia, and dashed out.

"Marina, can you get a glass of water for Grandad?" said Dorothy. The child did as she was asked.

Dorothy reassured her father that he would be fine, and put cushions beneath his head. Somehow, it was easier with Marina there; it gave both Seth and Dorothy something else to think about.

"Just lay still, Dad. Lydia's gone for the doctor."

"Don't want that young lad. Where's Dr Tanner?"

Calmly, Dorothy told him that it was years since Dr Tanner had retired, and that at forty-four Dr Blake could hardly be called a young lad.

Lydia soon arrived back, with the news that the doctor was following hot on her heels. Sure enough he came into the living room of the cottage shortly after Lydia.

"What's happened to you?" he asked, getting down on his hands and knees beside Seth.

"A pain. In my chest," Seth told him.

The doctor listened to Seth's chest.

"You've probably had a heart attack, Seth. Bed rest for you. No work for a few weeks," the doctor told him.

"Can you get him to bed, Dorothy?"

"I'll help her," offered Lydia.

"You'll do no such thing, I'm not having a lady seeing me in my long johns," Seth told them firmly.

They helped him up the winding stairs. Dr Blake left some tablets and told them he would call in next day.

"Are you alright then, Dad?" asked Dorothy, tucking him in. "I'll pop in when I come to bed, to see how you are."

"Right, girl," Seth murmured. He was ready for a good nights' sleep.

"Let's get you ready for bed, young lady," she told Marina, who had entertained herself looking at the pictures in the book of the film 'Gone with the Wind'.

Lydia bade them goodnight and left to go home.

When Marina was tucked in, Dorothy went down and sat by the remains of the fire, looking at the glow through the bars.

"Let him be alright, God. Please don't take him yet," she prayed quietly. There was no sign of Eddy. She glanced at the clock; it was late. He had changed his habits recently, and been more strange than ever. Her mind ran over the past, when her mother was alive, and gran.... She awoke with a jolt, cold and stiff. She gathered her cardigan and, switching off the lights, climbed the steep stairs to bed.

+ + +

On Easter Saturday, they all had a most wonderful surprise: Alice arrived unexpectedly.

"You couldn't have timed it better, Alice," Dorothy told her. "Dad's had a bad turn again. It's his heart. Dr Blake says he's to rest for six weeks and not work so hard."

"How are you getting him to rest, for goodness sake?" asked Alice.

"Well, he's obviously feeling poorly because he's been as good as gold."

Seth moaned and complained when he saw Alice, but was assured that no one had sent for her especially. Marina was thrilled to have both 'aunties' together. They went walking up the hill, picking bunches of primroses to fix to the trellis screen in church for Easter Day, as generations of children had done before. As they walked, they played games of make-believe, listing what they would do if they had a thousand pounds. Then they played a game where each told a paragraph of a story in turn. Marina enjoyed it, and so did Dorothy and Alice.

The doctor came each day and told Dorothy to keep her father as quiet as possible.

On Easter Saturday afternoon, they baked Easter biscuits and lardy cake and later went round to the church with their bunches of primoses.

"Ah, we have an extra helper," cried Douglas Glover when he saw Marina. Matthew and Lydia were helping to prepare the church for a joyous Easter Day.

"Your Dad alright, Dorothy?" asked Lydia.

Seth was liked in the village and people were perturbed to hear about his illness.

While they were out, James Hawkes, Seth's nephew, visited his uncle. James was Seth's brother Arthur's son, and was married with a young family. An elderly friend was sitting with Seth while everyone went to the church, and he took James up to Seth's room.

"Hello, lad," said Seth, pushing himself further up on his pillows.

"Hello, Uncle Seth." James bent forward and patted Seth's shoulder.

"How's things with you, lad?" Seth asked his nephew.

"Fine. Dad sends his best. Sorry to hear you're poorly. He'll be along himself soon."

"He keeping alright? And your Mum?"

"Yes. Mum had a bad patch in the winter, but she's alright now."

"And your Ruby and the children?"

"All well. Growing up fast."

"So what brings you to see me in my bed?" asked Seth querulously.

"I was speaking to Dad about you. You may need help to keep the Smithy going while you're laid low."

Seth peered at him silently. James cleared his throat.

"I've done any bits needed around Drakes Farm, though we brought the horses to you for shoeing..."

Seth interrupted him.

"You came to me when you were still at school, didn't you lad?"

"Yes, Uncle Seth. I knew it was what I wanted from then on."

"Why did you not say something, lad?" asked Seth, exasperated.

"Dad said there was only enough work for one man..."

"Paaa," spluttered Seth. "I've been worrying about the amount to be done, trying to think who could take over... thought you were settled at Drakes Farm, that they needed you."

"They've got enough hands now, cousins growing up, you know."

"You've made me feel better, lad. Go and get a glass of ale for us from the larder."

"Should you...?" began James.

"Should I, be blowed! I'm not that ill. Go and get it!" He exploded.

Thus it was, that on Dorothy, Alice and Marina's return, they found Seth, James and Walter the neighbour, enjoying a few glasses of ale in Seth's sick room.

Dorothy could not help but smile, for her cousin's visit had obviously improved her father's spirits. He told them of the plan, and how he would show James the ropes as soon as he was well. Dorothy and Alice nodded and responded enthusiastically, pleased that Seth would have company and help when he returned to work.

"Come again when you can, lad," instructed Seth, "and we'll talk more about the work I'm taking on these days."

The women left to make tea. There was an air of celebration and everyone's spirit was lifted at the thought of Seth's working again, but not so hard.

When James had left, Seth kept them talking in his room, full of ideas and looking forward in a way he had not for a long time. The evening meal was a happy one, as Eddy was pleased to see Alice, and his strangeness of recent weeks receded. Alice entertained them with news of the hospital; she was always amusing when speaking of her work. She told them of their cousin Anne, now thirty but still unmarried.

Later, upstairs in her bedroom, Alice told Dorothy that she was in love with a married consultant, and was conducting an affair with him.

"But that's adultery, Alice!" said Dorothy, shocked.

Alice shrugged.

"Better than breaking up a marriage," she commented.

Dorothy would never understand her sister's attitude to men. She did not know all the details of her various affairs, but knew that she had been more circumspect since the tragedy of Theo's death and the loss of her baby. Dorothy had had opportunities for what she regarded as misbehaviour, but her one great love had left her wanting nothing if she could not have love within a happy marriage.

"Aren't you afraid of being found out?"

"No chance of that. He comes to my flat and nobody from the hospital lives anywhere near Portobello Road."

"Is he handsome?" asked Dorothy, intrigued.

"Wonderful!" Alice assured her. "You should come up to London for a long weekend. I'll introduce you!"

"That's an idea. When Dad's better, I'll take you up on that," said Dorothy.

They gossiped and Alice showed her sister her clothes, including a suit and frock in the New Look. Now that the war was long over, designers were taking advantage of being allowed to use more material and the New Look included long flowing skirts in contrast to the short, skimpy frocks of wartime.

"It's good to have you home," said Dorothy fondly.

"It's good to be here," said Alice.

Dorothy snuggled into bed with Marina, feeling at ease with life and looking forward to one of her favourite times of the year: Easter Day.

MAY 1950

Diana was staying with her parents to await the birth of her baby. Lydia enjoyed fussing over her daughter and Matthew liked having her about. Dorothy was lunching with them, and later they were going for a walk.

Lydia had been able to refurbish School House since the war, and the dark terracotta paint in the dining room had given way to Regency striped wallpaper and elegant red curtains. There was even a new carpet, a square of Axminster surrounded by polished floorboards. In the drawing room, armchairs had been re-covered, and chintz curtains framed the arched windows. It was, as ever, cosy and friendly, with vases of flowers, the smell of baking, or a meal cooking, pervading the polished house.

They sat around the dining table and Diana was telling Dorothy that her husband would be joining her at the weekend, when she suddenly stopped speaking and Dorothy knew from the expression on her face that she was having a contraction.

"Why oh why do babies always arrive in the middle of meals?" laughed Matthew.

"It's not exactly arriving, dear," responded Lydia.

"Shall I see if I can get hold of Jenny or Gillian?" offered Dorothy.

"We'll phone them," said Lydia.

Jenny was as busy as ever with her partner Sarah. Gillian, who now had a family of her own, worked in tandem with Penny, who was Scottish. It turned out to be Gillian and Penny on call.

"They'll be here directly, don't fret," said Lydia, reassuringly.

Diana was having contractions every ten minutes, and Matthew was glad to leave his womenfolk to get on by themselves. Lydia, efficient as ever, had the room prepared for the birth, with everything the midwives would need. Dorothy was overcome with excitement but Lydia remained calm and comforting.

"You make us all a nice cup of tea," Lydia told Dorothy when the nurses arrived.

"Looks like a fast one," said Gillian, when she had examined Diana. But she was wrong; the nurses left again at tea-time when nothing seemed to be happening. Then just as Matthew came in again at six o'clock, Diana's waters broke.

"He's waited for his Grandad!" joked Lydia.

"Haven't you had that baby yet, Diana?" teased her father.

"I'm trying, Dad, I'm trying."

At eight o'clock, Diana's husband, Donald arrived.

"I'm in time then?" he asked breathlessly, having run from his car.

"Plenty of time, son," chortled Matthew.

The midwives returned at ten o'clock, and it looked as if some progress was being made. Matthew and Donald drank brandy in 'fortification and celebration', as he explained to Lydia.

At ten minutes past midnight, Diana gave birth to a baby girl.

"May we call her 'Lydia', Mum?" asked Diana, moist-eyed afterwards.

"A bit complicated, dear, isn't it – two of us in the family?"

"Can't do better than having two Lydia's, as long as this one's as nice as the first," said Matthew, putting his arm around his wife.

They left the new mother to rest, and went downstairs to drink hot toddy's.

"Here's to both Lydia's, and Diana, the new Mother," said Matthew.

Dorothy went home with mixed feelings. Across the years, she had dealt with babies and children, but not until tonight had she ever felt envious. Perhaps it was that her friend Lydia was a grandmother, but then Lydia was seven years her senior. Maybe it was that, previously, Dorothy had thought there would be children for her one day. At thirty-eight, time was fast running out. It was strange; she had no children, Alice' chance had been taken from her, the same applied to Eddy, and it was only her brother Seth who had four children, and he was not with them, or his wife.

Such is life... she thought, as she walked home through the warm spring night.

+ + +

Chapter Six

AUTUMN 1950 – AUGUST 1952

Dorothy had popped in to see her Aunt Louise and Uncle Gordon, and was dismayed to find them both extremely depressed.

"Our Victoria and Alan are emigrating to Australia," explained Louise, and just saying it reduced her to tears again.

"I wouldn't mind, but it's so far away," she added, between gulps.

"They'll be back, dear," comforted Gordon.

"'Course they won't. It costs a fortune to come back. We'll never see them, or June and Joseph again."

Dorothy did not know what to say. What her aunt said was true, it did cost a great deal of money to return for a visit.

"When do they go?" enquired Dorothy.

"Two months. They had word yesterday," said Louise.

"I didn't know they'd applied," said Dorothy.

"We didn't say anything, hoping it wouldn't happen," said Louise.

"Will they sell up?" continued Dorothy.

"We'll sell for them and arrange the transfer of money. It takes six weeks by boat, you know," said her aunt.

"They're beginning to sell their furniture and belongings now," said Gordon. "By the time they're actually in Australia, it should be more or less complete."

Louise began weeping afresh.

"Don't take on so, Aunt Louise," said Dorothy. "You'll make yourself ill."

"They're making me ill," sobbed Louise.

"Don't say that, love. It's their lives, it's a great chance. All that sunshine – great for the children," comforted Gordon.

Dorothy stayed for a cup of tea, and thought privately that it was going to be a long two months, and that Aunt Louise would

211

only begin to get over it once they had gone. She vowed to visit her aunt and uncle often once Victoria, Alan and the children had departed. Gordon saw Dorothy out, and told her that there was to be a farewell party the weekend before the family left, at the end of October.

"We'll be there, Uncle Gordon," said Dorothy.

Seth and James were having a cup of tea in the living room when she arrived back at the cottage.

"What's all this shirking?" she joked.

"We've worked hard today, haven't we?" James told her.

"Oh yes. Getting along like a house on fire. James doing most of it, in fact."

"Sir Oberon's horses take us half a day a week," said James.

"I saw old Lady Moira in church last week, she's good for her age. Must be two years now since Sir Matthew went," said Dorothy.

"Sir Oberon says Mrs Howard is coming home for good," said James.

"Who is Mrs Howard?" asked Seth.

"Was Miss Fidelia, apparently. Anyway, it's his sister," clarified James.

"Uncle Bill knew them quite well, didn't he? Looked after Captain Julian years ago," said Dorothy.

"Looked after Mrs Howard too, if you believe the gossip," said James quietly, in an aside to Dorothy.

"James!" said Dorothy, shocked at her cousin.

"What's that?" Seth had become hard of hearing.

"Nothing, Dad. Nothing for you to worry about," said Dorothy, grinning at James.

"How're Gordon and Louise?" asked Seth.

"Very upset. Victoria and Alan leave for Australia the first week in November."

"What? That's terrible! Why are they going all that way?" he exploded.

"More sunshine?" quipped Dorothy.

"Ridiculous! Why people should want to leave this beautiful country, I don't know...."

"They say Australia is a beautiful country, Dad."

"But it's the other side of the world! These young people...."

"It isn't long since we sent people there as a punishment," said James.

"Quite right too," said Seth with finality.

"They're having a farewell party, last weekend in October. Will you come?" asked Dorothy.

"I'll say I'll come – to tell them how foolish they are," said her father.

James took his leave of them.

"See you tomorrow, Uncle Seth," he said.

"Right, lad. Tomorrow."

When he had gone Seth told Dorothy that it was the best thing he had done in years, to take on James.

"He's a nice lad, hard-working. And he's family," said Seth contentedly.

"That's good, Dad. I'm very pleased that you're happy." She kissed his head as she passed him and went out to the kitchen to start the supper.

OCTOBER 1950

Dorothy was standing in the butcher's department, at the back of the grocer's shop. 'Department' was too grand a word, for it was only a counter at the front of the abattoir. Graham was slicing bacon for her, and talking about the Harvest Supper Dance which they had been to with their grown-up daughters.

"You should've seen her, Dorothy. She looked a picture, and so did Judith."

"Did she meet a nice lad, and were there any suitable for me?" laughed Dorothy.

"Seems your family's sorted out already, Dorothy Hawkes, with that brother of yours and that Iris."

Molly Roberts stood behind Dorothy, her prim mouth fixed in a disapproving thin, straight line.

"Hello, Mrs Roberts. What's that you're saying?" asked Dorothy pleasantly.

"Your Seth. Disgraceful," she said adamantly.

"Oh yes?"

"He's got Iris Murchison living in the cottage with him at Briersham. Thinks he can get away with it now her mother's passed on."

"I don't believe that anything my brother does is your concern," stated Dorothy.

"You're as bad as he is, you cheeky monkey."

Dorothy decided to ignore the woman, and told Graham that she would collect her order later on. She was flushing deeply as she made her way through the grocers shop, calling goodbye to Rosalie and Rosamund.

When she got home, she said nothing to her father, and decided to allow her temper to cool before she went to Plumtree Cottage later that day. She had still been visiting every other day to clean, tidy and leave snacks for Seth. If what Mrs Roberts had said was true, he had been duping her.

Dorothy collected her bike from the shed and called in at the barn to tell Seth she was going to Briersham. As she rode along, she looked at the autumn countryside and was glad to live in Abbots Ford, even if there were inquisitive elderly ladies living there as well. She made herself a cup of tea at the cottage, and wandered from room to room. It had been her home until she was seventeen and reminded her of her mother more than Orchard Cottage did. She peeped into the downstairs bedroom which she and her sister shared. It was used as a storeroom these days, but she could remember the arguments and fun they had experienced there. She returned to the scullery and sat drinking her tea.

It was nearly half past five when Iris opened the scullery door and came in.

"Hello, Iris," said Dorothy.

Iris stopped in her tracks, shocked to find Seth's sister there.

"Surprised to see me?"

"Yes." Iris did not know what to do; she could not be sure how much Dorothy knew, but it was obviously strange that she should be letting herself in like this.

"I just came...."

"Don't try explaining anything. I know you live here now. How long?"

"Two weeks."

"Then why did Seth not say something?"

"He was scared."

"Of what?"

"Of you."

"Of me?" Dorothy was astounded.

"Yes, of you and your holier-than-thou ways."

Dorothy could not believe her ears.

"You always disapprove of everybody. Just because you're a dried up old maid."

Dorothy had not meant this meeting to be confrontational, and she did not understand why Iris should be so bitter. She was too shocked to respond.

"You're the reason we haven't got together sooner."

Dorothy must have looked surprised, for she carried on.

"Don't look so stunned. Seth told me how you were always nagging him not to see me, and how you'd make sure his Dad took this cottage away from him."

None of this was true but Dorothy did not want to become embroiled in a row. She gathered her things and dashed out to her bike, cycling as fast as she could back to Abbots Ford. What would she do when she saw Seth? The hateful, nasty toad!

She still said nothing to her father, because she did not want to anger him. She knew that she would have to break the news to him soon, before anyone else in the village mentioned it. In the meantime, she needed to recover from her meeting with Iris, and decide what she would say to Seth the next time she saw him.

Dorothy was working in the kitchen when there was loud knocking at the door of Orchard Cottage. It was Dr Blake.

"Hello!" She was not expecting a visit to her father, and was surprised to see him.

"Dorothy, sorry to call in like this. I said I would. There's some very bad news. Your Aunt Jessica has died suddenly of a brain haemorrhage. Bill is in a bad way. I know you've your father to care for, but young Louise and John are so shocked that they're not much help at the minute. Can you go up there soon?" He carried on talking, initially to impart the information; but also because he was allowing Dorothy time to take it in. She went to sit down.

"Oh dear Lord," was all she could say. "What do I do, Dr Blake?"

"You get yourself along to Peartree Farm and I'll break the news to your father. Is he outside working in the barn?"

"Yes."

"Go along then, off you go. I'll tell him you've gone up there."

Dorothy pulled herself together, and collected her coat and hat.

"Will you tell my father I'll be back in time for supper?" she asked.

"Yes, and I'll break it to him gently. Is James still here?"

"Yes."

"Good. See you later."

Dorothy's mind was in a whirl of confusion as she walked up Church Lane. Poor Uncle Bill! Aunt Jessica was only fifty-four; that was not old.

She let herself into the kitchen at the farm house. Bill was sitting at the table looking into space.

"I'm so sorry, Uncle Bill, so sorry," said Dorothy, going to him, touching him on the shoulder.

"Don't know why…" he murmured, obviously still shocked.

Young Louise and John were sitting in the living room talking quietly.

"Dorothy, I'm so pleased to see you," said Louise.

"I'm so sorry about your poor Mum," Dorothy told them. "Where…?" she began.

"Dr Blake arranged to have her taken to a place at Steeple Burstead."

"Have you eaten?" asked Dorothy.

"No – we didn't want to."

"I'll make something light. Even if you have a few mouthfuls…."

There was a knock at the door, and a neighbour called in shocked at the news. There was not much response from Bill and Dorothy spoke with them, accepting their condolences on behalf of the family.

At eight o'clock that evening, Will and his wife, Polly, arrived. Their two small children were safely in bed, too young to take in that one of their grandma's had passed away, but in the safe care of the other. Will wept against his father's shoulder, while Polly stood crying silently. Dorothy moved efficiently among them, making drinks which were not drunk, and snacks which were not eaten.

"She was young to go, Dad," said Will, brokenly.

"She didn't suffer," said Polly.

"When are we going to tell Grandad Powers?" asked John.

Jessica's father still lived up the road.

"Tomorrow, son. Early tomorrow," replied Bill. It was the first thing he had said all evening, and demonstrated that he was beginning to take it in, and how the news was going to affect other people.

Before she left that night, Dorothy spoke privately to Will.

"Your Anne will have to be told. Shall I telephone Alice at the hospital tomorrow, and she can break the news?"

"Yes. Thanks Dorothy. That's a good idea," said Will gratefully.

"Then it's up to her what she decides, isn't it?"

"Yes."

She was glad to leave the house, so clothed in grief. Dorothy had always liked Aunt Jessica, and was desperately sad; but not being a partner, son or daughter, or even a sibling, she did not feel the all consuming loss which those people felt that night.

Her father was full of questions when she returned.

"When did it happen, girl?"

"This afternoon, Dad. Luckily Louise was at home with her because she'd felt so bad."

"And she went, just like that?"

"Yes. Lost consciousness, and was gone by the time the doctor got there."

"Shock for them all."

"Yes. Uncle Bill hardly knows what he's doing and the others are wandering around in a daze."

"When's the funeral?"

It was rare for Dorothy to lose her temper, especially with her father, but she came close to it now, after the afternoon and evening she had experienced.

"Oh, Dad, I don't know, it wasn't discussed," she snapped, with a suspicion that her father's questions were puerile. He did not ask any more and they ate their late meal in silence.

Eddy took in the news of his aunt's death without comment.

Dorothy felt frustrated. Why did these menfolk never seem to take anything seriously? Sure enough, they were devastated when someone really close died; but it had to be a wife or a mother, someone they relied upon absolutely. Could they not put themselves in another's place for a moment, and imagine how those people felt? They asked silly questions, or there was no reaction whatever!

Dorothy was tired and emotionally drained, or she would have had the patience to understand that her father and brother felt helpless at other's loss. They were not expected to offer succour, or to cook meals, or to be capable of running other's lives for a short time, while they grieved. So they got on with their own lives as best they could, while everything changed around them; coping with the echoes of their own griefs, which were so deep that they were never far away.

"Poor Bill," said Seth quietly.

"Aye, and poor children," said Eddy.

Dorothy went about the business of clearing away their meal.

+ + +

It was one of life's foibles: the timing of Jessica's death meant that the farewell party for Louise and Gordon's daughter, Victoria, took place before the funeral; so it became a low-key affair. Louise had never looked upon it as a celebration in any case, more of a wake, which in the present circumstances, was curiously apt.

Everyone knew that the family had suffered a recent bereavement and as most were sad to bid Victoria, Alan and their children goodbye, it was a muted gathering that last Saturday in October, and they were leaving on Tuesday.

Helen had brought the children from Bristol to say farewell to their second-cousins, and they were looking forward to seeing all their relatives. People were dotted about the cosy lounge, and Louise and her brother, Bill, sat commiserating each with the other on a sofa.

The doors were closed on this chilly late autumn day, so that when someone knocked, Emma, Louise' elder daughter, answered. At first she did not recognise the woman standing there.

"I'm Anne. Your cousin Anne."

Emma was completely nonplussed, so Anne continued:

"I understand my family are all here because your sister is off to Australia soon?"

"Yes – oh yes. Come in." Emma's mind was racing. *How many years was it, since Anne had left? She remembered Anne's falling in love with Joshua and how she had never forgiven her father for parting them, and blaming him utterly! She and Anne had become good friends, but Anne had turned her back on Abbots Ford.* Emma led the way.

"Mum, Uncle Bill, look who's here!"

Louise looked up and her mouth dropped open. Bill took seconds longer to take in who stood before him. Before he could speak, Will called out.

"Anne!"

Her sister Louise and other brother John crowded round kissing her, hugging and asking questions all at the same time. Other members of the family joined the group, welcoming her. Bill stood up. He had not seen his eldest daughter for thirteen years, when she had left without saying goodbye. Jessica had never understood the bitterness Anne had felt towards her father; indeed neither had Bill himself. Anne had not known that though her father was instrumental in having her lover, Joshua, sent away, he had not been the one to do the deed. Neither did she know the cast-iron reason why it had been necessary.

Bill looked at her. She was the image of her mother at the same age. Anne gazed at her father, while all around them people still uttered cries of greeting and pleasure. He had aged; not just the last thirteen years, but in the past three days. She knew that instinctively. His hair was grey and his eyes were dull and sunken from grief and lack of sleep.

"Daddy," she called him by her girlhood's name. "I'm so sorry."

They embraced and wept, but such was the emotion of the occasion that nobody minded. The words said everything. 'Sorry' for her mother's death, the wasted years, not explaining. Anne had her own grief and regret to confront, but at this time, it was what the family needed: to be almost whole again.

Victoria was glad that something had diverted her mother's attention from her imminent departure. She did not know that fate held yet another diversion for them all.

Helen and her children were enjoying the afternoon because it was some time since they had visited the village, even though Helen's own family also lived there. Nobody had given a thought to whether Seth might put in an appearance at the family gathering, because he was a law unto himself. Everyone was surprised, therefore, when he not only arrived not long after Anne, but had with him his lover, Iris. He talked with his cousin, Victoria, about the adventure she was embarking upon and started to make his way round the room.

"Dad!" Edgar was pleased to see his father.

The other children went to him and talked nineteen to the dozen and all at the same time. Seth laughed.

"Hold on, one at a time." He swung young Flora up and turned to Iris.

"You know our Flora, Iris, don't you?"

"How dare you? How dare you introduce our daughter to your – your, tart!" Helen shouted.

Dorothy went over and spoke quietly, firmly, "Helen", but she was too late. Helen had reached out and brought a stinging slap across Iris' face.

"Just a minute..." pleaded Seth.

"What did you expect, Seth? That we would all be one big happy family?" demanded Helen.

Seth the elder had walked slowly over to them, with the aid of his stick.

"That's enough. You're in someone else's house. Seth, take this woman away. She doesn't belong here. This is a family occasion."

Seth could do nothing but obey his father. Without a word, he took Iris' hand and stalked out.

"Well, Mum," said Victoria quietly in her mother's ear, "you won't have time to cry when we're gone, because you'll be so busy with all the gossip."

NOVEMBER 1950

The funeral for Jessica was the day after Louise and Gordon's daughter had left the country. The weather was cold, wet and dismal, for the rain did not cease. They no longer used a horse and carriage, and a sleek black limousine, the like of which she had never ridden in life, carried Jessica to her last resting place.

Douglas Glover conducted the service and the church was crowded with family, friends and neighbours. All his children supported Bill; both his daughters, Anne and Louise and daughter-in-law, Polly, were there for him. His sons, Will and John, wore their best suits and black ties. *Jessica would have been proud of them all* he thought to himself. Dorothy, Louise and the girls had worked together to provide the food for the wake.

The house did not seem the same to Bill without his wife. He could not settle. In the middle of proceedings, with his home full of people, he went off out, up the hill. Will and Anne followed at a distance. The weather was so foul and the day drawing in so early, it was best they follow him, especially as he had not worn a coat. Brother and sister talked as they went, filling in the lost years, Will telling about their mother's last few days.

"Did she mention me?" asked Anne.

"Always mentioning you," he smiled. "They're proud of you," he added.

221

They reached the top of the hill and caught up with their father.

"Here, Dad, put these on," said Will, helping him into the coat and giving him a hat.

"She loved it up here," said Bill, looking out into the darkening mist of rain. "Can't believe she won't come up here ever again." His voice broke and they clung together, in the misery of grief that is the world, when someone that you love is gone.

SPRING 1951

Alice could not make up her mind whether to go home for Easter or not. Marina was going to stay with Dorothy, and once again, travelling alone by coach. Sue, her mother, put her on at Victoria, usually asking a kindly lady to keep an eye on her, and Dorothy met her in Bristol. If Alice decided to go, they could travel together by train, which halved the journey time. It took five or six hours by road and only two and a half on the train. Alice had not been home since Easter last year because she was still in love with Mr Andrew Hoggart, Consultant Orthopaedic Surgeon at St Mary's Hospital, where she was a Nursing Sister. She was seeing him tonight, and needed to make up her mind about Easter, so that they could make arrangements for the holiday if she decided against going home. *No, I can't be bothered* she thought. Dorothy had said that Seth was much better than he had been, and although it would have been enjoyable to visit Abbots Ford, she would much rather spend time with Andrew – if he could get away. His wife, Alexandra, insisted he be around when their children were home from boarding school for the holidays. So the time they could snatch together was precious, especially at this time of the year.

Alice hummed as she went about the flat, dusting and tidying. She was not by nature tidy, but Andrew complained if it was too chaotic when he came. She watered her window-boxes, and encouraged the spring flowers which were just appearing, with a kind word or two.

They were going to a little local restaurant for a meal because Alice was not a good cook. She looked at herself in the mirror. "Not bad for getting on for forty-one," she told her reflection. Her hair still looked the same dark-honey colour, though it sported the odd grey one here and there. Her pale blue eyes looked out on the world as glacially as ever, but the years had endowed them with more expression than before. She rouged her high cheek bones and applied lipstick, something she did not do on her visits home where it was still frowned upon and considered 'fast'.

The doorbell rang and she went down to let him in. They kissed, briefly, because of her make-up and she led the way upstairs.

"Do you want an aperitif?" she asked.

"Yes. I'm exhausted. Busy clinic," he answered.

She poured him a gin and tonic and herself a whiskey with soda.

"Cure anybody?"

"No, but didn't kill anyone today, either," he laughed.

"Was that bitch McDonald on duty in out patients?"

He nodded, gulping his drink.

"Was she still after your body?"

He nodded again.

"I don't know how your wife lets you out when you're so devastatingly attractive to women," she commented, deadpan. She always called her 'your wife', never Alexandra or Alex, as he did.

"Those idiots in radiology have fouled things up again," he said dispiritedly.

"I thought we agreed not to talk shop," said Alice.

"You're the only one who understands," he said.

"Talk away then."

He followed her into the bedroom with his drink, explaining about lack of clarity if radiologists were less than careful, and how it affected diagnosis.

"Come on, I'm ready."

They arrived at the Bistro in Notting Hill Gate and sat at a side table. The candles were lit and the décor dark and sensuous. Wonderful aromas wafted through and they chatted while they looked at the menu.

"Are you ready to order, M'sieur-dame?" asked the waiter.

They agreed they were and Andrew ordered for them both.

They began with the fish soup, followed with steak and had seasonable vegetables. When they had almost finished the second course, Andrew looked serious.

"I've had a job offer abroad," he told her.

"Are you taking it?"

"Alex doesn't even know about it yet."

"What about your family?"

"Doesn't matter – you know they're always away at school through the term. Where they go in the holidays hardly matters to them."

"Where is the offer?"

"America"

She caught her breath sharply.

"Does it matter to you?" he asked.

"What a bloody silly question, of course it matters. I love you," she answered.

"I'm talking to them at home over Easter. I'm worried about my parents," he told her.

"How do you mean?"

"Well, they're elderly, and if the job went well, it's a question of virtually emigrating there."

She did not say, *What about us?* She knew, had always known, how ambitious he was. A mere love affair would not keep him in England. She lightened the mood by telling him amusing things about patients and their colleagues, including all the gossip.

"Are we part of the jungle telegraph yet?" he asked.

"No, I've been very discreet," she told him smugly.

They ate a dessert, had coffee and paid the bill. Andrew hailed a taxi, although it was not far back to the flat.

She poured him a brandy after helping him out of his jacket.

"If I don't do it now, I'll be too old," he told her, returning to the theme of their earlier conversation.

"I'm forty-five in two months."

"You don't look it," she told him, massaging the knots of muscle around his shoulders.

"They want someone my age, but as I say, I won't get the chance again."

She leant across the back of the chair, massaging his shoulders and chest. He pulled her head round to kiss her on the mouth.

"Come to bed," he murmured.

They got into bed naked and spent a long time caressing one another. He was an expert lover, and when they had first made love, she had asked him if this was so because of his knowledge of physiology, or because of practice. He had laughed out loud, but had not graced what he had thought of as a ridiculous rhetorical question, with an answer. He still slept with his wife, but said he needed her, Alice, also. He liked the fact that she was independent of spirit, and was not aiming at marriage, nor nagging him to leave his wife and family. He took her out to meals, the theatre occasionally, bought her expensive jewellery and clothes, and she was satisfied. They lay smoking cigarettes afterwards, not speaking. It never occurred to either of them that each was using the other, especially as they genuinely liked one another, and the other's company.

"I'll have to go, it's getting late," he said, getting up and starting to dress.

"I'll wait to hear from you," she said, knowing the form.

He leant over to kiss her before he left.

"Stay there, you look comfortable," he told her.

She lay for a while after he had gone, allowing her thoughts to run. *Yes I shall go home for Easter,* she thought. *I need to see them all.* She decided that she would arrange it the next day, and slept soundly that night.

EASTER 1951

"Well, this is nice," said Seth. "All of you here together for once."

It was Easter Saturday, at tea-time. Marina had gone out with Lydia and Matthew and Seth was at the cottage without Iris. Dorothy poured the tea and Alice passed sandwiches round.

"How's London?" asked Seth, her brother.

"Much the same. Everyone is full of The Festival of Britain."

"Yes, there's a coach trip going up for a visit," said Dorothy.

"They'll be too exhausted to go round the Exhibition by the time they get there," said Eddy sourly.

"You haven't been to see Helen and the children lately," commented Seth. "Any reason?"

"Busy," said Eddy shortly.

Dorothy and Alice began talking animatedly, sensing unease between their brothers. Dorothy had been aware that something was wrong, because it was a long time since Eddy had gone to see Helen in Bristol. She could trace it back to the strange period Eddy had experienced last year, but was, as yet, unaware of its cause.

"You're looking better, Dad," Seth told his father. "Work going alright?"

"Yes. James is a good lad. I only work a few hours in the middle of the day now."

"How's Uncle Bill?" asked Alice.

"Not himself, but at least Anne comes home regularly now," said Dorothy.

"Who is running the house?"

"Louise, of course. She's still working at the shop and I don't know how she manages. She's been going out with that Barry Harris for three years now and they seem serious. Maybe she'll marry and then what will happen?"

"Uncle Bill and John will have to look after themselves, or get a housekeeper," said Alice.

Alice asked about Charles and Amy.

"Nobody sees them these days. They went to live together in Bath three or four years ago, and I haven't seen them since," Dorothy told her.

"Bad do, that" muttered their father. "Never saw a man so different from his father as Charles Henty. It's that dreadful mother of his."

"Is she still about?" asked Alice.

"Yes, and that horrible husband of hers. He's a nasty piece of work," put in young Seth.

Lydia came back with Marina, and Eddy and Seth teased her for her curled hair.

"Looks as if she's had a fright, does Lucy," crowed Seth.

"Leave the girl alone – it's the fashion for young ladies such as she," said Grandad Seth.

"How are you, Lydia?" enquired Alice, thinking privately that she did not look well.

"I'm alright, dear, thank you," responded Lydia, in her cheerful way. She did not stay for a cup of tea, because she had Diana and her little girl staying and wanted to return home.

"Lydia is a lovely baby," Marina told them, of Lydia's ten-month-old granddaughter. "She was laughing when we tickled her."

"I remember you when you were a baby," Alice told her.

Seth searched out a bar of chocolate for Marina, who sat looking at a photograph album until bedtime.

Seth and his brother went off to the Partridge Inn, while Dorothy and Alice played 'Beat Jack out of Doors' with Marina once she was ready for bed. Since her last visit her mother had had another baby, a brother for Marina, of whom she was inordinately proud.

"His name is Hamish," she told them.

"And does he make a lot of noise?" asked Dorothy.

"Well, he is only small, and can't speak yet," replied the little girl.

It was definitely time for bed now, and Alice said goodnight, before Dorothy took her up.

"God bless Grandad Seth, Uncle Seth, Uncle Eddy, Auntie Alice and Aunt Dorothy," she added, after saying prayers for her parents, grandparents and new baby brother.

"It's been a lovely day, Aunt Dorothy," she said as Dorothy tucked the sheets into the full softness of the mattress.

"That's good, dear. Easter Day tomorrow!"

Dorothy went downstairs with the wonderful, secure feeling she always had when little Marina was staying. She looked forward to a gossip with her sister. *There are none like family*, she thought as she went down the steep stairs, *even if some of them are very odd.*

LATE SUMMER 1951

As the summer progressed, so did Lydia's illness. She attended hospital in Bristol two or three times, and each time Dorothy went with her. On the last visit, Matthew drove them, saying that as school had broken up for the summer holidays, he was free to go. The truth was that he knew that the journey would leech all her strength. They were jovial as they sped through the lush countryside towards the city. Lydia was as amusing as ever, and as they had seen a great deal of Diana and baby Lydia she would talk endlessly about the child's latest attainments.

The doctors did their best, but eventually, it became clear that Lydia would not recover. The couple both had reserves of strength to call upon: a strong belief in God, a good marriage and family, and a hardworking life had given them both more than they felt they deserved. Nothing was said between Dorothy and Lydia, or even between Lydia and her children, as far as Dorothy knew. She assumed that Matthew and Lydia had discussed her prognosis, and the effect upon them.

By the end of August, Lydia was too weak to look after her home and cook for Matthew. Dorothy helped as much as she could; at least Iris now took care of Seth and Plumtree Cottage. Vera was at her parents' home for the school holidays now that her mother was ill. Dorothy and Lydia sat in the shade of the sycamore trees in the garden of School House. The roses still bloomed and geraniums and Busy Lizzies were rioting in the flowerbeds.

"I feel so lucky to be able to sit in the peace and tranquillity of this garden," observed Lydia.

"You've worked hard to make it this lovely," said Dorothy.

"I have good family and friends," continued Lydia, ignoring the compliment.

"Nothing more than you deserve, you're a good friend to everyone."

"I worry about them, Dorothy. They'll need good friends."

Dorothy was too moved to say anything. She understood what her friend meant, the message she was imparting.

"I hope you won't desert them," went on Lydia.

"No," said Dorothy, struggling to maintain control.

The nurses began to help Dorothy with bathing and caring for Lydia when she could no longer do those things herself. Lydia told Dorothy how glad she was that the school term had begun, because Matthew needed to concentrate on something other than her decline. Lydia's children spent more and more time with her, just sitting and talking to her, or reading, or listening to the wireless with her, if the pain was not too bad. Dorothy felt privileged to be able to help her friend and demonstrated endless patience and love in her dealings with her. Even being gently washed became a torture for Lydia, and Dorothy devised ways to try to diffuse the pain; playing her favourite music, using scented water, warmed towels, telling her all the gossip if she was well enough.

AUTUMN 1951

Dorothy was included in every family gathering. She gradually became closer than ever to Diana and Vera, who grew to rely upon her. Matthew remained a law unto himself, becoming more bluff than usual, to conceal how heartbroken he was. Lydia had had a good day that last Saturday; the pain lessened, and she felt well enough to sit in a chair. Diana and Donald, with baby Lydia, Simon, Theresa and Vera were all there to lunch, which Dorothy cooked. The baby toddled about the room, speaking her own special language and giving great pleasure to her grandparents. They had always been a family which was happy to spend time together and this was a special time. No one betrayed the experience by showing sadness, and there was much joking and laughter. At teatime, Lydia felt tired and Vera and Diana helped her to her bed. Dorothy sat with her until she slept and then went home.

When Dorothy called in before church next morning, a dry-eyed Matthew told her that his wife had passed away during the night. Dorothy wept, and Matthew continued,

"The children are on their way." He was distracted, in keeping busy, though doing everything automatically.

"Is there anything I can do?" asked Dorothy.

"Have you time to make lunch for us?" he asked.

"Yes, yes. I'll go back home and prepare something simple for Dad and Eddy and return to do something for you people."

"Thanks Dorothy."

None of them felt able to attend the service that morning, and word went round that the headmaster's wife had died, at only fifty. Other close friends called by to see if they could be of help, and Matthew had to tell them he had not had time to think, and could they call again in the coming days?

Jenny and Gillian called in to lay Lydia out, for she was still in her room at School House. No one could eat the lunch Dorothy had prepared, but they sat around the table anyway. They talked of inconsequential things and Matthew could not tell of their mother's last hours in a cohesive way, but informed them in short vignettes.

"She was very proud of you all. You were her life."

His headmasterly directness saw him through.

"She loved you, how she loved you. And little Lydia."

His daughters and daughter-in-law were weeping.

"She told me how proud she was that another little 'Lydia' would carry the torch for her now."

"Father, don't," said Simon. It was too much, too soon, for him.

Dorothy had been pottering between them in the dining room and the kitchen, trying to help, but keeping out of family grief. She took them a pot of coffee, and Diana gratefully allowed her to take young Lydia out into the garden. So the family grieved for their wife and mother alone. Tears ran silently down Dorothy's face as she held the tiny child's hand and walked beneath the autumn sycamore, where she and her friend had sat, only a few weeks ago. She had many friends in the village, but Lydia had been special to everyone. She had been one of those people, without side or malice, who lit up others' lives when she touched theirs. How would her family go on without her? In the depths of their grief, they could not know that the gift which Lydia had endowed to them, was that her love, in life, had made them so strong that they would weather this tragedy and move on in time to be grateful for having known her and with memories to warm their hearts whenever they thought of her.

+ + +

Alice was visiting the Festival of Britain during the last week of the exhibition. She and a colleague from the hospital were astonished by the displays and technology on show, and the size of the spectacle. Their feet were sore and they complained to one another of the lack of seating.

"They want to keep people on the move, they don't want us sitting down to rest," said Pauline, her friend.

"Well, if I don't sit down and rest, I shan't be able to keep on the move," said Alice laconically. "Let's have some lunch."

They found a restaurant and were lucky to secure a table. Alice was elegantly but comfortably dressed in a suit with a gored skirt. It was russet tweed with a brown velvet collar, and she wore a small brown velvet beret to set it off, on her honey hair. They sat, laughing and relieved to rest their feet.

"What shall we have?" asked Pauline.

"Nothing too much," said Alice, "or we'll never be able to continue touring the exhibition."

They gossiped and looked around at the other people there. Folk had travelled from all over the country for the occasion, and Alice thought she could pick out those who were not Londoners.

"Don't be unkind," chastised Pauline. "After all, you're not really a Londoner yourself."

"What! After over twenty years?" she said, indignantly.

"You still speak with a Somerset burr."

"Yes, but in spirit I'm a Londoner," she insisted.

They were ordering their meal when she caught sight of him. She had not seen him for a month or six weeks. They had not quarrelled, but he was still trying to persuade his wife to go with him to America, and had considered it advisable to spend as much time as possible with her. He was at his most attractive, laughing and attentive. They had all four children with them, obviously still at home at the end of the holidays. He had always avoided describing his wife to her. When Alice had asked if she was attractive; all he had said was, 'She's alright, a typical housewife'. Alexandra was beautiful. She had a perfect oval face and her blonde hair was carefully permed in the fashion of the day and made a halo around her head. She wore discreet but flattering make-up, and a chic tan Princess line coat. The children were equally attractive, their ages ranging from twelve down to four. They were all fair-haired and blue-eyed, and sat enjoying their meal, used to eating in restaurants. Alice' eyes flicked down to the menu. Pauline did not know of her affair with Mr Hoggart, so she could not allow her dismay to show. She looked over at the family surreptitiously and carried on speaking to her friend. Suddenly, Andrew caught her eye and they both looked away at once. She could not bring herself to look at him again, and, fighting a feeling of nausea, she picked at the meal she had ordered. Pauline chivvied her.

"Eat up. You need all your strength for the rest of the tour."

Alice was sick at heart. How could he? With a beautiful wife, and a family like that? How could he have made her feel so beautiful, so worthy?

"I don't feel well," she told Pauline. "I think I'm going to have to go to the 'Ladies'."

When she returned, they had gone. She realised that while she had never mentioned it to him, secretly she had harboured hopes that, one day, he might want only her. Now she knew that Alexandra and the children were an important part of his life, and saw with crystal clarity, where she herself fitted in.

"I really am going to have to leave," she told Pauline. "You stay on here, don't waste the opportunity. I'll take a taxi home."

"If you're sure... by the way... while you were gone, Mr Hoggart and his family stopped by to say 'Hello'. Such a lovely girl, Mrs Hoggart. He's a lucky man, but then he's dishy too!"

Alice thought she would vomit over the table and Pauline.

"You look a bit green," Pauline told her.

"See you tomorrow at the hospital," said Alice, and, as fast as she decently could, made her way to one of the exits and hailed a cab. On the way home she felt numb, too numb to cry. She sat huddled in the corner of the seat, peering out as London rushed by, then stopped as the cab became snarled up in traffic.

"Busy time this," commented the taxi-driver. "The Festival has brought out the tourists," he added. He did not appear to notice that she had not replied, and carried on with a running commentary on the journey, road conditions and life in general.

Alice was never more glad to see Portobello Road. She paid the driver, tipping him moderately, and stumbled up the stairs to her flat.

Will I never learn? she thought, as she lay on her bed looking at the ceiling. *What is it about me? Why am I so self-destructive?* "Why can't I find a nice man of my own?" she said out loud.

The telephone broke the silence, shrillingly. It was Dorothy, who was distraught.

"Lydia Ashton died in the early hours of yesterday morning," she told her. "Isn't life unfair?"

"Yes, it bloody-well is," said her sister. "Yes, it bloody-well is."

SPRING 1952

The country had been deeply saddened by the death of King George VI at the age of fifty-six. The strain of unexpected kingship leading him to the country's helm during the traumatic time of the Second World War was thought to have shortened his life. His Queen did not retire, but remained, to become a valuable national asset and support for the new young Queen Elizabeth II, her elder daughter. Some people from the village had travelled up to the capital, to witness the lying-in-state of the King, queuing for hours to stream past the catafalque in Westminster Hall which bore the coffin.

Charles Henty was visiting his mother, Beatrice, who had recently been unwell. Robert and Rebecca's Amy was still living with him in Bath, to everyone's surprise. Not long after they arrived in Abbots Ford, Charles was called back to Bath on business, and because they had intended staying for a few days, he left Amy behind. He had found a niche for himself in antiques, and although living in Bath, travelled the country regularly in search of bargains and treasures. On his return to the village, he was travelling far too fast, as usual, and in avoiding a tractor being driven by Robert's grandson, Matthew Davis, crashed into a tree and was killed instantly.

People in the village attended the funeral out of respect for Charles Henty's brave father, killed in World War I and the Henty family. Beatrice was prostrate, and Amy pathetic in her grief. Both women had had to be supported at the internment, such was their emotional state.

Neither of Amy's parents could bring themselves to attend and support her, but she went to see them the day afterwards. A strained atmosphere prevailed at their cottage; it had been a long time since they had spoken.

"I am sorry about the accident," began Rebecca.

"Mum, Dad, Charles and I were married last Christmas Eve," she blurted out, before anything more could be said.

Rebecca began to cry, and Amy could not be sure whether through happiness or grief.

"We're glad about that much anyway," said her father gruffly.

"And I want to tell you that I am three months pregnant."

Rebecca gasped, and Robert stared at his daughter.

"You're spawning his young 'un?" he asked.

"Yes," she answered defiantly.

"I hope you're taking good care of yourself," said her mother, who had herself experienced late pregnancy and childbirth.

Robert got up and went out abruptly, as if he could no longer contain his feelings.

"Yes, Mother, I am."

"Does his mother know?"

"Yes, she and Derek were at the wedding and we told her about the baby when we arrived. Charles was as pleased as Punch." She began to cry.

"You'll have to try to get over it, dear, for the sake of the child. You'll make yourself ill," her mother told her.

"I loved him so much, Mum," cried her daughter. "He wasn't how Dad thought he was."

"Demons got to that boy at times," said Rebecca, cradling her daughter's shoulders. Amy sobbed, and Rebecca comforted her. *At least she's come home,* thought her mother. *She'll need us now she's expecting his child.*

Robert paced the garden, metaphorically shaking his fist at the gods.

"There is no justice in heaven or on earth," he muttered. "No justice that forces me to share a grandchild with that Jezebel."

SUMMER 1952

The telephone rang at Peartree Farm House, and Louise answered.

"I'm afraid he isn't here just now. Can I take a message?" she said. She wrote a name on the pad, and turned to her fiancé.

"Someone for Dad, that Fidelia Howard at Salisbury House."

"Come and sit with me," suggested Barry.

"Are you sure you want to move in with Dad and John?" she asked.

"If we live somewhere else, we know what'll happen. You'll be running backwards and forwards, doing everything in both households. I want to see something of my wife once we're married."

"Dad says we'll redecorate, and choose the wallpaper by ourselves, if we want."

"We'll take it as it comes. Plenty of time," he said, kissing her.

They were to be married on a Saturday in August and everything was in hand. The reception was going to take place at the village hall after the wedding at St Mary's. Barry was dark haired, cheekily handsome with laughing grey eyes and was of medium height. He continued to work as an electrician, travelling about in his van.

They listened to music, and her brother John came in and talked for a while before his preparations to go out for the evening. He was a charming young man of twenty-two, who had been a tower of strength to his father, Bill, and sisters, since their mother's death.

Shortly after he left, Bill himself came in.

"There's a message for you on the telephone pad," she informed him. He went to look, and they could hear him dialling a number.

"Hello, could I speak to Fidelia."

"Speaking"

"It's Bill. You left a message to ring you."

"Hello, Bill. How are you? I was terribly sorry to hear about Jessica."

"Yes. I miss her. What can I do for you?"

"Can you come for a meal one evening?"

"Yes," he replied.

They arranged a mutually convenient time and Bill rang off, wondering why she had got in touch with him.

He soon found out. They were sitting in the dining room at Salisbury House, alone. Nothing seemed to have changed since he had last been there, all those years ago. Another lifetime.... Fiddy looked both elfin and elegant, despite her age. Her hair had faded to an attractive sandy-blonde colour, and she still favoured floaty material, except that the cut was different in accordance with the present day fashion. A simple diamond sparkled on each earlobe, and she was her most charming. They talked of family matters, Fiddy asking about Louise and John.

"Isn't Louise marrying later in the year?"

"Yes. Nice enough chap. Barry Harris," said Bill.

"And what about Anne? Do you see her?" enquired Fiddy.

"She came home when her mother died. First time in years," he said.

"Did you ever explain anything?"

"No. She thought I had arranged for Joshua's banishment."

"He's coming back. Visiting Salisbury House. With his wife and two children," she stated, hard voiced.

"Don't you like her?" he asked.

"Not really, but then I haven't seen a lot of them."

"Why are you telling me this?"

"He says he wants to see Anne. I thought I ought to warn you."

"Thank you."

"I thought too, that it was time we enjoyed a meal together, if only for old times' sake," she smiled.

Her smile still had the power to melt his heart, and he told her so. Later in the evening, Lady Moira joined them for coffee.

"How are you, Bill?" she enquired fondly. "Julian sends his regards."

"Thank you, Lady Moira. I have many happy memories of my time here with him."

When she retired for the night, they spoke again of their son.

"We'll have to stop him contacting her," said Fiddy.

"Shouldn't be difficult."

"He's found out where she's working in London, it doesn't have to be in Abbots Ford."

"What are we to do?"

"Maybe you'll have to tell Anne after all."

"No, I couldn't. Never," he said firmly.

"See how it develops. If John gets in touch with her, you'll have to......."

He took his leave of her, thanking her for a pleasant evening.

"We must do it again," she said, kissing him lightly on the cheek.

"Drive home carefully," she called, as he closed the car door.

She watched as his car disappeared down the gravel drive, and turned right towards the village, and home.

+ + +

It was a while since Matthew Ashton had had all his family together; Christmas, in fact. Dorothy had called in to share part of the special day with them, but it had not been the same. They all missed Lydia too much, and Dorothy had made her excuses and left after speaking to them all, finding out how they were, and playing with little Lydia.

Matthew had someone in to do the house four times a week, and on those days she cooked him a meal. His family invited him to their homes on Sundays, or they all met at School House and the girls took over the cooking. On the odd occasions when his meals were not organised, Dorothy took something round to him. One Thursday when she went round, Matthew told her he was having them all over that Sunday.

"Would you join us?" he asked her.

"Yes, I'd like that," Dorothy told him.

"You won't have to cook, the girls will do it," he explained.

"I don't mind helping," she told him.

"I know that, Dorothy, but I want you to have a meal you haven't had to prepare."

"Lydia used to say that," she mused.

They smiled, remembering.

The lunch was enjoyable, and there was good news. Simon's Theresa was expecting a baby at Christmas, and Diana was pregnant again. They celebrated, and agreed that Lydia would have relished their news. They liked talking about her; how she would have reacted, what she might have said.......

After tea, Simon and Theresa had to go home. They waved them off, promising to meet up again soon. Gradually, the others left until there was only Matthew and Dorothy left.

"Would you like a cup of coffee?" asked Matthew casually.

"Yes, why not?" smiled Dorothy. "I'm in no particular rush to get home."

They sat talking about the coming events; Dorothy was as excited as if it were her own family. They talked about Lydia as they had not before, either to one another or to anyone else. It was late when she returned home, and he kissed her on the cheek when he left her outside Orchard Cottage.

"Thank you for coming, I've enjoyed it," he told her.

"Goodnight, Matthew," she replied, comforted for having had the opportunity of talking about Lydia with someone else who loved her.

AUGUST 1952

Louise had had her dress made by the workroom in Bath, having designed it herself. It was cream brocade, with a 'sweetheart' neckline, and cut on the cross so that it flowed smoothly over her slim waist and hips. She wore a lace veil, loaned by Barry's grandmother, held in place by a small marcasite tiara, lent by Barry's aunt. Bill wiped his eyes when he saw her, and again when he saw Anne in a rose-pink version of the bride's dress. Louise and Flora Hawkes and Will's daughters May and Janet, wore cream frocks with rose pink sashes.

Dorothy went along to help them dress, and to calm her Uncle Bill's nerves. Alice was home for the wedding, and she chivvied her father and Eddy. Fidelia Howard was in St Mary's for the service, and she smiled at Bill as proudly he walked up the aisle with his younger daughter. Fiddy was intrigued about Anne. The affair between her son, Joshua, and Anne had taken place fifteen years before, and she wanted to see how she looked at thirty-two. She was pleasantly surprised as Anne was tall and slender, with pretty blonde hair and friendly blue eyes.

Louise never took her eyes from Barry while she walked towards him, as Trumpet Voluntary played, thus becoming Organ Voluntary. They had waited a long time for this day. Having decided to marry shortly before Jessica died, they had shelved all plans because of the bereavement. Barry looked into her eyes as he made his vows, and it was obvious to all how much they loved one another. Even the two smaller bridesmaids behaved well, and Barry's brother was both amusing and sincere when he replied on their behalf and said that he wanted to marry all five of them.

Dorothy had invited Matthew to accompany her to her cousin's wedding.

"It'll cheer you up, you don't go out much socially these days, do you?" she had said. "In any case, Louise was once a pupil of yours, even if it was only for a year. Wasn't it your first year in the village?"

"So she was," said Matthew, amazed. "My goodness, that makes me feel extremely old!"

It seemed the most natural thing in the world when the village headmaster attended the wedding of a former pupil, as a friend of the family.

Dorothy had gone to more trouble than usual over her dress for the wedding. Usually she favoured tailored, rather severe clothes. On this occasion, she had gone to Bristol especially, and bought a frock and matching jacket. It was a pretty floral print, silky material. The frock had a full skirt and a sleeveless bodice, while the jacket hung loose in a swagger-back. She had bought a head-hugging hat in matching pink tulle, which flattened her dark hair.

"You look very fetching," Matthew had told her, and she had blushed girlishly. They sat beside each other at the reception, talking and laughing with other guests, most of whom they both knew well.

Later in the evening, a band came along and played popular tunes for them to dance.

"Shall we?" asked Matthew, after watching an attractive leading dance by the bride and bridegroom. Dorothy was not used to dancing, but Matthew was good at it and it was easy to follow him. She saw her father watching as they went by, and gave him a little wave. She had removed her jacket because it was warm; her face was flushed and her eyes shone. She could not remember when she had enjoyed herself so much.

When the time came for the newly married couple to leave for their honeymoon, they all went outside and waved them off, throwing confetti and rice. Dorothy and Alice made a point of keeping close to their Uncle Bill. People began to drift away once the couple had gone.

Alice sat talking to Anne whom she knew well as they met often in London, and now worked at the same hospital.

"Another one gone and we're still here," laughed Alice.

"Not for the want of trying!" agreed Anne.

"Got anyone serious these days?" asked Alice.

"No. But your Dorothy looks as if she's keen on old Matthew!" she observed.

"Don't be silly," mocked Alice. "He's too old! Dorothy may be no spring chicken, but she can do better than that!"

They helped to clear away tables and chairs and Alice asked if Dorothy was ready to walk their father home. Eddy was in the vicinity but young Seth and Iris had not attended the wedding at all.

"Matthew said he'll walk me home," Dorothy told her.

"Oh, all right. See you later," said her sister.

They had to walk past School House on the way to Orchard Cottage and Matthew asked her if she would like to go in for coffee as a nightcap.

"Certainly," she said.

He pottered around in the kitchen, having first put a record on the gramophone. It was calm, peaceful classical music and Dorothy asked what it was.

"Mozart," he shouted from the kitchen.

He returned with the coffee, and they discussed their musical likes and dislikes. Matthew played Rachmaninov and Vivaldi for her, then some music from the show 'South Pacific'.

"Oh I know these alright," she said delightedly. "I hear them on the wireless." She hummed along.

It was late when he finally walked her home, and the cottage was in darkness.

"I have enjoyed the evening," he told her.

"So have I, and thanks for the music." She giggled in the darkness.

"Night," he said quietly, and turning away, he disappeared into the pitch black of the evening.

"Night," she replied, and feeling her way carefully, let herself into the slumbering cottage.

+ + +

Bill was recovering from the nuptials and having a restful day. Anne had three more days at home before returning to London, and work. She decided to take a deck-chair out to the back of the house where there was a small patch of grass, and sun herself. She was wearing a white sundress with turquoise spots, and thought she looked attractive in it. She lay back in the chair and closed her eyes. If she opened them fractionally, she could see the hill. It occurred to her that she had not taken a walk to the top on this visit, and should do so before she left. She could hear bees buzzing around, the low mooing of a cow in the distance, and the sound of machinery working to gather in the wheat. *I miss this part of country life,* she thought. *Perhaps it is time to come home and settle down.* She had almost fallen asleep, when a familiar voice said,

"Hello. Just as beautiful as ever."

She opened her eyes, disbelievingly. It was him; it was Joshua.

"Hello, Josh," she said quietly, belying the frantic beating of her heart.

He sat on the grass beside her, looking even more handsome than he had fifteen years ago.

"How are you?" he asked.

"Fine. How about you?"

"Pleased to be back. Pleased to see you," he replied.

"Where did they send you?"

"All over the place," he said, morosely.

"Are you married?" she asked.

"Yes. You?"

"No."

"I wish I weren't. It was a mistake," he told her.

"I missed you."

"And I you."

"I left Abbots Ford."

"I heard."

"Why were they so against us?"

"God knows," he responded.

"I've never stopped loving you, you know."

He looked at her, eyes full of pain.

"There have been other men...." She told him.

"Naturally."

"How did you know I was here?"

"I asked Mother, asked around in the village."

"You were interested enough to enquire?"

"Definitely."

They smiled at each other, and he took her hand.

"Anne......."

Bill, who had been having a nap upstairs, got out of bed and stood looking at the hill as he always did. His eyes followed its contours and ran down towards his own farm. He looked fondly down at Anne sitting out in the sunshine. Who was that with her? He knew him but could not immediately place him. His heartbeat quickened as realisation dawned on him. Joshua! He quickly ran a comb through his hair, pulled his shirt and trousers on, and went downstairs.

"What are you doing here?" he barked.

"Just visiting," replied Joshua, getting to his feet.

Bill's emotions were mixed. Joshua had no business being there, yet he felt proud of him, all the same.

"It won't work, you know," Joshua continued.

"What won't work?" enquired Bill.

"You and Mother have tried for years to keep us apart. It's no good any more. We love each other too much. It's still there, Bill."

"You're a married man," stated Bill.

"Only in name. I've left her."

Bill's face went ashen, and his breathing increased alarmingly. Anne got up from her chair, worried.

"Get my tablets, Anne, quickly," he ordered.

Anne rushed inside the house and Bill slowly followed, assisted by Joshua. She held the two pills out to him on her hand, and gave him a glass of water with the other.

"Here, Dad." He sat down on a wooden chair in the kitchen, getting his breath.

Anne and Joshua watched him, sometimes looking at each other, puzzled.

"Are you feeling better now, Dad?" asked Anne.

Bill nodded. Anne put the kettle on to make tea.

"I'll go, and come back to see you later," said Joshua.

"No, Joshua" said Bill, becoming agitated again.

Joshua looked at Anne and shrugged.

"I've something I must tell you both," he said, fighting for breath again. Anne made a pot of tea and they went through to the sitting room.

"Sit down, both of you."

They both obeyed without protest.

"I never thought I would have to break this news to either of you. It won't do any of us any good, but you've made it necessary."

Anne's mind was running haywire, trying to think what her father was going to tell them. Instinct and circumstances told her it was something extremely unpleasant. Joshua just thought he was making excuses to thwart them yet again, and listened cynically.

"This will come as a dreadful shock to both of you," he warned.

"Yes, Dad. Go on," advised Anne, leaning forward.

He began, stumbled over the words, and tried again. It was one thing to tell Anne, but both of them! What would the truth mean to Joshua? How would he take it?

"Oh God," groaned Bill. "That summer, up at Salisbury House, looking after your Uncle Julian...."

"Yes," Joshua nodded encouragingly.

"I fell in love with your Mother."

The young people nodded again, waiting.

"I had an affair with your Mother, Joshua."

Neither of them spoke, so Bill continued.

"I didn't know it at the time, mind, not until much later. She didn't tell me, didn't say anything."

"Never a clue." Bill shook his head sadly.

"About what, Dad," prompted Anne.

"About the baby!"

"What baby," asked Anne and Joshua in unison. They still had no idea what Bill was trying to tell them.

"You." He looked directly at Joshua.

"Me?"

"You were the baby."

It took a while to sink in. It could only have been seconds, but seemed like hours.

"You are my father?" said Joshua, utterly incredulous.

Bill nodded.

"Never!" he laughed, without mirth.

"It's true. Ask Fiddy. Ask your Mother."

Joshua was so busy taking in this momentous news, that he forgot about Anne. But Anne was assimilating the connotations of what her father had said.

"He's my half-brother?" she asked in disbelief.

"Yes. As you are my daughter, so he is my son."

Joshua put his head in his hands.

"No, no, no, no, no," he said, his voice gradually rising.

"Nothing can change the facts. What I have told you is true."

Anne looked from Bill, to Joshua, and back again. Her head was spinning, her mind reeling.

"Did Mother know?" she asked.

"No, never," he replied.

"Thank God for that much," she said, and slipped from her chair and on to the floor, in a dead faint.

When she came round, she found that Joshua had lifted her on to the sofa, and Bill was holding smelling salts under her nose.

"Don't worry about a thing, everything will be alright," Joshua told her, stroking her hair. He stayed until he was sure she had recovered, and then left, telling her he would be in touch. He did not find it necessary to say anything more to his father and went without a backward glance.

Bill felt miserable and rejected. The situation had been of their making, they had not listened to reasoned warnings. His affair and its results had been a separate issue, until these two had complicated it by falling in love. He had made only one obvious mistake in a good and hardworking life, and now he had alienated his eldest daughter yet again and disappointed his and Fiddy's son.

"Shall you tell the others?" asked Anne.

"Something I'll have to think about," he whispered, almost to himself.

There is a destiny..., he thought, sadly.

He did not even have the comfort of Louise about the house. She was happily on honeymoon in Devon, and knew nothing of all this. What if it all came out? It was all so long ago, no one would be interested, would they?

+ + +

Chapter Seven

JUNE 1953 – EASTER 1956

Louise and Gordon's house was full of people, excitedly waiting for the Queen to emerge from Buckingham Palace in the golden coach, with Prince Philip at her side. They had followed the preparations with interest; many people had not seen a state occasion of this magnitude and splendour. The previous Coronation had, naturally, not been televised.

Louise and Gordon's television set had only recently been installed and was like a magnet to their neighbours. Gordon decided that, should family or friends arrive while the set was on, they would immediately switch it off, initially out of politeness: 'We don't have the wireless blaring when people come, do we?' as Gordon had said. Secondly, they had experienced friends sitting through a whole evening's programmes, not uttering a word, just staring at the screen. Gordon was indignant. 'Did they come to see us, or the television?' he had asked Louise.

On this occasion, people had been invited specifically to see the Coronation.

"Here she comes!" shouted Emma.

People who had never been to London watched, fascinated, as the golden coach came out through the main gates of the palace and round the memorial to Queen Victoria. The military band struck up, playing 'God Save the Queen'. The microphones picked up everything, including the jangling of the horses' harness in the mounted divisions of the Household Cavalry, and of those animals pulling the heavy coach. The crowds cheered as soon as they caught sight of the coach, and carried on all along the route. The Queen looked beautiful and incredibly regal, for one so young. The family and their friends watched, mesmerised by the sights and sounds being captured, as they happened, over a hundred miles away.

Seth, Dorothy's father, went out to walk around the garden, complaining of the darkness in the drawing room. The level of the technology made it necessary to have the curtains pulled in daytime, so that the images on the screen were clearer. The screen itself was extremely small, being a nine-inch tube, but it had a magnifying window over it, which helped to enhance the picture marginally. Dorothy followed him outside.

"Are you alright, Dad?" she asked gently.

"Mmm."

He walked around Louise and Gordon's beautiful garden, talking to Dorothy about the different plants. Bill joined them, so Dorothy left the two men to their own devices. Emma and Stephen were visiting with Margaret and Ewan. Bill had brought Will and Polly, with their daughters, Janet and May. Louise and Barry were coming later, with John and his girlfriend. Then there were the ubiquitous neighbours; about twenty people in all. There were many willing female hands to cut sandwiches and make tea, for no one would have wanted to leave the television set to eat a proper meal that day. Even Seth went back to check on Her Majesty's progress through her capital, to her coronation. There was something to interest almost everybody; the horses, the apparel, the music, the architecture, the people. There was a mass 'Aaaah' when Prince Charles, aged four, appeared on the screen standing between his grandmother Queen Elizabeth the Queen Mother, and his aunt, Princess Margaret, to witness the actual moment of crowning. There was absolute silence and concentration in the room, as the Archbishop of Canterbury raised the crown high above the Queen's head, and brought it down slowly, making an unremarkable, if highly-born young woman, into a crowned and anointed Queen.

"Vivat, Vivat Regina" shouted the choir and peers.

The ordinary folk in that room and around the country, watched an ancient ritual in a way no one had ever been able to before, and many of them were filled with awe. The moment of high drama over, another team of helpers went out to the kitchen to produce yet more tea and sandwiches for the participants; for that is what they were, sharing the ceremonial with their new

Queen, albeit with the assistance of electronic eyes. It was to become a joint folk memory and the beginning of a phenomenon which would alter society as much as any other single thing in the Twentieth Century.

OCTOBER 1953

Matthew was taking the entire school to a cinema in Bristol to see the film of the Coronation. It was being paid for by the Local Education Authority, because they wanted as many children as possible to see it. The coaches were paid for by the school. Matthew needed as many reliable helpers as he could muster, and Dorothy was an obvious choice.

"You don't mind, do you?" he had asked her.

"Of course not."

They had been meeting regularly since Louise and Barry's wedding. Occasionally they invited Marcus, Lydia's brother to join them for a meal, which Dorothy cooked. People began to invite them together, accepting them as a couple, even though, as far as they were concerned, they only met out of habit and convenience.

The coaches left the school at ten o'clock and Dorothy arrived before nine to help organise the first aid kit, name badges and drinks while Matthew and his two teachers, Thelma Wright and Thomas Murray, sorted out registers, tickets and the payment for the coaches. As the other helpers arrived, Dorothy was pleased to see that one of them was Sarah Ingrams, the young doctor's wife and local nurse.

"Hello! Didn't know, you were coming."

"Mr Ashton says it's always useful to have me along in case of accidents."

"Yes, I know, but should you be....?"

"I'm fine – it'll be alright." Sarah was three months pregnant, but after having three miscarriages, all concerned were taking extra care.

"Well, if you're sure...."

"I told Jack it's no good behaving as though I were a piece of porcelain. What will be, will be."

Dorothy silently thought that while it was a healthy attitude, she herself would not undertake to travel thirteen miles in a coach along bumpy lanes to accompany over a hundred children to the cinema, if she were in Sarah's shoes.

"Take it carefully, anyway. It's good to have another pair of hands and eyes around with these rascals," Dorothy told her good-humouredly.

They had a good day. The journey was smooth and the youngsters enjoyed visiting a cinema. Although films were shown in the village hall, most of them had not been to a movie theatre before. They were well behaved and watched the film of the Coronation spellbound. On the journey home, they were full of questions because seeing the film had brought all their lessons on the subject to life for them. Few had had the chance to see the ceremony on television. On their return, everyone dispersed, the children happily reporting their adventure to their parents.

Earlier in the week, Matthew had suggested that Dorothy join him for a meal after the trip.

"I'll ask Mrs Bunce to make enough for two," he told her.

"Why don't I cook, and we'll ask Marcus – we haven't seen him for ages," suggested Dorothy. "I know, why don't we ask poor Penny as well, she never gets out," she added enthusiastically.

Matthew pulled a face.

"Don't be such an old stick-in-the-mud," Dorothy cajoled. "Penny is very nice."

Penelope Thorndyke, widow of Giles, had taken a long time to recover from her husband's death. Once again Tradewinds was home to a grieving and inconsolable widow. As in Esmée's time, the gracious and elegant house became run-down, the garden overgrown and unloved, as the lady of the house lost her love of life. They had been an unlikely partnership, the young sophisticated social butterfly and the older man with a past – but their marriage had fulfilled them, even if it had not produced any children after Penelope's miscarriages. They had had nine happy years together and she was lost without him. Dorothy had been busy piecing life together after the war when Giles died, but after a suitable length of time, she and Lydia had gradually coaxed Penelope out into village life again. Strangely enough, Penelope had discovered a minor talent for watercolour painting, especially houses and animals, and eventually she began to make a little money from her commissions. When Lydia died, Penelope became a friend in the background to Dorothy; nothing intrusive, but they had both thought a great deal of Lydia and missing her was a bond. Every few months, Dorothy would be invited to lunch at Tradewinds – never the other way round – and the two women would chat while Penelope did her tapestries and Dorothy her embroidery. So it seemed like a good idea to entertain her now and make a foursome with Marcus.

"Oh, alright...," agreed Matthew, grudgingly.

On the evening, Dorothy, who had her father's and brother's meals 'organised' because she knew it would be a hectic day, popped home to serve theirs up before doing the same back at School House. Seth was disgruntled.

"Always dashing off somewhere," he complained. "No one to talk to now."

"You've got Eddy," she pointed out.

"Eddy doesn't say much," retorted Seth.

"That's because you don't say much to him."

"Can't see why you're rushing off again anyway," said her father, returning to his imagined neglect.

Dorothy carried on with her jobs, ignoring his complaints, and being patient with him. She was going whatever he said and that was an end to it.

Matthew was in affable mood. He welcomed his brother-in-law, Marcus, warmly. He was warm but quite formal with Penelope because they had not met often. He made the introduction with his habitual bonhomie.

"Have you two met before?" he asked.

"No. I don't believe I've had that pleasure," replied Marcus taking Penelope's hand. Marcus was too straightforward and too much of a gentleman to hold Penelope's hand longer than propriety would allow, but he was obviously impressed. He was a vague but charming academic, based at Oxford University. He and Dorothy got along well, but there had never been any romantic spark between them, however much his sister Lydia had pushed them together. From the beginning of the evening, Matthew and Dorothy felt surplus to requirements, because the couple were obviously attracted. Penelope had quietened down since her single days, and her bereavement had endowed her with an air of vulnerability. They brought out the best in each other, and the meal went swimmingly. The four sat far into the night, talking and laughing. Marcus was to stay at School House but ventured to offer to walk Penelope home along the pitch-black main road.

Matthew was helping Dorothy to tidy up the kitchen.

"Leave it for Mrs Bunce in the morning," he said, yawning.

But Dorothy could not do that. He was wiping dishes while she washed them. They talked over the events of the day, laughing about one or two incidents involving the children.

"You are very good with them," he said admiringly.

"Well, my training...," she began.

"Ah yes. I always forget about your life before Abbots Ford," he said with heavy irony as though quoting the title of a book.

"What do you mean?" she asked intrigued.

"What I said. Your life before you came back to take care of your family in Abbots Ford."

"That's not all I do. There's the clinic. With my experience in nursing...."

"All wasted," he observed.

"That's your opinion," she answered tartly, tears threatening to sting her eyes.

"It's valid," he told her.

"Valid but not necessarily kind."

"I thought I could be honest with you, not merely kind," he said almost jeeringly.

"When it might hurt my feelings?"

"You know I would never wittingly hurt you." His voice was thick and he turned away. It was an odd relationship. She had shared so much of his pain over Lydia's loss, and they had shared a love of her, each in their different way. She felt awkward with him for the first time. He seemed to have changed the parameters of their relationship by making a valued judgement on a decision she had made affecting her life. Moreover, he disagreed with what she had done. Her voice broke as she spoke.

"Well, what would you have me do? My Mother was dying... my Dad didn't know what to do next...."

"And you were the only member of the family who could do it?" he asked sarcastically.

"Yes," she shouted. "Yes."

"Really?" he challenged her.

"Yes – really. You know Alice..." she paused. "I don't have to make excuses for my family to you."

"Nobody asked you to," he retorted.

"I feel hurt, Matthew. You think I'm wasting my life – how do you think that makes me feel?"

"Only because I care about you. Anyway, that isn't what I said."

She did not know how to cope with the situation, and Marcus would be returning soon.

"I'm awfully tired, Matthew. It's been a long day – you'll have to forgive me. Things are quite tidy in here now...."

"Of course. I'll get your things," he said quietly.

He came back with her coat, hat and bags.

"I shouldn't have asked you for more time this evening," he said as he helped her into her coat.

"No, I've enjoyed it," she said, sniffing. "I feel a bit off-colour – perhaps I've a cold coming."

"I hope not," he smiled. "Everything would grind to a halt if you were incapacitated."

She looked at him intently, checking his eyes for irony but the remark seemed genuine.

He walked round to the cottage with her, as he usually did, and they did not tarry or talk. Dorothy said goodnight and went in. As she prepared for bed, she looked into her mirror and pulled at her hair. *A permanent wave would be a change for my hair,* she thought. *I'll make an appointment tomorrow.* She loved her feather bed; it was like a cocoon, into which she snuggled, hiding away from the world. She opened her book, but her eyes read without seeing as her mind wandered. She wondered why Matthew had been so dogmatic about what her life involved; what business was it of his anyway? Had she been working as a nanny, she would not have lived in Abbots Ford and would not have known the Ashton family at all. No doubt there would have been other friends. What right did he have to judge her, or her family? Her thoughts ran on to Marcus and Penelope and she made a mental note to speak with Penny soon... I haven't wasted my life, have I? .... Her book fell to the floor with a thud, and she did not waken.

SPRING 1954

After the meeting at Peartree Farm House, Joshua had left Abbots Ford immediately. Gossip had it that he had had a terrible row with his mother before leaving suddenly. Anne had cut short her holiday and left the next day. It was like a nightmare for Bill because it was all happening again. Anne did not write, telephone or visit; the amnesty after her mother's death was over. He often wished that he and Fiddy had told them at the outset; how much bitterness and heartbreak it would have avoided. He had lost them both now, probably for ever. He made the best of it, as he was lucky enough to have Louise and Barry, John and Will and Polly with their family. He had turned sixty in February, and did only fractionally less than before on the farm. He had taken time one Saturday afternoon to walk to the top of the hill. It was manna for the soul in springtime. He and Jessica had always made a point of going, if only to see the primroses. He could remember walking the route with his mother and elder sisters, Flora and Louise. As he passed the fields, he could recall his pride at being allowed to help his father, Will and elder brother, Charles when he was a boy. How the years had flown. People had been taken, and new people came. He adored his grand-daughters, Janet and May, and now Louise had told him that she was expecting a child in October. He looked into the distance, trying to ascertain what the weather might do, then back at the earth, casting an expert eye over the condition of it. He bent to pick up a handful, and was crumbling it through his fingers when he spotted a couple walking up the hill behind him. He had become short-sighted and did not recognise them, so he disregarded them.

"Dad?"

He looked slowly round, for he recognised the voice. It was her, and she had Joshua with her. He stood, his joints creaking, but not painfully.

"Hello." He looked at both of them.

"Hello," said Joshua, smiling diffidently. "We saw John. He said you'd come up here."

Bill nodded. "How are you?"

"We're fine," replied Anne.

"We needed to talk to you," said Joshua. "We couldn't go on like this, not seeing you."

Bill began to carry on up the hill, and they walked either side of him.

"We had to see you, to tell you that we are together."

The words hung heavily in the air.

"What do you mean 'together'?"

"We're living together, as man and wife. People accept it, because nobody knows," said Joshua.

"But what if they did? And isn't it illegal?" asked Bill. "In any case, I don't believe it's right."

"We weren't brought up together, Dad," said Anne.

"Hadn't even met...," put in Joshua.

"And we're half, not full, brother and sister," concluded Anne.

"Mmm, still can't be right though," said Bill.

"We weren't thinking of having children," stated Joshua.

Bill shuddered.

"I don't know...," he said, defeated. He knew he would not change their minds.

"We can even continue to come and visit, no one knows, do they, Dad? Not even Louise, John or Will?"

He shook his head, indicating that no one else knew, but also his disapproval of the entire business.

255

"It doesn't make it right, no one knowing," he said after a while. "God knows."

"God put us in this predicament, and you and Mum." accused Joshua mildly.

"I'm sorry for that. We should have told you straight away. Didn't think it would go on for years and years."

"Mother knows," said Joshua.

Bill was surprised, and looked into Josh's eyes for the first time since they had told him.

"What did she say?" he asked.

"Same as you. She liked Anne though."

"She suggested a meeting with her and you and you and us," explained Anne, "but we knew it would be to try to stop us, and nothing will do that, so we said no."

Bill smiled to himself. *Not many people have said 'no' to Fiddy.*

"We just want you to know, and to try to accept it," said Joshua. "We don't even want your blessing," he added.

"Give me time," he said quietly. "It's something I'll need to get used to."

They had reached the top, and all three surveyed their surroundings.

"Nothing like it, anywhere," said Joshua, breathing deeply.

Anne watched her father's face as he narrowed his eyes, trying to focus into the distance.

"We may not want your blessing, Dad. But at least try to understand," she said gently.

He nodded, mute in his confusion.

Once they had walked back down the hill, saying little, Bill asked, awkwardly, if they were staying anywhere.

"Oh that's alright," said Joshua, "we're in a hotel in Bristol."

"What are your plans now?"

"Well, we thought we would stay and say hello to Louise and Barry..." began Anne.

"I think I would make that another time," advised Bill. "I'll say you had to dash away."

They realised that the news they had brought had devastated their father so much, that he wanted them to leave as soon as possible.

"We'll see you again, soon," said Anne, biting back the tears.

"Yes, we'll keep in touch," said Joshua.

He stood at his gate, waving them off, as they drove away. He thought his heart would break. They both looked so happy, and it was all wrong. He walked up the path with a heavy tread, feeling desperately old.

AUTUMN 1954

Seth derived great pleasure from working with James, his nephew. They had worked in tandem for over four years, and James often said that it was better than working with his father because Seth was not as critical. James had learned much from his uncle and was grateful. They were as busy as ever, because while some customers wanted the experience of the older man, others wanted the innovative energy of the younger.

They were working on a special memorial in iron, for the churchyard. It was to be dedicated to the men of both World Wars. A man called Gilbert Didcot had designed it, and the three men sometimes worked together, pooling their expertise. It had been commissioned by the Lord Lieutenant of the County, as a gift to the village. Seth was proud of the work, and when James took over, he was involved, supervising and giving advice. Dorothy took an interest in the piece and enjoyed hearing about their progress or the problems they encountered in its execution. She worried that Seth was working too hard, because he became more and more breathless, and crotchety while at home in the cottage.

"You're overdoing it, Dad," she would say to him. "You ought to take more care at your age."

"What do you mean, my age?" he had snapped. "Winston Churchill was older than me when he led the country to victory."

As she had no answer to that, she had to let him carry on, lulled by the knowledge that he was happy working.

He was looking forward to another family gathering. Helen was coming with Edgar, Louise, William and Flora. Edgar was almost eighteen and well on the way to manhood.

It was four years since Iris had moved into Plumtree Cottage with Seth, where Dorothy had confronted her. Four years, also, since the altercation between Helen and Iris at Victoria's farewell party. Time had cooled feelings, and Helen had a 'man-friend' herself these days; but discretion dictated that Helen's friend and Iris had made prior arrangements on the day their partners were visiting Orchard Cottage. Helen drove herself and the children from Bristol in her little Morris Minor, to a warm welcome from Seth and Dorothy. Edgar shook hands with his grandfather, and twelve year old William followed suit. Louise and Flora, thirteen and ten, brought examples of their embroidery as gifts for Seth.

He took them out to the Smithy to look around. Afterwards, they remained out in the orchard while Seth went back inside to talk to the others. The orchard was mature now, the trees tall and productive. There still lay scattered around pieces of machinery and even one or two old vehicles, a car and a small truck. William and the girls climbed into the cab of the truck, pretending to drive to wherever their imagination would take them. Although the gear-stick moved realistically, and the wheel turned, a chicken had nested on the dashboard at some time, ruining the illusion. Edgar had gone back into the cottage when his father, Seth, arrived. They were pleased to see each other, and Seth talked to his son about his work as an apprentice printer in Bristol.

"So you still like it, then?"

"Yes, I've just started my third year," replied Edgar.

"You still go to college once a week?"

"Yes, that's really interesting."

"That's when you do the theory?" put in Dorothy.

"Yes, and some practical work. It's good being away from Rycarts' for the day," he added.

Dorothy got up to organise tea, just as Eddy came in.

"There you are boy! How are you?" He greeted Edgar before anybody else.

"I'll lay the table," offered Helen.

When she brought out a chocolate cake, Seth was pleased.

"I only get chocolate cake when you come," he fibbed to the children.

The grandfather clock chimed and struck five.

"I've always liked this room," said Helen.

Nothing much had changed over the years. The carpet Louise and Will had made when they married, was still there, if a little threadbare. Flora had renewed and mended it once she and Seth had moved back to the cottage. Chairs and a sofa replaced the horsehair chaise longue and leather chairs, but Seth's leather chair remained, continually being mended by him.

"It's a shame Alice missed this," observed her father.

"She says she's going to have time off to come home at Christmas," said Dorothy.

"You'll all have to come again then," said Seth, pleased with the idea.

"Yes, Grandad, that would be lovely," said Flora.

The time passed too quickly, and Helen said it was time for them to leave.

It was quiet when they had gone; young Seth stayed for a while, talking to his brother, but their father retreated into silence, sad that it was over.

"Cheer up, Dad," said Seth. "Christmas isn't that long. It'll be nice to get together with Alice home."

"Mmm."

Seth did not broach the subject of Iris with his father. He had it in mind to include her in the Christmas visit, if only because they planned to marry just before the festive season. Helen and he were awaiting the completion of their divorce, but only Dorothy knew about it. None of them wanted to tell their father.

"I'll say cheerio for now, Dad," said Seth.

"Yes. Goodbye, Son," replied his father.

When she had tidied up, Dorothy turned the wireless on to listen to a play. She sat on the sofa and took out her knitting.

"This is a winter pullover for you, Dad."

"Nice colour," he remarked.

They sat contentedly, listening to the play. When it finished, Seth cleared his throat to speak.

"I do appreciate how you look after me, girl."

"That's alright, Dad. I enjoy it," she told him, truthfully.

Later that night, Seth Hawkes, the love of Flora's life, kind and loving father, loved grandfather and friend, died in his sleep.

His family was grief-stricken, but Dorothy perhaps most of all. James Hawkes wept openly when told the news. The funeral was held on a beautiful early November day when the mist stays low, and the cold is crisp, not cruel, and the wood-smoke drifts over hedges. They laid him next to Flora, and his children remained, when the others walked back to the cottage.

"They're together again, at last," said Alice.

"He was never really himself, once she had gone," said Seth.

Eddy put his arms around Dorothy's shoulders.

"You did your bit, girl."

Dorothy could not stop weeping. Her father was not a man to have favourites, but somehow, she had always been her Daddy's girl. And now he was gone. She could not take it in, could not believe it. He had always been there; running everything, organising things, even as he grew older.

They had brought out the old carriage, and James had a perfectly black horse, called Beauty. Seth had gone to his rest in style, James had seen to that. He could remember Seth, and even Tom, grooming a horse and burnishing the harness, polishing the carriage, for a funeral. In turn, it had been done for him.

The churchyard war memorial had been completed only two weeks before Seth died, and it became his own. Sir Charles Harvey suggested that James should engrave extra words at the base:

Seth John Hawkes
1886 – 1954
Village Blacksmith
1916 – 1954

NOVEMBER 1954

Polly and Will had brought their children Janet and May to see their new little cousin, baby Jessica. Louise had carried on working at the shop until the late summer, and had become bored at home waiting for the birth of her baby, even though there was plenty to do. The child had arrived on time at the end of October, to the delight of her parents and family. Bill had taken a great interest in the preparations, as Louise and Barry still lived at Peartree Farm House with him.

Jenny, the nurse had retired two years earlier and Sarah had a new girl working with her, Fiona Cooper. It was Gillian and Penny who had attended Louise. The birth had been protracted, but normal, and the baby weighed almost eight pounds. She was dark haired like Barry, and although it was difficult to tell what colour her eyes would be just yet, they were such a dark blue, that they could guess they would be brown, also like her father's.

Janet and May were fascinated with the baby's tiny hands and feet. They were eight and six respectively, yet already cooing maternally to their tiny cousin.

"Can I hold her?" enquired Janet.

"Better not, dear," said Polly.

"Perhaps when she's up for her feed?" suggested Louise.

"You can see the family resemblance," said Will.

"I can see Mum in her," agreed Louise.

"How are you feeling?" asked Polly.

"Not too bad, a bit tired," smiled the new mother.

"If you want any help...."

"So far, so good. Dorothy has been cooking for us since Jessica was born, and doing goodness knows what else," explained Louise.

"She's kind, Cousin Dorothy, isn't she," said Polly.

"She says she's grateful to be busy just now after Seth's funeral last week," explained Louise. She had been unable to go because it was only days after Jessica came.

"Yes, I went with Dad," Will told them.

"Did you? How were the family?" asked Louise.

"Dorothy was very upset, they all were, in their own way."

"Understandable," commented Polly.

They all went downstairs, just as Bill came in through the back door.

261

"Hello!" he said, surprised and pleased to see them.

"We've been to see the new baby, Grandad," May told him.

"Yes, she's as lovely as you two, isn't she?" he said.

"Didn't you want a grandson this time Dad?" asked Will.

"No, all my lovely girls are what I want."

Bill had not seen Anne or Joshua since their visit in the spring, after which he had been deeply depressed for some weeks. Louise had been worried about her father, being completely unaware of the truth, yet knowing that Anne had removed herself from the family circle yet again. The coming child, and the announcement in July of John's engagement to his girlfriend, Gillian, had gone some way towards improving their father's low spirits, and now the birth of Jessica had given him something to celebrate.

The family had tea together, and the girls were thrilled to be able to hold Jessica when she awoke for her feed. Barry came in from work, and was obviously proud of his baby daughter. He took a hand in 'burping' her, and was already adept at holding a small baby. Polly teased her husband that he had been hopeless with their girls.

"And I'm having nothing to do with this one until she's bigger!" he laughed. "So don't expect me to hold her!"

Polly, Will and the girls reluctantly left for home, Polly whispering to her sister-in-law, "You've made me all broody again!" as she went.

In the car on the way home, Polly remarked to her husband that his father looked much happier.

"Yes. I don't know what Anne thinks she's playing at, but whatever it is, I'll have a few things to say to her when she turns up again."

SPRING 1955

After Dorothy and Matthew had their discussion about her choices in life, Dorothy had withdrawn herself from his private life, only dropping in occasionally. They still met regularly because of her voluntary work for the school, and both were now on the

Parish Council. Her withdrawal had been both subtle and gradual, and neither party had found it necessary to comment upon it. Matthew had attended Seth's funeral, knowing that Dorothy would appreciate his support.

He waylaid her when she was spending an afternoon working in the school office.

"Diana mentioned that they haven't seen you for a while, and you've never even met Simon and Theresa's baby, Matthew."

"That's true," she smiled.

"What about coming this Sunday?"

She raised her eyebrows and looked at him.

"Can you come to lunch? The children will all be there."

"That would be very nice," she agreed. "What time?"

"About twelve-thirty?"

She nodded, and he disappeared to carry on with his work. She could hear his voice booming at the top class of oldest children. He was a disciplinarian, and strict with his pupils, but none left the school unable to read, write or compute numbers.

Dorothy still missed Seth. She thought she saw him walking through the orchard, or up Church Lane, or disappearing into the kitchen. She thought she heard his voice or smelled his pipe. She still had to look after Eddy, but he materialised at meal-times and disappeared afterwards, almost without a word, and no longer sat in the living room in the evenings. Dorothy did not know where he went, but Seth's passing had had its effect on him.

Seth and Iris had married quietly before Christmas as planned, and Iris was expecting a baby in the autumn; she was thirty-seven, which was late to be having a first baby, but they were looking forward to it. Seth realised that his father never would have understood, nor accepted the situation. It had worked in the end, because he had always taken responsibility for his children, and continued to pay for their keep. He saw more of them now that he and Helen were leading their own lives; Louise and Flora often stayed the weekend with their father and Iris at Plumtree Cottage; only William refused to go.

James Hawkes continued to work in the Smithy and Dorothy enjoyed having him out in the orchard, and giving him dinner each day, with herself and Eddy.

Dorothy prepared carefully for her lunch at School House. She wore a grey tweed skirt and a full-sleeved white blouse with a revered collar. She looked in the mirror, and decided to add a Fair-Isle waistcoat which she had knitted herself. She had been pleased with the result of her first permanent wave, and had continued to have curly hair. She looked in the mirror again, smoothing the skirt over her slim hips. Dorothy never wore make up or jewellery, except for brooches, and today, not even that. Her brown button eyes looked back at her. She looked pale, and was thinner than ever; her cheekbones were prominent anyway, and now the skin stretched tautly over them. It dawned on her that she did not look well. Not ill, exactly, but not well either. She pinched her cheeks, hoping that the colour would improve her appearance. "Oh well," she told her reflection, "it doesn't matter anyway!"

She arrived on time, to an enthusiastic welcome from Matthew's family. The children were lovely, for young Lydia was almost five, and Diana's son Richard almost two. Simon and Theresa's baby, another Matthew, was four months old. Diana, Theresa and Vera fed the little ones first and Lydia sat up to a second small 'lunch' with the grown-ups.

"We were so sorry to hear about your father," Diana told her.

There were murmurs of agreement around the table.

Family gossip oiled the conversation, but there were odd silences, demonstrating that the old, easy relationship between them all had weakened. Dorothy helped them with the washing up, and was about to make her excuses to go, when Diana and Donald made moves to leave. When they had waved them off, Simon and Theresa decided they ought to take the baby home, and Vera left with them.

"Isn't it quiet, now they've all gone?" said Matthew, with relish.

"Yes," she laughed, "but the children are so sweet. And it was lovely to see everyone again, after so long."

Matthew sat on the piano stool and Dorothy leaned on the piano.

"Why has it been so long?" he asked, looking at her intently.

"No reason."

"You've been avoiding me, haven't you?"

"No, just trying to keep busy."

"Yes, I know. I'm sorry. But you have been avoiding me."

"I was upset when you said I've been wasting my life."

"That was ages ago!" protested Matthew.

"I don't see why that matters," countered Dorothy. She turned to go and collect her things.

"Don't leave," said Matthew.

She was surprised; his voice sounded as if there was a plea in it.

"Why not?"

"Because I want you to stay."

"I don't understand. What's the matter. Are you ill?"

He had followed her into the hall and they stood facing each other.

"No, you don't understand. You don't understand how I feel about you."

Dorothy was stunned. She had never thought of him in that light. Matthew Ashton! Lydia's husband? She was embarrassed, and reddened

"Oh Dorothy," he said despairingly. "You're such a child in some ways!" He was exasperated with her.

"I'd better go," she said quietly.

"I'll walk round with you."

He helped her on with her coat, and, turning her slowly to face him, kissed her gently on the cheek. He had kissed her on the cheek before, but not with the infinite tenderness he showed now. They walked round to Orchard Cottage, and he kissed her again.

"In you go, my dear," he said.

Dorothy did as she was told, confused and amazed by the events of the afternoon.

"See you during the week," he said, and waving, turned and went back home.

JUNE 1955

Robert was an elderly man now, and tended to look back on his chequered life. His wife Rebecca had died and he was filled with remorse, for he felt that he had not done the best for her. His family, five children, fifteen grandchildren and two great-grandchildren tried to comfort him, in vain. He and Rebecca had loved each other dearly and their marriage had never been dull. Only he knew how guilty he was, but his regret extended to the bitterness which had soured his life and sometimes, their marriage.

With Rebecca's encouragement, Amy had begun to visit them, when she came to Abbots Ford to see Beatrice. When she had the child, the November after Charles' crash, Robert and Rebecca' grandson, Matthew Davis, whose tractor Charles had been trying to avoid, had taken them to Bath to visit her and the baby. Amy had attended her mother's funeral, but left straight away, because she still felt ill at ease with her father. Soon afterwards, her eldest brother Robbie, had got in touch with her to say that they were all worried about Robert, and could she come to Abbots Ford again to see him? His son, Matthew, drove to collect her and little Charles, and took them to her father's cottage. She lifted the little boy down on to the path and turned to thank Matthew.

"Aren't you coming in?" she asked.

"No. I'll call back later for you. Mum says you're coming for tea?"

She nodded.

"About an hour?" he asked, and she nodded again. She looked at the cottage, set high above the road. She was apprehensive about the visit; she knew she would miss her mother's presence. She held little Charles' hand, and walked up to the front door. She knocked and waited. She could hear shuffling footsteps, slowly coming nearer. Naturally, she had seen her father at the funeral, but she was unprepared for how frail he had become in so short a time.

"Hello Dad."

"Hello, Amy. Are you coming in?"

"Yes. Dad."

"Who is this?"

Amy was not sure how to respond. Did he really not know whose child this boy was?

"It's Charles, my son, Dad."

The little boy looked up at the elderly man, and repeated, "It's Charles, Dad."

"This is your Grandad, Charles. Say hello to Grandad."

"Hello, Grandad," said the two and a half year old child.

Robert looked down at him. Amy's boy.

"What did you say his name was?"

"He's named after his father, Dad. He's called Charles."

"Hello, Charles," said Robert.

Amy made a cup of tea, not sure that her father was taking in what she was saying. While she was in the kitchen, she heard Robert talking to Charles.

"Your Grannie loved you very much. Do you remember Grannie?"

Charles said something about 'Grannie, Grandad and Charles'.

"Yes, Grannie and Grandad love you Charles."

Amy came out with the tea.

"What is he gabbling on about?"

"He and I are having a talk," said the old man.

They drank the tea, and Robert asked where she was living.

"It's a nice little house in a village near Bath. We bought it when we knew the baby was on the way," she told him.

I'm glad you're settled, Amy," said Robert. "Your Mother was glad too."

When they were leaving, Robert tapped her on the arm.

"Here's something for him," he said, giving her an envelope. "A little something."

"Thanks, Dad." She kissed him goodbye.

Matthew had returned to pick her up.

"My eldest grandson, and my youngest," he smiled.

He turned to Matthew and said,

"He's got the look of the Davis's about him, but he's a Henty as well."

Matthew and Amy glanced at each other, and Amy lifted Charles into the back of the car.

"Bye, Dad," she waved. She cried as they drove away. He had known exactly who her son was, and still accepted him. Perhaps, after all these years the bitterness was fading after all.

+ + +

Dorothy was giving the living room a good clean. She really wanted to decorate, but Eddy was against the idea. She had taken the curtains down and stood looking at the uneven bulging walls. Her grandparent's dresser still stood against the main wall and she decided to take all the china down and wash it, before doing the cobwebbing. As she stood washing the serving plates in soapy water, she realised why she had not done all this at the more traditional time, in the spring. She had been depressed, and ordinary, everyday activities had taken all her energy. It had been a sad winter, and her dark feelings had continued into the season of renewal and growth. She smiled to herself, remembering some of the occasions on which the plates had been used. She could picture Flora, her mother, or Aunt Elsie, or even Gran, setting food out on them, in readiness for a gathering, or placing a joint ready for her father or Grandad Will to carve....

"Hello"

She was jolted from her reverie by the voice.

"Sorry, I made you jump," smiled Matthew.

He was standing at the open kitchen window, in front of where she was working. She was nonplussed, wondering how she must look. She was wearing an old crossover overall over clothes she kept specially for heavy work, and her dark hair was protected from dust by a scarf.

"Hello, Matthew. I must look a mess," she said.

"You look fine to me." he offered. "Indeed you look happy, working away there."

"I'm summer-cleaning," she told him.

"Summer-cleaning?"

"Late spring-cleaning!" she explained, laughing. "What can I do for you?"

"Any chance of a cup of tea?" he asked.

It occurred to her that it was unusual to see him out and about at this time of the morning, during term time.

"Yes. Come in. I'll put the kettle on. Time I was having a cup anyway."

She pulled the scarf off her hair and ruffled it up, hoping it would look presentable. She was undoing the ties to take off her overall as he walked through the door.

"My goodness, we are busy!" he commented, seeing how bare the room looked without benefit of curtains, ornaments, pictures and lamps.

"Are you sure you can stop?"

"Yes. I told you. I've been on the go since nine."

She poured the tea and sat on the arm of the chair near the table, where she sat at mealtimes. Dorothy looked at him, expectantly, because he had the air of a man who had something to tell.

"Thelma told me before school this morning that she wants to leave at Christmas," he said.

"She's nowhere near retirement age, is she?" said Dorothy.

"No."

"Then why?"

He did not know. Thelma Wright had been at the school a few years before Matthew had taken over as headmaster, but must still be only in her mid-forties. They were a good team, the three of them. As the roll had increased, Matthew had taken on Thomas Murray. In a small community like Abbots Ford, the change of an established teacher was an issue. She could see that it was worrying him. They discussed the repercussions, and what type of person he would need to replace Thelma.

"It's a shame you aren't qualified!" he said, only partly in jest.

"Well. I wouldn't be, having 'wasted' my life," she smiled.

"You know what they say about sarcasm," he said lightly.

"Anyway, I could never work with you, Matthew."

He was genuinely surprised.

"Why ever not?"

"Because you're bossy, self-opinionated and brash."

269

He was lost for words and sat, opening his mouth to speak, but nothing emerged.

Dorothy laughed out loud, and he could not help but join in. Before she was aware of what was happening, he had got up, walked over to her and was kissing her on the mouth. Taken aback, she struggled mildly at first, but then sat passively while he kissed her. He stood back, flustered.

"I'm sorry, Dorothy. I didn't mean to...."

She was not going to let him down lightly.

"What?" she questioned, looking him straight in the eye, but with laughter waiting to burst from deep within her at his discomfiture.

"Taking advantage..." he started to explain.

"Of what?"

He began to apologise and explain again before becoming aware that she was teasing him.

"You minx," he shouted, surprised at her response.

He approached her again, and putting his arms around her, kissed her lustily.

At first, she remained passive, as before; but then she was aware of a response within herself which she had never experienced. She began to return the kiss, but pulled away, wary of the feelings being aroused. They looked at each other with new eyes.

"Dorothy?"

"I... I don't know what came over me," she stuttered, turning away.

"I think you do love me, as I've loved you."

He moved close to her, kissing her expertly and authoritatively, and she allowed herself to float on the seas of sensation he was creating.

"Oh Dorothy! I've waited so long...." He wanted to kiss her again, but she pushed him away, laughing happily.

"Matthew! We can't, I mean we're busy people!"

"Can I see you tonight" he asked eagerly.

"Well, no, I've arranged to go to see Louise and..."

"Can't you cancel it?"

"No," she laughed again at his impatience. "No, I can't – not at such short notice. I'm baby-sitting."

"Where's Bill? Can't he baby-sit. I'll come with you." he added, delighted at the notion.

"No, you can't. I'll tell you what we'll do. Come round tomorrow after dinner," she told him.

"No, there's Eddy. Can you come round to me, and we'll have dinner together?"

She concurred, and he kissed her once more, lightly and exuberantly.

He was no closer to a solution for the problem about which he had, ostensibly, come to see her; but his step was light as he left to return to his work.

SEPTEMBER 1955

Gordon and Louise had been winding down their involvement in the shop for a number of years. They were in their mid-sixties, and felt it was time to retire completely. They wanted to visit their daughter Victoria in Australia before they were any older; it was five years since her departure with her husband and family. So they came to an arrangement, and handed the business over to their niece, Louise. Louise had been working in the shop since leaving school, and had, for a long time, dealt with the workshop in Bath and had a major voice in design. Baby Jessica was nearly a year old now, and so far, Louise had relied on the goodwill of family and neighbours to baby-sit whenever she went to work. She and Barry decided to employ a full-time nanny for Jessica, because it would be unfair to continue to ask relatives to look after her; they had lives of their own, after all. They did not use a local girl, but went to an agency, who sent a number of people for interview. Louise found it very difficult, because Barry opted out and left her to make the choice alone. After much heart-searching, she chose a Scottish lass by the name of Margaret MacIntosh, who was nineteen. So that Margaret had her own room, Louise' brother John moved in with his Aunt Louise and Uncle Gordon, who had a huge house and no family left at home. Everybody was pleased with the arrangement, as the two homes were only minutes apart in any case.

Louise invited her aunt and uncle to a celebratory dinner. Her father, Bill, was present, of course, as they sat around the table in the dining room and talked animatedly as they enjoyed the meal.

"When does this girl arrive?" asked Gordon.

"On Monday."

"And you're sure about it?" This from Louise, her aunt.

"Jessica will be fine. She loved Margaret. Anyway, she can bring her down to the shop any time, to see me," said Louise happily.

She had thought it through carefully.

"When do you go?" Bill asked his sister, changing the subject.

They talked about the coming trip to Australia. Gordon and Louise were using the six week journey there, and on the way back, as holidays in themselves. 'Cruising round the world', as Gordon put it. They were excited about seeing Victoria and her family again, and promised to take many photographs. They were leaving in two weeks time, and would arrive in Australia in high summer.

"Shall you enjoy a 'hot' Christmas?" asked Barry.

"As long as we can spend it with Victoria, Alan, June and Joseph, we don't really mind," said Louise.

"It'll be a change from England," added Gordon.

They drank to the voyage, and the visit, followed by toasts to Louise' ownership of the shop and Jessica's new nanny. It was an enjoyable occasion, where almost everyone had great events to look forward to. Bill looked at his sister's and daughter's faces, and took comfort in their happiness and joy.

OCTOBER 1955

Marcus had courted Penelope in his own quiet way. They had both been hurt by life and approached it with caution, unwilling to let it trip them up again. At the beginning of their relationship,

Marcus had been discouraged by the fact that Penelope still lived at Tradewinds which had been left to her, solely, in Giles' will. She rarely saw his sister, Madeline, or her family nowadays.

When news leaked out that they were to marry, there was gossip in the village. At one time, Matthew's name had been linked to Penny's because folk remembered how Lydia had tried to pair off Dorothy and Marcus. When the four met regularly, people had jumped to the wrong conclusion. It was an extremely quiet wedding. Marcus had no family left, except his sister's widower and children, who all rallied round. Both Penelope's parents had died, but her sisters attended the quiet service at the tiny chapel on the estate, where she had married Giles. They all went to great lengths to retain the privacy of the ceremony, ordering everything from Bristol, rather than locally, to plug one of the main ways these things can leak out. All the guests stayed the night before the wedding at Darnley Hall as guests of Penny's eldest brother. A friend of Marcus officiated at the marriage at eight o'clock that morning. Penelope looked elegant in a pale grey woollen suit and with a grey velvet turban on her head. Their friends and family were delighted that two such deserving people had found each other, and the day went well, with lunch being the wedding breakfast.

Marcus took her away to Oxford for the honeymoon, to the small house from where he had conducted his academic career. Penny was in such demand once his colleagues had met her, that they stayed on for longer than they had intended. Indeed, when they returned, Penelope confided in Dorothy that they were considering selling Tradewinds to buy a larger property in Oxford. They had planned to retain Marcus' small house because he would have to live there during term, but Penny was enjoying university life so much that, she was preparing to uproot herself to live with her husband all the time.

Dorothy had difficulty in refraining from confiding in Penny about her own relationship with Matthew. She was as sure as she could be about her feelings but wanted to keep them close to herself for a while longer. In any case, there were unresolved issues regarding her responsibility to her family. The fact that Marcus at forty-nine and Penny at fifty-one had launched themselves into matrimony, encouraged Dorothy. It made the whole situation seem feasible. Matthew had squeezed her hand at Penny's wedding, and smiled encouragingly. Everyone was living their life, while Dorothy remained a spectator. She could feel her attitude changing. Times were changing. The music emanating from the radio these days was witness to that: squawking and squalling, young men screaming out as if in pain! To add insult to injury, Marina had spent her last holiday with her ear glued to the wireless, trying to pick up the signal from Radio Luxembourg which played that type of music most. Dorothy felt old, yet she was only forty-three. It was wonderful to see Penny and Marcus so happy, but when would it be her turn, she wondered silently.

DECEMBER 1955

Christmas! thought Dorothy. *How many happy memories one can conjure up.* She was baking batches of mince pies for the school Christmas dinner. It took her back to her mother's preparations for the festive season. She had found herself thinking back a great deal to her childhood, and the time before her mother died, since Seth's passing. Dorothy was excited about Christmas. Both she and Eddy were going to School House for dinner on Christmas Day, and Matthew's family were all coming. She could not remember when she had cooked for so many people. Since the summer, the relationship between Dorothy and Matthew had developed, and though they were not lovers, both found it difficult to maintain the proprieties. Matthew was so besotted with her that he had been pleading with her to marry him, but Dorothy took his proposals with a pinch of salt.

"One day I'll say yes, that'll surprise you," she teased.

"I wish you would," he responded.

They spent happy evenings at School House or Orchard Cottage, talking, eating, playing cards, listening to the wireless or playing records of their favourite music. They had attended the Harvest Supper Dance together, and been surprised at their welcome as a couple. It had crossed their minds that some people might gossip or disapprove, but this had not happened. All people saw was a nice, deserving couple who had fallen in love. Many had never understood why Dorothy Hawkes had remained single, but the simple fact was that she had always put family first. Not all fathers and brothers were as easy to live with as Bill and John, and not all prospective husbands as understanding as Barry had been. Later, when she delivered the pies to School House, Matthew seemed suffused with excitement.

"Quickly, put those down. I've something to show you."

He led her into the drawing room, where something stood in the corner, covered with a sheet. He blew a mock fanfare with his voice, and whipped the sheet away. There stood a television set. Dorothy had never thought that television was something she had time for; she was always too busy.

"Come and sit down. The evenings' programmes begin in ten minutes," he enthused.

"Matthew, I haven't time…" she protested, half heartedly.

He pulled her on to the sofa, and playfully imprisoned her in his arms.

"Say you'll stay, just for half an hour," he insisted.

"Oh alright," she laughed. They kissed, ever more urgently, and Matthew's hand strayed to the neck of her blouse, and down to her breast.

"Matthew, no." She was giggling, but she could not allow such intimacies. He respected her feelings, but was incapable of completely controlling his own. They sat cuddling on the sofa, watching an engrossing current affairs programme. When it finished Matthew commented,

"There, that wasn't so bad, was it?"

"Very enjoyable. Now, I've plenty more to do at home."

"Make this your home, then we can be together all the time. All the time," he repeated, emphasising **all** and leering at her.

"Matthew Ashton, do you think of nothing else?" she chided.

"I mean it. Marry me."

She looked at him; he was serious. He had always been serious.

"There's Eddy...."

"Eddy is a man of forty-one, more than capable of looking after himself," reasoned Matthew.

"He can't, you know. He can't cook."

"Something can be worked out. Say you'll marry me. You've sacrificed so much of your life. Think of yourself, for once", he said.

"Think of you, you mean," she parried.

"Seriously, think about it. I love you. You love me. We enjoy being together," he told her.

"I will, I promise," she said.

Matthew was exultant; he could see that Dorothy was assimilating the idea, and approaching acceptance. It was not that she did not want to marry him; she was worried about her brother. If the problem could be dispatched, he was sure that they could name the day.

+ + +

Alice had not been home since her father's funeral, or the Christmas after he died. In fact she had avoided returning at all, until now. She had written a long letter to Dorothy, explaining that she was handing in her notice and leaving the hospital. *I'm too old for all this now,* she had written. Dorothy was horrified. Forty-five was not 'too old' as her sister had said, not if you were fit and well. *I am coming back to Abbots Ford to live. I hope there's room at Orchard Cottage for me.* Dorothy's mind raced. How long was it since they had lived together? At least twenty-five years! Mother and father had been there then! Still, it was Alice' home as much as hers, and she had no right to dissuade her. Dorothy merely mentioned that Alice was returning 'for the holiday' to Matthew, because she wanted to think about the situation by herself first.

When Alice arrived, Dorothy could see that she needed a break, for she was in a state of nervous collapse. She came the weekend before Christmas and they spent the entire night talking. Andrew Hoggart, Alice' lover, had not emigrated to America, and their affair had carried on, enlivened by a jealous row between them, after Alice had seen him with his wife and family. It had continued to be a stormy relationship, culminating recently in Alice going to Alexandra, his wife, to ask her to give him up. Alexandra had laughed in her face, asking her if she knew how many times she has had experienced this scene.

"You mean someone else has come to see you like this?" she had asked incredulous.

"My dear lady, if only it were merely some *ONE*," she had replied, sarcastically.

Later, when she could think clearly, Alice had thought that Alexandra and Andrew actually deserved one another. They were like piranhas, feeding off each other, each needing the other, as well as other people. Alice was so upset that she had decided then to return home for good.

"Just relax and enjoy Christmas," advised Dorothy.

In the circumstances, Dorothy organised a family get-together, and invited Seth and Iris with their baby boy, Seth, born in September. Even Eddy managed to put in an appearance, looking ever more dishevelled. It was the Monday before Christmas Eve, and they had decided to meet for a cup of tea, rather than a meal. Seth and Eddy believed that this was because it would be their only chance to see Alice, because they knew that Dorothy was spending Christmas Day at School House, and Alice usually stayed only a short time.

"Is he a good baby, or like his father" Alice asked Iris, smiling. They had left little Seth at home in bed, being cared for by a friend.

"He's good, like his Dad," defended Iris.

"Will you be here long enough to come and see us," asked her brother.

"It's strange you should say that," said Alice, "because I'm home for good."

Alice had been 'home for good' on a number of occasions through the years, so Seth and Eddy were not unduly surprised; at least not as surprised as they would have been if they had been aware that it was genuine this time.

"So you three will be sharing the cottage?" smiled Seth.

They nodded, and he laughed.

"Well, I'm better off out of it, even with another new baby at my house."

Alice gave them a brief outline of why she had decided to come home.

"I'll give you six months," said Eddy, and then to the others: "She'll be off again."

Dorothy said nothing of her plans. A solution had been formulating in her head ever since she had received her sister's letter. Her talks with her had revealed that she really was disillusioned with London life. "It's not what it was, Dotty. It's turning nasty," she had said.

Dorothy felt guilty that her sister's misery was her salvation. She hugged her thoughts to herself, picturing Matthew's reaction. A whole new life! Living in School House! The Headmaster's wife: Matthew's wife. The connotations of her decision impinged upon her mind, and sent a shiver of excitement through her body. She could hardly wait until Christmas in two days' time, when she would tell him of her decision; tell Matthew, that, yes, she would marry him.

+ + +

The fire crackled and leapt in the grate and the lamps were lit in the drawing room of School House. The curtains were drawn against the cold hostility of the night. Furniture gleamed warmly in the subdued light, while the decorations on the tall tree glittered and sparkled. It had been a wonderful Christmas Day. Matthew's children were all there, and his grandchildren had given the festival true meaning. They had attended church that morning, to be greeted by folk equally enjoying the company of large families. The atmosphere had been one of familial love and community spirit; it was one of those occasions when Douglas Glover was glad that he had chosen the ministry.

Christmas dinner had been an event of riotous hilarity and goodwill. Both Alice and Eddy had accompanied Dorothy, and

Lydia's unmarried brother, Marcus, was visiting. While Vera and Theresa entertained the children, Diana helped Dorothy with the cooking. Matthew's eyes caught Dorothy's during the meal and the love between them was plain for all to see. Dorothy came in for much teasing from Alice, and Matthew's daughters, but still she said nothing.

Once the children were in bed, for they were all staying the night, the grown-ups settled down with drinks, and looked forward to a lighter, but none-the-less enjoyable, meal together.

"Do you remember Christmas during the War?" asked Matthew. "I remember how Lydia would save up ingredients through the year to try and make Christmas the same as usual." He smiled fondly at the memory.

"Do you remember when she tried turnip grated in the Christmas puddings?" said Diana, and everyone was convulsed with laughter, most of all Dorothy. They talked of old times, Matthew's children recalling happy memories of their own childhood. Marcus could remember japes into which he, Lydia and their sister had become embroiled. Dorothy, Alice and Eddy became weak with laughter and reduced the others to a similar state, with tales of their childhood at Plumtree Cottage.

Dorothy informed them that the meal was ready, and they filed into the dining room obediently. She had made an effort, and the room looked inviting. Holly decorated the picture frames, and red candles burned amid a holly decoration on the table. Matthew nodded to her approvingly.

When they had eaten, Matthew refilled everybody's glass.

"I have an announcement to make. 'We' have an announcement to make," he corrected himself.

He looked around at the faces at his table. His children, his and Lydia's, looked at him with growing anticipation; Lydia's brother; Dorothy's brother and sister. How would they all react? What would they think? He was a man aged fifty-five, and Dorothy was forty-three. He would prefer their approval, but he was going to marry Dorothy whatever anyone thought.

"Dorothy has agreed to be my wife, and as of today, we are betrothed."

Pandemonium broke out, as everybody spoke at once.

"How wonderful."

"About time!"

"We'd given up on you…"

"You dark horse, Dorothy."

"When?"

"Congratulations, Matthew. I'm so pleased," said Marcus.

They were all kissing Dorothy, and shaking Matthew by the hand. Even Eddy got up and said quietly to his sister, "You deserve it, Sis."

It was a merry gathering there, that Christmas Day in the evening. They had all known grief and tragedy, and the loss of loved ones, but tonight there was no war, no grief, or loss or tragedy. Only unfettered joy, and happiness that two people whom they loved had made the right decision.

Marcus held up his glass.

"Dorothy and Matthew."

The others stood and did the same.

"Dorothy and Matthew."

Matthew looked at Dorothy and then at his family and friends. He had not thought to have this much happiness in store, after his life with Lydia. He was not an overtly emotional man, but he could feel the tears welling up inside him. He swallowed and cleared his throat.

"We're getting married in the spring. At Easter," he told them. "Naturally, you're all invited." Then he held up his glass and toasted his wife-to-be.

FEBRUARY 1956

Margaret MacIntosh, Jessica's nanny, was a great success. Louise had the best of both worlds, knowing that her baby was happy, and she, herself, able to carry on with the job she enjoyed. It had even worked well that her brother, John, had moved out when Margaret arrived, because Louise and Gordon had someone looking after their house while they were away in Australia. The visit, and the voyages there and back, were spread over nine months, a long time to leave a house unoccupied. Margaret was a pleasant, friendly girl with dark curly hair, blue eyes and an open face. Bill had taken a great delight in baby Jessica and it turned out that Margaret was good company about the house as well.

Bill had still not seen Anne and Joshua since their visit when they told him they were living together. On the odd occasion, he and Fiddy had continued to have dinner together at Salisbury House, so they kept in touch.

It was a winter's day when the telephone rang before Bill had gone about his work. It was Fiddy.

"Bill," she said, and he knew that she was upset.

"What is it, Fiddy?" he asked.

"Mother died in the early hours of this morning."

"I'll be round directly," he told her, and hung up.

He changed into his suit and drove to Salisbury House. Fiddy greeted him and dissolved into tears.

"My dear. Don't distress yourself. Lady Moira had a good life," he comforted.

"Julian and Olivia are on their way," she told him.

"Where is Oberon?" Bill had never liked Fiddy's younger brother, but he had never come across him or his family, on his visits to see Fiddy.

"Out riding," sniffed Fiddy. She ordered coffee to be served in the library. Bill sat close to her holding her hands, which in turn held a sodden handkerchief. The coffee arrived, and they sat sipping it, while Fiddy told Bill the details of her mother's last few hours, punctuated by more weeping.

"There's one thing I think you should know, Bill," she said. "I didn't say anything before, for fear of worrying you."

Bill paled, wondering what she was going to say.

"Mother's will. She's left a cottage in the village to Josh," explained Fiddy. "She told me some time ago. I think she knew whose son he really is, but we never spoke of it. She didn't know who Anne was, either; just that she was the girl Josh lived with."

Bill said nothing.

"What if they return here to live?" asked Fiddy.

"Surely they won't...?" said Bill.

"Even if they did, we're the only ones who know what their relationship is to each other," stated Fiddy.

"But if anyone ever found out..." began Bill.

"No reason why they should," observed Fiddy.

"Anyway, we'll worry about it if it happens," Bill told her. "You look after yourself and try not to get too upset."

She nodded silently, tears trickling down her cheeks again. She had told him when the funeral would take place.

"Do you want me to come along on Friday?" he asked.

She nodded.

"I'll go to the church," he said.

"No, come here."

"Are you sure?"

"Yes. You're a friend of the family. It'll cheer Julian to see you as well," she assured him.

He kissed her gently.

"I'll see you at, what, ten o'clock, Friday morning?"

"Mmm," she agreed.

"Ring me if you need me," he instructed.

"Yes, I will."

He left her then and drove home with myriad thoughts in his mind. Lady Moira had always been kind to him, a charming lady. Times were changing rapidly, the old order was being transmogrified. What would 'Captain' Julian be like nowadays? Would the spectre of Anne and Joshua never go away?

He drove back to Peartree Farm, and went into the house. Margaret greeted him cheerfully.

"Hello Mr Henty. There was a phone call for you, from your daughter Anne. Says, can you ring her at this number because she needs to speak to you."

"Thank you, Margaret." Bill went to change back into his working clothes, more worried than ever.

+ + +

Douglas Glover had always found the ministry interesting and rewarding. He certainly experienced the light and shade in people's lives. He liked working in a village, because he was able to grow to know his parishioners and become involved in their lives. The different strands of his work were demonstrated that week in February.

On Friday, he officiated at the funeral of Lady Moira Johnstone, widow of Sir Matthew, inhabitant of the parish for over fifty years. Her family was distraught, for even though she had lived a long and interesting life, they realised that she had been the one component holding them all together, for they knew no loyalty or filial duty to one another. Rev. Glover was interested to see that Bill Hawkes had accompanied Mrs Fidelia Howard, and equally seemed at ease with Mr Julian Johnstone. He did not know the history of Bill's links with the family, and Bill and Fiddy had been discreet over their continuing friendship.

Later that day, he was called urgently to the home of Dr Jack Ingrams and his wife, Sarah, to baptise their new baby who had been born two months early. Sarah had given birth to their first child, Philip, in April, 1954, to their delight, after so many disappointments. They were pleased to find that she was expecting again last summer, and now little Christine had arrived precipitately, endangering her life, and necessitating the urgent baptism. Martin and Emily Blake and Bonnie Newman, Ellie Bates' daughter, stood as godparents during the short service, while Sarah's parents waited anxiously, her mother sniffing and blowing her nose at regular intervals. The ambulance arrived to transport the tiny mite to the hospital in Bristol, where they would fight for her life more easily. Douglas Glover stood in the cold wind with the others as Jack went off in the ambulance with the child. There were enough people to comfort Sarah, and she wanted her husband to be with their daughter. Douglas had a few quiet words of prayer alone with Sarah before he left, and marvelled at her bravery.

The following day, he officiated at the wedding of someone he regarded as a family friend, when Matthew's youngest daughter, Vera, married David Bishop, whom she had met years ago, at college. Vera was a radiant bride, dressed in white brocade, cut simply and ruched across the bodice. She chose two friends to be her adult bridesmaids, and Diana's daughter, Lydia, as the little one; they all looked wonderful in cornflower blue dresses. Matthew found it strange to give Vera away, only weeks before his own wedding to Dorothy. He took his youngest child proudly up the aisle towards handsome David, who had waited so long for her. Douglas Glover kissed the bride, marvelling at the ability of the human spirit to transcend everything unpleasant, and maintain its faith in the future, regardless of experience. He liked to think that people could do this because of an unshakeable belief in God. His wife, Esther, was a guest at the wedding, and they went together to School House, where they were gathering before being conducted to the reception in the School Hall. Both could remember well the days when Lydia Ashton reigned in her domain. They smiled tenderly at each other, happy to participate in the regeneration of the family.

God or mammon, Douglas thought blasphemously to himself, *people will never cease to amaze me.*

EASTER 1956

Dorothy sat contemplatively, looking into the oval mirror on her bedroom wall. Her sister was dressing in her own room, leaving her to prepare in peace and quiet for her wedding. She knew beyond doubt that she loved Matthew, and he her; she had never been more sure of anything. After today, she would no longer be a spinster, but a married woman. Her role would change, as would people's perception of her. She could feel the spirits of other people about her. As she sat, she realised that Flora, her mother, would have prepared for her wedding to Seth in this very room. Had she felt the same? She had been a young girl of eighteen on her wedding day, but Dorothy was middle-aged. Even so, she felt like a bride; she was a virgin. She tried to take in the enormity of what she was about to do. She had shared her life, all her life, but never in a marriage. Matthew would not be an easy man to live with, she knew that much. She was apprehensive about her wedding night, but had not felt able to speak to anyone about it; certainly not Alice, and least of all Matthew himself. She had no qualms about running School House, for she was practiced and confident about that.

Dorothy was not one for frills or flounces, they did not flatter her. So she had chosen to get married wearing a suit. It was moss green tweed with a flared skirt and fitted jacket. Under it, she wore a cream blouse with her mother's cameo at the neck. She had chosen a tan felt hat to match her shoes and bag, and she now put it on and jammed a hat-pin through it, anchoring it to her head. She had a swagger-backed jacket to wear over the suit if it turned cold, and she let it remain on its hanger for now.

She was delighted to be marrying Matthew at Easter, when the church was bedecked with spring flowers, especially primroses, her favourite. The sun was doing its best to peep through a light covering of clouds, but it was early yet. The wedding was scheduled for midday, and it was still only ten o'clock.

"Why are you ready?" asked Alice, who was washed, but not yet dressed.

"I'm getting married. Remember?"

"Am I likely to forget?" Alice smiled at her sister. "Have you eaten anything this morning?" she continued.

Dorothy admitted that she had not.

"Right. I shall make your breakfast, on your wedding morn," she informed her.

She disappeared downstairs to the kitchen, while Dorothy checked on her packing. She and Matthew had gradually moved all of her personal belongings into School House over the past few weeks. Matthew had had the bedroom redecorated according to Dorothy's choice and instructions, and promised that they would do the rest of the house in the coming months. Dorothy heard the shouting at the same moment as the smell of burning reached her nostrils. She rushed downstairs as fast as the old staircase would allow.

"What's happening?" she called.

"Nothing, Sis," replied Eddy. "You just get ready."

Dorothy ran into the kitchen, which was obscured with black smoke.

"What happened?"

"Alice was frying the Bride's Breakfast," Eddy told her.

The three were standing in the blackened kitchen, when a voice called.

"Anyone at home?" It was Seth.

"What has happened here?" he asked.

"Don't ask. Alice has been cooking," Eddy told him.

"Pity you, Ed. This is what you have to look forward to now." His brother guffawed while Eddy scowled. Dorothy was keen to clear up the mess then and there, in her wedding clothes, but they managed to dissuade her. Both her brothers promised that they would help Alice later.

Seth was giving his sister away. Eddy had been asked, as the elder brother, but was too shy. Seth looked darkly handsome in his 'good' suit, and Louise and Flora wore their best tartan frocks to be their aunt's 'flower girls'.

Marina had come for the wedding, among many other friends, and she was staying at Bill's during this visit to Abbots Ford. People had travelled from all over the country to witness Dorothy's marriage to Matthew, as well as a large number of local friends and family; it was to be a surprisingly big wedding.

Dorothy was nervous. She carried a small posy of spring flowers as she held Seth's arm and went up the aisle to the hymn, 'Love Divine'. Douglas Glover was kind to her and gently took her flowers from her, placing a hymnal in her hand. Matthew was concerned that Dorothy looked so pale. He whispered to her,

"Are you alright?" and she nodded acquiescence.

His concern gave her strength and she smiled at Donald as he began the well-loved service:

"Dearly Beloved, We are gathered here together, in the sight of God and of this Congregation......"

Dorothy smiled at Matthew. It was a weak and wan effort and he smiled back encouragingly. The only people absent were Dorothy's Aunt Louise and Uncle Gordon, who were not due back in Britain until the summer. It was a special service because of the commitment of the couple, and their separate histories.

When they emerged from the church, the churchyard was filled with villagers. It seemed that every schoolchild and its parents, and every baby Dorothy had ever weighed, every mother she had ever counselled, were there waiting to greet them. They cheered and waved, and the couple laughed with delight.

The reception and wedding breakfast went by in a blur of speeches, congratulation and laughter. She could not believe so many people had turned out for them. Matthew was at his best and made a witty and well-received speech. They circulated together after the meal, thanking people for their gifts and attendance, enjoying seeing so many family members and dear friends.

It was time to leave on their honeymoon. They were to spend two nights in London, then carry on to Scotland for a week. Alice was crying copiously, and Eddy and Seth were obviously struggling with their emotions.

"Bye Sis," said her brothers, kissing her shyly.

"Bye, Dotty," cried Alice, through her tears.

For them, it was tantamount to saying 'goodbye' to a parent, even though she was the second in the family. Dorothy had usually been there for them all, especially since Flora died. She had kept the family together, and looked after them. She had represented stability, in war and in peacetime. Now she was to embark upon a life of her own, where Matthew would come first, and with a ready-made family. She kissed them all.

"See you soon."

She got into their car.

"All right? Ready?" checked Matthew.

She nodded.

A crowd waved them into the distance, carrying on until the car was out of sight.

"Sure you're alright, Mrs Ashton?" asked Matthew again.

"Yes, I'm fine, I really am." She gave him a glowing smile. "Never been happier, its' been a wonderful day."

"Nothing to how your life's going to be from now on," he told her reassuringly.

Dorothy watched as the scene sped by, leaving Abbots Ford behind. They travelled towards Bath, towards London, as Matthew drove them through the countryside, towards their future.

THE END